LISTENING TO THE QUIET

LISTENING TO THE QUIET

Gloria Cook

severn House

This first world edition published in Great Britain 2001 by
SEVERN HOUSE PUBLISHERS LTD of
9–15 High Street, Sutton, Surrey SM1 1DF.
This first world edition published in the USA 2002 by
SEVERN HOUSE PUBLISHERS INC of
595 Madison Avenue, New York, N.Y. 10022.

British Library Cataloguing in Publication Data

Cook, Gloria
  Listening to the quiet
  I. Title
  823.9′14 [F]

ISBN 0-7278-5793-2

Typeset by Palimpsest Book Production Ltd.,
Polmont, Stirlingshire, Scotland.
Printed and bound in Great Britain by
MPG Books Ltd., Bodmin, Cornwall.

To Roger, for always being there. Vicki and Dave Jones, Yvonne C. Craine, Mary Cross and Jenny Cook for their constant encouragement and friendship. Also Joy, Tina, Heidi, Claire, Margaret S., Margaret D., Roger S., Sarah, Natalie, Joan Sheppard in Canada and Kerith Biggs at Darley Anderson Agency. Special mention to Joanne Willoughby; without her interest and belief in me this book would not have been written.

One

'You're back then. How was it?'

'You know what funerals are like, Alistair,' Joanna Venner answered her brother, as he helped her take off her hat and coat. 'It was awful.'

'I'm sorry, Jo. You look cold. Come into the sitting room. I'll order some tea.'

'No, thanks. I want to have a serious talk with Mother. Straightaway. While I'm in a suitable mood.' Jo glimpsed herself in the hall mirror. Her eyes were red and puffy from weeping. She flicked irritably at her bobbed, reddish-brown hair; why did it refuse to fall sleekly in front of her ears? She tugged at the waistline of her plain black dress. Fashion at the moment might dictate that her shape was to be desired and envied, but she was ashamed of her almost flat chest and boyish hips, and wished she had feminine curves. 'Blast. I have only to spend a few nights under the same roof as Mother and I start fretting again about my appearance.'

'Mother's upstairs in her room.' Lounging against the newel post of the stairs, Alistair stroked his chin thoughtfully. 'I'd have thought you two would have become closer after all those years apart. Believe it or not, I actually missed you. Are you returning to Hampshire so soon?'

'No. I'm going somewhere Mother is most definitely not going to approve of. If I were you, I'd keep my head down all evening.'

'What's it all about?'

'Let me get this over with first. I'll explain later.'

'It sounds intriguing, little thing. Want me to go up with you?' He lazily puffed out a cloud of smoke, adding to

1

the confusion of fittings and furniture, which, like the enormous fir tree, were overadorned with brightly coloured tinsel, baubles and streamers, begging for Twelfth Night to be over. The interior of Tresawna House – stately, built high up on the windswept cliff at Carbis Bay – was an unmarriageable blend of elegant Georgian origins and brash modern art and loud decor; the latter their mother had talked Alistair into buying, to show off to her latest acquisition of social acquaintances. Jo felt little allegiance to the house; she had few happy memories here.

'Thanks, but I'll do this by myself,' Jo said resolutely. Whenever they were together, she and Alistair quarrelled tit for tat, hell-bent on bettering one another's deeds or witticisms. Sibling rivalry apart, and Jo's resentment at Alistair's easy passage through childhood in comparison to hers, he was quietly supportive of her hard-won achievement in breaking free from their mother's demands and expectations and forging her own life. Confident and unhurried, he was not afraid of asserting his authority over their pretentious mother. Jo loved and respected him for it. 'You've got to live with her after I've left. We'll be able to see each other regularly this time though. I'm not going very far away.'

'Jo, wait. Be careful,' Alistair counselled gravely. 'Mardie Dawes called on Mother while you were out. You know how Mother hates having what she calls her mystical aura disturbed after the fortune-teller's visits.' He let out a snatch of laughter, sharing a trait of Jo's, of switching moods rapidly in a manner others found disconcerting. 'I listened at the door. Mardie told her the usual old tosh about a new man coming into her life and her acquiring a fortune within the next year or two. Then, after warning Mother to watch out for trouble with her kidneys this winter, she babbled on about someone's mysterious wanderings and that a certain death was not what it appeared to be or something. Don't know what that has to do with Mother, she's hardly been out of the house since she contracted influenza back in November. I nearly gave myself away, I was laughing so much.'

'I find it hard to understand how a cynical woman like Mother entertains such an obvious charlatan,' Jo scoffed.

'She's like you, little thing. Fascinated by anything out of the ordinary.'

'You'd never catch me parting with good money for something so blatantly fabricated. The old woman is a nuisance to the people of Parmarth. Anyway, if she really could see into the future she would have told Mother that she's in for an upset, although, as it concerns me, only a minor one.'

Jo slowly climbed the dark oak stairs to her mother's bedroom, resigned to what would be a confrontation. Katherine Venner had scorned everything Jo had said or done from childhood, while totally approving of her son, who had turned out exactly as a gentleman of education and privilege was expected to be. Married to a young lady of substance and accomplishment, Alistair was successfully expanding a private yacht-building business established on his late father's banking fortune. Jo knew that this time she would receive not only the usual scorn at her hopes and dreams, but a round of utter hostility.

As Jo expected, her mother viewed her as she always did, with slight irritation and an entire lack of interest. It was an overcast day, but enough light streamed in through the tall windows to illuminate Katherine Venner's firm outline. Nudging her fifty-fifth year, she had retained her courtly bearing and was still attractive, albeit hard and aquiline. Buffing her nails at her dressing table, she was flashily turned out in a multicoloured crêpe dress. Her softly waved hair, golden-red by courtesy of her hairdresser's products, obliged her by lying in perfect symmetry. Jo saw new additions in the room she had rarely entered. On the mahogany bedside table, an ugly bronze statue of a naked man cavorted under a painted-glass lightshade. Brightly painted flatware and glass paperweights were peppered among the more graceful porcelain figurines.

'What do you want, Joanna?' Katherine jabbed a cigarette into a jade holder. 'I asked Emma to make sure I was not

3

interrupted. I want time for a long meditation before getting ready for my dinner party.'

'Emma wasn't about when I got back. I shan't keep you long, Mother. I've something to tell you.'

'If it's not about accepting a suitable proposal of marriage I don't want to hear it.' Katherine pursed her glistening crimson lips. She always overdid her make-up and overplucked her eyebrows. 'Why the black dress? You look like the lead of a pencil. And you've spent too long outside in the wind, your eyes are an unsightly colour.'

'I'm wearing black and my eyes are red because I've just come from Celia's funeral,' Jo snapped, controlling the lump rising in her throat, not about to let her mother see the extent of her grief over losing her closest friend. Katherine could make Jo feel like a badly constructed drawing, one that Katherine seemed always to be seeking to rub out and reassemble to her own specifications.

'Really, Joanna! You know I loathe that woman's name being mentioned.'

'How else could I answer your question? I'm sorry you still feel so hostile towards Celia. Have you forgotten how good she was to you when Father *and* Bob Merrick were killed?'

A tiny blue vein throbbed on Katherine's temple, indicating her gall at Jo's direct attack. 'Joanna, you are too old to be sent to your room. Do you want me to slap your face?'

'Certainly not.' Jo found it difficult to imagine this woman had actually carried her inside her body and given birth to her. They were like distant strangers. No, more like two people merely on antagonistic social terms. 'You ought to remember that if it wasn't for your affair with Bob Merrick I would never have met Celia. She did you a service befriending me and keeping me occupied while you met your lover on the moors.'

'I don't wish to discuss that kept woman.' Katherine ground her teeth, incensed that Jo should remind her how she had used her as a child as cover for her own adultery. 'Now go away.'

4

'I haven't told you my news yet.' Breaking from her mother's hostile disregard, Jo went to a window and looked out across the bay. It brought back more hurtful memories of her home life. A little further downcoast, lacy white spume was riding the heavy winter waves surging towards St Ives' Porthminster beach. Jo had painted this scene several times, outside on the cliff. Once, seeking Katherine's acknowledgement, she had showed her one of her paintings and had been scorched by her remark, 'The sea is like the contents of an inkwell and the figures on the beach look like dead ants on crushed biscuits.'

'I'm not listening.' Katherine returned to her nails.

'Before Celia's sudden death,' Jo persisted, 'which you so unkindly saw fit not to inform me of, but left to Alistair five days later, I had arranged to leave Hampshire and go to live with her. I'm changing schools. I'm going to teach at Parmarth.'

'You're what? You've left the young ladies' academy? To lower yourself even further by teaching in a worthless primary school, and you even dare to bring your disgrace near to home?'

Squaring her narrow shoulders, Jo looked her mother straight in the eye. 'Mother, teaching is a worthwhile profession and taking a position in the village where I have so many happy memories is something I wish to do. I don't intend staying there for ever. I have other far-reaching plans. There is nothing wrong in following one's desires – if they're not selfish.'

'Oh, you choose to make another jibe at me? You are opprobrious and ungrateful. As for teaching, it's an option for women who have no hope of making a good marriage. You are plain and shapeless, Joanna. Your seemingly high intelligence is another of your displeasing features, but you have the advantage of your father's trust fund. It is of ample proportions to ensure a gentleman of good repute will take the bait. Yet rather than look forward to your father's benevolence in the future, you live on a meagre salary and now, presumably, you will earn even less. You have deliberately chosen to go against his wishes.'

Jo was not prepared to be merely swept away. Celia had taught her many things, one of them to stand and fight for her right to be heard. 'Father died when I was very young, and there was nothing in his will expressing the wish that I meekly hand over my inheritance to someone else. You're just bitter that Father left you nothing. I don't understand your objections to my lifestyle. You've broken away from convention yourself, refusing half a dozen marriage proposals since you were widowed. And for years you've mixed with women who have chosen an academic career, or who earn their livelihood in the arts, in films, or the theatre. Most of them have never married. Why is it so different for me? It's because you've always despised me, isn't it? Because I wasn't the sort of sweet, pretty child you could show off as a compliment to yourself.'

'Yes, Joanna, you've always been a disappointment to me, and I'll never forgive you for becoming so attached to that wretched Sayce woman, for taking her money to sponsor your time at college. Teach in that pathetic little village if you must, but you will not do so from under this roof.' Katherine took a furious puff on her cigarette.

'The house belongs to Alistair and he'd make me welcome for as long as I chose, but as I don't want the atmosphere to be contentious for him and Phoebe, I have made other arrangements now that I cannot live at Cardhu.' Jo made no attempt to keep the mocking out of her voice. 'Mercy Merrick has been in touch with me. She's offered to let me stay at Nance Farm.'

Rising to her well-shod feet, Katherine advanced on Jo, snarling. 'Is there no limit to the lengths you will go to insult me? You're actually going to stay with that other despicable woman?' She halted, as if she could not bear to be close to her daughter. Contracting her eyes, she dropped her voice but still vented pure sarcasm. 'Do you perhaps get some kind of perverse pleasure from having the Trevail brothers pulling you about?'

6

'My plans do not involve getting back at you, Mother. Staying at Nance Farm is simply a practical arrangement. I won't waste any more time with explanations. You could never understand my reasons for wanting to teach at Parmarth.'

'Now Celia Sayce is dead you have no reason to stay in Cornwall. Ask Alistair to arrange your reinstatement at the young ladies' academy.'

'Can't you bear the thought of me living so close to you, Mother?' Jo ridiculed calmly. 'I'm going to teach at Parmarth. There I shall feel close to Celia even though I won't have her company. I will not change my plans.'

Katherine gave a malicious smile. 'I think I know what your reasons were for intending to live at Cardhu. You were hoping the Sayce woman would value you so much in downgrading your ludicrous career and keeping her company in her old age that she'd leave you her house and money. She had no family and it was well known in our circles that Sheridan Ustick kept his mistress in comfort.'

'That's a vile thing to say! I loved Celia. She encouraged me to make a success of my life, to achieve my ambitions. She was the mother to me you should have been. What I do with my life is none of your business.' Jo made what she thought was a fairly graceful withdrawal to the door. 'I'll see you at dinner.'

'I won't have you at my table tonight,' Katherine uttered through her teeth.

'I want to meet Ben Nicholson. I'm interested to learn about his new approach to painting, something you will only pretend to understand.'

'I'm quite sure Mr Nicholson and the rest of my guests will have nothing in common with you, Joanna. They're real achievers, while you're off to stagnate in a place that's so primitive it belongs to the Dark Ages. We shall see how long you'll endure living without the basic things like piped water and the luxuries you're used to. When do you intend to leave for the farm?'

'At the end of the week.'

'Make it tomorrow. Be sure you keep out of my way until then. I have no wish to set eyes on you again until you apologise to me and plead that you have come to your senses.'

Two

A covered wagon rumbled down the main street of the solemn little village of Parmarth. Ignoring the curious faces popping up at many of the lantern-lit windows, Luke Vigus headed his young working horse round the back of the forge to the stable space he rented.

He took his time in the yard unhitching the wagon and securing the wares he plied all over the West Penwith area. He had just fixed up a good deal in a pub, and also had a load of stolen lead piping hidden on board. He should have been feeling pleased over the large profit he'd make, but in grim silence, he stalled, groomed and fed the horse, then leaned for long minutes on the animal's warm neck.

When he left the stable, icy raindrops, borne on a cruel wind, lashed his body, wetting him through in seconds, freezing his flesh. He sought no shelter. Facing the stable door, he cupped his hands and lit a cigarette, drew in deeply, then in a defeated manner, turned and leaned against the whitewashed wall, crossing one heavy boot over the other on the cobbles.

Tall, well set, dressed in dusty working man's garb, badly in need of a shave, his mouth taut, pale blue eyes compressed, he stared at the angry indigo sky and sighed in edgy discontent. He would rather stay here and perish in the extremes of the weather than go home.

It was a few days into a new decade, but 1930 offered no sense of hope, no fresh start for him. He was a young man. All he should have had on his mind was making a living and enjoying himself, not being dragged down by unsought responsibilities.

When the coldness had seeped into his bones, diluting his frustration to a manageable level, he strode down the village hill to the Engine House Inn and stayed there until closing time.

'You got anything for me?' Jessie Vigus demanded, the instant he got inside the door of their one-up, one-down cottage.

Glaring at his mother, Luke hurled back, 'You got something to eat for me?'

'There's only the end of a loaf. I ain't got nothing else in, Luke. How was I to know you was coming back? You're on the road for weeks. Got a fag?'

Scowling, he ripped out the cigarette clenched between his lips and tossed it at her. Her hair wispy and prematurely grey, her body bloodless and emaciated by years of alcohol abuse, she was too unsteady to catch the begrudged offering and tottered drunkenly to retrieve it from the filthy stone floor.

Luke winced at the sight and smell of her. Jessie never washed the family's clothes, rarely washed her body. Lew Trevail was a rotten dirty bastard for going with her and fathering another child to drag him down.

The baby whimpered, the pitiful, neglected sound of miscomprehension of an infant starving. Luke glanced down at his youngest sister, lying in her own filth in a corner of a drawer, half pulled out of the dresser. Marylyn's skin was grey and biscuity, her eyes staring unnaturally out of hollow sockets. Pity his mother's promiscuity and drinking habits hadn't rendered her infertile.

'You can't expect keep if I don't get no bloody food.'

'I bet you've had a drink.'

'I work flaming hard! I deserve a drink. I'll give you nothing. Where's the couch? I need something to sleep on when I'm here.' He glanced at his other sister and his brother, six and seven years old, huddled pathetically in worn-out clothes at the stone hearth in a vain attempt to get warm from the smouldering twig fire. 'And the kids' good clothes and shoes I bought 'em? You've sold them, you bitch! What for? A few shillings' worth of Mardie Dawes' homemade poison?'

'Luke, please,' Jessie appealed as she got the shakes. She had trouble striking a match.

'You can go to hell.' He searched the cupboard built into the recess next to the fireplace. Pulled out a small tin that had once contained boot polish. Took off the lid. 'Bloody empty!' Gone was the money he'd left for Rex to buy food, milk and candles, and to pay the rent. He'd left more than enough for the month he'd been away. He wouldn't have minded so much if there was something to show for it. Jessie must have beaten Rex, and probably little Molly too, until the boy confessed where he had hidden the tin. It would account for their fresh bruises.

Rex and Molly were used to the verbal abuse of their mother and brother on the few occasions Luke was home, but they were not listening to the quarrel. They watched Luke from gaunt, hungry eyes, hoping . . .

Cursing his mother, Luke put his hands into his jacket pockets. Jessie watched him avidly, greedily, like a ravenous she-wolf.

'Here,' he said to Rex, 'I thought you'd still be up, and starving hungry. I've got something for you and Molly.'

Rex got up on bare, chilblained feet, held out eager hands. Jessie dived between her sons. Luke grabbed her by the arm and pushed her away.

'They can't live on fresh air, woman. The place stinks. Have you been sick again?'

While Rex and Molly gulped down meat pies and wrinkled-skinned apples, he hunted about, tossing the odd sticks of furniture out of his way. He kicked at a filthy rag and howled in disgust. A heap of dried vomit was underneath it, adding to the stench of urine and faeces which seemed to emanate from the very structure of the cottage. Luke pressed his knuckles to his forehead in shame and despair. This was his home, a cramped, dark and dank, sodden, mouldy cave.

Jessie made to run for the rope ladder that led to the upstairs room, which was reached through a hatch. Luke gripped her scrawny shoulder. In the worst language ever heard in Parmarth, he berated his mother. 'Clean it up or

11

I'll throw you outside for the bloody night. It's all you're fit for, the gutter.' He pushed her towards her offence. 'This place is worse than a god-damned pigsty!'

'You don't have to live here,' Jessie screeched, scrabbling with the rag. 'Just piss off and leave me alone.'

'I wish I'd never looked you up. You deserted me, leaving Gran to rear me. We were poor but everything was clean and not crawling with fleas. I always had food in my belly. I'd have gone off ages ago and never come back if it wasn't for the kids. I don't want to see any more of 'em in the churchyard. You go, you filthy whore! We'd be better off without you dragging us down.'

Seven children his mother had borne, each from a different father, none with the benefit of a wedding ring. Luke had been her first. He had dark gipsy looks, had spent a lot of time with gipsies and assumed his father had been one. He was cursed with the gipsy desire to keep on the move. Open spaces were as precious to him as the fresh air he breathed. Right now, he felt he was suffocating.

Dirty and wearily pale, Rex and Molly gorged the food without a murmur, gazing alertly at the pair scrapping and swearing.

Pointing at the baby, Luke asked Rex, 'She had anything today?'

The boy shook his scurf-ridden head.

'I'll go over to Nance Farm and get some milk. Mercy Merrick stays up late. Tomorrow I'm going to see about getting the baby adopted.'

'You can't go to the authorities, Luke,' Jessie wept, shaking uncontrollably, struggling to her feet, her self-abused state forcing her to lean against the dresser. 'They might wonder how some of the others died.' She became malicious, mocking him. 'If they put me away, I'll say you were in on it. Then we could both hang.'

Luke banged his fist against the cold bare wall. 'God in heaven, what have I done to deserve this?' There were times he was afraid he would give way to the utter disgust and loathing which cankered inside him for his mother and beat her senseless.

'If something better doesn't happen soon,' he whispered in despair, 'I just might . . .'

Three

In heavy silence, Jo sat straight-backed and implacable beside Alistair as he drove towards Parmarth. They were bumping along the narrow, winding coast road, which had recently been tarred and gritted for the first time, passing lonely farmsteads, running streams, stone walls, stretches of open moor, all flanked by gaunt boulder-strewn hills.

Alistair always motored idiotically fast and Jo clung to the door strap. Her luggage, heaped on the back seat, was under continuous threat of being pitched on to the floor of the black and yellow Bentley. The air inside the car was choked with the stench of Alistair's pipe and she wound the window down to draw in a welcome breath of crisp air.

She turned to gaze at the stony entrance of Bridge Lane. A short distance along the quiet thoroughfare, sheltered in a valley, was Cardhu, where she had proposed to live. It was down the lane, on the little flat granite bridge not far from the house, where, as a six-year-old, she had first met Celia. Jo had been washing muck and blood off her hands, knees and dress, after being dragged through a field with cowpats and thistles by the Trevail brothers. She had been brought to the area by Katherine, who had slipped away from the pretence of taking a country picnic, for an assignation with the boys' uncle, Bob Merrick.

Jo longed to get out of the car and run to the house where she had been treated with such genuine concern, sensitivity and love. This close to Cardhu, she was inspired once again to pursue her dreams, no matter how stupid and futile they seemed to others. She sighed, vexed that her feelings were dismissed in certain quarters.

Alistair crashed the gears as he took a tight bend and ignored her.

They rounded the next bend and the square tower of the village church came into view. Alistair swept the Bentley importantly through the village, making the few people who were about stare and comment huffily at the madness of some drivers.

Jo kept her eyes on the churchyard for as long as she could. Only twenty-four hours ago, she had shivered in the biting winds and wept over the simple coffin of the kindest, most positive person she had ever known. And she had been grieved that so few people had attended the funeral. Celia had been good to the villagers, employing from among them, during a time when jobs were scarce, a washerwoman, a seamstress, a delivery boy and a gardener.

She only caught a glimpse of the school and wondered what it was like inside. In a couple of days she would find out.

Taking her make-up mirror out of her clutch bag, she manoeuvred her head to get an overall view of her face. She touched the pink satin rose, blowing in the draught, on her slouch hat. Free again from her mother's cold disapproval, she was feeling lighthearted and full of purpose, and she looked it.

'Why care about how you look?' Alistair said impatiently. 'You're going to live in a primitive backwater. There won't be anything of what we take for granted. There's probably not even a cricket team. You must be mad coming to this place.'

'It's a perfect place to paint in,' Jo pointed out. 'Many important artists are using the moors these days for the clear, vibrant light and the glorious scapes, including Mother's dinner guest last night. There are writers and poets too.'

'You mean like that D. H. Lawrence fellow who once lived at Zennor, which we've not long passed through? If you paint like he writes, your work will be disgusting.'

'You just don't understand what he's trying to say!'

'Well, all I can say is, I truly hope you don't.'

'Oh, shut up.'

15

Jo felt the Arctic coldness seep through her fur-collared coat. She sniffed the air. She had not lost the senses she had acquired of what the weather had in store. A heavy shower of rain was imminent.

'Close the damned window,' Alistair barked. 'It's freezing in here.'

Jo complied, then replied tightly, 'I'd appreciate it if you knocked out your pipe.'

'For goodness' sake.' He thrust the pipe at her and she was forced to remove its offending matter herself. 'You can't expect me to approve of this stupid plan of yours, so stop sulking.'

'I never sulk, as you well know. I thought you could see things my way a little, that's all.'

'You hate it when I take Mother's side, don't you?'

'I simply don't think you're being fair.'

'I've driven you to this blasted little place, haven't I?'

'You could be more gracious about it.'

'You could be more grateful. You want everything your own way. Always have. Well, if you make a pig's ear of it, you've only yourself to blame.'

'Have I ever asked you to take the responsibility for my mistakes?'

'No.'

'Well, shut up and drive carefully. I'd like to arrive at Nance in one piece.'

Jo's eyes were drawn constantly to the forsaken works of the Solace tin mine. Laid bare to the weather, set close to the cliff edge a quarter of a mile away, the buildings were silhouetted against the murky, darkening sky, dominating the western horizon as they had done for eighty years.

Hunching his shoulders over the steering wheel, Alistair tacked a path to avoid muddy puddles and the heaps of manure left by livestock. 'I didn't really see any harm in you taking up a career, Jo, but to seek such a lowly position, to teach creatures who aren't worth the bother, is inconceivable. It's pathetic.'

A mix of determination and indignation became Jo's

16

expression. 'When I come into my trust fund, Alistair, I'm going to strike out on my own. Open a school for girls, where they will be given every encouragement to strive for their ambitions, like Celia Sayce did for me, and I shall provide scholarships for girls just like those who live in Parmarth. And the children here are not creatures and they are worth every consideration. How dare you take such a high and mighty attitude towards the lives of people you know nothing about?'

'You don't know them. The Sayce woman kept you all to herself. Besides, their families are as poor as church mice. They won't welcome someone of your background.'

'I may not know this generation of children but I once mixed with some of the villagers.' Jo was aware that she knew little of the conditions most of her pupils lived in but she felt an empathy with them. She knew what it was like to be considered of no value. Now she was back on the beloved moors where she had gained her freedom, where she had been loved and nurtured, she no longer cared about Alistair's views, or her mother's.

'What, those scabrous brothers?' he scoffed. 'Hardly a recommendation.'

Jo saw no need to justify her actions and fell silent again, reintroducing herself to the moors. The high ground of the coast road afforded spectacular views of the carns and mighty tors, the cliffs and the seaboard.

While she savoured these familiar sights, the first freezing raindrops hit the windscreen. Winter had its harsh grip on the surrounding land. The uninitiated might see only its barrenness and the bleak derelict engine houses, the towering chimney stacks and ugly slag piles; tragic memorials of Cornwall's once thriving tin and copper industry. Jo, however, saw life and purpose. The vast sweeps of bracken, dead gorse and heather, and the huge granite boulders were coloured in living, vibrant browns, russets, reds and every shade of grey. She sensed the presence of the ancients who had trodden the long-vanished paths, felt the very spirit of the land. She had come back, and it was as if during her absence this soul-stirring beauty had been waiting for her.

Nance Farm's rambling buildings were situated either side of a bend in the road, and sheltered by high grey stone walls from the vagaries of the wind and rain which swept over the West Penwith moors, the most westerly moors of Cornwall, with unrelenting regularity at this time of the year. Next to Cardhu, it was Jo's favourite place to come back to.

Alistair stopped the motorcar on the road. 'Much more sanitary than the farmyard, I'm sure,' he muttered darkly.

Jo did not wait for him to help her alight. 'Don't worry,' she smirked, 'you won't spoil your shoes.' A path of straw had been laid over the thickly muddied ground, from the wide, open farm entrance to the front door; a thoughtful gesture by Mercy.

Within minutes they had deposited Jo's luggage inside the porch, then stood gazing at each other, many a remark lying unspoken on their lips. An intense steamy smell threatened to clog their nostrils, but if Alistair noticed the fouled air he chose not to mention it.

He smiled faintly. 'I don't want to leave you here, little thing.'

'I'm a grown woman, Alistair. I can look after myself.'

'I hope you know what you're doing. Well, you can always find a telephone and get in touch if you need me, I suppose.' He kissed her cheek, and before she could reply he left her.

Outside in the rain, she watched as he reversed the Bentley into the yard and drove away, waving until he was out of sight.

Then she turned her back on her family's disapproval, to relish every inch of the rugged, neglected aspect of the two-hundred-year-old farmhouse. The roof had been slated in 1919 when the thatch had caught fire, taking away some of its charm. A coat of dark green paint had been dabbed on the window frames and splashed on the door, without the old paintwork first being sanded down. Dust, grit and mud had gathered carelessly against the doorstep. The long narrow flowerbeds either side of the porch, once proudly tended by Mercy's good-natured grandmother, were empty quagmires.

Rubbing the rusty horseshoe nailed to the door for good

luck, Jo stepped inside the friendly, cavernous confines of the dwelling. She carried her suitcases and vanity case along the passage and left them at the bottom of the steep, bare, wooden stairs, then made for the kitchen.

In the event Mercy's two boisterous border collies were inside, she opened the door cautiously and peeped round it. There was no sign of life, but the room was busy and welcoming with the succulent smell of lamb stew simmering in a gigantic saucepan on the iron range, which was incorporated into a huge open chimney. There was enough space for a small person like Jo to sit in the chimney and blissfully toast herself. A massive granite lintel stretched the length of the wall and protruded to form a narrow, untrue mantelpiece. The cooking overpowered the farmyard's primitive odours. In a few minutes Jo would not notice the unpleasant smells. She hugged herself in sheer contentment. She had always enjoyed coming here, where social class, position, wealth and beauty did not matter, where she had always felt wanted.

She hung her wet coat on the door knob of a tall oak cupboard then warmed herself in front of the great stone fireplace, its higher stones long blackened by soot.

The farmhouse had only the most basic of furniture, mellowed with age, but was heated all through; the walls were constructed of huge boulders and Mercy kept roaring fires. The table, made from wreck timber and long and wide enough to seat a fair-sized banquet, was set with preparations for a meal of similar proportions, although for just two people. Suspended from the ceiling was pig meat, bagged in cloth. Jo could almost taste the delicious ham inside it. She would enjoy living here. Mercy was not stingy with anything, fuel, food or affection.

At the back door, she peered across the yard, which was paved with rab, a yellowish clay formed from decomposed granite, and called out Mercy's name several times. Her eyes flicked from the ricks and animals' accommodation and she smiled as the hens, geese and ducks, which wandered at will, started a ruckus at her shouting.

She received no human reply; her friend must be out in the fields.

When Jo returned to the kitchen she found she was not alone. From hidden corners of the large orderless house, Mercy's three cats had crept forth and were blinking at her curiously. Sunny, a fat patchwork of ginger, white and black fur, leapt up on to the window sill over the huge stone sink. Jo followed her slinky movements and saw, propped up against the late Bob Merrick's cracked shaving mug, a note from his sister. The bold writing stated: *Dear Jo, In case I'm not here when you arrive, your bedroom's next to mine, overlooking the yard. Mercy.*

Before Mercy came in, Jo thought it best to change her clothes. Her dress was already attracting cat hairs and Mercy would bring the collies inside with her. More than once before Kip and Hunter had favoured her with a liberal coating of farmyard dirt.

She carried her luggage up to her room, where a hearty coal blaze was crackling in the grate, then she looked out of the dusty window.

Nance, sheltered by a bank of leaning sycamore and thorn trees, consisted of one hundred acres of hill and croft and thirty-five acres of arable land. The fields were rocky and exposed to the ferocious Atlantic gales, and crop growing, apart from animal feed, was impracticable, so that the farm concentrated mainly on animal husbandry. Mercy kept a small dairy herd, mainly Guernseys, which in fine weather Jo would be able to see in the sloping fields at the back of the farmhouse. Encircled by a low straggling stone wall was the paddock where horses were put to roam, and in the field nearest the yard a billy goat would be tethered to an old millstone, while his family of half a dozen grazed unencumbered nearby.

As a child, Jo had risked her mother's rage by covertly helping during the farm's busiest periods, bottle-feeding orphan lambs, broadcasting corn seed from a 'seed-lap' which had protruded grotesquely from her scant body. She was eager to pitch in again.

Changing into a skirt, blouse, cardigan and comfortable old slippers, Jo unpacked her things. It had been sensible to bring clothes hangers; there were none in the ancient wardrobe which stood on ugly bracket feet and smelled of camphor, used for treating woodworm. She hung up the lavender sachets she'd brought with her and left the wardrobe door open to let in the light. Thick, off-white, wax candles in glass jars and enamel candlesticks were dotted about the room. Jo would have use of a lantern to light the way to and from her room at night. It was all crude and basic, her mother would have hated it, but Jo would not mind foregoing the niceties of life too much.

There was a small square table which would be useful as a desk where she laid her pen and stationery and the letter from Marcus Lidgey, Parmarth's headmaster, confirming her post.

As there was no dressing table, she put her brush and comb, clothes brush, make-up, trinket jars and rosewater bottles on the chest of drawers, a chunky monstrosity of pitch pine, which also accommodated her small clothes and the rest of her personal things. Before putting her jewellery box away she opened it and gazed at an exquisite cameo pendant. She treasured this piece of jewellery most, a gift from Celia on her twenty-first birthday.

'You up there, Jo?' a loud voice rang out from the foot of the stairs.

'Mercy!'

Jo hurried downstairs down to her friend and landlady. They shook hands warmly.

'Have you been here long?' Mercy's large blue eyes searched Jo's face. 'Will you be comfortable, do you think? There's no proper bathroom. 'Tisn't like Cardhu.'

'I arrived about twenty minutes ago,' Jo replied brightly, dwarfed by her friend's bulk. Mercy was big-boned and well above the average height of a woman. 'And of course I'll be comfortable.' Nance did not boast a bathroom but there was an upstairs toilet, a tiny cubby-hole equipped with an Elsan, enamel bucket and little seat. 'It's good of you to let me live here. You're used to being on your own.'

'Maybe, but at times I've been lonely since Bob was killed. Come into the kitchen, stew's nearly ready.'

Jo happily braced herself to accept twice an exuberant welcome. She was practically knocked off her feet by the two long-haired collies before Mercy called them away. Catching her breath, Jo collapsed in the sunken rocking chair next to the hearth. 'I think I'd better use the front door when I come home from the school or church.' She grinned contentedly.

'I'll slap a bit of concrete down to the front door so you don't get your feet dirty,' Mercy said, plonking a huge mug of tea down on the fender, close to Jo.

'Don't put yourself to any trouble for me, Mercy.'

'Get on with you, maid. Won't have you teaching looking rough as rats. I'm proud of what you're doing.' Mercy was cutting thick slices of bread. She spread roughly half an ounce of butter on each slice with the lack of finesse she used while working. Although broadly built, she had a totally feminine shape, undisguised by the collarless flannel shirt and corduroy trousers she wore. While busy, she had a habit of clenching her big white teeth, adding extra lines to her forty-six-year-old face, which was weathered with a permanent redness. She was an attractive woman; well liked in the area.

'So your mother took it badly then?'

'Turned me out, damn her.'

'She still mixing with them arty types?'

'Yes. She finds this interest of hers a better cover for her affairs than when she used to cart me round with her.'

'I regret the day my brother met your mother.' Mercy's expression darkened. 'While she paraded herself round Penzance's streets on market day. It stopped Bob getting married and raising a family. But I'm glad to have met you, Jo, and I'm glad we're still friends.'

'So am I, Mercy. My mother's selfishness has caused a lot of pain over the years, but she doesn't always succeed in accomplishing her aims or I wouldn't be here now.'

'Well, never mind she. What did you think of Marcus Lidgey?' Mercy ladled out the stew.

'Mr Lidgey's younger than what one expects in a headmaster. I would place him at about thirty-five years of age. He was stern and precise at the interview, but I gathered he has some forward-thinking ideas for the school and the pupils, but unfortunately only for the boys. I shall see what I can do about changing his traditional views. Celia mentioned his name and appointment a year ago in a letter, and that he had a house at Penzance and taught in London before coming to Parmarth. What do the villagers think of him?'

Jo carried her tea to the table and sat down on the end of a long bench. Mercy had lit the oil lamps, and a glance out of the window showed night was spreading its inky fingers over the land. There were no curtains here or anywhere else in the house. Mercy had a simple philosophy for an easy life; if she never cleaned the windows there was no need for curtains.

'I've not seen him often. His widowed mother lives with him. She's crippled, practically housebound. He's devoted to her, hardly ever leaves her side. Keeps to himself mostly, but then there's nobody round here his sort can socialise with. You could change that. Said to be down on his luck. Why else would a man like he take a position round here? Talks with a plum in his mouth as you must've heard. He's church, of course. People respect him. The maids continually cast an eye in his direction. He's not bad-looking, don't you think?'

'I did notice.' Jo thought back to the dingy hotel room at Penzance where the interview had been held. The faces of the school's governing board, all gentlemen of good repute and flourishing businesses, were a blur. Her main impression of Marcus Lidgey was that although immaculately groomed, he seemed a little careworn. While he'd listened attentively to her answers to the stark questions forwarded to her by the stiff board members, he was restless, as if eager for the interview to be over. On the one occasion he had smiled at her, while shaking her hand goodbye, his intense dark eyes had softened at the edges. 'You must know more about him than that, Mercy. Gossip gets around just as quickly, I'm sure.'

'You know me, Jo. I'm not much interested in what people do.'

'Of course people could pass similar remarks about me. What is someone of my background doing teaching in a small primary school?'

'They already are. 'Tis best you don't say you aren't staying here indefinitely, they'll see it as disloyalty. You won't be accepted easily, you know that, don't you?'

'Yes, but I'll enjoy the challenge. It will be good experience for my future plans.' It would be five years before Jo's wealth was available to her, to found her school. Would Parmarth hold her interest for that long?

A plate of stew, enough to appease the appetite of three men, was placed in front of Jo. An odd knife and fork were sent skidding down the table towards her. Mercy was a wonderful cook and Jo took an appreciative sniff of the meal. 'I'll never manage all this, Mercy.'

'No matter. What you leave the animals'll gobble up.' Mercy laughed kindly. She sat on the stout chair at the head of the table, where once her brother had sat, swallowed a giant mouthful of food and waved her fork at Jo. 'I'll put a bit of fat on you before Easter, never fear. Now, my handsome, you can do what you like to your room but don't go bothering yourself with housework or anything outside.' Mercy looked at her next forkful of food and smiled secretly to herself. 'I've got plenty of labour on the farm. Still got Darius Pendower every day. Throw your washing in the washhouse. Kizzy Kemp'll see to it. There's sheets in the airing cupboard when you want to change your bed. I'll do the cooking. I prepare overnight for the next day. But help yourself to anything in the larder if you get peckish.'

'Thanks, Mercy. We didn't mention board and lodging. I'll earn nearly a hundred a year. I thought I'd give you six shillings a week. And I'd like to help out with a few jobs each day.'

'Three shillings,' Mercy said, giving Jo no room to insist on the higher remuneration. 'You're a friend. You're welcome to feed the poultry and number the eggs on the chart. I want you to treat this place like home. There's no furniture in the parlour, didn't really need it so I sold it one hard winter to buy cattle feed. The canvas on the floor has some life left in it. If you want to get a few bits together you can have guests in there. I always stay in here so they won't be no bother to me and I won't be no bother to them.'

'Thank you, that might be very useful.' Pictures flashed through Jo's mind of holding meetings, with Mr Lidgey's permission, for parents who were interested in their offspring's education and future.

'Got a drop of beer when we've finished eating,' Mercy said. 'Are you going to travel often to Carbis Bay to see Katherine?'

'I shouldn't think so,' Jo said quietly. Resting her knife and fork beside the remains of her meal, she stared grimly at the mismatched cutlery.

'Never mind,' Mercy said. 'You can't change the course of the sea nor the weather, and you can't change the ways of some folk. It was a great pity about Celia Sayce. I'm very sorry, Jo, I know how much you'll miss her.'

Jo's eyes filled with tears. 'I wouldn't have had much of a life if it wasn't for her, Mercy. My biggest regret is that she died alone. I wish she'd got word to me that she was so ill.'

Mercy looked solemnly at her paying guest. 'Jo, I'm sorry to have to tell you this, the news is out about Celia's circumstances. Gossip, some of it cruel considering how well she was accepted for an outsider in the village, started circulating shortly after she died.'

'So that's why there was such a poor attendance at her funeral.' Jo smarted. 'How narrow-minded can people be?'

'You're about to find out. You haven't lived in a village where everyone wants to know everybody's else business. I hope it won't make things hard for you.'

'I won't let it, Mercy. I knew it would take a while for the villagers to get used to my presence at the school, but I

25

thought coming to live at Parmarth was going to be agreeable. It isn't going to be, is it? To begin with I won't have Celia's companionship, but one thing I swear, I will not allow any disrespect to her name.'

Four

Marcus Lidgey sat rigid and tense at the dining table in the schoolhouse. Hardly tasting his cooked breakfast, he divided each forkful with his quick, correct movements, longing for the meal to be over.

What excuse could he offer to escape the woman directly across the table from him?

That he must attend to important work in his study? There were no exercise books to be marked. He'd finished the task at the beginning of the Christmas holiday. She would be aware of it. A letter to the school governing board? But she would know he had no reason to write to the board. He had seen each member recently, when Miss Joanna Venner's appointment at the school had been confirmed. Marcus had difficulty swallowing the next mouthful of food and gulped at his tea. A letter to the Jelbert twins' parents? He often had occasion to complain about their disruptive behaviour at school.

Becoming aware that his mother, of sparse appetite, was watching him, Marcus ate mindfully.

'You will invite Miss Venner to dine with us when you show her around the school tomorrow, darling?' Eleanor Lidgey's tones were powerful, husky and to the point.

She attempted to sit up straight but was gradually sinking into the ungainly heap that would anger her if she glimpsed her reflection in the glass of the long sideboard. An accident had reduced the mobility and strength of her spine, but not the magnetic expressiveness of her uncommonly beautiful face.

Against his will, she held Marcus's gaze. He had inherited her high forehead, perfectly proportioned cheekbones and finely moulded mouth, but while her dark eyes were darting and lively, his held no light, no enthusiasm, no life. She looked much younger than her sixty-two years, even, as now, when wearing no make-up. Her hair shimmered with a silvery incandescence. Eleanor seemed to be endowed with strange powers of inducement, and could draw people to her and hold them fast, and break them as quickly or as slowly as it pleased her.

'Of course, Mama,' he said, employing his deep and resonant voice carefully. All his interactions with Eleanor were reasoned out beforehand.

'I find it strange that she is to live at Nance Farm.'

'Nance Farm?'

'Yes, Marcus. Sally informed me; Russell Trevail told her last night that Miss Venner has moved in with his aunt. Such a terribly coarse family. I think it rather ill-considered of Miss Venner to be associated with them. The other Trevail brother is said to have fathered the latest Vigus child. It would be more suitable if Miss Venner could live at Cardhu, even though Celia Sayce is departed and the scandal concerning her past has finally broken.' Eleanor kept herself informed of all happenings in the village, despite rarely mixing with the locals, owing both to her indifference towards them and the constant pain in her back.

'It was her first intention.' Marcus shuddered suddenly. 'Cardhu is a lonely house.'

'Have you been there?' Eleanor asked sharply.

'No. I've had no reason to.' Marcus rubbed his temples. He was getting another of his headaches. 'I'm afraid I can't do anything about Miss Venner's living arrangements, Mama.'

'Talking of that Sayce woman. There was a long interval between her body being discovered and her burial, don't you think?'

'Was there?'

'Marcus, I do wish you'd take more interest in the village. Information about what is going on outside this horrid little house is diverting for me. I would like to have known Celia Sayce lived close by, rather than finding out for myself in the obituaries in the *West Briton*. Incidentally, has the Vigus woman turned up yet?'

'Oh, yes,' he replied hastily. 'Her elder son found her wandering on the moors late yesterday afternoon. I'm sorry I forgot to mention it. She had gone off on a drinking spree, apparently.'

'Again? That woman is a disgrace. To get back to Miss Venner, what will the vicar think of her living at a dirty farm?' Eleanor looked down over her regal nose. 'But, of course, her background is of no real consequence. Her mother was only a shopkeeper's daughter before she ensnared William Venner. He left her penniless, you know. She strayed from his bed once too often, and he divided his money between his two children. Tell me all you know about the young lady.'

Marcus painstakingly repeated the few details he knew of the newest member of his staff. 'Due to her past connections with Parmarth she was considered the best equipped candidate to realise the needs of children from a depressed mining district. I think her idealism rather foolish. She has excellent references and qualifications in English language and literature. Miss Venner has given up a position in an excellent academy, has halted, perhaps irretrievably damaged, a promising career. I am confident she will be good for the school. I should obtain exceptional results from her.'

He, in fact, had been the only member on the interviewing panel who had been keen to select Joanna Venner. While listening to the direct, enthusiastic answers to the questions put to her, Marcus received the impression the vicar and the others had been concerned she would bring dangerous new ideas with her. That she might encourage the children to think for themselves and not merely absorb their lessons in the usual parrot fashion. Marcus had seen her as an equal in class and interests. She was something of an exciting prospect rather than the staid spinsters who had also applied for the post. He had argued with great persuasion to secure Joanna Venner for the school. She might make his existence here a touch more bearable.

'Should you now? She has something in common with

you, descending to a lesser position. Although in her case it is voluntary.' Marcus flinched. Eleanor pushed aside her almost full plate. 'Never mind what she will do for the wretched school. We could make her future loss our gain. She could be the means of us getting out of this dreadful place.'

Marcus could not pass another morsel between his lips. For several minutes he had realised where the conversation was heading. 'What do you mean?'

'Don't pretend to be in the dark, Marcus. I shall get angry with you.'

'She's unlikely to fall for a story about one of your non-existent charities in this quiet place.' He was getting anxious. It grieved him he could no longer look forward to the professional relationship he had anticipated with Joanna Venner.

'Then there's only one other option: you'll have to seduce a substantial sum of money out of her.'

Marcus recoiled at his mother's immoral scheme.

'Is she pretty? It will be a bonus.'

A vision of Joanna Venner's compact features, pure complexion and vivid green-flecked eyes was imprinted on Marcus's mind. Small-boned, alert, resourceful, she had an original, sparky quality about her.

'Marcus!'

'A-actually, she has a rather quaint face.'

'Sally's met her. She's remarked that Miss Venner is a funny little creature, given to uneasy temperament. Never mind. As things are at present, she will have to do.' A pained expression burned the predatory mien off Eleanor's features. 'I'm in agony again. I shall have to lie down until luncheon.'

There were no servants' bells in the headmaster's house, which was dark, closed and uninspiring, and Marcus immediately leapt for the door. 'I'll call Sally.'

'No, my dearest boy.' Eleanor looked at him intently. 'Don't take her away from her work. You can settle me after you've carried me upstairs.'

A sudden shower of hail battered the window. It startled

Marcus but he longed to be outside in it. Anywhere but here right now. 'I really have to—'

'Come and get me, Marcus. At once.'

Too late. He'd left it too late to mention the non-existent letter. She had won, again.

Rubbing his sweaty hands on his napkin, he lifted Eleanor off her chair, carried her up to her room and laid her on the bed.

Before he could step away, she gripped the sleeve of his jacket.

'I have to get away from these moors, Marcus, darling. To live in a house that suits my position, where I can invite my friends, hold parties again.' She was harshly insistent about this every day.

With her other hand, she reached up and caressed his neatly cut black hair, ignoring the petrifying of his body and his silent plea to let him go. 'You're such a handsome boy. My precious. My own.'

She pulled him down to her and held him very close, for a very long time.

Five

Jo was standing in the middle of a dance floor, wearing a badly stitched gown which hung off her body in unflattering folds. The material was coarse and pricked her skin. She knew the other female dancers, all beautiful, curvaceous, in silks and jewels, were laughing at her, making cruel comments about her flat figure. She wanted to run away and hide her shame, but her mother was blocking the doorway, a list of spiteful remarks against her written all over her excessively made-up face.

A sound woke Jo. She raised her head off the pillows. It was strangely quiet, the room in total blackness until her eyes picked out the dark grey rectangle of the window. She recognised a light step. The bedroom was filled with the scent of gardenias.

'Celia?' In one rapid movement Jo was sitting up straight.

Celia was standing beside the bed, smiling down at her. Celia, so hauntingly lovely, statuesque, astute, assured, kindly. Jo was about to speak but she heard Celia's voice in her heart. 'No need for words, my dear. I've just come to say hello. Go back to sleep.'

She vanished, and Jo, forgetting her recurring tormenting dream, slept peacefully.

Creeping out of the back door of the schoolhouse, Marcus lit a cigarette. Dawn was streaking the sky, illuminating the desolate tors on the horizon into vivid looming shapes. The naked branches of the ash trees in the garden swayed like grotesque arms in the east wind. The water closet at the bottom of the path stood out stark and abysmal, like a tiny prison, with all the attendant horrors of such a place awaiting within.

He had risen from a hot sticky bed and come outside in just his shirt and trousers. But he desired the cold, hoping it would somehow slam precious moments of normality into his life. He filled his lungs with smoke. Normality. What was it like? Would he ever realise it? Not if landmarks of nature and everyday objects in his own garden seemed threatening.

A touch on his arm made his flesh leap. He exhaled the smoke in a strangled gasp.

'It's only me,' Sally Allett, the housemaid, whispered. She was clutching a blanket over her nightdress. 'You're jumpy. You'll catch your death. Come back to bed.'

'No,' he said sharply.

'Did you have another nightmare?'

'No. Is my mother stirring?'

'Didn't hear anything when I passed her door. Have you quarrelled with her?'

'No, of course not.' He glared at Sally's pretty, showy face, outlined by springy fair curls. 'Why do you ask that?'

'Sometimes I don't understand you two. You're so attached to each other, but she often raises her voice to you and you sink into long silences and try to avoid her.'

'Occasionally she becomes difficult, the result of her accident,' he said tersely, 'and I need some peace. Remember, Sally, it's none of your business.'

'Sorry.' She moved closer to him and he could smell the allure of her body. 'I didn't mean to pry. I thought I might be able to help.'

To check himself, he swallowed the saliva in his mouth. 'You do help. The girl that started this week to do the heavy housework, is she suitable?'

'Beth Wherry's a bit simple-minded but she works well.'

'Good. I want you to concentrate on my mother's needs. Keep close to her. Make sure she has everything she requires.' The more tasks Sally performed for Eleanor the less demand she made on him. It would make it easier to break the hold she had regained over him.

Sally's hand travelled down his arm to rest on his quivering palm. Her skin was warm and alive. She was the same age as Joanna Venner but different in every way. Sally had no ambitions except to obtain a husband and her own home. She was totally uninterested in what went on in the world outside the village. Her body was formed in bountiful curves, which she flaunted at men to look at, to use, and many had taken up the invitation.

She pressed herself against him. Her fingertips teased his wrist and he was aroused, instantly, agonisingly, but he did not want sex again. After lunch he had to present a respectable front to Joanna Venner. He had to be appealing, full of charm, if his mother's scheme was to succeed. He felt sick at what he must do if he was ever to find release from his miseries.

He prised the housemaid's fingers off him. 'Bring my breakfast into the study. I'll eat in there today.'

The unaccustomed smell of fried bacon and eggs filled the Vigus cottage. Rex and Molly had been sitting eagerly at the table for some time. Dishing up the meal on the few pieces of crockery their mother had not sold, Luke joined them.

'Eat properly,' he snapped moments later. 'Haven't you kids got no manners? The old woman's hung over, she won't come down and snatch it away from you.'

Heads bent over their plates, Rex and Molly shovelled forkfuls of food into their mouths a little less ravenously. Molly sniffed and wiped her nose on her dress sleeve.

'Mother took the Christmas presents you left off us,' Rex said, aggrieved.

'What? I told you to hide them away.' Luke sighed impatiently.

The matter was not discussed further. The doll and wooden puppet were gone, irretrievably, a fact of life.

'You staying home long this time?' Rex asked sullenly.

'A day or two.'

'Can I come with you when you go off again?' It was the same plea Rex uttered every time Luke set foot inside the door. Luke set aside the terrible wrench it gave his heart.

Molly whimpered, afraid of being left behind without Rex. She rarely spoke, speech having been beaten out of her from an early age. She was undersized and vacant-looking. A moron, an idiot, an imbecile, the villagers called her, and the local bullies bestowed far worse insults on her. Rex was the only person she trusted, the only one ever to be truly kind to her.

Rex was very protective of her. As far as he was concerned, Molly was all he had. 'Molly too?'

'Don't be daft. What about the baby? You know I can't take kids on the road. Please don't keep on about it,' Luke said, covering his guilt with a growl. No matter how hard he tried he could find no love for these half-siblings, from the mother he hated for her dereliction of the most basic maternal duties.

'Gipsies do.',

'We're not the same as gipsies. Anyway, I haven't got a woman to look after you, have I?' Luke was pleading now for Rex to understand his position. It served to make him feel even more callous for striving to hold on to his freedom. Why should the boy, who'd had one of the worst possible starts in life, care about anything more than his own and Molly's survival?

'Then bloody get one.'

Luke cuffed him on the ear for his cheek.

Rex glanced up fearfully at the low beams overhead. 'We're afraid, Luke. Mother said she'll kill us one day. She means it.'

'No, she don't. It's the drink talking. Finish your meal, then give Marylyn her bottle. I'm going out to get you something decent to wear. I promise I'll come back.'

'Mother'll only sell it,' Rex mouthed despondently.

Luke dropped his fork, his meal uneaten. He could not bear the despairing expression on his little brother's face. 'I'll threaten her with a good thrashing if she does. I'll get you some liquorice bootlaces. You'll like that, eh?'

'We need some shoes,' Rex said tartly, unreceptive of the bribe to shut up.

'I know,' Luke groaned. 'I'll see to it.'

'We're getting a new teacher,' Rex murmured, saying anything to keep his older brother interested in his and Molly's plight.

'So what?' Luke got up from the table. Rex and Molly's eyes were on his plate. They would clear it in seconds when he went out. 'Clean up this damned place, will you? It stinks. I'll be back in a couple of hours.'

When Jo woke again she basked in the peaceful warmth of her unexpected vision of Celia. Her little square clock on the mantelpiece indicated it was ten o'clock. Yawning, stretching, she jumped out of bed into the cosy atmosphere. Mercy had stolen in and lit a fire of coal and driftwood.

Jo looked out of the window over the yard. The rain had drifted away during the night and the sun was shining optimistically. She opened the window, which creaked on its old sashes. Noisy starlings were flitting about below, impertinently searching for titbits among the territorial hens, ducks and geese.

Directly across the yard reared a forty-foot barn, supported by massive granite pillars. Memories came flooding back. She had been a small child when Lew Trevail, then a robust boy, twice her age, carried her up the steps at its side, and climbed on top of the rough-wood roof with her. He'd left her stranded there, oblivious to the danger, and Jo, who had thought this a great adventure, could have tumbled off and been killed. Ten minutes later, when she had been about to jump off on to the haywain, which might have caused her serious injury, Mercy had rescued her. Jo grinned, remembering how Mercy had beaten Lew for his recklessness.

Darius Pendower, a bent-over old codger from Pendeen, a mining village two and a half miles away, emerged from the barn dragging a heavy sack on a sledge. He was about to take chopped mangolds to the fields to feed the cattle, who would get their ration outside today as the weather was dry. Darius had seemed ancient to Jo when she was a child. She pondered his age. Seventy? Eighty? He had to be at least eighty because Darius had worked for Mercy's grandfather. He was as much a part of Nance as the fields and buildings, a shy individual with platinum-white hair and a thick accent few people could understand. He moved very slowly. Mercy also employed Kizzy Kemp, an enormously fat woman, now middle-aged, and inclined to be lazy, in the washhouse and dairy. It occurred to Jo that the condition of her employees meant Mercy must perform most of the farm's tasks herself. There was a sense of familiarity and continuity on the farm which Jo had never experienced at Tresawna.

'Good morning, Darius,' she called out, cupping her hands to her mouth. Darius was hard of hearing and did not heed her. She watched him plod off.

'Hey, Shrewface!' A man she had not spied in the vicinity of the pigsty was waving to her. 'Heard you was here. What time of the morning do you call this?'

'Lew Trevail!' Jo looked down on Mercy's older nephew with disdain. 'What are you doing here?'

'Haven't come t'see you,' Lew shouted back, grinning mockingly, strutting through the cackling poultry with his hands thrust inside his heavy black belt until he was under her window.

'I gathered that,' Jo retorted rudely.

'There's hardly any work in the mines now, so Aunt Mercy took me on three months ago.' Lew guffawed as if it was a big joke. 'Didn't she tell you?'

'No, she did not.' Jo stared down at the craggy, insolent, dark looks which helped Lew succeed with just about every female he fancied.

'I'm looking forward to dragging you through the cow shit again, like at our first meeting. Never forget you running off like a scalded cat.' Lew bawled with mirth. 'Just imagine what the kids at the school would think, eh? Me and Russell know you for not being much of a lady, Jo Venner.'

'You had better not.' Jo shook with indignation.

'Put the kettle on then, maid,' Lew said, digging a cigarette out of his waistcoat pocket.

'Oh, very well, you darned nuisance. Give me a minute.'

'I'll be in for a big mug of tea drekkly.' Lew strode manfully back to the pigs.

'You're in good company,' Jo muttered at his proud back.

She was not vexed with Lew for long. It was his and his younger brother Russell's rough play which had led to the events which had changed the course of her stifled, formal life, bringing her to where she was now, in a career and a destination of her own choosing.

What kind of woman she would have grown to be if denied Celia's love and influence she had no way of knowing. She could not guess if she would have been weaker or more stubborn, painfully shy or brazen, becalmed or hopelessly frustrated. One thing Jo was certain of, she would always be thankful for the richest blessing of her life so far, the all-enduring love of Celia Sayce. For she was able to give and receive recommendation and criticism without docility or suspicion, to genuinely care for the pupils in her charge, to own real affection for Alistair, to trust and respect Mercy.

Jo washed and dressed in a hurry in the bedroom of the farmhouse. After lunch she had two appointments to keep, and before that she must entertain one of her old playmates.

Six

Feeling desolate and emotional, Jo opened the wrought-iron gate at Cardhu, walked along the path that cut through the lawn and stopped to gaze at the house. Protected by a five-foot stone wall, it was small in comparison to Tresawna House but much larger than the wayside cottages of the local people. An ashlar-fronted building, with a thick chimney stack at either end, it was graced with large double windows and a front door overseen by a decorative porch. When Jo had first come here she'd decided it exuded the same cheerful friendliness as its owner. A house to be noisy in, to dash up and down the stairs, to flit from room to room without first having to tap on the door and await permission to enter. And no keys in the upstairs rooms where a naughty little girl could be locked in for hours at a time.

The house was now padlocked, the windows shuttered inside, presumably by the solicitor acting for Celia's estate. It had stood here in princely isolation for thirty-seven years, built for Celia by her lover. Although the ever-present winds buffeted the moor, the house seemed surrounded by a cathedral calm.

The front garden was well tended, but Jo wondered if it would be the case if former miner, John Wherry, caretaker of the Methodist chapel, had known before Celia's death she had been mistress to a married man.

The rose trees and many plants from the herbaceous borders had been dug up and taken away, a sacrilegious act by selfish vandals. The proud-looking stone eagles which had guarded each side of the front doorstep were missing, the guilty damp patches suggesting they had been stolen only hours before. Jo was relieved to see the gardenia bushes had not been touched. Celia's favourite flower, she had chosen a partially shaded spot, in humus-rich soil for them, and had kept them trimmed in shape. The white, delicately fragrant, double flowers would soon be in bud, if the frost could be persuaded by mist and low cloud to keep its cruel fingers at bay.

The house was desolate without its owner, who, despite being terribly lonely here for so many long years, had loved it so much. Her heart raw and aching, Jo walked round to the back of the building.

Moving with animal effortlessness, Luke cast a practised eye round the interior of the small stable. He was disappointed. Ponies had not been kept here for years. There was nothing worth pinching, no feed stuff or spare tack for Lucky, no tools, no odds and ends.

Outside, under the lowering grey sky, Luke glanced about warily, a little on edge. This place had always seemed lonely, further away from life and habitation than it really was, but now the owner was newly dead, had died within its walls, he half-expected to see Celia Sayce's spirit loom up in front of him. He wouldn't hang around long. Anything worth stealing in the garden had already been taken away. After trying the garden shed and outhouses he would seek entrance to the house.

His long strides were brought to a halt at the corner of the house when he found himself face to face with a stranger.

'Who are you?' Jo bluntly asked the man suddenly in her path, someone who had no right to be here by the look of him. A gipsy? His skin had an olive tone, his hair coal-black, falling carelessly across a hardy brow, but his sharp pale blue eyes, although guarded and restless, were less suspicious than those of the gipsy clans she had encountered. She did not take him for a farmhand or casual labourer. There was colour in his clothes, boldness in his stance. He had a free-living air about him, held his bare head at an angle hinting of his own mastery.

'What are you doing here?' she demanded when receiving

40

no reply. He had seemed slightly startled at her arrival; now he was smiling in a lazy, inquisitive manner.

'I saw it first,' Luke said, warm and insolently, taking time in collecting together his cigarettes and matches. What an interesting little piece she was. Standing out clear and firm, hair the colour of autumn bracken, kind of prettily aloof, staring at him with intense curiosity, undisturbed at finding him trespassing on what was likely a relative's property. She looked familiar, then he knew where he had seen those black-lashed, wide-set intellectual eyes before. Eyes that had told her story then, as now, of her possession of conviction and vigour, and a trace of disdain.

'Are you saying I'm here to steal something? Is that why you're here?'

He smiled as if the accusation amused him. 'I'm reliving memories of an old friend.'

'You knew Miss Sayce?' Jo asked suspiciously. She could not place him, and a man of such astonishingly good looks, an instant friendly smile, candid, decadent eyes and such a forthright bearing was not easy to forget.

'Not as well as you did.'

'I beg your pardon. How could you possibly know who I am?'

'I recognised you from a painting inside. It's set in a prominent place, so you must have been very important to the old lady.'

Jo moved up to him. Luke eased his footing, casually placing his hands on his hips. He kept his eyes on her, and Jo did not drop hers from his dark face. For several seconds, without invitation or rebuff, embarrassment or a bid to gain supremacy, each searched the other's expression, digging deep, delving wilfully. It became more than inquisitiveness. Equanimity of sorts, strangely not unwelcome for two very individual people who demanded their own space, was being set up.

'Miss Sayce never mentioned anyone like you to me.' Jo's voice was a touch softer, conversational. 'What connection did you have with her?'

'As I said, we were friends.'

She responded to his smiles, which came readily one after the other. She was in no doubt this man operated on wit and guile, was a quick thinker, adept at talking himself out of tricky situations and she was sure his reason for being here was not at all innocent. 'I don't believe you.'

Luke lit a smoke without lifting his gaze from her. He was enjoying the banter, sensing a haughty madam of her birth, but a free spirit, one who could take kindly to gentle mocking. 'We did business together is nearer the truth. I'm in the demand-and-supply business.'

'A dealer.' Jo was satisfied with the explanation. 'I thought it was something like that.'

She walked past him and peeped through the window of the nearest outhouse. A fan of emotion sent moisture behind her eyes. There among the miscellany of old lanterns, stored apples and garden furniture were her childhood toys. The hobby horse, hoop and toboggan, all crafted by the village blacksmith, one of the few mourners at Celia's funeral yesterday.

Luke followed her, pressing his hand against the outhouse wall above her head, towering over her. He liked her invigorating perfume and drew in a long breath of it. It was a healthy, young smell and stimulated all his senses. He felt she had something new and unique to offer.

'Are you a niece of Miss Sayce's?'

Jo moved to the lawn, passing over the stepping stones until she was standing at a green-painted swing. She gave it a little push, and told the man at her side, 'I met her nineteen years ago, on a hot sunny day, on the bridge down the lane. I was hurt and lost and she took me back to my mother. We became close friends. I shall never forget her.'

'Those who cared for us never leave us.'

Jo looked at him, smiled her appreciation at not getting a platitude but a sincere word of comfort. A cherished sadness had formed on his brow. He knew what he was talking about. Who had he lost? Who was he?

'Do you live in Parmarth?'

'Not often.'

'May I know your name?'

'Luke Vigus. Pleased to meet you . . . ?'

Jo accepted his hand and felt his firm fingers wrapping around hers. 'I'm Jo Venner. Yes, it's been interesting.'

Then a lift of her brows intimated that their meeting should come to an end; she needed to be alone.

He gave a small nod of understanding. 'I'd better go. I hope we meet again before I go off on my travels.'

He left without a goodbye. Jo sensed he avoided goodbyes. She watched his strong, athletic outline, his loose, confident way of walking, until he was out of sight. She thought him both straightforward and complicated, most definitely attractive, and a little exciting. Was he a thief? Had he stolen Celia's stone eagles? It seemed unlikely. She knew him somehow. He would not have stayed and made himself available to her if he'd committed an offence here. Whether he had been about to was another matter. Her mind drifted over his every word and smile, before, while sitting on the swing, she found Celia again.

Celia had often said she would leave Jo her house and money. Was it wrong to hope she really had? It would provide Jo with more security and a greater independence. The house featured a bathroom, upholstered furniture, silverware and genteel crockery, books and a piano, all of which, despite feeling quite comfortable at Nance, Jo would be glad to have the use of again.

Unknown to her mother, Alistair paid a small allowance into her bank account each month, but to have her own means before her trust fund matured and to possess property would make her . . . someone of importance? Noteworthy? Was it what she desired? Katherine's spiteful remark about her cultivating Celia's friendship for selfish ends repeated itself in her mind.

'No,' she said aloud and the word was snatched away by the wind, as if nature itself recognised an unfair accusation. Jo could honestly say it was her love for Celia, her desire to return all the years of Celia's care and affection, which had made her want the position at the insignificant local school.

Jo's mind went back down over the years to the stream a short distance down the lane. While trying to make urgent repairs to her unkempt appearance, she had felt someone watching her up on the little bridge, and she had been mightily relieved to find it wasn't her mother who had discovered her.

A lady in her middle years, wearing an embroidered long-coated linen suit and a large hat with a double bow – fashionable wear for this quiet backwater – called down to her in pleasant unfaltering tones, 'Are you hurt badly? Did you take a fall?'

'It's nothing really.' Jo explained how, thanks to the Trevail brothers, she came to be in her predicament. Looking closely at her surroundings for the first time she realised she was lost.

'That was very unkind of those two boys. Don't worry, I'll take you back to Fern Field where you've left your picnic. I'm dressed this way today because I've just had company but I'm wearing my walking shoes.' The lady held out her ungloved hand to help Jo out of the stream. 'My name's Miss Celia Sayce. I live a little further along the lane. And who are you, dear?'

Dripping like a pond leaf, Jo pulled on her shoes and stockings. 'I'm Joanna Venner. I prefer to be called Jo but my mother insists on Joanna.'

'Which name do you think portrays your true character?'

'Jo,' the little girl replied emphatically.

'Then I shall call you Jo.' Celia Sayce smiled warmly, and Jo instantly liked her. 'And you may call me Celia. I know the Trevail brothers. A noisy pair of ruffians from the village. Their father is a tinner. Do the boys themselves worry you, Jo, or is it just their rough play?'

'They use awfully naughty words and my mother would be cross if she knew I'd even spoken to them, but it would be good to have friends of a sort. My brother rarely plays with me. I've got nobody really.'

'Well, Jo, the next time the boys cut up rough, be sure you return the compliment. And you could suggest to your mother that you wear older clothes while out playing.'

Jo's mouth dropped open. Celia Sayce was suggesting a combination of disrespect and wickedness. 'I don't think my mother would approve, Miss Sayce.'

'I'm sure she wouldn't but perhaps I could persuade her. Now do call me Celia.'

Jo frowned; it felt uncomfortable calling adults by their first name unless they were servants.

'Come along, Jo. We'll take a short cut across the moor to the farm.'

When they reached the end of the rough narrow lane and had crossed the St Ives road, they were tramping through coarse springy grass and patches of heather on the open moor. Jo's shoes were becoming more and more scuffed, her stockings snagged, but she was unconcerned. It did not seem to matter in Miss Sayce's company. In Celia's company.

Celia strode along, loose-limbed, head up, surprising Jo when she broke into a cheerful whistling. 'I can't offend anyone out here on the moor, so why not?' She laughed.

'Yes, why not?' Jo shouted, her echo returning to her and encouraging her to be even more carefree. She ran on ahead, plunging through the foliage, bounding round clumps of gorse and bramble, skirting crops of fern, finally leaping up on a high granite boulder. She whooped and trilled. She felt silly. She'd always wanted to act silly. Her mother's most constant rebuke was, 'Joanna, stop being silly at once!'

When Celia reached her, however, she was unsure. Grown-ups were apt to change their judgements in unfair and inexplicable ways. She blushed and hung her head.

Celia lifted her chin. 'Be as energetic as you like, Jo. Be yourself. I don't believe in us conforming to rigorous ideals, of having to restrain our natural spirits.'

Jo knew she could trust Celia's word. With a gleeful scream, she jumped off the boulder, forgetting everything drummed into her from the moment she could understand an order. It was as if something heavy and choking had seeped out through her flesh and bones, something that had been crushing her soul.

'See the hole in the top of the boulder, Jo,' Celia said. 'It's been formed by centuries of wind and rain. There's a legend which says if you look through the hole and see one of the small people, you'll have your first-born child stolen away by them. Another belief is the hole was made by the local giant, Holiburn, tossing a stone in play at it. If one can find a stone which fits the shape exactly, then that person will be imbued with the giant's strength. The moors have many legends. I hope I shall have the opportunity to tell you more of them.'

Jo absorbed the information, her thin lips moving, silently repeating Celia's tales. She was certain her new friend was an encyclopaedia of interesting facts, and although she lived in a remote area, kept up with all the current news and had a strong opinion about everything.

'Celia, have you ever climbed that hill up there?' Jo was pointing to Carn Galver, one of the most beautiful tors on the moor, which provided a dramatic backdrop to the farm.

'Yes, Jo. I climb to the top at least half a dozen times every summer.'

'Will you take me there one day?'

'Certainly, dear. I have a strong feeling that you and I will become very good friends.'

Jo hoped so with all her heart. She needed a friend more than anything else in the world. Although Alistair was showered with everything he wanted, her mother denied her the company of other little girls at Tresawna House. Apart from these moorland picnics her mother had suddenly acquired a strong leaning for, the only time Jo got away from home was twice a year when she was packed off to stuffy relatives in Norfolk. She did not attend a school, but had her lessons with a severe governess, excruciatingly boring lessons in which Jo was unable to discuss any scintillating information she procured. She longed to learn more and more and to pass it on, and already cherished the ambition of becoming a teacher in a proper school. A progressive school, where girls could achieve more out of life than merely becoming wives and mothers. It was something her parents would never agree to.

'Celia, are you going to get married one day?'

Celia did not answer straightaway and Jo apologised. 'I'm always being scolded for being too curious.'

'I don't mind what you ask me.' Celia took her hand and gave it an encouraging squeeze. 'I'll tell you about myself. I would love to have had children but, of course, I've never had a husband. I live alone and get rather lonely in my big house. I'm keen to see you again, Jo. I'm sure we could get along well.'

'Would you have liked a little girl like me?'

'Exactly like you, Jo, dear.'

Jo was set on impressing her new friend. Recently, she had listened in on a conversation her father had conducted with a group of gentlemen luncheon guests (rarely being spoken or listened to, Jo had acquired the habit of eavesdropping and collecting information) and the male gathering had branded Emmeline Pankhurst and the suffragette movement as a 'scourge on the British Empire! Women who did not know their place. Outrageous!' 'Celia, are you a suffragette? They stand for women's rights, don't they? I don't understand much about it but I think it must be a good thing.'

'You have got an old head on young shoulders.' Celia did indeed seem impressed. 'I totally admire their stance. If I did not live quietly in this part of the world I would be fully involved with the Movement.'

Jo was delighted with Celia's response in taking her seriously, and with the thought that perhaps Celia really *was* slightly wicked.

Next, she wanted to know, 'Are you worried about the war in the Balkans? My father frowns and says it could spread and involve our country.'

'If it does, I don't think it will affect us very much, my dear.' On that point Celia was to be proved tragically wrong, when just a few years later her lover, Katherine's lover, and Jo's father were all killed in the Great War.

47

They walked on towards the outlying fields of Nance Farm, the question-and-answer session, which was to become a feature of their relationship, in full flow.

When they approached Katherine Venner, who was pacing furiously among the ferns, near the pony and trap, Jo clung to Celia's hand. Tension formed throughout her body.

'Where on earth have you been, you disobedient girl? Look at the state of you! Where is your hat?' Katherine's face pulsed with wrath as she gripped Jo's arm and shook her violently. She delivered a resounding slap on Jo's leg.

Jo's hand flew guiltily to her bare head. She had forgotten Russell Trevail had swiped off her dainty straw hat, that she had not retrieved his trophy from him. The unsedate passage from Bridge Lane had added more tangles in her long, ringletted hair, the old-fashioned torture her mother insisted she endure every day. She could expect more punishment when they arrived home.

'I've brought Jo back safely to you, Mrs Venner. There was no need to strike her,' Celia intervened forcefully.

Katherine glared at Celia Sayce. Then, 'I know who you are! How dare you talk to my child?'

The strength of her mother's hostility left Jo shocked, but she had no need to be afraid.

'Mrs Venner, I know why you're here and why you've brought Jo with you,' Celia continued, completely unruffled. She was the more graceful figure, looming some four inches over Katherine, but it wasn't her advantageous height which made her the dominator. 'In the circumstances, I think you and I should form an alliance, don't you?'

An alliance was formed between the two women that day, and it was always hostile on Katherine's side. Jo was to spend time with Celia while Katherine enjoyed her picnics. During Jo's first visit to Cardhu, Celia mentioned she'd ask her mother if she could sleep over at times.

'Do you think she'll really say yes?' Jo said, hoping desperately it would happen.

'I'll do my best.' Celia laughed. 'I can be quite determined.'

48

'That's just how I'm going to be when I grow up.'

Celia had drawn her into her arms and hugged her affectionately. 'It's how us women often have to be, Jo.'

There was no history to Cardhu, but Jo had found love inside the house, and it had been loved in. Jo had never met Sheridan Ustick. When Jo reached womanhood, Celia had told her how desperately she had loved him, how she'd tried not to fall unwisely for a married man, but after it had happened how she could not give him up. There had been no question of him deserting his marriage and children. His wife had not been a hard or unloving woman, but when Sheridan was killed she had set her lawyers against Celia, demanding she leave Cardhu immediately. To help her come to terms with her grief, Celia had been able to prove Sheridan had gifted her the house outright and she had never heard from Mrs Ustick again.

Now Cardhu was to get a new owner.

Seven

'Thank you for coming to me last night. If only it wasn't too late for us to be together. I'm going to the school when I leave here,' Jo whispered tearfully beside Celia's grave. And in the same way she had informed Celia of all her movements when her friend was alive, she told her about Katherine's reaction to the news of her post at the village school, about staying at Nance, and the gipsy-dark man who had brought a little colour to her sad pilgrimage at Cardhu.

She had applied for the teacher's post at Parmarth following news of the vacancy in one of Celia's regular letters. Informed of the governing board's decision the same day as the interview, Jo had celebrated with Celia in a tea room at the top of Market Jew Street, in Penzance. Celia's response to Jo's request that she come to live with her had been joyful, as if she was expecting a beloved daughter home.

'If it's what you really want, my dear,' she had said in a typical unselfish statement, 'then I shall be delighted to have you with me. But are you sure you want to leave Hampshire?'

'I'm certain it's the right thing to do. Lately I've felt I'm slipping into a life of routine and monotony, and that's the last thing I want. I need an even greater challenge than teaching young women, who, in the main, will achieve their aims. Perhaps, before I go on to found my own school, I could inspire one or two of the village girls to seek better things.'

'Careful, Jo.' Celia had smiled. 'You'll be accused of putting unethical notions into their heads.'

'We'll see. Parmarth will give me a breathing space and it

50

will be wonderful living at Cardhu and wandering the moors, to be with the person I love the most.'

They had parted at the railway station, Jo to travel back to Hampshire to hand in her resignation, Celia to return home to make the arrangements for her indefinite stay at Cardhu. Then a sudden cold had turned into pneumonia and Celia had died. Snatched away from Jo, as Sheridan Ustick had been snatched away from Celia and Bob Merrick from her mother. Although Jo's father had also died in the war, Jo's visits to Cardhu had not been stopped, as she'd feared. Years later she discovered Celia had paid her extravagantly spending mother for the privilege.

As there was no one to erect a memorial to her friend, Jo resolved to have a granite headstone inscribed herself: 'Celia Mary Sayce   Died 17th December 1929   Aged 69 years', and add, 'Sadly Missed'.

'I've picked some snowdrops from the clump you always admired in Bridge Lane, my dear,' she said emotionally. Tenderly, she placed the white posy on the mound of wet earth, next to the only other flowers there, a wreath from herself. 'I haven't really wept for you yet.'

In the windswept graveyard, high up on the moor, Jo wanted desperately to release the grief building up inside her. She must wait until the meeting with the headmaster was over. It would be a painful interlude. She should have come here afterwards. Holding off her tears, she left the churchyard for her appointment with Marcus Lidgey.

Jo had taken little notice of the heavily buttressed church building two days ago, but a hasty glance revealed that the leaky roof was still in need of renovation. The vicarage nearby seemed every bit as bleak and rundown. There were no funds anywhere in Parmarth for improvement. The grey stone, slate-roofed cottages were shabbier than before. The thatched-roofed public house, flanked by uneven outside steps rising to its upstairs rooms and guarded by a bent iron rail, had not altered or changed hands. Nor had the few other places of business. The Methodist chapel, nestling at the bottom of the hill, was in need of fresh brown paint and plaster.

At one time over eight hundred people had packed into the parish, excavating and dressing tin ore at the Solace Mine. The mine had closed in 1912, two months after Jo's first presence in Parmarth, and she had been aware of the apathy and depression, the unnatural quietness which had settled over the village like a shroud. Subsequently, as the men sought work elsewhere, the number of inhabitants had quickly halved. The numbers were still dwindling.

It was no surprise to Jo to hear a violent argument coming from number 2 Tregersick Road, a tiny cottage squeezed in between its larger neighbour and Pascoe's General Store. Without pausing to listen, she heard every word clearly.

'For crying out loud, you stupid old fool! I told you where I put they blasted matches. What have you got for ears? Old Jolly Retallack's shirt?'

'I wouldn't be asking you if I knew where they bleddy were, would I? You useless excuse for a woman.'

Verena and Abner Jelbert quarrelled on a daily basis. Villagers had acquired the habit of being ready to duck as they passed the Jelberts' abode, to avoid being struck by a hurtling missile.

Suddenly there was a terrified yelp, the wrenching-open of a door, and Jo turned round to see Scamp, the Jelberts' wire-haired, long-bodied, greyish mongrel being kicked out of the house.

'Get out my way, I said, you bastard.' Jo watched, horrified, as Abner Jelbert delivered two blows, one on the dog's head, the other on its side.

'Stop that!' Jo rounded on him. 'There's no need to be cruel to the dog.'

Squat, sallow-faced, unemployed miner Abner Jelbert spat out the dog-end between his fat purple lips. 'Mind your own bleddy business. I don't need an outsider telling me what to do with me own bleddy dog.'

Verena, tall, stern-eyed, wearing a cross-over pinny, appeared in the doorway. 'Who've you upset now, you old fool?'

'Only this fancy bint here. Had the cheek to tell me off for kicking the bleddy dog.'

'Serves you right. How many times have I told you to leave Scamp be? Anyway, don't you recognise she? 'Tis Miss Venner, she's what's going to be the new teacher.' Verena smiled self-consciously at Jo. 'I wish you well at the school, Miss Venner. You'll have our twins in your class.'

'Oh, really,' Jo replied coolly, 'I shall look forward to meeting them.'

'Stuck-up cow.' Abner spat a ball of black phlegm on the ground. 'Kids'll never understand a word she says.'

'Stop it.' Verena cuffed him round the head, and the couple went back inside to pursue their current disagreement.

'Just like old times with those two at it hammer and tongs, eh?' said a woman, who had come out of the newsagent, sweets and tobacco shop she owned, on the other side of the general store. Paula Hadley, of full and stately bust, wearing round-rimmed spectacles, all the better for spotting quarry to gossip about, had recognised Jo immediately. 'It seems only yesterday Miss Sayce used to bring you into my shop for sherbet lemons. Be strange having you back here as teacher. What does your mother think about it?'

'Mrs Venner was rather surprised,' Jo replied evenly, ready to fend off any more personal questions.

Paula Hadley was gazing intently at her. 'You haven't grown much. Good luck to you is all I can say, specially with those Jelbert twins.'

'Thank you, Mrs Hadley, I'm confident I shall manage them. While I'm here, may I order *The Times*? It can be delivered at Nance Farm with Miss Merrick's newspapers.'

'Certainly. Heard you was staying at Nance. *The Times*? That's what the 'master reads.'

'I'll step inside now and give you a week's payment in advance.'

Mrs Hadley's remark on Jo's appearance caused her to hope she was suitably dressed to meet the headmaster. There was no reason why she shouldn't be. Her Hampshire dressmaker had interpreted all the latest fashions to Jo's satisfaction. Even so, a picture of Katherine's scathing face entered her mind and Jo was brushing the fur collar of her coat with gloved fingertips. She licked her handkerchief and stooped to wipe off the moorland dirt accumulated on her high-heeled shoes during the walk to Cardhu and the village.

Quickly, she viewed herself in the glass of the shop window. There was nothing misplaced about her clothes, she told herself, and it did not matter how little she filled them out. She was a teacher, not a social butterfly looking for a husband or a lover.

She glanced at the news stand outside the shop proclaiming the day's dramatic international and local headlines. *German Ex-Chief of Staff implicated in plot to overthrow Soviet regime. Man killed by freak wave: St Ives.* Jo had once thought the people living in this remote area would take little interest in events outside their domestic boundaries, but Celia had informed her that Paula Hadley made an agreeable profit on all her print trade.

As she progressed to the counter of the dark, cluttered shop, Jo grew nostalgic at the delicious smells of fudge, butterscotch and sherbet lemons, and the sweet scent of good-quality tobacco. Two rows of pipes stood in their accustomed place beside the ornate Edwardian till. Neat shelves of newspapers, magazines and sixpenny love and adventure story books lined the lower regions of the walls. At the head of a small queue was Miss Teague, the infants' class teacher.

'Miss Venner.' She beckoned to Jo. 'How good to see you. Welcome to Parmarth. Do serve Miss Venner first, Mrs Hadley.' She raised her chin in the manner of a turkey. 'I understand she has an appointment shortly with Mr Lidgey.'

'It's very kind of you, Miss Teague.' Jo greeted the three other customers, women of varying ages, as she produced her purse from her handbag.

Miss Teague had a mediocre face, was short and chubby, her age well past forty. Jo had seen her on half a dozen occasions before but Miss Teague had not spoken to her until now.

'Not at all. I do hope you'll like it at the school. It won't be what you're used to.' Miss Teague gave an overstretched smile.

Halting at tapping chips of treacle toffee off a tray for Miss Teague, Paula Hadley listened for Jo's reply, as did her other customers, whom Jo suspected were gathered here to exchange tittle-tattle.

'I'm sure I shall,' she said brightly. When she had paid for the newspapers and tucked the day's edition of *The Times* in under her arm, she bid the women, 'Good afternoon.' She knew, without looking back, they would form a huddle to talk about her.

'Do you think you'll get on with her?' Paula Hadley asked Miss Teague.

'I have grave doubts,' Miss Teague told the huddle importantly. 'She will not fit in easily among us. I was hoping a friend of mine, Miss Martin, who recently lost her place at St Mevan's primary school when it closed for lack of pupils last month, would obtain the post.'

'She shouldn't have no trouble,' Ellie Blewett, an elderly woman, wearing a thick hairnet underneath her black felt hat, said good-naturedly. 'She used to run barefoot 'cross the moors with the Trevail boys and my grandson, Mick.'

'It's easy to run barefoot when you've got umpteen pairs of shoes to put on when you get back home,' the shabbily dressed niece of Verena Jelbert, holding a newborn baby, remarked sourly. 'There's something strange about her coming to the likes of Parmarth, if you ask me. The 'master's too good for this place too and that's another mystery. Perhaps she's his fancy woman. Come here to carry on their affair.'

'You've got an evil and a jealous mind, Biddy Lean.' Ellie Blewett remonstrated with the young mother. 'She's staying with Mercy Merrick. She's a good judge of character and that's good enough for me.'

'Don't forget who Bob Merrick was meeting in his fields,' Miss Teague said, making Paula Hadley stop hammering again at the toffee.

'Well, there is that, I suppose,' Ellie Blewett mused.

'She's likely just as immoral as her mother and Celia Sayce,' Biddy Lean muttered, adjusting her baby's washed-out, passed-down clothes. 'That sort sticks together. High and mighty in their fine houses but common as muck underneath.'

'We've no right to judge Joanna Venner; she probably didn't know Celia Sayce was a fallen woman,' Paula Hadley said in a superior tone. 'This Mr Ustick died in the war. He might have been a hero. Miss Sayce spent many years alone. I think she was very lonely, and it was good of Miss Venner to want to come to live with her in her old age.'

'Of course, you're bound to take a stand for Celia Sayce,' Miss Teague replied tightly. 'She spent good money in your shop. But it isn't you who has to work with Joanna Venner, who, I fear, may share some of the radical ideas I heard Celia Sayce express.'

There seemed to be a lot of men loafing about the village and most of them spoke to Jo. Looking into their faces, she witnessed the despair and humiliation of men out of work. The redundant miners and their sons and daughters still in the area had turned to farm work, fishing, stone-breaking, service in a big house, or the docks at Penzance to earn a living, but there was a chronic shortage of jobs. Jo saw facial resemblances among them. Many of the villagers had intermarried. To offend one of them might also offend a brother or a cousin.

Sally Allet left the schoolhouse front doorstep she was scrubbing to talk over the garden gate. 'Hello, Jo. This is a turn-up for the books, you coming here to teach. I'm the headmaster's maid, well, housekeeper really. There's not many of my old class round here now, most have moved away.'

After what Lew had gloatingly told her, while drinking the teapot dry in Mercy's kitchen, Jo felt uncomfortable facing the girl who had occasionally joined them and Russell in their childhood pranks. 'You'll have to watch yourself with that headmaster,' he had said. 'I reckon he's knocking off Sally Allett. Got her all to himself, which is a pity, 'cause she used to be very obliging to me and others, up in the mine ruins.' But Lew wasn't likely to see innocence in any situation involving a man and woman.

'You've turned out very pretty, Sally. Just like everyone said you would.' Jo glanced at her wristwatch. 'I'm afraid I can't stop. I'm meeting Mr Lidgey at the school.'

'I know,' Sally said bluntly, and Jo thought she detected a trace of possessiveness in her demeanour. 'He left the house a few minutes ago.'

Jo set off again with fast steps. She was not late but it would appear bad form to keep Mr Lidgey waiting.

Sally returned to the doorstep, knelt down on the sacking and slammed the scrubbing brush on the hard granite, thoroughly disgruntled. She should have ordered Beth Wherry to do this, then Joanna Venner would not have seen her working at something so menial. Even though Marcus admired her femininely moulded body, the other woman's fashionably neat, almost curveless figure, clad in tailored clothes, made her burn with envy.

Jo saw Marcus Lidgey standing outside the school gates. He was rubbing the back of his neck, twisting the briefcase in his hand. Although casually dressed, he seemed a little flustered.

Before Jo reached him, she had to pass another young woman she did not particularly want to look in the eye: Gweniver Pascoe, wife of the proprietor of the general store, whom Lew had boasted to be his latest conquest. Kizzy Kemp had come inside the farmhouse kitchen at that moment and confirmed it. Shifty in features, Gweniver Pascoe crept past her.

'Good afternoon, Miss Venner.' As Marcus Lidgey came forward, Jo noticed he had a studied, slightly stooped walk. 'I understand you are living at Nance Farm. I trust you had a comfortable journey there and have settled in.'

'Thank you, Mr Lidgey.' She returned his firm handshake. Jo took a moment to drink in the rather bleak, single-storey building of the Church of England primary school. The rab playgrounds, one each for the boys and girls, were both indicated by thick letters carved out of the front wall. Lew and Russell had crowed about breaching the high surrounding walls many times to skip lessons.

'You will find it a completely different environment to what you are used to, Miss Venner,' Marcus said as he unlocked the teachers' diminutive entrance.

'I'm sure I shall find it agreeable.'

He ushered her inside the infants' classroom. 'You know already there will be sixty-one pupils on the registers for the new term. Miss Teague takes the infants' class. You will be taking over the middle class from Miss Choak. I, of course, take the upper class. Did you know Miss Teague and Miss Choak at all?'

'I met Miss Choak once, briefly. I've just renewed my acquaintance with Miss Teague.'

'Miss Choak has retired to be with her family at Morvah. I'm sure Miss Teague will do all she can to help you settle in.'

He took three sheets of foolscap paper from his briefcase. Jo noticed the initials 'B. Mus.' engraved on it – he was a Bachelor of Music. 'This is a suggested timetable for you and a report on each child in the middle class, Miss Venner. I like the pupils to be well turned out. If a child is going to make something of himself it starts with him taking care of his appearance.'

Jo carefully folded the papers and put them into her handbag.

The infants' classroom was cramped. There was a sandpit and redundant household oddments for use as toys. A sprig of dried holly left over from Christmas threatened to fall off the top of a happy picture of Jesus with small children at His feet.

As the tour of the classrooms continued, Jo found the interior not as cold and forbidding as she had imagined it would be. The walls were painted in cream, pink and blue. Mercy had mentioned a temperamental, smoking, black stove which heated the ancient, creaking water pipes running along the walls, but it had been replaced by open fireplaces.

A folding wooden screen, which looked new, divided the middle and upper classrooms. There was the inevitable large map of the world with pink areas denoting the British Empire, which all the pupils would view each day at morning assembly. Some inspired artwork adorned the walls. Jars of what looked like very basic scientific experiments, labelled with boys' names only, sat on the high, deep window sills. Jo frowned at that.

She silently admired the harmonium which replaced the out-of-tune piano she had heard being played when she had passed this way with Celia.

'The school has an orchestra of sorts,' Marcus said with some pride, 'with a few new instruments. Shortly after I took over as headmaster, Miss Celia Sayce, with whom you were acquainted, made a generous donation to the school.'

Jo bit her bottom lip to forestall a show of emotion. In this little school of no repute, she was overwhelmed with the reality of Celia's death. 'The donation was typical of her kindness. It was Miss Sayce who encouraged me to follow my chosen profession.'

'I see. Please accept my condolences on your sad loss,' he said softly. There had obviously been a very close relationship between the two women; sympathy of this kind could only endear him to Joanna Venner.

'Thank you, Mr Lidgey.' If his remarks were a true representation of his character, Jo was confident she would achieve a good working alliance with the headmaster.

'I hope you will find your desk comfortable, Miss Venner,' Marcus said, as he motioned for her to lead the way round the other side of the screen. He made sure he did not follow her too closely. He was sure it was unintentional, but she was wearing a sensuous perfume. It stirred him. God damn his wretched mother! It was difficult for him to form a natural association with any woman, but when he was supposed to quickly seduce the one he was presently with to secure a large portion of her money, it was well-nigh impossible to act with the desired formality. He hoped his nervousness was not on show.

'I'm sure I shall, Mr Lidgey.' The wooden floor was polished and she could see her reflection in the brass lamps on the walls.

'Good. The usual offices for the staff are connected to the children's cloakrooms. I think this is all you need to know for now. I shall look forward to seeing you here at eight o'clock next Wednesday morning.'

He moved away. Jo thought she had been dismissed. Before she headed for the door, she allowed herself a covert glance at him, to see if there was anything about him that matched Lew's crude assertions that he was a libertine in regard to his housemaid. His features were well drawn and held a natural sternness, his wide mouth was given to tension. He looked closed, singular, but rather than scandalous, hinted of being a constant, dependable character, if somewhat fidgety.

He turned back almost immediately, having picked up a folder off her desk. 'Y-you have a question, Miss Venner?'

'No, no,' she said quickly, castigating herself for her impropriety. She should not have been staring at him. Her memory had served her right: he was an attractive man.

Her apparent interest in him gave Marcus a little hope. He smiled, releasing some of his unease. 'Miss Venner, will you be free to dine with my mother and me on Friday evening? I will send Davey Penoble, the blacksmith, in my motorcar to collect you.'

'I would be delighted to, Mr Lidgey.' She would look forward to the occasion. If it was a success it would consolidate her new position.

'We shall expect you at seven o'clock.'

When they were back at the school gates, Jo's attention was drawn directly across the road. In front of a tiny cottage in the middle of a long row of similar homes, Abner Jelbert was talking to a tall man with untidy black hair, a dark complexion and unwavering eyes, which were set fully on her. Luke Vigus was leaning against the window sill of the grimy building, smoking, his thumbs inside his trouser pockets. Jo noted again his extraordinary looks. Competition for Lew with the local women?

'The older man is called Abner Jelbert,' Marcus informed her.

'I know him. I've been told his twins are in my class and are very disruptive.'

'Indeed, they are. The other man is Luke Vigus. A rather undesirable character, older brother of two more of your pupils. I'm afraid you'll find problems of a different kind in their case.'

'I met him just a little earlier today.'

Nodding at Jo, Luke muttered testily to his neighbour, 'Who the hell does that miserable schoolmaster think he's staring at?'

A short time ago, Marcus Lidgey had knocked on the door and reprimanded him for not ensuring Rex and Molly attended school regularly. 'I want none of your complaints, specially during holiday time. Tell my mother, not me,' Luke had barked at him.

'In the absence of a father, they are your responsibility, Mr Vigus,' Marcus had returned obstinately.

''Tis nothing to do with me. Bugger off.' Luke had shut the door in the headmaster's face.

'Don't tell me she's his bit of fluff?' Luke remarked to Abner.

'Nah.' Abner chuckled. 'She's the new teacher. You probably haven't seen her before, you being away most of the time. She used to be friendly with Celia Sayce. Mercy Merrick's brother used to shag her hoity-toity mother. She's got a sharp tongue on her. She's living at Nance now; a strange set-up. Sweet-looking little thing, don't you think?'

Lighting another cigarette from the butt hanging out of his mouth, Luke blatantly studied the skimpy form in the fur-collared coat across the road. He would have been very disappointed if she had turned out to be Lidgey's mistress. 'She's not bad at all. The school kids won't know what to make of her.'

'She's no soft touch, Luke.'

'You reckon? Let's have a drink.' Luke strode up the hill to his wagon behind the forge, where he had a crate of beer on board. Abner followed eagerly on his heels.

'The Viguses are a misfit family,' Marcus said wearily.

Jo recognised a plump, unwieldy woman, wearing a faded paisley headscarf, a shapeless wool coat with a dipping hemline and carrying a floppy straw bag, heading towards them.

Irene Trevail's thumping steps slowed and stopped in front of the two teachers. 'Hello, my luvver. So 'tis true then about you coming here to teach. Been taking a look round, have 'ee?'

'Good afternoon, Mrs Trevail.' Smiling, Jo held out her hand. 'It's good to see you again.'

Irene Trevail shunned a handshake and gave Jo a hug and kissed her cheek. ''Twill be more than a nine-day wonder having you round here. Shame Miss Sayce passed over before you could settle in at Cardhu. I can mind she now, sitting in Mercy's kitchen, not too proud to drink tea with us while you went off with my boys. Never mind, like Lew said, you'll be nearly as well at home at Nance. I'm on the way there now, to get my weekly eggs, butter and cream.'

She raised her plump, thread-veined face to Marcus, who was staring at the two women in something akin to disbelief. 'She used to play with my boys backalong, 'master. As wild as the wind, she was, and could fight like Tom Henna's cat. She's dressed to death now, but there's many a time I've seen she looking like a mimsy pulled through a furze bush backwards.'

'Really.' Marcus smiled as if he was charmed by the tale. He was unnerved. Joanna Venner had been under the influence of the nonconformist Sayce woman, and if she could behave like an Amazon, she would not be a pushover.

'Mrs Trevail is the sister of Miss Merrick, whom I'm living with. I've been friends of the family for many years,' Jo explained.

'I see.' Marcus was growing anxious. The Trevail woman was intent on a time of chatter and he had no wish to be included. The struggle to appear courteous was making his head ache and he was beginning to feel unreal. He felt the first prickings of an outbreak of sweat. Soon he would find it hard to breathe. These occurrences, when he was suddenly rendered panic-stricken, were becoming more frequent. The only thing that made him feel normal again was a long period alone or to play one of his musical instruments. 'You ladies obviously have some reacquainting to do. If you'll both excuse me. I'll inform my mother she'll be able to meet you on Friday evening, Miss Venner.'

'Didn't expect him to hang about.' Irene stared after him, as he strode off in the opposite direction to the schoolhouse. 'He takes the occasional drink in the pub but never mixes with the likes of us. Come to Heather Cottage for a cup of tea, Jo, and meet Father. Can't wait to hear all your news. I'll walk with 'ee to the farm later.'

'I'm sorry, Mrs Trevail, I was about to—'

'Oh, come on.' Irene linked her arm through Jo's. 'Russell's just got home from his shift at the Geevor. Thank the Lord, he's still in work, at least for now. He'd loved to see you.'

'I'm very sorry, Mrs Trevail.' Jo swiftly disentangled herself from the former miner's wife. 'I was about to say I'm expected elsewhere. I'll call on you and Mr Trevail some other time, I promise.'

She hastened back through the village and wandered on to the moor. Alone at last, she was overwhelmed with grief and, her breath coming in frantic gasps, she began to weep.

Eight

'Hello, darling.'
      'Mother?'
   'Oh, Joanna, why are you ringing this number?'
   'It's my home, isn't it?' Jo answered her mother as crossly
as she was questioned. 'I thought you might be interested to
learn that I've settled into Nance.'
   Impatient sigh. 'I haven't got the slightest interest in what
you're doing there. Get off the telephone. I'm waiting for an
important call.'
   As sarcastic as the words would come. 'From the very
young, wild-haired artist fellow I saw lurking about the
grounds of Tresawna before I left? Are you bringing your
affairs out in the open these days? How very modern. May
I speak to Alistair now, please?'
   'No, you may not,' Katherine snapped, and Jo knew she
was barely restraining her fury. 'Try later.'
   'But the landlord of the pub is kindly allowing me to use
his private telephone. I don't want to have to come—'
   Katherine severed the connection.
   'Horrid cow,' Jo hissed at the receiver in her hand. She
would have phoned back immediately but her mother would
only cut her off again. The casual chat she was hoping to
have with Alistair would have to wait until another time.
   'Couldn't get through? Bert's said I can use the phone
next.'
   Jo found herself looking over her shoulder at Luke Vigus.
If anyone but him had overheard her moment of pique she
would be horrified, but for some reason she felt at ease in
this man's company. She put some pennies down on the

landlord's sideboard to pay for the call. 'I'm sorry to keep you waiting.'

Luke was there to arrange to pass on the stolen cargo on his wagon. 'I'm happy to wait if you've another call to make.'

'I haven't, thank you.'

After they changed places at the sideboard, and Jo was preparing to go outside into the sharp-as-ice evening air, Luke said, 'I'm going for a drink after this. Care to join me?'

'No, thank you. I must be getting back.' It would cause a scandal if she walked into the public bar with this man, but part of her wanted to accept his invitation. Even in the gloom of the pub's little parlour she saw his eyes reflected all the colours of the sky.

Which dress should she wear tonight? Jo held up her calf-length, blue-green evening dress and a less showy affair in pale pink with a simple neckline. What sort of fashions prevailed at the schoolhouse? These quiet parts were at least two decades behind the rest of the world. How old was Mrs Lidgey? Was she a woman of flair or an ancient granny-type? Jo wished she'd asked Mercy more about Eleanor Lidgey.

Jo knew the evening dress was the obvious choice. The invitation wasn't to take high tea, and Parmarth's headmaster was a league above the average incumbent of a small village school. So it should be the evening dress. But it fell straight from the shoulders and flattened the tiny amount of bosom she had.

'Damn it! Damn you, Mother! Why do you have to keep making your wretched point about my body being so underdeveloped? Why do I care, for goodness' sake? You're not worth it.'

Flinging the garments on the bed, she undressed completely and approached the full-length cheval mirror she had seized from one of the farmhouse's spare bedrooms. Did she still look like an adolescent girl? Or a boy even? Her waist was nipped in, her hips flowed in gentle angles.

65

Surely she didn't look like a boy? She turned sideways. Her breasts protruded from her body, not much, but it proved she was not totally flat-chested. Is this what a grown woman was meant to look like? Would a man find her body attractive?

She took her breasts in her hands. They were not heavy and full, as she so desperately desired them to be, but they possessed a definite shape and when pressed together they formed a tiny cleavage, thank heavens.

She liked the sensations of her own touch. It was a sinful act, but she did not quickly take her hands away and pull on her underclothes. Jo recognised her sexuality, her feelings, her needs. She saw her arousal as normal. One day she hoped to cross paths with a man who could satisfy all her needs, as Celia had found in Sheridan Ustick. Marriage figured at the bottom of her agenda. Until such time as a sense of equality and fairness prevailed, women teachers who became wives had to give up their careers. If she found the right love, faithful and discreet, a man she could love as deeply and enduringly as Celia had loved, she would have the best of all worlds. Maybe it was a selfish desire, but it was what she wanted.

While putting on her cameo necklace her thoughts turned sorrowfully to Celia. If only she had lived to take a role in this new chapter of her life. Denied her friend's affection and inspiring advice for ever, Jo felt a measure of unease about the future. As she applied her make-up, she grimaced at her uncertain reflection in the mirror. She was experiencing one of her darker moments. Celia would have been encouraging about her presentation for this dinner, but she had been beautiful and distinctly feminine, as was her wretched mother, whose cruel words about her plainness echoed in her ears yet again. People had noticed them, whatever they had worn.

'Do I look all right, Mercy?' She put the anxious question when downstairs.

Mercy glanced round from scrubbing her hands at the kitchen sink. 'You look fine to me. Pretty dress.'

'But does it suit me?'

'Yes, I s'pose so. I don't know much about fancy clothes. Pity Lew's gone home. He's an expert on what looks good on a woman. Mind you,' Mercy broke into gales of laughter, 'he's more expert at what a woman looks like when he's taken them off her.'

'Oh, you're no help at all, Mercy.' Jo sighed, checking she had her comb and a clean handkerchief in her evening bag.

Leaning against the sink, Mercy surveyed her paying guest. 'Why the long face? You're not nervous of the Lidgeys, are you?'

'No. I was just wondering if I looked the part, that's all.'

'Part of what, for goodness' sake? You're going out to eat, you're not part of the menu. Where's the girl who used to play barefoot over the moors? Not caring if she looked like a gutter urchin?'

'Sometimes I think part of her is buried with Celia,' Jo murmured despondently.

'Nonsense. What did she teach you all those years? To be yourself, to make the most of your life and give no mind to the daft expectations of others. No one's better or more important than anyone else. We're all different. Good advice, remember?'

Jo relaxed and let out an ironic laugh. 'Thanks, Mercy. I needed to be reminded of that. I should have come straight to Parmarth and not gone home first. My mother always has a bad effect on me.'

The sound of a motorcar was heard stopping in the lane. 'Here's your ride,' Mercy said. 'Enjoy yourself.'

Jo slipped on her coat and wrapped a chiffon scarf round her head. 'I want to thank you, Mercy. It's good to have your support now that I'm without Celia's.'

'How did you come to drive for Mr Lidgey, Mr Penoble?' Jo asked the blacksmith, while making herself comfortable in the front seat beside him in the black and red Ford coupé, which was in tip-top condition. 'He must be the only person who's ever had a car in Parmarth;

even Miss Sayce chose to walk or ride her pony everywhere.'

While he answered, Davey Penoble kept his keen eyes
focused on the narrow bumpy road. 'He don't like leaving
his mother at night. It was at night time the accident
happened.'

'What accident was this?'

'When she fell down the stairs and damaged her back.
Happened about a year ago, apparently. In her house on the
seafront at Penzance. Sally says she likes to have company
when it gets dimsy, so he always stays home. Must be a
boring life for him, but it helps me to earn a couple of extra
bob servicing the car and 'tis a pleasure to drive.'

'Poor woman,' Jo said.

She watched Davey Penoble's heavy, calloused hands carefully turning the steering wheel. She had become acquainted
with him when Celia had commissioned a new wrought-iron
garden gate from him, a speciality of his, incorporating his
initials. The gate now hanging, perhaps forlornly banging
on its decorative hinges, in front of the lonely house on this
cold blustery night. Davey Penoble could hammer out a tool
in minutes, and also as a farrier and wheelwright, expertly
make or repair a horse's shoe or cartwheel. Differing from
the traditional blacksmith's build, he was rangy-bodied,
quiet-faced. Nearing middle age, he lived alone in the little
cottage next to his work place.

Jo considered he must be hunted diligently by the spinsters
of Parmarth. Her mother liked to consort with hard-working,
ordinary men. Men with meaty hands and sweat and grime
on their bodies, who spoke coarsely, but Davey Penoble
would not suit her requirements. He lacked the sort of
overt masculinity and hint of something wild and primitive
which Katherine sought. Perhaps she ought to introduce her
mother to the thrusting-male adult version of Lew Trevail,
Jo thought astringently. Luke Vigus was another prospect.
Jo shrank from her last thought; he was too pleasant for her
mother to taint.

'I was surprised to hear about your appointment at the

school. Mercy told me about it,' Davey explained. 'People are wond'ring exactly why you've come here to teach.' He chanced a quick look at her before concentrating on his driving. 'If you don't mind me saying so, isn't it a step backward?'

'You could look at it that way. I'm surprised that people can't see the main reason for my taking this opportunity was to live with Miss Sayce. You know how close we were.'

'Pity she didn't live t'see this day, then.' As they neared the village, Davey slowed the car at a spot where a wide expanse of creeping willow bushes grew on a low bank. He bent forward over the steering wheel, peering into the shadows as they were lit up by the headlights.

'Are you afraid of running over an animal?'

'No, I'm afraid of running into Mardie Dawes. She waved me down just here as I was driving to Nance and I couldn't get rid of her until I bought one of her potions.' He tapped his jacket pocket and said wryly, 'I'll be all right if the rheumatics ever play me up.'

'I haven't had the misfortune to meet up with her yet.'

Davey stopped the motorcar smoothly outside the school-house and helped Jo out. A chill wind gusted down the village street, snatching at her chiffon scarf. Jo shivered violently. Her evening dress and coat offered no real protection to her small bones against the harsh moorland weather. Davey lit the way to the front door with his storm lantern and rapped on the door.

Sally Allett opened the door and invited Jo inside. Davey left to park the motorcar round the back of the house, then to pass the evening away in the Engine House Inn until he returned to collect her.

'Perishing tonight, isn't it, Jo?' Sally addressed her as an equal rather than her master's guest. 'Here, give me your coat and things then I'll show you into the sitting room. They're drinking sherry.'

'The food smells delicious, Sally,' Jo said, unconcerned at the lack of ceremony.

'It's just roast beef. They don't go in for nothing fancy here.'

A deep throaty sound, edged with distinct displeasure, indicated someone did not approve of Sally's familiarity. Marcus was bearing down the hallway towards them. 'Come along, Sally. Don't detain Miss Venner with idle gossip. Good evening, Miss Venner. I'm delighted you have arrived safely. It's an extremely cold night.'

A deep-throated voice called out from the room at the end of the passage. 'Marcus, dear. Do come.'

'Please excuse me for a moment,' Marcus said pleasantly. 'I'll see what my mother wants.'

'They're very close,' Sally said, laying aside Jo's outdoor things to dispose of properly later. 'He puts himself at her beck and call, nothing's too much trouble for him. Mind you, he can be moody, fierce at times. You had better watch out.'

Busy studying her image in a gilt-edged mirror, Jo missed the mischief gleaming in Sally's pretty face. 'It's always good to hear of families who are close. How do I look?'

As the housemaid took full notice of Jo's appearance, her face hardened. The 'funny little creature' was wearing a dress Sally could only dream of owning. The height of fashion, the silk sheath accentuated the limited contours of Jo's figure in a beguiling manner. The discreet amount of carefully applied make-up took away all hint of sharpness from her delicately formed features. Diamanté slides sparkled in her hair, sweeping the chin-length bob away from her neat ears. Joanna Venner looked poised and assured.

'You'll do. Follow me,' Sally said curtly.

Marcus was bending over his mother's armchair, as if making sure she was comfortable. 'Mrs Lidgey has been greatly looking forward to meeting you, Miss Venner.'

'I can speak for myself, Marcus,' Eleanor said. Releasing his wrist, she manoeuvred him aside and extended her hand to Jo. 'You are very welcome, Miss Venner. Do sit close to me. I'm very grateful to have another woman's company. Miss Teague was invited, of course, but she rarely

70

socialises of an evening, and the vicar is still away on a speaking tour.'

'I'm delighted to meet you, Mrs Lidgey,' Jo replied. Before sitting on the sofa, close to her hostess, she felt her hand being explored by the woman's long tapering fingers.

'Sherry, Miss Venner?' Marcus remained on his feet, anxious the evening would go well and for it to be over. Eleanor had just threatened to smash his violin if he did not turn on all his charm to the young lady. He could take his violin up to his room, but his mother would only ask Sally to bring it to her, then she would pretend to drop it.

'Yes, please, Mr Lidgey,' Jo said, her eyes flickering on him for a few moments before returning her attention to his mother.

Eleanor Lidgey's long neck was encircled with a Queen Mary-style pearl choker. Her gleaming silver-white hair was swept up in dramatic peaks towards a centre parting. Jo found herself noting the elegant shades of her lipstick and eyeshadow, how her eyebrows naturally formed the shape of birds' wings in flight. Dynamism, candid maturity, shone from her quick dark eyes. Her every cast and motion declared social grace.

Finally, Jo glanced round the room and decided the few pieces of refined, Edwardian furnishings had come from Mrs Lidgey's house at Penzance. A harpsichord, its lacquered woodwork deeply scratched, a cello and a full-sized violin took pride of place in a corner. Otherwise it was a drab room with no outstanding features. The Lidgeys looked out of place here. Jo was curious about their lives before they came to Parmarth.

Sherry glass in hand, she enjoyed a strictly feminine conversation with Eleanor. Then Jo noticed her body was gradually slipping, no, collapsing in on itself. She did not pity the woman, there was nothing frail about Mrs Lidgey despite her disability. If she could stand up straight she would be as tall as her son. From the evidence of the ivory-framed family photographs, she had once been an active woman.

71

Jo glimpsed her late husband in the wedding photograph, a small, boyish-looking man.

'I lost my husband many years ago, when my son was a little boy,' Eleanor said. 'I used to live at Penzance, in far larger and more comfortable surroundings, of course.' She looked directly at Marcus. 'But it's so good to be close to one's family, don't you agree, Miss Venner? You've chosen to lodge at one of the local farms, I understand. Could someone not motor you over from Carbis Bay every day? Tell me about your past connections with Parmarth.'

Jo wondered if Mr Lidgey was uneasy about the way his mother was interrogating her. His eyes kept shuffling to the clock, he was shifting on his feet. She had expected this curiosity and answered, not altogether untruthfully, 'I became acquainted with Miss Merrick many years ago when my pony threw a shoe while I happened to be riding past Nance Farm. We formed a close and enduring friendship. The conditions of the farm are quite civilised actually.'

'I'm pleased to hear it. How many people live at the farm?'

'Just Miss Merrick. Her brother was killed in the war.'

'Some fine men died in the war, men with loose associations with Parmarth. I must mention, Miss Venner,' Eleanor smiled apologetically, 'that I knew Sheridan Ustick. I appreciate how his death must have been a terrible loss to Miss Celia Sayce, your late friend.'

Marcus repeated the rumbling sound in his throat he'd given in the hallway. He wanted to dash across to his mother and order her to shut her mouth. She had demanded he be pleasant to their guest. Why did she have to indulge in thinly veiled tactlessness, which might offend Joanna Venner? Why must she always make life harder for him?

'Mama, perhaps Miss Venner would be interested in our plans for the garden this spring.'

Jo sipped her sherry awkwardly, but perhaps it was better Mrs Lidgey aired her knowledge about Celia and Sheridan Ustick. She had spoken so pleasantly.

'If I may ask, because there are so many different tales circulating, what was it Miss Sayce died of?' Eleanor continued in the same soothing tone. 'It seemed such a long time before she was buried. I hope there were not any problems.'

Marcus clenched his fists until his nails seared his palms. He felt revoltingly lightheaded. Why must his wretched mother keep taunting their guest? If Miss Venner discerned the true nature of her questions, he sensed she would not easily forgive such unadulterated prying. It would make it harder for him to gain her trust.

'It was two or three days before it was discovered Miss Sayce had died. She had no family. Her solicitors had to make the arrangements for her funeral.' Jo volunteered the information to avoid more speculation. Celia was resting in peace, and Jo would strive with all that would prove necessary to keep it that way.

There was a tap on the door and Sally announced the meal was ready. Marcus lifted Eleanor to a more upright position then handed her her two walking sticks.

Jo gazed above the overmantel at a portrait of him in gown and mortar board, holding his degree certificate. Painted about ten years ago, there was a semblance of hope and aspiration about him that was not evident now. Presumably he had served in some way during the war – his age dictated he would have been just old enough to enlist – but had he been a schoolmaster all his adult life? Why was a man of high academic and musical abilities apparently wasting his talents here? Meeting the unfathomable gaze in the black eyes in the portrait, she felt his reason for being in Parmarth was not as simple as hers.

Marcus said courteously, 'I'm afraid I cannot offer you my arm, Miss Venner. Would you kindly follow us to the dining room.'

When Eleanor was on her feet, Jo saw her right hip was slightly out of alignment with her body. Nonetheless, she was an imposing figure. Jo followed as she shuffled slowly to the next room, supported by her son.

At the table, Marcus was too nervous to join in with much of the conversation, only politely halting Eleanor, who monopolised Jo with sparkling chit-chat, to pour more wine for the two women. Jo noticed he ate half-heartedly and drank copiously. After the meal, he escorted them back to the sitting room then left them to their coffee.

The moment he closed the door, Eleanor became rather sad. 'It was a shame there was no other gentleman available tonight to keep Marcus company. Sometimes I fear he must get very lonely. Well, never mind our problems,' she said, shining with enthusiasm once more. 'You seem to enjoy living at the farm. Such an inappropriate place, but you're adventurous, I should think. Do you find all those animals and things of nature refreshing?'

Jo was pleased Eleanor Lidgey seemed to understand her values. 'Actually, it is invigorating.'

'I'm sure your mother doesn't approve.' Eleanor's next words were spoken as if in great alarm. 'Oh, please forgive my frankness, Miss Venner. I fear I shall offend you. I'm afraid I have a tendency to speak exactly what's on my mind. I interrogate everyone for every scrap of news. My disability has left me almost entirely housebound and I am bereft of scintillating company. I rather hoped you and I could be friends. The vicar calls occasionally but it's not the same as female companionship. Miss Teague used to come but I found her boring. I feel you and I could entertain each other. You will come again, Miss Venner? Do say you will, and often.'

'I shall be glad to.' Jo smiled, eager to make her hostess feel she had no need to apologise. Eleanor Lidgey was outspoken but utterly charming. 'You were right about my mother. Neither she nor my brother are happy about me teaching here, but I chose to follow my own path.'

'Really? Excellent.' Eleanor smiled approvingly.

Shortly, smelling faintly of tobacco and brandy, Marcus rejoined them. He contributed small talk to the conversation, undertaken with warm smiles often aimed at Jo, but Jo noticed he diligently watched his mother, sometimes with marked anxiety. At a quarter to ten, he glanced darkly at the clock.

Eleanor stalled him by mentioning the school. 'Has Mr Lidgey informed you, Miss Venner, that the staff, when not on playground or dinner duty, often take tea here? You would be very welcome to join us. It will save you eating in cramped conditions and help cheer an otherwise lonely day for me.'

'No, I did not know, Mrs Lidgey.' Jo glanced at Mr Lidgey, who smilingly confirmed it. 'I shall enjoy spending time here.'

'I'm sure you will do very well at the school,' Eleanor continued, ignoring Marcus's restless movements. 'As you are familiar with the village you will understand something of the children's problems. The Jelbert twins will require a firm hand. The Vigus children rarely attend, in fact they are not often seen outside their cottage, which apparently is no better than a hovel. My son and the authorities are always chasing them up. The boy has the most unspeakable habits and the girl never stops whimpering. You will like Ann Markham. She is very attentive, and although she lives on a farm she manages to come to school scrupulously clean.'

'I'm sure I shall have a reasonable idea of their backgrounds,' Jo said, disturbed to hear more unfavourable things about the Viguses. If true, why did Luke Vigus, who seemed to own an agreeable disposition, allow the situation to carry on? 'I hope to put it to good use. I've seen a few of the children about the village and spoken to them.' She would have liked to have seen more than the collection of either saucy or suspicious faces, including a couple who had deliberately hidden from her, but guessed that if the children weren't earning a few pennies or doing jobs for their parents, they were off playing on the moors.

'I'm confident you'll be a credit to the school.' Marcus smiled at Jo again.

His eyes crept back to the clock. He was anxious to pack his mother off to bed quickly. A river of sweat was running down his back. He had to get outside, let the wide open expanses of the moor calm him. He was concerned that Joanna Venner, astute and perceptive as she was, would notice his discomfiture. It would not be as difficult to romance her when alone with her. Prolonging the evening would not serve him at all.

'You taught young ladies before,' Eleanor said. 'Will you be able to cope with small boys?'

'I taught at a mixed primary school for six months before joining the academy,' Jo said.

Marcus consulted the clock again. It was five minutes past ten o'clock. 'Mama . . .'

'Are you going to play something for us, Marcus, dear?' she fielded him, then asked Jo, 'Which instrument would you like to hear, Miss Venner?'

Jo was denied the chance to answer.

'I think you have stayed up long enough, Mama,' Marcus stated recklessly. 'Davey Penoble will be waiting to drive Miss Venner home.'

Eleanor's mouth stayed open in mid-sentence. She looked about to argue but suddenly smiled. 'See how he cares about me, Miss Venner? Very well, Marcus. I know I ought to go to bed. I am tired. Thank you for coming, Miss Venner. Please do call on me again shortly.'

Jo expressed the necessary compliments to Eleanor while Marcus called for Sally.

'Stay with Mrs Lidgey,' Marcus ordered her. 'I'll see Miss Venner to the door.'

Taking Jo's outdoor things from Sally, he ushered her along the hall then helped her into her coat. 'I do hope you have enjoyed the evening.'

Jo replied truthfully that she had, but she wondered if it was the same for him. He looked heated and she wondered if he had caught a fever.

With a final ingratiating smile, Marcus opened the door and deposited her safely into Davey Penoble's lantern light.

He locked up. A hand on his arm pulled him round roughly. 'I saw you running your eyes over her,' Sally tore into him. 'Well?'

76

He ran a heavy thumb down Sally's cheek. 'Whatever I think about her, you're the one who's here, aren't you? Help me get my mother to bed.'

'Come back after Sally's finished with me, Marcus,' Eleanor ordered, as he stepped back from her bed.

When Sally left the room, Marcus reluctantly returned. Eleanor would only keep ringing her bell if he didn't. She took his hand. It seemed the more he longed to get away from her the more unnatural strength she called on to keep him prisoner. Only minutes ago she had admitted she was tired, now she was breathing lustily, had him in a vice-like grip.

'Hoping to slip away somewhere, were you? Foolish boy. You'll never, ever get away from me. The Venner girl is young and lissom, has a spring in her step. You know what to do?'

'I could do the task better if you allowed me free rein,' he said irritably.

'You aren't capable of making your own decisions, Marcus. You change the way you feel moment by moment.'

'But even if I do manage to induce her into my bed it doesn't follow she'll hand her money over to me.'

'Stop worrying. I'll think of something. Win her over soon, then you can tell me all the intimate details of your conquest. You'd like that, wouldn't you?'

He would not. And he could not answer his mother. Capitulating to her again, he switched off his mind, his feelings, his emotions, in the same way, out of self-preservation, he had taught himself many years ago.

'Now kiss me like you did as a boy, my darling. Show your mama just how much you love her.'

When she arrived back at Nance, Jo found Lew in the kitchen. He was wearing a clean shirt and had combed his hair. All her senses were instantly alert. 'You're not usually here this late. Why have you returned? Where's Mercy?'

'Gone for a yarn over Boswella Farm. Mercy said how pretty you looked in your evening dress. I wanted to see for myself.' Lew's handsome dark eyes were searching her body, as intrusively as if he was actually touching her. 'You look and smell beautiful, Jo. I'd never have thought you'd turn out to be a dazzler.'

He came closer and closer. Jo squared her balance. His smile was full of charm. Here was male sexuality at its most blatant, and despite his scandalous reputation, Jo was not left unstirred. 'I think of you as a big brother, Lew. You always treated me like a punchbag but you were never cruel to me like Russell. I hope we can be friends, but take warning, there will never be anything stronger between us.'

His dusky eyes stole a few more seconds of liberty then he shrugged his shoulders. He knew how wildly Jo could fight. 'Pity. I'd like to make love to you, Jo. I know what a woman likes. It would be good for both of us.'

'I'm not here looking for romance, Lew. Certainly not a casual affair.'

'We could be anything you like to each other, Jo. Think about it. You're not like other women. A tart like Sally, or a narrow-minded prim-skirt, or a quiet little homebody. You're your own person. You look for more out of life. You're totally a woman, Jo, and a very alluring one.'

Jo did not shut out his compliments, even though they were probably made only out of his hope for yet another sexual conquest. They filled her to the very roots of her femininity with confidence.

Bending his head, Lew put his lips over hers. His huge rough hands came to her waist, kneading the silk of her clothes against her skin. Jo's body leapt into life. The arousal he provoked in her took dominance over her good sense. She kissed him back, tasting him, trying him.

Lew pulled her in tightly against his body, sliding a hand up over her back, already seeking to unfasten her dress. It felt good to be up against him, but it wasn't overwhelming. He was a sensitive, knowledgeable kisser and his hands weren't too direct or hurting her, but he wasn't exciting her enough. He wasn't what she was looking for. For Jo, there had to be much more. Her power of reasoning returned. There were too many complications to yield to him. He had good looks and an overpowering virility, but he was a heartless philanderer. And he was Mercy's nephew. An old playmate. Something of a brother to her, as she had mentioned earlier.

Pushing his arms away, she drew back from him. 'No, I'm sorry. This is all wrong for me.'

'Don't, Jo. Just give us a chance.'

'No, Lew.' She made a cut-off motion with her hands. 'It's no use trying to talk me round.'

He took a moment to catch his breath, nodding regretfully. 'Pity, but if that's the way you feel, fair enough. Friends it is then. All that's left to say is welcome back. I reckon you're going to shake up this place.'

Nine

Sixteen pairs of inquisitive, seven-to-nine-year-old eyes were fixed solidly on Jo. Most of the children were poorly attired. The girls, outnumbering the boys by nine to seven, were dressed in jumpers and skirts, with the odd dark gymslip, and strapped or lace-up shoes. The boys were in short grey trousers and jerseys or jackets, a few with the addition of a tie. Many of the children had gaps in their mouths from losing milk teeth.

Jo smiled broadly at her class. It was an overcast morning. The oil lamps were lit, but with the windows high up, designed to prevent outside distractions, the pupils at the back were in a semi-gloom; the domain of the shy and the mischievous, until she got around, out of inevitable necessity, to moving some of them forward.

'Good morning, children. My name is Miss Venner.' She waited for a respectful response. The only reaction was open mouths, a variety of blinking and stares. She put a little more authority into her voice. 'Before I go on, you must return the greeting to me.'

From the front row, a fair-haired, bright-eyed girl, sporting the traditional wide ribbon on the crown of her head, chanted in a heavy Cornish accent, 'Good morning, Miss Venner.'

A mumble of 'Good mornings' and a lot of tittering followed.

Jo continued, 'If you look to my left you will see I've written my name up on the blackboard. I shall now mark the register and try to get to know some of you before assembly.'

She scanned their avid faces. A few of them she had seen

in church on Sunday. A boy in the middle row of desks, with chickenpox scars on his face, was busy picking his nose and he quickly withdrew the offending finger when her eyes fell on him.

She sat down at her desk, which was scratched with ancient graffiti; one cheeky word by Lew's hand, he had told her to look for it. Fresh oil had been put on the rusty parts of the desk's ironwork. Earlier, Jo had put her handbag and personal effects in the top drawer. She had tried the three lower drawers and found the bottom one too stiff to open. She would mention it to Mr Lidgey. She had forgotten about the caretaker, Frank Burthy, who also ran a small farm shop. Did he still work here? She was glad she had brought her own cushion to compensate for the hardness of the chair.

There was an outbreak of murmuring. She silenced it with a stern look.

'I'm Arnold Jelbert, miss,' a scratchy voice suddenly piped up from the back row of desks.

'I know who you are, Arnold Jelbert. I spoke to you last week. Be quiet until I reach J in the register, please. You will address me as Miss Venner, not miss.'

Arnold, untidy, tow-haired, with large protruding ears and a countenance that shone with mischievous intent, made a silly noise. 'She's prettier than old Miss Choak,' he said, chuckling, then made to pinch the boy sitting next to him.

'Arnold, if you move or speak again you will stand in the corner. Sit up straight, do not slouch. Do you understand?'

'Yes, Miss Venner,' the boy mouthed without a particle of respect.

There was a shuffle as other pupils sought to correct their posture. Then a sniff came from somewhere. There was always one pupil with a persistent sniff, something Jo could not abide, owing to the obstreperous way her father had performed his snuff habit. She gazed at the boy who had been picking his nose but he was not the guilty party. From her handbag she extracted the supply of small handkerchiefs she had made from clean, cotton feed bags. 'If anyone needs one of these, do ask,' she said, putting them on

81

the edge of her desk. 'You must return it to me washed and ironed.'

The sniffer went quiet.

Picking up her fountain pen, she began to mark the register. 'Mavis Best.' She glanced up. Silence. 'Is Mavis Best present?'

The fair-haired girl with the good manners put her hand up. 'Gone down with measles, Miss Venner.'

'Thank you. Ann Markham, isn't it?'

'Yes, Miss Venner.'

'Teacher's ruddy pet,' Arnold was heard to whisper disgustedly.

Jo chose to ignore him. Ann Markham beamed proudly. Used to classrooms separated by thick walls, Jo managed to shut out the young voices on the other side of the wooden screen, but every now and then, Marcus Lidgey's exacting tone broke through her concentration.

When Jo got to J she called out, 'Arnold Jelbert.'

'You already know I'm here,' he scoffed.

Putting her pen down, rising swiftly, Jo strode down the gangway through the desks to an accompaniment of hushed gasps. 'To the front of the classroom, Arnold Jelbert. In the corner by the door.'

'But I haven't done anything,' he protested.

'You've been cheeky three times.' Jo put her hand on his back and gently pushed him along to the corner of humiliation; no doubt a worse punishment would follow if Mr Lidgey chose to enter the room at this moment. 'I never ignore anything three times. Class, take note.'

She had less trouble with Arnold's twin, Gillian, a female replica of him with long plaits and round glasses, who took no pains to disguise her amusement at her brother's early defeat. Jo was resigned to the certainty that the Jelberts were always going to be a problem. They were never disciplined at home, unless Abner deemed their behaviour warranted a belting.

Jo moved on swiftly to the last names. After the Lidgeys' comments on the Vigus family, it was no surprise to find Rex and Molly Vigus were absent.

'Kenneth Willis.' There was no reply. Jo glanced up from the register. 'Is Kenneth Willis absent too?'

George Lean, the boy who had been picking his nose, nudged the boy sitting in front of him. The boy lifted his head off his arms and rubbed his eyes dozily. 'What?'

'Are you Kenneth Willis?' Jo asked rather sternly. 'Were you asleep?' She softened when she saw how thin and pale he was. She assumed he was feeling poorly.

'Yes, miss. Sorry. Present, Miss Venner.' Kenneth Willis blushed to the roots of his wavy red hair.

'Well, do try to stay awake, Kenneth.' Jo smiled at him.

'That's not fair,' Arnold complained from the corner. 'I got sent here just for talking. At least I can stay awake.'

'You will return there after assembly if you do not curb your tongue, Arnold,' Jo threatened lightly.

At nine fifteen, the screen was folded back by two boys in the headmaster's class, then the two lower classes, three nervous first-day pupils among them, filed in and stood in straight lines for assembly. Jane Lawry, short and chubby, shyly asked Jo for a makeshift hanky. She was clinging to the hand of her best friend, Susan, who was the younger sister of Beth Wherry, the new skivvy at the schoolhouse. Jo smiled as she handed Jane a handkerchief, then she carefully watched the one disabled child in her class to see if he required help. Norman Pascoe, from the general store, skinny and owning an effortless smile, hobbled along expertly with the aid of a stick.

Hymn books were passed out. Jo stood on the platform, two humble steps behind Mr Lidgey. She had brought her own hymn book, a leaving present from the staff of the academy. Miss Teague, chin thrust forward, lips pursed piously, played 'Morning Has Broken' on the harmonium. The singing flagged before it really began. His face stern, Marcus waved his arm in an arc, and as he led the children with a strong tenor voice, they found their best voices. Miss Teague smiled brightly, but avoided looking at Jo.

After the prayers and a few words on the Epiphany, Marcus formally introduced Jo to the school. The children welcomed her with one voice. Marcus nodded at her. Jo stepped forward and thanked them, with a friendly smile. Marcus noticed her confidence. She was dynamic, totally appealing. He was drawn to her. Carrying out his mother's scheme could prove not to be such a burden. Ensuring she saw his encouraging smile, he buoyantly ordered the classes to divide again.

'How are you enjoying your first day?' Eleanor asked Jo, when she joined her in the sitting room of the schoolhouse during the mid-morning break.

Before replying, Jo asked her, 'You do not feel me too forward in coming here so soon?' At odd moments she'd found herself thinking about Eleanor Lidgey and had been anticipating the company again of this forthright woman.

'Oh, no, I'm delighted. I told Marcus that he mustn't put you on playground duty today and to send you here. You can come back at dinner time.'

'Thank you. Actually, I feel I'm already beginning to establish myself at the school.'

'I'm so glad.' Eleanor smiled a smile that was spellbinding; Jo couldn't take her eyes off her. 'The tea tray is prepared for us, my dear. Would you be so kind as to pour? I like mine very strong with just a dash of milk. Help yourself to biscuits.'

While she served the tea, Jo talked about her morning. 'I gave the class a simple arithmetic test to start off with, then, not wanting to tax their minds on the first session of a new term, I began reading *The Wind in the Willows*. I shall take English next, and reading and geography this afternoon. I'm singling out the characters; the difficult, the lazy, the bright and those of limited abilities. The Vigus children were among the four absent. Looking back over the register, Rex and Molly Vigus's record of attendance does not include a full week for the last three terms. I think, with Mr Lidgey's permission, I'll follow them up sooner rather than later.'

'I admire that. Put my tea on the little table beside me, dear. It's lovely to have someone sweet, young and fresh waiting on me. You are going to be a treasure to Marcus and me, I'm sure of it.'

As Jo put the cup and saucer down on the appointed place,

Eleanor placed two of her fingers on the back of Jo's hand and rubbed them in a circle. It was like being touched by cool silk but Jo did not like it, nor Eleanor's sultry tone.

'Do you know anything of the Vigus family's circumstances from your old days in the village?' Eleanor asked.

'No.' Jo sat down with her own tea. 'It would be useful to learn all I can before I teach Rex and Molly.'

'I can enlighten you. They're dreadfully poor and live in far worse conditions that any other villagers. The mother's morally loose. She's an alcoholic and spends all her money on bootleg gin, produced apparently by some old witch who lives on the moor. There is an adult son who is little better, so I'm told. If you do call on them, I would be happy if you'd report back to me. I may be able to help. My son is running out of ideas on what to do about them.'

Eleanor glanced towards the door and lifted a finger to her lips. 'Ah, he's here. I don't want him to think I'm meddling in his affairs.'

Marcus quietly helped himself at the tea tray and sat on the chair furthest from his mother. Jo felt conspicuous while Mrs Lidgey commented on the details of her shell pink, accordion-pleated skirt, matching jumper and long cardigan, because Mr Lidgey was also looking intently at her. 'Your shoes are so stylish. How did you manage to keep them pristine on the muddy roads?'

'I wore boots to the school and changed into shoes when I arrived.'

'Very sensible. I trust you have brought an umbrella with you,' Eleanor chattered on. 'The forecast on the wireless said it will rain this afternoon.'

Marcus raised an eyebrow, interested again in Jo's reply. Jo did not appreciate being subjected to such personal scrutiny. 'Miss Merrick suggested I take my umbrella, but before I set out this morning I could see for myself that rain is inevitable.'

'Really?' Marcus said. 'Because you are used to moorland weather?'

'Yes. I am looking forward to taking the children outside for nature studies.'

'Good, good.' He nodded. 'Have you met with any problems?'

'No. I should point out I have one pupil away with the measles. I hope we're not about to be hit by an epidemic.'

'I can set your mind at rest. There was a run of measles before Christmas. Mavis Best should be the last case. Is there anything else? I want you to be perfectly comfortable.'

Jo made no mention of the appalling habits of some of the children, of having had to stop Gillian Jelbert from digging scabs off both her knees, of reprimanding Norman Pascoe for taking a sweet out of his mouth and passing it to George Lean, who had promptly put it into his own. 'The bottom drawer of my desk is stuck fast.'

'I'll inform Frank Burthy.' Marcus drank the last of his tea. 'I have to get back, Mama. I have lots of paperwork to do.' He darted to his feet and was standing at the door. 'Do not rush yourself, Miss Venner.' Then he was gone, before his mother said something to embarrass him or demand a peck on the cheek.

'You'll find Marcus very caring.' Eleanor smiled proudly.

'I'm sure he is, Mrs Lidgey.' Jo was experiencing his accommodating nature for herself.

'Why not call me Eleanor? I'm keen for us to be friends. I may call you Joanna?'

'Yes, of course,' Jo said, pleased at the suggestion, but she had resisted the desire to grit her teeth. Eleanor had resonated her full name in exactly the same way her mother did; Jo did not want to think about that woman today. 'Well, I really must go. I need to freshen up.'

'Please do use our amenity. Marcus has gone to the expense of installing one across the hall for me. It will be more dignified for you than using the convenience at the school. There's a mirror in there. You can attend to your hair although it's not necessary. You are well turned out. A refreshing sight for me after seeing only inferior clad individuals in the village.'

'You are very kind,' Jo said, flattered by the compliments. She admired Eleanor's uncomplaining spirit; several times

86

she had flinched and dashed a hand round to her back but had not mentioned the pain.

Eleanor suddenly moved her misshapen body forward. 'No. It is you who are kind, Joanna. I know an old woman like me requires a lot of patience.'

'Oh, nothing of the sort, Eleanor.'

As the morning wore on, Jo adapted her teaching methods to suit the abilities of her charges. She constantly checked the report Mr Lidgey had given her and found they were accurate for each pupil. They had a variety of skills, and while pressing the brighter children to do well, she was sympathetic with the slower ones. This was how she taught. If the children did well, she rewarded them with praise. If they wasted her time or their intellect she chastened them. She encouraged them all, but even at this early stage it was obvious the majority had little interest in their lessons with the prospect of a poor future, the boys of obtaining dead-end jobs, the girls expecting only to marry. Jo hoped to change their attitudes. Arnold Jelbert fidgeted but was not required to stand in the corner again. Jo knew he was saving up his mischief for another day.

Miss Teague supervised the children's dinner-time meal of homemade sandwiches and pasties. The mothers of the children not going home to eat took turns to collect all the fare and meet the children at the school gate.

Eleanor offered Jo some of the lentil soup she and Marcus were to eat. She declined and regretted it. Unpacking the pasty Mercy had made for her – the pasty Jo had cut in half for it was so big – she found it overflowed her plate. Marcus glanced at it then looked down into his soup bowl with, what Jo determined, was a smirk.

He had been considerate all morning but she wasn't going to allow him to make fun of her. 'Would you care for some, Mr Lidgey?' she asked with a similar expression, pushing the plate towards him.

'What? Um, no, thank you.' Breathing heavily, he picked up his soup spoon.

When Jo left, Eleanor beckoned Marcus to her.

'What is it, Mama? I'm busy.'

She slapped him violently across the face. 'You embarrassed her, you bastard. You need to get the girl to fall in love with you, and as soon as you possibly can. I'm not staying in these wretched circumstances a moment longer than I'm forced to.'

In an uncontrollable rage, she castigated him over the subject she had brought up many times in the last year. 'If you had taken the trouble to keep in touch with me and my affairs, instead of getting yourself involved in a sordid scandal, you would have realised the tin-mining industry was sinking into decline and I was about to lose my meagre assets. It's all your fault! You did this to me. It was my state of anxiety that caused me to fall down the stairs, making me a cripple. Well, it was your petty perversions which sent you skulking back to Cornwall. Now you must make up for it. When you get back to the school, make sure you work hard to win over that tender little shrew.'

Ten

It was raining steadily and the moor was fogbound when Jo made her way home. She strode along under her black umbrella, recalling the success of her first day.

There was a sudden thud behind her and her shoulders were grabbed. She lashed out with her elbow and tried to bring the umbrella down against her attacker.

'Stop it, Jo,' shouted a familiar voice. 'It's me, Russell.'

Her fury surpassed her moments of fright. 'Why couldn't you say hello properly, you fool? You were always jumping out on me.'

'And you were always fighting me off.' Slipping his hands in under her arms, the younger of the Trevail brothers lifted Jo's limbs until she was standing before him like a scarecrow. She was about to force them down, when he said, 'Let's have a look at you then.'

Twisting her lips in contempt, she allowed him a moment's perusal.

He mimicked her expression, then gave his verdict, 'You're lovely.'

'You really think so?' She thought she would collapse with shock, both her former rowdy playmates actually paying her compliments. Or was Russell about to take his back and insult her?

He grinned and kissed her cheek. 'Lew said you'd grown into something worth looking at. I agree with him.'

'You look rather good yourself, Russell.' He shared most of Lew's stalwart features, but while his had a lesser touch of commonness, they hinted of his slyness. He was always quick to pick a quarrel.

89

Russell put his arm round her shoulders in the natural way he'd done occasionally when he and Lew had escorted her back to Cardhu, after they'd romped together on the moors. Keeping his head at an angle away from the umbrella, he walked on, taking her with him. 'Do you like it at the school?'

'I do,' she said, watching her ankle boots forge patterns on the bemired lane. There was the pungent smell of saturated foliage. 'Tell me about the Viguses, Russell. I'm interested in them because two of the children are in my class. I've met Luke Vigus. Does he do his best for the children?'

'You'll never see those brats at school. Jessie Vigus has had heaps of children, never a husband. Some of them died. As for Luke, he turned up on her doorstep a few years back. He must've been her first. Comes from Germoe. 'Tis said he nearly got done for burglary. His story goes, that when his grandmother, what reared him, died, he was curious to meet the mother who deserted him. He's still up to his tricks. Constable's round to his cottage quick as lightning when something goes missing. Some reckon it'll be prison for him one day. I don't think so. Luke's too artful. He's a bad'un. A drifter, never stays in Parmarth more than a few days at a time.'

'I see. What a terrible way for the younger children to live.' Jo was deeply disappointed to learn so many negative things about Luke Vigus. 'How about you, Russell? How are things at the Geevor?'

'Price of tin's still dropping.' He sighed grimly. 'The way it's going, 'tis reckoned it'll be down to less than a hundred and twenty pounds a ton by the end of the year. I'm drilling in Victory Shaft. Only hope the work lasts, or I'll be off, abroad maybe like so many others. So, apart from teaching the local brats, what else have you been up to since you got here?'

'I've settled into the farm. I've been walking the moors. I've been to many of the places where we used to play – where I tried to play alongside you and Lew,' she ended accusingly.

Russell gave a snorting laugh. 'You were a tough little

bugger. We liked to amuse ourselves with you, but when we wanted to get rid of you it was always a hard job. You should've been a boy. Have you been to Cardhu?'

'Yes. It was sad seeing the house, where I'd spent so many happy hours, locked up and deserted. It may soon belong to someone else.' It hurt to express those last few words and she was suddenly consumed with jealousy at the idea of strangers living in the house which should rightfully now belong to her. Jo widened her eyes at her mercenary thought, but it was exactly how she felt. She had become the most important person in Celia's life. Celia had influenced her life more than any other. They had loved each other. Cardhu was special to her. She longed to learn the fate of the house.

'Aye, it's locked up tighter than a barrel. Just as well, or its contents would've walked straight out on to Luke Vigus's wagon.'

Jo said nothing, wondering if Luke Vigus really did steal the stone eagles.

'Wish I had a house like that.' Russell sounded gloomy. Jo lifted aside the umbrella to look up at him. 'When are you going to call on Mother and Father?' he said moodily. 'She's all excited about it. Keeps baking fresh cake for you. It wouldn't hurt you, you know.'

'I do know, Russell.' She sighed heavily. 'I'm beginning to feel guilty about leaving it for so long. Tell Mrs Trevail I'll pop in at the weekend.'

'She had a fright last night.' Russell chuckled. 'Jessie Vigus knocked on the door, demanding money for her baby.'

'Do you think it's Lew's baby?'

'She's the dead spit of him.'

'How did your mother respond?'

'Sent her away with a flea in her ear. Jessie Vigus is a dirty bitch.'

Jo could understand Mrs Trevail's disinterest in her grand-child, there were too many rumours of others scattered abroad, but Jo felt a stir of concern for this particular baby. 'If Rex and Molly are still absent from school at

91

the end of the week, I think I'll arrive on their doorstep. They obviously need encouragement.'

'You can't do nothing for 'em, Jo. Jessie'll only try to get money out of you. I gave her a shilling once to buy milk for the baby and she spent it on booze. She don't care about the kids going to school.'

'Well, I can try.'

Russell pulled the umbrella out of her hand and held it over them both. 'How did your dinner go the other night,' he said into her face, 'with the schoolmaster?'

'It was quite enjoyable.' Jo was intrigued by Russell's interest.

'I'm fond of Sally,' Russell admitted, turning crimson with embarrassment. 'Do you think the 'master's interested in her?'

'Of course not. I've noticed nothing of the kind,' Jo lied diplomatically. She had seen the intimate way Sally Allett treated her employer, while jealously watching for signs of anything more than a professional attachment between her and Marcus Lidgey.

'Look, Jo, I've asked Sally to walk out with me and she said she'll think about it. Will you put in a word for me? Point out I'm in work. That I'll do the right thing by her.'

Jo wasn't on the kind of terms with Sally to say such a thing to her, and she was sure it would prove fruitless anyway, but it was unwise to refuse Russell's request. He was capable of causing trouble at the schoolhouse. 'All right, Russell, I'll see what I can do.' She smiled placatingly.

'Thanks, maid. I gotta go. See you soon.'

Shaking her head, she watched him walk away, turning up his coat collar against the drenching rain.

Jo was in the kitchen laying the table for tea. The two dogs, sprawled in front the hearth, suddenly sprang to their feet, whining and prowling at the back door. They could be finicky animals when Mercy wasn't there and Jo let them outside. Before she closed the door against the rain, the dogs shot off into the gloom, barking loudly. Mercy, who was in the cows' shippen, bawled at them to shut up.

The dogs kept fussing, and Jo peered across the yard to see what might have alerted them. A sudden gust of wind made her blink and recoil. Perhaps the weather was making the dogs skittish.

Then through the darkness and downpour, amid a guard of leaping, sniffing collies, a pair of small children appeared, holding hands.

'My goodness!' Jo ran to them in her slippers. 'Whatever are you doing out in this weather, without coats too? Come inside and get warm and dry.' She was alarmed to see the boy and girl were wearing inadequate shoes and the girl had a ragged cardigan without a single button on it. Kip and Hunter were bounding round them and she ordered them off.

The children backed away. 'We've come t'see M-mercy,' the boy said through chattering teeth. 'We w-want milk.'

'There's no need to stay out here,' Jo said kindly. 'I'll fetch Mercy for you. Go inside to the kitchen.' She moved towards the children, but the boy drew the girl back.

Mercy was there. ''Tis all right, kids. She's my friend. Inside with you, like she said.' She didn't wait for them to obey but picked up a child in each arm and carried them into the farmhouse.

'Who are they?' Jo exclaimed, shivering on her heels. 'Gipsies?'

'You know you've never seen gipsy children in their state,' Mercy said sternly, as she put the children to sit in the huge chimney. 'This is Rex and Molly Vigus.'

'What!'

'Calm down, Jo. You're scaring 'em. They trust few people and no wonder. Leave this to me. You fetch some towels and blankets.' Mercy threw the rough towel at the sink over Molly's dripping head.

Stepping out of her saturated slippers, Jo raced to the airing cupboard, which overhung the staircase. She pulled out as many towels and blankets as she could carry. When she returned, the children were drinking chicken broth directly out of bowls in trembling dirty hands. Mercy held up a warning finger. Silently, Jo put the bundle on the table.

'I'll get you some milk, Rex,' Mercy said. 'Bring the can back tomorrow.'

Rex nodded. His face was marked with suspicion, but he and Molly would get fed again when they returned the can. Luke had left Parmarth that morning, saying he was meeting a contact at Gwithian and he would be back in the evening. Not trusting Luke to keep his word, and knowing their mother would thrash him and Molly until he handed over the money Luke had given him to buy milk for Marylyn, Rex had taken Molly to shelter among the tombs in the churchyard until he was sure Jessie had drunk herself into a stupor. Now he had come for the milk, with which he would feed Marylyn, hoping his baby sister had come to no harm during the day. He unknotted his frozen fingers and the precious pennies rolled out and clinked on to the floor.

'Keep your money. I've plenty of milk. 'Tisn't my way to sell the surplus if a neighbour needs some.'

Rex snatched up the pennies and stuffed them inside his soaked shirt.

While keeping her eyes on the children, Jo cut bread. Mercy buttered the slices thickly and swapped them for the empty soup bowls. The bread was wolfed down.

'Mercy,' Jo whispered, incensed, her heart aching with pity and concern for the children. 'They're starved. They're half naked. They're crawling with fleas. The girl has weeping sores on her face.'

Mercy clamped a heavy hand on her shoulder. 'Now don't go getting ideas, Jo. You can't do much to help 'em. Every time someone's intervened on their behalf their mother gets nasty and beats them more than ever. She sells any good clothes they're given.'

Jo knew it was wise to keep her counsel but her mind was ticking over. When the children had eaten a large slice of seed cake, gulped down a mug of hot, spiced milk, she said to Mercy, 'Is there any way of getting them home without them becoming half-drowned again?'

94

'I'll hitch up the wagon. They can hold a tarpaulin over their heads.'

'I'll come with you. I'll explain who I am and perhaps it might persuade them to come to school tomorrow.'

Minutes later, Mercy, in oilskins and a waterproof hat, was urging her two workhorses along the murky road. Jo, clad in her raincoat and boots, a wool cloche hat pulled down over her head, sat on the straw in the back of the wagon helping Rex and Molly prop up the tarpaulin. She had a horn lantern wedged between her feet so they weren't in total darkness. She felt guilty to be so well wrapped up while the children could only huddle in borrowed blankets. As the wagon lurched and rolled, she changed her voice to less modulated tones and talked about being their new teacher. Of how she used to visit the village and play on the moors.

'Are you coming to school tomorrow? Rex. Molly. I'd like to get to know you properly.' Neither answered, or looked at her. She told them about some of her childhood pranks, but still there was no response. Jo had known the children for less than half an hour but she was worried that, indeed, little could be done to help them grow up into normal, well-adjusted adults. From the notes of Marcus Lidgey's report she knew they were both illiterate and innumerate, had a small level of concentration; in other words were retarded, probably the result of wilful neglect. Rex had only just come up from the infants' class this term, and because Molly, although a year younger, relied on him so heavily she too had been elevated. Thinking about their amusing, swarthily attractive, older brother, Jo was angry over the way he was letting the children down.

The rain pounded on the tarpaulin, but Jo's concentration was drawn to the sound of Molly's harsh breathing. Jo rocked with indignation. If they existed in this dreadful condition, what was the fate of the baby, Lew's child?

Mercy was heard calling to the horses. The wagon was pulled up. Rex and Molly tossed aside the blankets, grabbed the milk can and scampered away, leaving Jo tangled up in the tarpaulin.

When she was able to jump down on to Parmarth's oozing

95

street, she saw Luke Vigus beckoning to the children in the poorly lit doorway of the cottage. He shouted, 'Thanks, Mercy, thanks, teacher,' then shut the door.

Jo made to follow the children, but Mercy grabbed her arm.

'What are you doing?' Jo protested. She hardly heard her own voice above the howl of the wind and beating of the rain.

'I've told you, you can't do anything, Jo,' Mercy shouted, wiping rain water away from her eyes.

'But Luke Vigus must be made to see that he shouldn't send the children out into the rain as he did tonight. I can't go home and say nothing about it.'

'It'll be seen as interfering and'll only make things worse.'

'Then I'll see Mr Lidgey.' Jo scrambled forward again.

Mercy pushed her towards the wagon. 'You can't disturb him on a night like this. Wait till morning. We're going home.'

'No, I won't wait! Something has to be done now.'

Sitting at the desk in his study, Marcus was clenching a pencil in his fingers, his knuckles white and bursting. How could he have been so stupid, so off-guard, as to allow his mother to burrow her clutches into him again? In London, he'd shut the abuse, starting soon after his father's death, out of his mind. When shame-filled memories caught him unawares, somehow he'd convinced himself it had all been a terrible nightmare.

He snapped the pencil in half and rubbed the splinters between his thumb and fingertips. Wishing he could do a similar thing to his mother.

He had just managed to coax her to retire early, then got away from her by pleading a mountain of paperwork. He could not bear her touching him, of having to kiss her lips. He had weakened her mastery of him tonight by holding her fast until he'd crushed the strength out of her. Then he had tossed her invasive hands aside to lie limply, in mock innocence, at her sides.

If only she had died in the fall down the stairs. Had it been an accident? She was quite capable of engineering an accident to make him take full responsibility for her, to punish him from escaping her for twelve unfettered years. How she gloated at his downfall from a senior tutor in the music college. Even his behaviour there had been a consequence of his upbringing. Eleanor had tainted every composition of his life. He could never be honourable, attain self-respect. Never experience love with purity and true self-giving.

'Were you nice to her? Did you use your charm on her? Are you sure you smiled at her enough, to make up for making her look a fool at the luncheon table?'

'Yes, Mama,' had been his repeated answer to her interrogation on his conduct that afternoon towards Joanna Venner.

His mother had laboured her point and he had reiterated his cooperation with her selfish plan until he thought he'd lose his mind and scream and swear at the defiled virago. Sometimes he hated her so much he plotted ways of shutting her up for ever. He imagined himself calling Sally away from the bathroom then drowning her in the bath. Smothering her with a pillow. Collecting fungi from the moor and poisoning her. Feeding her extra pain-killing pills. He had formed an endless list of murders since returning to Cornwall, resulting in him hating himself as much as he hated his mother, because he knew he lacked the courage to carry out any of his escape plans.

Suddenly he wanted to thrust the broken ends of the pencil into the palm of his hand to eradicate his mental torture with physical pain, to purge his filthiness, to imbue his impure thoughts with something right and clean for once. Just once. With all his being he hated his mother for corrupting him, making him perverted, and in a moment of temporary madness, he hated the girl he was to lure into his mother's latest self-seeking scheme. He needed cruelty. Wanted to inflict cruelty. Then he was afraid. Afraid that one day he would lose his mind and turn one of his fantasies into a terrible reality.

There was an urgent knocking on the front door and he swiped the tears from his eyes.

Moments later he rose from his desk, to view the incredible spectacle of Joanna Venner in the room on this storm-tossed night, dripping on his rug. Was he seeing things? He clenched his guts to get a grip on himself. She was in obvious distress, but in the effort to appear normal he could neither offer the comfort she required nor exploit the situation providence had unexpectedly thrown him. And he felt ridiculously amused at the rather pathetic sight of this dainty, drenched person.

'Miss Venner, you simply amaze me. I did not expect to see you again today, particularly in the guise of a refugee.'

'I'm sorry, Mr Lidgey, but I have to see you on a matter of some urgency,' Jo panted.

'Has Nance Farm burned down? Are you without shelter for the night?'

'No, I . . .' It took some moments before Jo realised he was being sardonic. 'This is not a situation for cynical humour. Miss Merrick and I have just—'

'Are you cold?'

'What?' she snapped.

'You're shivering, Miss Venner. If you are cold, please do take the benefit of my fire.' He gestured towards the hearth.

Jo shifted her shoulders and raised her head. 'Mr Lidgey, are you going to listen to me or am I wasting my time?' There was a knock on the door and she thought she would swear.

Sally came in with a tea tray. 'I took the liberty of making Miss Venner a hot drink, sir. It's what Mrs Lidgey would've ordered, if she was still up.'

'Thank you, Sally,' Marcus said tonelessly, and although he did not look at the housemaid, Jo was not insensitive to the intimate rapport travelling between them.

'I can't stay,' Jo stressed, almost at the point of frustration. Damn the man's pussyfooting display of genteel manners. If she had gone to an ordinary house, the occupants would have wanted to know straightaway why she was there and been eager to do something about her exigency.

'Have you had a misfortune, Jo— Miss Venner?' Sally asked, holding out a cup of tea towards her. 'I was some worried to see you standing on the doorstep like that, leaking wet, splashed all over with mud.'

Jo took the cup and saucer and rattled them down on to the desk. 'My friend and her horses are outside in this terrible weather,' she seethed, furious that the headmaster and his lover should make fun of her. 'Could I get to the point, please?'

'I've just peeped out the front-room window and saw Mercy heading for the forge. She'll shelter her horses in the stable,' Sally said pertly. 'Are you in trouble?'

Jo was about to snap, 'It's none of your business,' when Marcus said sternly, 'Sally, take Miss Venner's outdoor things to the kitchen and dry them.'

Sally's jaw dropped. Jo could see she had not expected to be dismissed. She pulled off her hat, slipped out of her raincoat and thrust them into Sally's hands.

Glaring at her, Sally flounced out of the room, slamming the door.

Marcus motioned again at his well-tended coal fire. She moved towards it and held out her hands to the flames, which were twisting convulsively from the draught coming down the chimney. She relaxed. If Mercy was comfortably occupied, she would exploit Marcus Lidgey's time in explaining why she was here.

He followed her with her tea in his hand, smiling kindly. Marcus had managed to get himself under control. 'I owe you an apology, Miss Venner. You took me by surprise arriving suddenly on my doorstep, looking as though you'd been through a whirlwind, bursting with ardour. It diverted me from my boring paperwork and I couldn't resist indulging in a little repartee.'

So he thought her an object of jest, did he? Dampening her anger, for it would not help her reason for being here, Jo sipped the tea then set the cup and saucer down on a bookshelf. He was looking at her hair. She put up a hand and met a confusion of damp kinks. She must look a mess. No matter. Her appearance was not important at this moment.

'Rex and Molly Vigus came to Nance Farm a short

99

time ago to buy milk for their baby sister. I was shocked to see the appalling condition they were in, from wilful neglect, and I would hazard, a certain amount of cruelty. Their brother doesn't seem to care very much about them. Something must be done immediately. I felt I had to inform you straightaway.'

'And what do you expect me to do?' he asked calmly.

'Take immediate action to ensure the children are treated properly. Telephone the authorities, write to someone,' Jo retorted, her voice rising. Wasn't the damned man interested?

Marcus's face was quiet. 'Let me assure you, Miss Venner, that everything that could be done for the Vigus children has been attempted. Many people, myself included, have pleaded with Jessie Vigus to behave as a responsible mother. The family have been given food, clothes, bedding and furniture, often by others who could ill afford to part with them. Jessie Vigus thwarted the good intentions every time. She sold everything to nourish her drinking habit.'

'But things can't be allowed to continue as they are, Mr Lidgey.'

'I agree with you and they won't be. The next step will be for the children to be taken away and put into an orphanage. The authorities are reluctant to do so while the elder brother is trying to provide for the family.'

Jo tossed her head towards the ceiling. 'I've just mentioned how ineffective he is. The only thing he will do for the children is teach them to drink, swear and steal.'

'He does try. We can't invade the home to keep checking on his efforts.'

'Well, whatever he's doing it is obviously falling miserably short,' she said huffily. 'You must get in touch with the authorities again.'

'If I may say so, it is easy to stand on one's moral indignation and suggest that. But have you thought about what it would do to Rex and Molly to be uprooted and forced out of their home? To live the rest of their childhood in a cold institution amongst total strangers? To many children, whatever sort of home they are brought up in, it is usually better to them than no proper home at all.' A heavy weight descended upon Marcus. He had repeated the comments Miss Teague had made about the Vigus children, views he did not necessarily share. He knew that life in an institution might be more easily endured than an unforgivably abused existence in the home.

Jo brushed back her damp hair and walked towards the desk. The passion seeped out of her. 'You're right, Mr Lidgey. I'm sorry. I've been thinking with my heart instead of my head. The children's plight touched me deeply.'

'I've no doubt your heart has a large capacity for compassion. I will consider the problem of the Vigus children anew,' he said softly. He ventured to her side. 'Please sit down. Have some more tea.'

'No, thank you. I've disturbed your work. I must go and find Miss Merrick.' Jo faced him, determined again. 'Mr Lidgey, I have to tell you that if Rex and Molly do not attend school tomorrow or Friday then I shall call on their mother at the weekend.'

'I advise against the notion,' he said gravely. 'Leave it to me.'

'I'm sorry, but I cannot. It may have come to your notice that the baby, Marylyn, is Lew Trevail's child. I have some influence on him and somehow I feel I have a duty towards the little one. I will not forsake it.'

101

Eleven

L uke rolled up the bedroll he used when on the road. Unable to bear sleeping under his mother's roof for this visit home, Luke had pitched his wagon on the moor, close to the outskirts of the village. Lighting a cigarette, he opened the canvas at the back of the wagon and looked outside. The air was damp and chill, the sky heavy, threatening and grey, but he had everything he needed inside his moving home. A photograph of Gran, the woman who'd reared him, a change of clothes and his latest stock of goods: bolts of cloth, household wares and garden tools to sell to the street traders at Penzance, and a concealed stash of stolen silver to pass on to a fence in the same town. When the wagon was empty he'd travel over to Hayle, pick up a haul of timber, taken illegally from a timber yard, and sell it on to a small boat-builder at St Ives. Then he'd deal strictly legitimate for a few weeks, to keep the law off his back.

Last night he had gone home to check on the kids. The cottage appeared deserted at first. He thought Rex and Molly had crept off to bed, and their mother had wandered off again. He hoped she had fallen foul of a forsaken mineshaft or something equally dangerous. Then Marylyn whimpered hungrily in her drawer and he found Jessie hopelessly paralytic on the floor next to the dresser, beside two empty illegal gin bottles. Hefting her over his shoulder, he carried her up the rope ladder and threw her down on her filthy mattress. Why couldn't she suffer the fate of others when in this condition, to be sick and choke herself to death? Luke believed she only stayed alive to torment him.

'Oh, hell, where have you two gone?' he'd groaned at Rex and Molly's empty mattress.

Recognising Mercy Merrick's voice outside, he knew that out in the cold and rain was the answer. He had called his brother and sister inside and thanked his neighbour and her lodger for their kindness. He had done his bit, so what right did the new schoolteacher have to glare at him accusingly? Sighing with discontent, he knew the answer to this second question, and what he must do about it. He'd have to shelve his plans to take off to the north of the county for the next few weeks.

Washing in the stream before going home to see the kids got some breakfast, he wished he could wash away his moral obligations.

Rex and Molly were eating porridge in their ragged nightclothes when someone rapped loudly on the door. Afraid it was the 'truancy man', after eyeing Luke nervously and receiving a nod from him, they clambered up the rope ladder with their bowls and spoons.

Leisurely firing up a cigarette, Luke finally answered the door.

It was Marcus Lidgey, wearing a silk tie and the dark suit he taught in, of a style and cut that was the envy of every man in the village. He was carrying a briefcase, presumably about to start his day's work.

'What the hell do you want?'

'You must have a very good idea.' Marcus frostily held up his hand, determined he would not have the door slammed in his face this time. 'Are Rex and Molly attending school today?'

Taking a long puff on his smoke, Luke said defensively, 'I s'pose so. My mother will see to it.' He knew it was unlikely.

'Can't you make sure they get ready?' Marcus enquired stubbornly.

Overhead, Molly coughed, a painful blaring sound.

Marcus frowned impatiently. 'She's caught a cold, from being out in the rain last night, no doubt. I've been informed of the children's excursion to Nance Farm. If you don't want your brother and sisters to end up in an orphanage, Mr Vigus, you will have to ensure they are more suitably looked after from now on.'

'I know that,' Luke swore. 'You bloody do-gooders should be telling Jessie this, not me. 'Tisn't my fault if she's pissed most of the time and doesn't behave like a proper mother.'

'In the circumstances, you ought to assume parental responsibility.'

'Oh, really?' Luke snarled, dangerously close to losing his temper.

'If your mother can't or won't take proper care of her family, you should find someone who will,' Marcus barked, his own temper rising at the roughcast dealer's indifference.

Luke placed his hand on the door. 'Have you finished?'

'Yes. The fate of your family is in your hands, Vigus.'

As Marcus swung angrily away on his heel, Luke kicked the door shut. 'Sanctimonious bastard. It isn't schooling the kids need most.' At this moment they needed him. But he needed his freedom. He had some hard thinking to do to work things out satisfactorily for all their futures.

Twelve

'Who's she?' Keane Trevail asked his wife. He had just limped into the kitchen of Heather Cottage, having paid a call to the outside earth closet. Shutting out the draught, hanging his jacket on a hook behind the door, he lowered his hefty body, fronted by a sagging paunch, down gingerly on the chair at the head of the table. He sat directly in front of the dresser, which made it difficult for his family to fetch and put things away in it.

''Tis Joanna Venner. You remember she. She used to play with our boys backalong. Used to stay at Miss Sayce's.'

'Eh?' Keane stroked his full grey-streaked beard, shifted awkwardly to get comfortable on the knitted-covered cushion. He had not been fully mobile for ten years, after suffering a crushed foot at the Carn Valley Stamp. 'Oh, she that's the teacher now?'

'Jo's been to the shop,' Irene said. 'She bought me a bag of peppermints and this for you, Father.' She proudly put a two-ounce packet of Gold Flake on the scrubbed table, before pouring her husband a huge mug of tea.

Feeling slightly embarrassed, Jo waited for Keane to thank her.

His heavy breathing, due to a spot of miner's lung congestion, filled the stuffily warm room. 'Kind of her,' Keane told his wife, and Jo realised he usually spoke through Irene. 'She can stay for dinner, if she likes.' He reached for his cigarette papers and matches on the dresser, next to his most prized possession, his miner's hard hat.

'I'll get on with the pie,' Irene said, returning to the

105

making of the rabbit pie on the table, the job interrupted by Jo's arrival.

'I wish I could stay for dinner, Mrs Trevail,' Jo said regretfully. She felt at ease in the shabby little home. She was getting used to the smells of residue of cooked cabbage, stale tobacco and liniment; there was a large bottle on the dresser, probably used to ease an arthritic joint. 'I have other business this morning.'

'Never mind, perhaps another time.'

Jo watched Irene sprinkle coarse flour over a rolling pin then roll out a lump of greyish dough to complete the rabbit pie. Irene made a homely figure, hairpins falling out of her thin, grey bun, bobbled slippers on her feet. Jo considered asking Mercy to teach her to cook.

Sucking on a cigarette, making his ragged breathing noisier, Keane studied Jo as if she was a slice of meat brought in from the butcher's horse and cart.

'She's still like a yard of pump water. A woman should have a bit of bum and bosom. She haven't got a face like a mare's backside though. Could get herself a husband, I s'pose, and live a proper sort of life. I mind, when she couldn't get her own way with Lew and Russell, she belonged to look like a ferret had put his arse in under her sharp little face.'

'Keane,' Irene chided him, turning crimson. 'You're being rude.'

'It's all right.' Jo could not help laughing. She knew Keane was not being offensive. Then she fell into wishing she did have a 'bit of bum and bosom'. Thrusting her shoulders back she tried to appear more rounded.

He finally spoke to her. 'Well then, maid, what are you on upon, coming back to these parts like this? Bet your mother was mazed with 'ee.'

'She was.' Jo smiled to herself. Before calling at Heather Cottage, she had rung Tresawna House from the parlour of the Engine House Inn again. Emma, the maid, had fetched Alistair to speak to her. Alistair had sounded jolly, admitted reluctantly that he was pleased she was settling in at the school. When she enquired how Katherine was, he had replied resignedly, 'Oh, you know Mother, she's how she's always been, little thing.'

Jo knew her name was never mentioned at home by her mother, unless in a derogatory tone.

Quickly putting the rabbit pie into the coal-burning, cream-coloured Cornish 'slab', Irene stood in front of the range, cutting off the heat, folding her arms across her aproned bosom.

'How did your first week go?' Irene asked her.

'I think it went very well. I feel I've known the children for ages. There's one boy, Kenneth Willis, who keeps falling asleep.'

'He would, poor little soul. His father works him like a donkey, labouring wherever he can get them both work. I knew you'd settle in here,' Irene went on triumphantly. 'Told you so, didn't I, Father? Miss Sayce, well, I won't say nothing about her private life, we being good chapel people, but she was good to you, Jo. You'll understand the kiddies better than that old mare Miss Choak. Used to crack Russell's knuckles with the ruler nearly every day, she did, the miserable old so-and-so. Do you get on with Miss Teague?'

'She seems a little distant. I'd like to get to know her better.' Miss Teague had been coolly polite to Jo all week. She did not avail herself of the schoolhouse during the breaks and Jo suspected she resented her visits there.

'You won't get much out of she.' Irene shook her head. 'Likes her own company mostly, though she can be charitable. She'll probably come round when she gets used to you.'

'Funny thing 'bout that schoolmaster.' While filling his pouch with Gold Flake, Keane kept his watery gaze on Jo.

'What's funny, Mr Trevail?' Jo would not indulge in gossip about her superior but she was hoping to learn something more about Marcus Lidgey.

'You never asked yourself what he's doing here? Clever man like he could get a much better job. Doesn't have t'be a schoolmaster at all, I'd have thought. Plays beautiful music, I've heard un a time or two. Gotta car, a few posh bits of furniture went inside the 'master's house the day he moved

107

in, but he ain't got nothing else. He's ruined, been up to something bad, if you ask me. Watch out you don't get involved in it, maid, whatever it is. If you find out—'

'I'm really not interested in Mr Lidgey's private affairs, Mr Trevail.' Jo felt it was time she interrupted. She consulted the clock on the mantelpiece, flanked either side by the cheap plaster ornaments she remembered Lew and Russell winning at the Corpus Christi Fair. 'Is that the time? I'm afraid I really must go. Thank you for the tea.' She was sure she would taste Irene's bitter-strong brew on her tongue for the rest of the day. 'I'll see myself out.'

'Next time you come just walk straight in, my luvver.' Irene smiled warmly. 'No need to knock, we never do round here. Come and go by the back door if you like.'

Jo put her raincoat on and left by the back of the cottage. Before she got through the back kitchen, she was set upon by Russell. He was unshaven, bleary-eyed and smelled manky, having rushed out of bed after the late shift at the Geevor mine.

He grabbed her arm. 'Have you spoken to Sally yet?'

'Yes. She's thinking about it,' she lied shamelessly. Jo had totally forgotten Russell's request she act as romantic go-between.

'Ask her if she'll meet me up by the ruins.'

'The mine ruins?'

'Where else do you think I meant?' he muttered impatiently. 'Set up a meeting, let me know.'

'She doesn't get much chance to leave Mrs Lidgey.'

'You can always stay with that cripple to give her a break.'

'I can't order the Lidgey household.'

'You can damn well try.'

'I don't have to do anything for you.' Jo's eyes shone with a threat.

'I'm sorry,' Russell wailed. 'It's just that I've fallen for Sally. Do what you can for me, eh, Jo?'

She opened the door, letting in the fog that was covering the moor. 'I'll have another word with her now. Go to the ruins tomorrow afternoon. If she's not there, you'll know she's not interested.'

I hope you enjoy your trudge through the mire for nothing, Russell Trevail, Jo said to herself while making her way to her next port of call.

No one answered the Viguses' front door. Jo looked through one of the small windows, which had shutters hanging off at the sides. The remnants of a pair of coarse curtains were drawn across the dirty glass. Rather than knock again and create curiosity, she lifted the wobbly latch and peeped inside.

She recoiled at the stench that hit her like a wash of corruption, as if it had a life force seeking to cut off and destroy all that was pure and natural. She hastily raised a hand to cover her nose. Outside, the fog had reduced visibility to a few yards; in the cottage the filth and gloom hid the corners, making everything dark and ominous. 'Hello, is anyone at home?'

The room appeared to be empty, then she saw a movement in the bottom drawer of the dresser. Alarm grew inside her. She thought it was a rat. She was afraid of rats. The conditions the Vigus children lived in were worse than she had feared. Summoning up her courage, Jo crept inside and approached the dresser. There was another movement. She flinched. But there was no scurry of brown fur, no twitching pink nose, no big sharp teeth. A pale, nearly naked thing undulated in the drawer. Then she was rushing to it, falling down on her knees. 'Oh, my God.'

Marylyn Vigus was lying on her back, on a scrap of cloth. A dirty, urine-drenched muslin nappy was tangled about her legs. She must have kicked off her inadequate covering, which was also soiled. Her movements were fretful, her tiny blue-white mouth puckering, her eyes huge, sunken, vacuous. How had she survived the bitterly cold night?

Jo touched Marylyn's cheek with her fingertip. The baby turned her head, mouth frantically searching for nourishment. Gingerly, Jo lifted the soiled nappy aside, then pulling the silk scarf off her neck she placed it over the tiny body. While frightened she would hurt the baby, she gradually lifted her into her arms. She felt weightless as she sought something to suck. Jo's heart ached for her. Resting Marylyn half on the dresser surface for security, she unfastened her raincoat and brought Marylyn in against her body, hoping to warm her.

'Dear God,' she breathed, 'what can I do for you?'

Marylyn mewled like a kitten. Jo looked anxiously about the room. There was nothing she could feed the baby with. 'Hello, Marylyn,' she whispered, 'I'm Jo. I'm going to do all I can to help you.' Marylyn had a definite resemblance to Lew. When Jo saw him next she would demand he face up to his responsibility. She wished she had come here before. Marylyn, and Rex and Molly, desperately needed help.

The door to the cottage was opened. Jo braced herself for a confrontation with Jessie Vigus, who would almost certainly be outraged to find a stranger in her home. Jo would not let Marylyn go hungry again, even if it meant walking out of the cottage with her and ending up under arrest. Somehow she would ensure her presence here would not make things worse for the children.

Then Jo was holding her breath for a dispute with Luke Vigus.

Luke let out an oath of shock, nearly dropping the box of food held under his arm. For a moment, in the shadowy gloom of the hovel, he thought he was seeing a ghost. 'Oh, it's you.'

Jo backed away, afraid he would take Marylyn from her. 'Good morning, Mr Vigus.'

Luke's handsome tough features changed to an expression of indignation. 'You've got no right to walk in here. What do you think you're doing?'

Of all the bloody cheek! His first notion was to throw Joanna Venner out of the house, make her feel as small as a worm. Only there was nothing worm-like about her. The utter determination, the sense of power and authority she exuded, the accusation in her eyes over the state of the baby in her arms, made him feel less of a man. Joanna Venner lived at Nance Farm and had seen for herself how badly neglected Rex and Molly were. Now she was standing in the dirt and degradation of his home, for which he must partly bear the shame.

Jo gripped the baby tighter. There was no question of her backing down. 'I haven't come to interfere or patronise, Mr Vigus.' She had difficulty keeping the contempt out of her voice. 'I want to help the children. I would like to speak to your mother.'

Luke's face worked with indecision. He glanced at the empty dresser drawer. 'Put the kid back and get out. You do-gooders are all the same. You'll soon tire of helping a lost cause.'

He was not as hostile as Jo expected and she felt not all of his anger was aimed at her. 'I won't give up. I never give up. Listen to me, I have an idea. I've thought of nothing else since Rex and Molly came to Nance.'

'You can't do anything.' Luke ran a hand through his lank hair. All he wanted was to get away from her accusing green-flecked eyes. 'Get away from here for ever. My mother will throw it back in your face. The kids'd be better off dead. Pity she wasn't dead,' he ended bitterly.

'If you feel as strongly as that then you've got nothing to lose by letting me help you,' Jo pointed out quietly. She felt she was getting a tentative foothold.

'Who do you think you are, telling me what to do? You, who've got a whore for a mother.'

'We've both got whores for mothers, but it doesn't mean you or I or the children should suffer for it,' Jo retorted levelly. 'Does it, Mr Vigus? Have you no other family who could help?'

Luke considered her comments. This time when he had come back, the kids had never looked as hungry, battered, despairing. If nothing was done soon to improve their lot, Marylyn would follow the other babies to the churchyard. He had women friends on his travels, but even those he was on intimate terms with wouldn't take in three scruffy brats. No one in the village was likely to help again. It was thought an orphanage was the best option for the kids. But Rex had

111

begged him never to let this happen. He'd threatened he and Molly would run away from an institution, and God knows what would happen to them then.

Of course, he could stay home for good, keep an eye on the kids. But he couldn't bear that. He couldn't stand being in his mother's company. His throat swelled tight with despair. God, he prayed, near to tears, why aren't I as strong-willed as this schoolteacher seems to be? She can even look me the eye and admit her mother's a whore.

He stared at the door, and it seemed as if it had slammed shut on him, as if he was interred in a prison. He felt heavy chains forming around his heart, weighing down his soul.

Jo feared his long silence meant she was about to be expelled, her mission a failure.

He sighed sullenly, 'There's no one.'

'Not even a godparent?'

'The kids aren't christened. I've got a cousin at Germoe but she won't want to help with the way my mother is.'

'Then will you let me help? Please?'

'I'll listen to what you've come to say,' he replied grudgingly. 'Sit down. I'll see to the fire.'

Clearing dirt off a hard, bare chair, Jo sat down. Apart from two more chairs, the table and dresser, the rest of the furniture consisted of a three-legged stool and a worm-eaten chest.

'Sorry about that,' Luke said, embarrassed. 'I'll see about getting some more furniture.'

Keeping her raincoat wrapped round Marylyn, Jo watched while he lit a cigarette, then lighted a fire of sticks and dried furze. Even his simplest movements were made with impatient energy, a raw strength, like an animal of the wild. Jo sensed what it was costing him to permit her to stay, to say her piece, but she felt no sympathy for him. He had allowed his young brother and sisters to live in unspeakable poverty. Marylyn shifted feebly and whimpered in her arms.

'Where are the other children? And your mother?'

'The kids must be sleeping. The old woman's probably sleeping off yesterday's drinking binge.'

112

He pulled open the ragged curtains at the two front windows. Jo looked about the one-room living accommodation. It was not much larger than the bathroom at Tresawna House. The light that filtered through the accumulated grime on the poor-quality glass showed the dwelling an exceedingly grim, oppressive prospect. A child would not grow up with zest for life, with hope, in these surroundings. A dirty cushion and scraps of foul cloth which served as nappies were strewn about in piles of dirt.

'Ugh!' Jo leapt to her feet. Her lap was being soaked by strong-smelling urine. Her urgency frightened Marylyn, who bawled and stiffened. Throwing her saturated scarf to the floor, Jo gagged. She thought she would never get the stench of this place out of her nostrils.

'Have you got something to wrap the baby in?' she asked desperately.

'Do you still want to help?' Luke smirked.

'Yes.' Jo struggled out of her raincoat, while trying to pacify Marylyn. 'A little pee is of no consequence.'

Shaking his head at her choice of words, Luke eyed her as she lifted up her skirt and slip, tucking dry tweed and silk in underneath the wet parts of the garments. She was basically straight all the way down, but she was revealing a pair of lovely legs. Firm knees, shapely calves and neat ankles, all wet with his sister's dark yellow urine.

'Well? Have you anything for her?' Jo resumed her seat, making his eyes travel up to her indignant face. 'It's a cold winter day and the poor child is naked.'

He opened the cupboard built into the recess beside the fireplace and searched among its jumbled contents. 'Here.' He handed her a piece of ragged material and a discoloured baby's gown. He saw the lack of covers in Marylyn's makeshift cradle. Angels must have been watching over her last night. He pushed his next thought aside – that he should have been here last night, to make sure she got through it safely. 'I'll see if I can find a shawl. Sometimes Jessie doesn't bother to wrap her up properly.'

Very awkwardly, Jo wrapped the material about Marylyn's

lower half and tucked in the edges, hoping it would stay put. Then, while Marylyn struggled and screamed, she somehow managed to get the nightgown over her head and push her woefully thin, flailing arms through the ripped sleeves.

His strong features straining at his sister's distress, Luke passed Jo a shawl, a holey scrap of shapeless knitting.

At last, a little warm and comfortable, Marylyn's voice fell to pathetic whimpers but she still moved her head from side to side seeking sustenance.

Luke took a bloomer loaf out of the box. 'I've got some food, and milk for Marylyn. I always make sure the kids get plenty to eat when I'm here,' he said defensively.

'How often are you away from home?'

'That's my business,' he said gruffly. 'When I went away last month the kids had good clothes on their backs.' He passed Jo a curved baby's bottle full of milk, heated over his camp fire and kept warm in a towel.

Jo stared at the heavy glass object in her hand.

Luke pointed to the teat. 'You put that end in her mouth.'

'I know.'

He grunted. He'd stake the contents of his wagon that this young woman knew nothing about child care. 'I've just bought some new clothes for the kids to go to school in. They're hidden away. The old woman sells everything I get for 'em cheap to Mardie Dawes. Mardie doesn't care if someone's kids are running round naked, as long as she's making money out of it. She sells things on to tinkers, but I s'pose you know that.'

'Mardie's always been a nuisance,' Jo said dryly. If Luke Vigus was trying to win her over he had a hard task.

He kicked at the dilapidated fireplace. 'When I first came here I put up with my mother's ways because she was all I had. I was hoping she'd be like my gran, who brought me up. She promised to change, give up the drink, clean the damned place. She'd manage a couple of days then slip back. She can't give up the drink now, doesn't even try. I've almost got used to it, the kids suffering, the stink, the hopelessness of it. Poor little sods. They don't know what it's like to be looked after

114

properly. I do.' One reason for him not abandoning the kids permanently was because his grandmother would not have approved. 'I'm thinking of paying someone to look after the house and kids. It's the best I can do. I have to go on the road to earn their keep.'

Jo listened carefully, while anxiously watching Marylyn, who was having difficulty sucking on the teat.

'What's this idea of yours?' he asked tersely. How could he show gratitude to someone who showed him up as a selfish failure?

'When people tried to help in the past, no doubt they expected your mother to give up the drink. The way I see it, if she won't, then there's no use asking her to.' Jo adopted a softer tone. 'I was going to suggest the same thing you've thought of. It's a good start. Have you anyone in mind?'

Luke reached on top of the dresser, produced a long, sharp knife which he kept hidden there, and began cutting the loaf. 'Beth Wherry. She only works part time at the schoolhouse. I'm sure she'd agree. I'm hoping to persuade her father to let her come. They're a very religious family. I'm afraid he might not want the girl near my drunken mother.'

'I've met Beth. She's a sweet girl. If her father does agree, I'll do all I can to support her. The children can come over to Nance for meals at any time. Mercy Merrick will be pleased to welcome them.'

Luke looked with suspicion at the uninvited guest in his home. 'Why are you so keen to help? The kids aren't your responsibility just because you're Rex and Molly's teacher.'

Marylyn had finished her feed. Jo held the minute body against her chest, wondering why her face was contorting, her stomach agitating. She prayed Marylyn was not about to be sick. 'I didn't come to Parmarth to play the lady bountiful, if that's what you think. There would be no point in my taking on this more humble position unless I did my very best for the children in my class. How old is Marylyn?'

'Um, about three months. She was born just before Guy Fawkes Night. You have to pat her back, bring up her wind.'

'Wind? Oh.' Jo followed his instructions and was rewarded with a loud belch from Marylyn, and a smelly posset of milk down her bunched-up skirt. 'She must only weigh about twelve pounds.'

Luke turned away. He rubbed his stubbly jaw. Hurt came into his quiet tones, moving Jo to look at him again, and remember their first good-natured meeting. 'We could all do with better care. I must get cleaned up. Coming here's made me slovenly like my mother.'

'I'm sure you're nothing like your mother.' Jo smiled at him.

Thirteen

S ince her arrival at Nance Jo had kept a diary, written as if she were talking to Celia. She recorded each day at the school and each event spent roaming old haunts, all the places Celia had taken her to, even a stroll down the lanes, many so narrow that sledges instead of carts were still pulled by pack animals to convey goods and animal foodstuffs.

On one occasion she took a track past the abandoned twin engine houses and counting house of the Carn Galver Mine, situated directly across the coast road from the foot of Carn Galver itself. Soon, she was picking her way, as there was no obvious route, to reach the cliff over Porthmeor Cove, where she had learned to swim. The sea was huge. It pounded frustratedly on the dangerous, jagged granite far below her, and at the distant points, up and down coast. She would come back in the spring and picnic in the rocky places, where many times she had examined rock pools with Celia and collected driftwood for the Merricks.

Backtracking a short distance, she headed inland to the tall gaunt workings that had once been Parmarth's lifeblood, a place that had become another of her playgrounds; she could still hear the persistent roar of the ocean. Owned and lost by the Morvah Mining Company, all the mechanical equipment, including the forty-inch pumping engine, had been removed and sold at the Solace Mine's closure. The locals had quickly helped themselves to the massive timber beams and the bricks at the top of the tapering chimney stack, where the greatest strength of the construction had been needed, the latter requiring a precipitous climb. The remains of the engine house were strong enough to stand at least another century. Some of the stones had wonderful pink and blue hues incorporated in them, all were coated with mosses. The boiler house and sheds had been dismantled, their foundations, like the engine-house floor, encroached on by bracken, heather, gorse and brambles. Foliage, dead and skeletal, mercifully disguised the ugly attle as small hills.

She followed the course of one of the leats which had served the mine until it merged with the stream which eventually ran along Bridge Lane. And then she was standing on top of the desolate hill sheltering Cardhu. The house looked grey and isolated, bleak and empty, but Jo thought she heard Celia's voice in the wind calling her name.

Each time she closed the diary she marvelled that she knew these pleasures and had escaped the unfulfilling future her mother had planned for her. The day after she added the details of her visit to the Vigus cottage, she decided to climb Carn Galver.

The sky was dull, the cross winds bitingly cold, and Jo dressed warmly, seconding Granny Merrick's Burberry coat. She was only yards down the coast road when her hike was delayed by Mardie Dawes. She was dismayed at being accosted by this individual.

Mardie lived in a crumbling, ivy-invaded old miner's cottage in a secluded dip on the moor. Little was known about her except she had didicoi origins. In her long flowing clothes, she was apt to spring out on travellers and thrust her herbal products under their noses, or demand she tell their fortunes. One glance at her heavily shadowed, glassine eyes, gummy mouth and malevolent expression ensured the stranger, or unwary local, usually paid up quickly. Some people sought her help with a health or love problem, or to buy her other homemade commodity, strong gut-rotting gin. Jo found it extraordinary that her mother not only believed the old woman's ramblings but actually entertained her at Tresawna House.

'Hello, Miss Joanna Venner.' The old woman peered at Jo

through slit eyes, rather like those of an ugly newborn baby. A whiff of something offensively musky wafted from her.

Jo could not return a simple greeting and hurry away. Mardie would follow and push her wares on her, and she could move amazingly quickly for her age.

'Good afternoon, Mardie,' Jo said cautiously.

Mardie's hand dived into the deep pocket of the long, tasselled apron she wore over a red skirt. Out came an assortment of tiny, brown, cork-stoppered bottles. Mardie held one up. 'To make your pretty hair shine, m'dear, got nettle and rosemary in it.'

'I don't want anything,' Jo said ungraciously.

Mardie's greedy eyes landed on the marcasite clip on Jo's scarf. If unsuccessful at wringing money out of a potential customer, she would try to barter.

'You can't have it,' Jo snapped.

'I'll tell your fortune for sixpence.'

'No, thank you. Not now, not ever. If you'll excuse me . . .' Jo started away.

'Saw your mother the day before you left home.' Mardie stalled her, the wind tugging at the gold scarf wrapped round her head.

'I know. My brother told me.'

'She don't care much for you.'

Jo gazed steadily at the old woman and gave no response. She was not about to give this mischief-maker ammunition to widen the estrangement between her and Katherine.

Mardie seemed to be reading the circles of her eyes, delving into the flecks, intruding in the corners, as if she was seeing into all of Jo's thoughts, her hopes, her future. Jo reminded herself that Mardie was only a hindrance.

Mardie stared more deeply. 'Your friend, Celia Sayce, was good to me. Used to give me regular little presents. I hope you and me can do business one day.'

'I doubt it.' Jo sighed impatiently.

'I'll look for a way.' Mardie added a hard edge to her mocking tone.

At the sound of rumbling cartwheels heading towards

them along the straight stretch of road, Jo looked ahead. A powerfully built grey horse with a confident step was pulling a covered wagon.

The women waited silently, knowing Luke Vigus would not pass by them without some sort of greeting.

Luke brought his wagon to a halt and jumped down beside them.

'Here you are, Mardie.' Luke produced a silver coin of high denomination and placed it on the old woman's puckered palm.

Mardie ferreted about in her apron pocket then tossed him a rabbit's foot attached to a length of cheap metal. Grinning pleasantly, he placed it around his neck.

Jo wished the old woman would go on her way. She wanted to enquire from Luke Vigus when Rex and Molly were likely to attend school.

'Tell your fortune, Luke?' Mardie simpered at him.

'I don't need to be told I'm going to be lucky if I've got this, do I? You can keep up the supply I asked you about?' He winked at her.

'As long as I'm paid, your mother will get what she needs.'

Jo was reflecting on the nature of the business transaction the pair were referring to, when Mardie said to her, 'I'll be seeing Katherine again quite soon. Want me to pass on a message from 'ee?'

'No, I do not.' Jo turned her head from Mardie's offensive odours.

'Don't get hard like she.' Mardie wagged a bony finger at Jo. 'You're a nice little thing at the back of all your lip. Isn't she, Luke?' She winked at him, giving the effect of slicing her ugly face in half.

'I'm sure she is, Mardie.'

Apparently satisfied with her single sale today, snickering inanely, Mardie sauntered off along the road, heading for Parmarth.

'Why did you give her so much money?' Jo demanded from the companion she was left with. 'It only encourages her to make a nuisance of herself.'

'It don't hurt to keep the old mare happy.' Luke smiled and shook his head slightly.

Jo knew he was amused at her indignation. She peered through the open canvas at the front of his wagon and studied the contents. A brown horsehair couch, a roll of carpet, a mirror and a baby's cradle were part of the goods stowed securely on board. 'You deal in furniture?'

'Not usually. This lot's for home. Give me a day or two then you're welcome to come to the cottage and see the changes I'm going to make.'

Jo was all set to make a reply in a superior tone but there was something about this man that made her want to gain his trust. 'If I may ask, Mr Vigus, have you had any success in hiring Beth Wherry to help you out?'

'She's already started.'

'I'm pleased for you. I'm sure she will be good for the children. Does it suit your mother?'

'Naturally. The lazy bitch is quite happy not doing any work. I thought about what you said, about not expecting or hoping she'd give up the drink, so I've done something about it.'

'It that what you and Mardie were talking about?'

'That's right,' Luke said grimly. 'Mardie will leave a couple of bottles on the back doorstep every day for her. The kids are better off when she's drunk. She's getting too unsteady to bother them. With luck she'll soon drink herself out of this world.'

'I wasn't thinking along those lines.' Jo was shocked. 'And that's a terrible thing to say.'

'You must've heard all my story by now. You don't seriously expect me to have feelings for Jessie, do you? Anyway, from the way you spoke to Mardie just then, sounds like you've got no love for your mother either.'

'I don't wish her dead.'

'Then thank God you can say that.'

'I'm sorry things have been so bad for you and the children. When will Rex and Molly be returning to school?'

'Soon,' he replied guardedly. 'I'll see to it.'

'Well, if there's anything I can do to help them, as their teacher, I should like to hear from you. I must get on, Mardie Dawes has already delayed me. Good afternoon, Mr Vigus.'

Straight-faced, Luke said, 'Teacher.'

After cutting across the fields and roughlands towards the carn, Jo turned, and with the wind lashing into her body, she watched the wagon until it was out of sight. And wished she had found some kinder words for its owner.

Using energetic strides, she headed for the highest outcrop of the craggy shapes of Carn Galver, scaling the most used path, which was rough and soggy and virtually the bed of a stream. At times, to prevent the tops of her boots becoming saturated, she sidetracked on to reeds and marshy grass.

Jo knew some people found the moor frighteningly lonely. With its almost menacing splendour, it could be cruel to mankind and animal alike. It had given miners a precarious way of life, snatching away some of their lives and the wealth of nearly all the mine-owners. It relentlessly visited hardships on the farmers. Jo had never felt threatened out in this wildness, where it seemed to her there were moments when echoes of the past broke through from their place in eternity to merge with the present, and hint of something indefinable regarding the future.

Shadows of clouds scudded over the landscape, they, like the moorland, changing shape with every few steps she took. In everyday life, Jo had a need to be close to people, but the more she climbed, a strange stirring was gathering in her soul, a peace that went deep into the heart of who she was. She felt she could almost melt into the other world she sensed all around her, where Celia was now, and she stretched out a hand, as if she really could find a way to enter this heavenly dimension.

When she reached the top of the ridge, panting gently, the wind stinging her face, she could very nearly swear she discerned a living energy under her feet. The carn was the abode of the giant Holiburn, a rather passive giant, who, in return for cattle and sheep, had protected the local humans from the more aggressive Trencrom giant. Holiburn had married a farmer's daughter and they had produced a fine line of descendants. When Jo first heard the tale she believed Mercy, and her brother Bob, also of lofty, powerful build, were descended from the giant.

Standing defiantly against the elements, with a small sketchbook and pencils, she sketched the coast, shaped by its many headlands, coves, zawns and deep valleys. It was a shaky drawing and so was the following one, of the church tower of Morvah, the next mining village to Parmarth, but Jo was satisfied with her works of art. Also prominent in the same direction was Pendeen's church tower, Pendeen Lighthouse and the St Just mines, including the Geevor, where Russell Trevail worked.

In a deep valley to the south of Nance was the Carn Valley Stamp. Many unemployed miners found work there, crushing horse-drawn wagon loads of tin ore, which had been tediously sorted by hand from the heaps of attle. Sweeping in all directions were the small fields whose patterns had been determined by settlers of the Bronze Age and Iron Age.

She drew two scenes of the windswept moor and grey sky beating down on the horizon, then she scrambled across the ridge to the opposite end of Carn Galver, to take in the breathtaking sights inland. To the south-east was the forsaken engine house of the Ding Dong Mine, said to be one of Cornwall's oldest; it had seen an unsuccessful attempt in recent years to restart it. Beyond it, on the south coast, on a clear day she would just be able to make out the shadowy forms of St Michael's Mount and the Lizard. Seeking refuge this time against a massed formation of boulders, she sketched the whole landscape.

She became aware someone was watching her.

Luke was standing tall in the claws of the wind, his long black hair whipped back from his striking features.

He formed the main subject of Jo's next work, a clear and dominant figure in front of the magnificent backdrop. Her fingers steady as they flew swiftly over the paper, his likeness appeared lightly at first, then ever more boldly, as

123

if he was a vision from the other world become a reality.

She returned the sketchbook and pencils to the deep pockets of the borrowed coat. 'You'll freeze if you stand there much longer.'

'I wouldn't have noticed,' he said, closing in on her. 'I was enjoying the view. Can I see the drawing?'

'Not right now. I want to put some finishing touches to it. You have more life and colour about you than a simple pencil drawing can convey.'

'I'm pleased you think so.' He swept his eyes over the dramatic scenery. 'I like this place. I come up here when life wears me down, to think things through. To listen to the quiet. Do you know what I mean?'

'I understand you perfectly. I used to climb up here several times every summer with Celia before I went away to college. I miss her so much.'

'She knows.'

Jo smiled at him. 'She came to me the first night I stayed at Nance. She was like a mother to me.' Strange, that she could tell him these intimate things, things she had not mentioned to Mercy. She could open up to this man, whom her generous-hearted friend, called a 'no-good, thief'. 'You feel the same way about your grandmother, don't you?'

'She was the only person I've ever loved. We were poor but I never went without anything. She was always there for me.'

'Celia. Your grandmother. They could be watching over us now.'

'I've often felt Gran watching out for me.' Reaching out his hand, Luke lifted tendrils of wind-teased hair away from Jo's face. 'I like to look at you, Jo Venner.'

Jo lifted her fingers and touched his face, exploring the finely carved lines and angles she had drawn. The frank brow, high cheekbones, strong hawk nose, sensuous mouth. He was overwhelming this close. Jo stared into his eyes. Could she read into their vibrant blueness? She hardly knew him and everything she had been told about him was bad. But here, now, anything hidden from her did not matter. She felt them connect deeply.

He placed his hands gently each side of her face. When he kissed her she felt the whole rhythm of her body change. Stepping into the animal warmth of his body, she kissed him back with demanding pressure. The firm possession of his mouth bred unimaginable swells of pleasure which erupted inside the very core of her. She felt she had not lived before these intense indescribable moments.

She could feel the softness and the urgency of him as he took her fully into his arms. It was like being wrapped in a warm fleece. She revelled in the hard contours of his body, the powerful movements of his muscles, his strength and solidity. Breathed in his wonderful, intoxicating maleness, part of him clean and alive and desirable, another part pagan and uncivilised.

She was conscious of nothing in the world but Luke. She wanted to share his flesh. Out here in the wildness, in the wideness of time and space she gave her whole self to him.

Fourteen

'**G**et upstairs,' Luke ordered his mother.

'Eh?' Jessie mumbled idiotically, drawing close to getting inebriated. She was slumped on a chair, in a good mood, as she had been for the past few days, content to be given the drink she craved instead of begging, stealing or selling her body to pay for it.

'Beth'll be here in a minute. I don't want you in the way.'

'Oh? You laying her then?'

'Shut your filthy mouth, the kids are listening. I'm not like you. Anywhere with anyone. You know Beth's very religious. It took a lot of persuasion to get her parents to let her come here and work in this dump. I had to lie, say it was for your sake because you're making a real effort to give up the drink. They see it as part of her Christian duty, so if you don't want the Bible rammed down your throat, get up to your bed. Pity you didn't learn some religion when you were a kid, then you wouldn't have turned out to be a rotten little whore – that's what Gran used to say about you. From now on you've got to cut out your filthy habits. I don't want this place stinking like cat's piss ever again. Now get up the ladder or I'll take you up there myself and tie you to the bleddy rafters.'

Wrapping the bottle of gin inside her dirty dressing gown, Jessie began the precarious climb up the rope ladder. She paused, one leg, seamed with thick varicose veins, exposed to the thigh. 'If you think I've got a filthy mouth, you should mind yours. You swear every other word, my son. Have to watch yourself when that maid arrives, or if that schoolteacher shows her face here again.'

126

It was arranged for Jo to call at the cottage during the school dinner break, to introduce herself again to Rex and Molly on their home ground, to help them feel less threatened when they returned to their lessons. Luke prayed the two women would never meet; the thought of Jo seeing Jessie in her defiled condition filled him with shame.

'Get out of here,' Luke stormed, yanking a packet of Player's Weights out of his waistcoat pocket.

When his mother was out of sight, although not out of mind for she started singing a bawdy song, Luke motioned for Rex and Molly to follow her.

'We want to stay down here,' Rex protested. Thanks to Beth Wherry, he and Molly were now clean and tidy. She had cut their hair and they were wearing the second-hand clothes Luke had bought for them. The children had been treated for lice and scabies. Their lot had improved, but neither child desired to be near their mother. They did not trust her to stay cheery, were waiting apprehensively for her to resume lashing out at them for no reason, whether drunk or not. Molly began to cough hoarsely and Rex patted her back.

'I want a quiet word with Beth,' Luke coaxed sternly. 'I'm trying to make everything better for us in the future. There's some things grown-ups can't say in front of kids. Go on. Do as I say. It won't hurt Molly to have a nap. I want you looking your best when Miss Venner calls. Don't let your mother know she's coming. I'll buy you some toffee later.'

Beth Wherry entered as the children were at the top of the rope ladder. A modest, slow-moving girl, she was wearing clumpy shoes and a skirt longer than her coat, which was distinctly in a child's style. She was pink and soft and well scrubbed, and marked with innocence. Luke liked her. Everyone liked Beth. She gave the impression she would never progress past her present age. She was all things young.

'Hello, Luke. Are Rex and Molly coming down again? I promised I'd tell them the story of the Battle of Jericho.'

'You can do it later. I want to ask you a favour, Beth. A great kindness.'

Luke was soon to leave Parmarth to keep up his rounds. But he had a problem to sort out first, if all his and Beth's efforts were not to quickly backslide. He stubbed out his cigarette and looked at the girl intently. She had put her coat on a nail behind the door and was taking off her beret, revealing two long fair plaits and a fringe cropped close above her brows.

Shy at having his splendid, pale blue eyes fastened on her, Beth put on her apron and crept to the dresser to collect a duster and polish. At the end of every session here, her father asked her about Luke's spiritual state and she confessed she thought him a long way off being saved. Her mother worried about her taking a shine to Luke, but Beth, who saw Luke as nothing more than someone needing her help, truthfully replied that he always behaved with modesty.

'I'm going on the road again very soon, Beth,' he said pleasantly. 'I won't be back for a fortnight. I need someone to call in and make sure the kids get to school, to pop in often and keep an eye on Marylyn. To clean the place and get their meals.'

'I'll be glad to do all that,' Beth said in her whispery voice. 'I'll take Rex and Molly to Sunday School, if you like. I was going to ask you about it today.' It would be more comfortable working here with Luke gone. The sly remarks she was receiving from some villagers, about other services Luke might try to press on her, were embarrassing and upsetting.

'Thanks, Beth. I knew I could rely on you.' Luke piled on the charm. 'But, you see, I will still have a problem.'

'Is there anything else I can do?'

'I hope so. You know my mother hasn't given up the drink, don't you? I'm sorry I was deceitful, but I knew your father wouldn't have let you come here if I'd told him the truth. I'm worried about the kids' safety when I'm not here. Beth, could you sleep over? I'll pay you well.'

Sleet pattered frustratedly on the window panes. The wind rattled down the chimney, howled through the eaves. An early darkness invaded the room. Luke was desperate to gain Beth's cooperation. He ached to get away from the bitch upstairs, still giggling and warbling to torment him.

Beth bit her lip as she turned over his proposition. Her father was unlikely to agree to this but she wanted to help, even though the cottage was still an unhealthy place to sleep in. Rex and Molly were beginning to trust her and she doted on the baby. Beth knew people laughed about her, thought her 'a scat behind the band', but she felt useful here. 'It's not that I don't want to, Luke—'

Luke was right in front of her, ready with a multitude of pleas and lies to persuade her. 'You have to do it, Beth. The kids need you. You do see that? I've been thinking over all the things your father said to me. That the kids should be baptised, brought up to know about God. Miss Venner, their new teacher, is taking an interest in them. If your family was to help take the kids' welfare under their wing too, life will have a new meaning for them. Surely, your father would want that. I'm doing all I can, Beth, but I can't do it alone. What say I help you clean up this place then we go and see your father?'

'Goodness. It's like a different room,' Jo exclaimed, when Luke admitted her into the cottage, after her polite knock. The walls had been whitewashed, making the interior seem lighter and brighter. The stone sink, dresser, and cupboard doors were scrubbed clean. The worm-eaten chest was gone. Proper curtains hung at the windows, in pale green damask. The new material had come from Luke's wagon and Mrs Allett, Sally's mother, the local seamstress, had made them up for him. There was the smell of lavender polish.

'It's going to stay like this,' he said firmly. He desperately wanted Jo to approve his efforts.

They were face to face, both a little wary that the other thought their passionate moments on top of the carn a mistake. The moment passed. They knew there would never be another one like it.

'I'll call Rex and Molly down in a minute. First, I want to hold you.'

'I didn't sleep last night, thinking about you,' Jo said, crushed in his arms. She had lain in bed, reliving her first time of making love, awed at how perfect, fulfilling it had been. And gazing by candlelight at her drawing of him, to which she'd added just enough subtle colour to bring his strong features almost alive.

'Me too.'

They kissed. And the world revolved only around their intimacy, their caresses, their need to be close, until reluctantly they let their lips part and arms fall from each other's body.

'I've got everything sorted out,' Luke said, recounting the trying hour he'd spent in the Wherry household. He had used flattery on John Wherry's spiritual values to achieve Beth's assistance in the children's care, agreeing to have the three children baptised soon and attend Sunday School; Jessie need not know about that. Luke had then been given a bonus when Mrs Wherry offered to take Marylyn into her home every day while Rex and Molly were at school.

Jo took his hand. 'I knew you would do it, Luke.' She believed he was a good man, his faults brought about by the cruelty and selfish standards of his mother. Jo knew what a detrimental effect a rotten, unloving mother could have on a person's life.

Relieved that she felt proud of him, even though he did not really deserve it, Luke was confident at last about the future. He went to the rope ladder and called for Rex and Molly to come down.

Jo looked about for Marylyn. The baby was lying on her front in a cradle, straining to lift her head. No doubt, the little mite spent nearly every minute of every day in there, lacking the stimulation and the warmth of love. But she was well wrapped up and now would have the benefit of Beth or Mrs Wherry's daily care. Jo picked Marylyn up.

To Luke's horror, it wasn't Rex and Molly who descended to the lunch table he had prepared for them and Jo. Despite his protests, Jessie jerked herself down the rope ladder and pushed him out of her way. Then Jo was subjected to open hostility from her glassy eyes. 'I'm sorry, Jo. I didn't want you to meet her.'

'It's all right, Luke. Good afternoon, Mrs Vigus.' Jo stared directly into the drunkard's prematurely wrinkled face, bravely ignoring the woman's foul odours.

'Miss Vigus,' Jessie corrected her rancorously, teetering towards Jo on bare feet. She had already consumed half her daily liquid diet. 'I never was married. All my brats are bastards.'

'This is Miss Venner, the kids' teacher. So mind you keep a civil tongue in your head,' Luke hissed, growing restless as if he was short of breath, the effect of his mother's presence.

'Whatsh she d-doin' here?' Jessie's words came out slurred and she was forced to whip out a hand and press it against the wall to prevent herself tumbling to the floor.

'I'm sorry,' Luke repeated to Jo, utterly embarrassed she was witnessing Jessie at her worst. 'I'm afraid we won't get no sense out her today.'

'Don't worry,' Jo reassured him.

Jo was suddenly nearly pulled off balance as she was grabbed by a very unsteady Jessie. 'You come to t-tell me off 'bout the kids?'

'No, I have not,' Jo said harshly, shaking Jessie off, revolted at her touch. 'I'm here to encourage Rex and Molly that the school has something to offer them. I suggest you return upstairs and get dressed, Miss Vigus.'

'Why? Don't I look good enough for 'ee?' Jessie cackled. Leaning against the wall, she opened her blue dressing gown, which was filthy because she'd refused to let Beth wash it, and revealed flesh that looked near the state of mummification. The stench from her intensified unbearably. It was hard to believe she was in her early forties.

Jo felt sickened; Lew had gone with her. Although Marylyn had been starving, she thanked God the beastly woman obviously had no milk. The thought of the tiny baby she was holding in her arms suckling from those pendulous, withered breasts turned her stomach. Jo understood why

131

Luke hated every moment he spent under his mother's roof.

The gin and lack of food took their toll on Jessie. Shambling to the couch she collapsed on to it, fell into a deep sleep and snored loudly, open-mouthed.

'My God.' Luke ran his hands through his hair in despair.

There was a hammering on the front door. Luke stopped himself from uttering an obscenity out of sheer frustration.

'What do you want?' he snapped at Davey Penoble, on the doorstep. 'I've paid my stable rent.'

'It isn't that,' Davey answered quietly, but as if he had something sour in his mouth. 'Your mother hasn't paid me rent on the cottage for ages. You had plenty of money to splash out in the pub last night. Perhaps you can do the right thing by me before you sneak off again.'

Digging his hand into his trouser pocket, Luke produced some notes. 'Pay rent for this miserable place? You've got a flaming nerve. You haven't done any upkeep on the dump for years.'

'There wouldn't be any point, would there? I'll do the necessary renovations when the cottage has been made habitable again, not that I believe that'll ever happen,' Davey retorted. 'But to be fair, I dropped the rent accordingly a while ago. Jessie owes me seven pounds, eight and six.'

Counting out ten pounds Luke slapped the money down on Davey's palm. 'You've got what you wanted, now clear off!'

Davey bent his head in under the door frame. 'I'm sorry you've heard all this, Miss Venner.'

'The teacher and I are having a private conversation.' Luke pushed Davey away from the door and slammed it on him.

He sank forward, pressing his forehead against the door, too ashamed to turn round and face Jo.

Jo put Marylyn back into her cradle and went to him. 'Luke, what is it?'

'You shouldn't get involved with me. You can see how things are.'

'Were, Luke, how things were. And it wasn't all your fault.

132

I can see that now. You've sorted things out, remember. There's only the future now to look forward to. We'll both work hard to make the children's lives worth living. Do you want me to leave?'

'No.' Turning shakily, he worked up a smile. 'Stay, I like having you around.'

'I like being with you.'

'Good. Well, let's eat, for the sake of the kids.'

Before returning to the school, Jo drank the tea and ate ham sandwiches Luke made to the accompaniment of Jessie's dissipated breathing and Rex and Molly's suspicious silence. She told the children she was looking forward to having them in her class the next day. Luke bantered a lot, but his usual warmth and light-heartedness were missing.

When Jessie woke up she had no memory of there being a visitor to her home. She took a swig from her best love and sniggered at Luke.

Leaping across the room, he hissed at her ugly, mocking face, 'Just don't say a word. Not one word.'

Fifteen

Dawn was a long way off. Sounds of torment convulsed the schoolhouse. Disturbed by the groans, the cries of utter wretchedness, Sally lay listening in her own bed as Marcus fought demons again in his sleep. Many times she had asked him what his nightmares were about, but he would never say. Sally was glad Mrs Lidgey insisted on taking a sleeping draught every night to escape the pain in her back. She would be distressed to hear her son in such anguish.

Lighting her lamp, Sally padded across the shabby landing to her lover. Marcus was lying on his back, the bed covers wrested off his sweat-soaked naked body, his head jerking on the pillow, hands clenching the bottom sheet. Leaning over him, she shook him violently. It always took an effort to rouse him when he was like this.

Finally, he awoke, shuddering, muttering pathetically. Grasping her, he clung to her for comfort, almost as if he were a child and she his mother.

Closing her eyes to bear the pain of his terrible grip, Sally stroked his shoulders and wet hair. She crooned to him, kissed him. Gradually, he quietened. Soon, as she knew it would, her consoling incited him into fierce arousal, an immediate unstoppable need for satisfaction. He pulled off her nightdress, his mouth seeking her body in mastery as he reached for his protection.

Some time later, awash in her own perspiration, she said, 'The tinkers keep you well supplied with those things. Just as well, the number of times you need them.'

As always after their frantic coupling, Marcus settled with

his back towards her, remote, unreachable. 'Did you not finish the last time?'

'Do you care?' she asked, raising herself so she could look over his shoulder and watch his face in the lamp light.

'Of course. Are you complaining?'

'Not about your performance. You know exactly how to please me.' She put her arm over him; his flesh was agitated, hot and slippery. She could feel the impenetrable shell he had formed around himself, something she was sure he had perfected long before her swift seduction to his bed. She knew he wanted her to move away from him, leave the room. 'I'm thinking of walking out with Russell Trevail.'

'You would do well to stay away from him.'

'Are you jealous?' She knew it was a stupid question. If anyone could penetrate his fortress, it would not be her. But he owed her more than erotic sex and a good wage. He could give her a little of his thoughts, his hopes. He could pretend she meant something to him.

Sighing, he eased himself away and located his cigarettes. 'He's no good for you.'

'How do you know that?' she demanded accusingly.

'The fellow strikes me as hard and cruel. I've heard him picking fights in the pub.'

Sally was annoyed Marcus could only hand out negative advice on the one man who had ever shown a prolonged interest in her. She'd noticed the way her lover looked at Joanna Venner. Sally felt hurt, believing she was about to be spurned. He was bound to think the other woman more suitable for him. 'I probably will consider Russell. My only choice in this miserable life is to marry him or move away from this place.'

'Then move away, if it's what you want!' Marcus's nightmare was flashing through his mind in a series of distorted pictures. He, young and innocent, unprotected, being forced to gratify his mother's body; being touched, hurt. He was in no mood for Sally's prattlings, her ill humour.

'To become what?' Sally snapped bitterly. 'To go on being a servant? Another man's whore? A prostitute even? I'd be good at that, with all the things you've taught me. Before, all I did for men was to lie on the ground and stare up at the sky.'

Marcus winced. Sally had made him face the fact that the activities he had introduced her to were unhealthy. He was not only a victim of corruption, he was a corrupter. 'You could get a job in a factory, or a dairy or an hotel. You're not a whore. You're an honest, hard-working young woman.'

'That's not what most people think. I've been with a lot of the men round here. I even let Keane Trevail feel me for a penny when I was fourteen years old. I don't want to slave for anyone for the rest of my life, to service a rich man in the vain hope he'll marry me. Russell's sweet on me. I can handle him. Marrying him's my best bet.'

'Then bloody well do it!' Marcus stubbed out his cigarette and flung back the covers.

Stung to fury, Sally grabbed his arm before he could get out of bed. 'I know exactly how your mind's working. You want to drop me because you've got designs on Jo Venner. You'd soon marry her, wouldn't you? She's got breeding and ambition and best of all she's got money.'

'The Venner girl has many attractions,' he sneered. 'It sounds to me as if you're jealous of her. Is she what this is all about?'

'I admit it,' Sally retorted. 'I'm jealous of her but I also admire her. Jo's not as stupid as me, you won't get anywhere with her. She knows what she wants out of life. It's believed she came here only out of duty to Miss Sayce, but she won't stay long now the old lady's dead. She'll go off and make a success of herself, and she'll leave you here to rot with the rest of us. I've been comparing myself to her, that's what's upsetting me. I can see now that I've been wasting my time with you.'

'You're right, Sally,' he mouthed, suddenly twisting her arm. 'I am getting tired of you. You'll get more out of that worthless Russell Trevail than you ever will from me.'

'You bastard. I hate you!' Sally thrust his hand away from her. Leaping off the bed, she gathered up her night-dress, but before slipping it back on she glanced down slyly at her stomach, 'What if I told you I was pregnant?'

Marcus's eyes turned icy, sharded. 'I'd kill you.'

'Oh, really?' she mocked. 'I've had passion and coldness from you. Didn't ever think I'd get dramatics.'

Next moment he had her sprawled across the bed, his hands squeezing her throat, making her eyes water in pain. Dark shadows contorted his face. His breathing came in discordant rasps. 'I'd never ever let a child of mine be born. Do you understand, you putrid lascivious whore?' He uttered a stream of profanities.

Fearing he was becoming deranged, Sally gasped tearfully, 'Y-yes. Let me go.' There had been moments during their intimacy when he had been deliberately cruel, had used obscene language. Unnerved and offended at first, when she had realised it excited him she had willingly taken part, even enjoyed the acts. But he had never been like this before, horrifyingly vehement, breathing as if powered by an unnatural force. 'I-I was only joking, Marcus. I'm sorry.'

'I can make you very sorry, Sally. Don't forget it.' He thrust her hands underneath her body, trapping them there.

Then he threw his weight on top of her and subjected her to half an hour of terror and brutality.

Jo had a full class that morning. Molly was very nervous and shook when Jo separated her from Rex and sat her down to share a desk with Ann Markham. Ann's pleasant nature meant Jo could rely on her to encourage Molly. Otherwise, she took little notice of Molly and Rex to avoid them being teased. She took an interest in Mavis Best, who had recovered from the measles, and a boy called Adam Moore who was absent regularly owing to severe asthma attacks.

After assembly, she took the class for their daily arithmetic lesson, setting the simplest work for Rex and Molly, and Susan Wherry, who also had trouble with numbers. Rex bent his head over his blue exercise book, his tongue resting on his lower lip as he concentrated. Jo had no notion of it but she had gone up in his estimation after yesterday's visit, when

137

she had behaved in no way like a strict schoolteacher. Luke obviously trusted her and liked her a lot.

Molly was edgy and tearful and made no attempt to write in her exercise book. She stared down agitatedly at the page, as if she had no idea what its purpose was. Ann picked up Molly's pencil from the groove in the desk, then put it in Molly's shaking hand. 'Count on your fingers,' she whispered.

From the blackboard, where she was writing multiplication sums, Jo smiled to herself. If Rex and Molly settled down to their lessons she had only Kenneth Willis's problem of falling asleep in class to sort out. It was time she encouraged Ann Markham to look towards a far-sighted future. Ann had expressed the desire to become a nurse; she must be made to see it was possible with hard work and determination.

Suddenly Molly began to sob.

Jo dropped the chalk and turned round. 'What's the matter, Molly?' she asked gently.

'She's done number one in her knickers,' Gillian Jelbert shouted gleefully. 'It's dripping down on the floor.' Like her twin brother, she was sitting near Molly, at the front of the class, where Jo had moved them during the first week of term. The class broke into an uproar of laughter and aimed scathing abuse at Molly. She began to wail.

'Silence!' Jo ordered, but although the volume dropped the children kept giggling and whispering.

She was walking towards Molly and was dismayed when the girl began to shriek and shrink away from her. 'It's all right, Molly, dear. I'll soon make everything better for you.' She looked anxiously at Rex, sitting at the other end of the class and leaning over his desk as he watched his sister with a mortified expression. Jo would get him to take Molly home.

'Got habits worse than ruddy gippos,' Arnold Jelbert sneered in disgust.

'Arnold Jelbert, stand in the corner and don't you dare say another word,' Jo hissed at him. 'The rest of you be quiet or I shall punish you all severely.'

She tried to lift Molly up off her chair but she clung to

her desk and screamed. 'Molly, calm down,' she pleaded tenderly. 'You know who I am. You can trust me. I'm going to ask Rex to take you home.'

From the corner, Arnold chanted, 'Teacher's pet, knickers all wet.'

The rest of the class laughed uncontrollably. Arnold repeated the chant and some of the children joined in. Rex got up and was heading for his sister, but he changed course and kicked Arnold's leg. Arnold cried out and the two boys began to fight.

'Silence!' Jo called out. 'Stop that at once!'

But the children thought the wetting incident, Arnold's cruel cheek, and now the fight, too hilarious to be able to stop their mirth. For the first time in her teaching career, Jo feared she was losing control of her class.

Suddenly, apart from Molly's loud and mournful wails and Arnold and Rex's struggles, all went quiet. Jo looked over her shoulder. Marcus Lidgey had come through the partition. His face was forbidding. There was a belated scuffle as the class, except for Molly, shot to their feet in respect for the headmaster's presence.

'What is going on here?' His voice lashed the air.

Arnold and Rex stopped fighting and stood straight and still. Red-faced, their fearful eyes were on the headmaster. Molly's weeping turned to racked sobs.

Jo felt extremely uncomfortable. The man who usually offered her his total support was glaring at her with accusation and intolerance. 'I'm afraid Molly has had a little accident, Mr Lidgey.'

He advanced on them. 'What sort of accident?'

Jo's cheeks flamed for Molly's shame. 'She's wet.'

His harsh expression remained unaltered. 'I'll arrange for one of the girls in my class to take her home. She must be unwell. She can take the rest of the day off.' He turned his black eyes on Arnold and Rex. 'You boys stay there until the mid-morning break, then you will report to me.' He did not look at Jo again before returning to his class.

Jo was on playground duty. She felt disturbed when Arnold

139

and Rex emerged, long after the other children, displaying sore, red left hands, the hand they did not write with. Arnold had tears in his eyes but acted as if it was all a great joke. Rex glared at Jo as though he blamed her for his pain and humiliation, and Molly's too. Jo's heart sank. On his first day back at school, she had failed to gain Rex's trust. And she had assured Luke she would take care of his brother and sister at school. It did not seem fair that Rex should be caned when he had only been driven to lash out over his sister's terror and acute embarrassment.

The next period passed smoothly except for Arnold's constant fidgeting and mutterings. Gillian kept nudging Mavis Best and giggling. Jo moved the twins to the desk nearest hers, and while teaching on prehistoric times, she stood over them. They wrote and drew as diligently as the rest of the class, but before allowing them home for dinner, she warned them that the next time they misbehaved she would be calling on their parents.

Eleanor Lidgey was expecting her, but first Jo intended to cross over the road.

'You are heading in the wrong direction, Miss Venner,' Marcus said from behind her on the road.

Not knowing he was there, she nearly missed her footing. Facing him, she began, 'I'm going—'

'I know where you are going and I forbid it.' He loomed over her, his hands clasped behind his back.

'I shall only be a moment then I will be joining Mrs Lidgey.'

'That is not the point. I will not allow you to single out any child as a special case. It's not fair on the other children and will create ill feelings among them and their parents. Molly Vigus has many problems, and if you show too much regard for her it will inevitably lead to more teasing.'

Jo was livid with his decision. Surely he did not expect her to take no more action over Molly's predicament. 'But Molly may be there alone.'

'She is not. When the girl returned, she informed me Luke

Vigus was there. Molly was safely delivered home, she is his responsibility now.'

'I'll go after school is finished.' Jo turned on her heel and headed for the schoolhouse.

Marcus walked beside her. 'It's a great pity you have become emotionally involved with two of your pupils. If you cannot treat Rex and Molly as you would the other children you are not going to give your best to the school. You do see this?'

'Yes, of course,' she answered tartly, uncomfortably acknowledging he was speaking the truth. She would not have rushed off to another child's home.

When they were in the hall of the schoolhouse, he continued, 'You must distance yourself from the Viguses.'

'I can't.' She would not. 'Marylyn is just a baby. I care deeply for her.'

'You must. As the mother is of no use, I have sent a note to Luke Vigus, asking him to call on me to discuss Rex and Molly's problems. You have admirably played your part in bringing the children back to school. Now I'm asking you to keep your association with the family out of school hours.'

Jo's face worked in sheer disquiet. If she was to teach successfully in Parmarth, to be able to look for the right moment to approach Marcus Lidgey with her own ideas for the girls' education, such as their receiving science lessons, she must abide by his request. She conceded by dropping her eyes and joining Eleanor in the dining room. He followed her in.

'I'll pour your tea, Miss Venner,' he said in a soft, warm voice, to please his mother.

Jo was annoyed at this sudden pleasantness.

Marcus was, in fact, in torment again. Sickened with himself for raping Sally, he had apologised, appeased her by giving her five pounds to buy new clothes, blamed his nightmare for unnerving him and making him behave like a mindless savage.

He must leave Sally alone. It was not fair to keep taking advantage of her while what she really wanted was a settled

141

future. He had been grateful to have a woman with strong sexual needs readily available, but Sally was beginning to annoy him. She had brought him to breaking pitch and he had been violent towards her. He feared what he might be capable of in the future. This had made it hard for him to face Joanna Venner this morning.

He found her more appealing each time he saw her. He admired and respected her. She was a sensitive, accomplished teacher. He'd studied her devotion to her pupils, not above comforting a muddy, fallen child in the playground against her body. He ached to have her. But how could he treat her like a trollop, introduce her to acts beyond the comprehension of her intelligence and decency? He could not bear to think he might contaminate her. If he had acted kindly over Molly Vigus's tribulation, and she had been grateful to him, he'd feared he might have done something to compromise their growing friendship, something to revile her.

He had never had such fears before. What was happening to him? Sometimes he was afraid he was going mad. But he was charged with the task of manipulating her into caring for him. If she succumbed to him he knew he would not be able to resist her. She would be immeasurably sweet in the taking, and he was terrified he'd sink into the squalor of his unnatural desires.

He ran his fingers despairingly through his hair. If only he could make up his mind what to do. Before he really did go mad.

His mother smiled at Jo with faked charm. 'Joanna, don't you think it's time you and Marcus were on first-name terms? You should become friends. And it's time you dined with us again. Isn't it, darling? Marcus.'

Her tones cut through his mind, shredding him, destroying his last scrap of peace. 'Um, yes, Mama.' Suddenly, he knew what he had to do. Somehow he must find a way and the strength and courage to carry it through.

During a period in which her pupils read individually to her, Jo's attention kept wandering to listen to Marcus's voice expounding a geography lesson on South Africa. One moment his intonation was soft, then it boomed, became muffled, then distinct. One moment he was jocular with his class, then he was snapping at the pupils. Jo frowned. Was he ill? He had displayed a change of moods today with startling rapidity.

The middle class joined the upper class for a session of the school orchestra. Marcus decided which child should play each percussion instrument. As part of their punishment, Arnold and Rex were denied participation and were made to stand in a different corner, facing the wall of the upper classroom. It was an effort for Jo not to cast sympathetic glances at Rex.

Jo was to perform on the harmonium. She had not played it before and needed to practise. The children tittered, and Marcus scolded them harshly over her first failed attempts to perform 'Early One Morning'. She felt utterly embarrassed at her clumsiness in the presence of a musical craftsman. She could sense the headmaster's displeasure as he hovered over her and pressed the right key.

Jo could not doubt the quality of his teaching. When she had conquered the harmonium, the children relaxed and there was a sense of them being eager to please him. He conducted them until he was satisfied they had reached a good pitch and rhythm. Then he played the cello, accompanied in the string section by Jane Lawry, Susan Wherry and Adam Moore who, thanks to Celia's donation, each played a three-quarter-size violin; Marcus was giving them free after-school lessons. Norman Pascoe played his father's trumpet passably well. Jo was heartened by the music lessons the children were receiving from the headmaster, which, like the boys' science lessons, were not usual in many primary schools.

Jo sneaked glances at Marcus. The tension in his dark face was fading. It seemed the music was reaching him deep within.

When the school day was over, Jo wished she had not promised Eleanor she would return to discuss the lady's spring wardrobe. She wanted to see how Molly was, to talk to Luke about her. To add to her frustration, the vicar was there, newly arrived back in Parmarth from his speaking engagements at a training seminar at a Dorset overseas mission.

The Reverend Silas Mountebank, a bachelor in his late fifties, whom she had met at her interview, explained he was asked occasionally to give lectures on his missionary work in the Philippines. He seemed, strangely, a little shy of her, as he looked down over a pair of half-spectacles. His dark suit and thinning white hair were both of a severe cut. Eleanor had told Jo beforehand that he was a man who cherished peace and quiet, and quickly became harassed when things did not run smoothly. If he had witnessed the wilder side of her nature, Jo mused, perhaps he would have selected another of the candidates to teach in the school.

He finished his tea hastily. 'Well, if you'll excuse me, ladies, I really do have to see to my greenhouse and then I have a meeting with the churchwardens. Please do tell Mr Lidgey I shall be at the school for final prayers on Friday afternoon.'

'We won't see much of him,' Eleanor said, after he had gone. 'He prefers to be in his garden.'

Marcus stayed on at the school to take a forty-five-minute music lesson. Arriving home, he raised his eyebrows at seeing Jo ensconced in the sitting room with Eleanor. They were looking at ladies' clothing catalogues.

'Joanna is kindly helping me choose something new, Marcus, dear,' Eleanor said smoothly. 'I've explained I can't afford to dress in the style I'm accustomed to but I couldn't possibly call on the local seamstress. Far too provincial.'

'Of course,' Jo agreed. 'Miss Sayce used to send away for her clothes.'

Marcus avoided his mother's eyes. 'It's very good of you, Miss Venner.' After a sharp intake of breath from Eleanor, he ventured, 'Joanna.'

'She's going to be a treasure to us, isn't she, Marcus? Why don't you stay and eat with us, Joanna, dear,' Eleanor crooned.

Marcus sighed inwardly. The music had relaxed him and he would prefer to spend time with Joanna alone. She had smiled at him just prior to leaving the school, forgiving him for his earlier curtness, and he did not want his mother's overbearing presence to spoil things before he had the chance to make amends properly.

Jo saw the tenseness snagging again at Marcus's features. She enjoyed his and Eleanor's company, yet the more she came here the more she was finding the atmosphere bleak and confining. 'Thank you, Eleanor, but Mercy is expecting me. Actually, it is time I was going.'

'Another time,' Marcus said graciously. 'I'll show you to the door.'

Having seen Jo out, he had intended to slip away to his study, but first he faced up to Eleanor. 'There's no point looking at those catalogues. We can't afford new clothes.'

'We shall when you've succeeded in the task I've set you. And not rubbish like this.'

'You'll just have to sell your jewellery.'

'I will never do that. It's all I have left of my old way of life.'

Marcus was suddenly angry. 'Why should I put things right? If you were normal, you'd get yourself a wealthy lover.'

Eleanor threw the catalogues at him.

Jo went straightaway to the Viguses. Luke was alone, preparing to leave Parmarth. He took her immediately into his closest embrace.

'I'm sorry about Molly's distress today, Luke. I felt so helpless when I couldn't comfort her.'

'It wasn't your fault, Jo,' he said, kissing her, caressing her. 'There's no need for you to worry about the kids. Mrs Wherry's agreed to take Molly in with Marylyn till she's well enough to go back to school. I took her to the doctor's this afternoon; he said she's got an infection. He's given her some medicine. She's tucked up in bed right now. Rex is amusing her with some puppets I got 'em. Marylyn's already looking better now she's fed regularly, getting some attention. Before

145

I leave, I'll tell all this to that damned headmaster. Should satisfy him.'

'If people really knew you they would see you are a good man, Luke.'

Folding her in closer to him, he murmured against her lips, 'I'm glad I met you. I'm going to miss you when I'm gone.'

It was foolish of her to stay here alone with him, risking gossip, her position at the school, but she could not tear herself away. She ran her fingers over his face, burning his image into her mind for the lonely days ahead without him. 'Hurry back.'

All was quiet, they would not be disturbed. It was a long time before Jo slipped away from the tiny cottage.

Sixteen

Jo dismissed her class but asked Kenneth Willis to stay behind.

Standing wanly at the side of her desk, Kenneth shivered in almost threadbare clothes, although neatly patched. 'Please, Miss Venner, I've got to get off home. My dad'll be waiting for me.'

'I will not keep you long, Kenneth,' Jo said kindly, noticing the shadows under his eyes were more pronounced. His skin was stretched and pallid. He smelled as if he had not washed for days. 'But first I want to talk to you about your falling asleep in class. It won't do, you know. If it continues, I'll have to mention it to Mr Lidgey and speak to your father about it.'

'No, don't do that, miss.' Kenneth's chin wobbled as he fought to keep tears in check. 'I promise not to fall asleep tomorrow.'

'If you come to school tomorrow. You did not attend Monday or yesterday. I've been told you accompanied your father in combing the beaches downcoast, following the sinking of the cargo ship which foundered off Cape Cornwall at the weekend. Is this true?'

Hanging his head, Kenneth nodded feebly. He stifled a sob. Jo knew his need to weep came not from fear or despair but utter exhaustion.

Taking the boy's hand, Jo continued probing gently. 'And you walked there and back, in the rain and sleet, sleeping rough at some stage.'

Kenneth nodded again.

'Has your father got work for you to do after school today?'

He nodded once more, pathetic, defeated.

'What is it you will have to do?'

'Gather kindling, feed the pig, cook the supper. Other things.' Kenneth yanked his hand free and started to head for the cloakroom door. 'My dad's not a horrible man. He's got no regular work, that's the trouble. I've got no mum, see? We make do the best we can.' He was nearly shouting now.

'I know that, Kenneth.' Jo rose and caught up with him. Mercy had filled her in on the facts concerning Joel Willis and his only child. Joel Willis did not drink or gamble or waste the money he earned. He was a proud man, determined to pay his own way, would never accept charity. The father and son were very close. It was Joel Willis's needlework on Kenneth's jumper and short trousers. 'But while I respect all that your father does, he has a responsibility to send you to school every day, fit and well, able to learn your lessons. I'm sure he would understand if I was to have a word with him and I'm sure you would welcome a little more rest. Wait there, please, Kenneth, while I write a note for you to take home to him.'

Like a fidgety colt, Kenneth restrained himself and stayed by the door. She knew he would rather spend his days working with his father than attend school.

Turning to her desk, Jo saw Miss Teague had entered her side of the partition. Hatted and coated, umbrella in kid-gloved hand, the infants' teacher dropped her eyes, but Jo had the notion she would like to make an arid comment about the latter part of her conversation with Kenneth. The cloakroom door was opened and banged shut and Jo was too late to prevent Kenneth running home.

'It's a sad story.' Miss Teague primly rerolled her umbrella. 'But I'm sure you've been told about Clarrie Willis's tragic death, three years ago from tuberculosis.'

Jo was becoming increasingly annoyed about Miss Teague's thinly disguised antipathetic remarks in regard to every aspect of her life. Cowardly darts of contempt had been aimed at her lodging at the farm, her friendship with Celia, the poor attendance at Celia's funeral, Jo's 'posh' voice, her almost daily cups of tea with Eleanor Lidgey. A reference had been made to Bob Merrick's 'lady-love', and comments about the length of Jo's visits in the Vigus cottage when Luke was at home.

Jo had not expected Miss Teague to welcome her without misgivings. She had been informed, courtesy of village gossips, of Miss Teague's disappointment over Miss Martin, late of St Mevan's school, not securing the post she held. But Jo had tolerated enough.

'I'll speak to Kenneth tomorrow, if he's present. Tell me, Miss Teague, would you approach the problem of his sleeping in class in a different manner to me?' She strode purposefully towards her colleague.

'Well, I . . .' but Miss Teague could not come up with a contrary statement this time. 'No. You have every right to speak to Kenneth's father.'

'You resent me coming here, don't you, Miss Teague?'

'Why should I feel that way?' Miss Teague coloured awkwardly.

Eleanor was right. The woman was a mouse, afraid of a direct attack; she was sly, underhanded. Jo gathered up her personal things from her desk but kept a constant gaze on the other teacher. 'Gossip works both ways, you know, Miss Teague. It circulates particularly in the sweet and tobacco shop.'

'Oh, I did happen to mention . . . I'm sorry. I thought you unsuitable for the post here, but, yes, you have the right to reprimand me, Miss Venner. I should not have judged you prior to your starting work.' Miss Teague's tone became ingratiating. 'You have made good progress with your class already, most notably in the way you've tackled the Viguses over the children's living conditions. I don't know what you said, but whatever it was it seems to have worked.'

'What I said is, no doubt, the source of much speculation. I hope my effort will prove successful and we'll actually see both Rex and Molly regularly in school. I would like us to work in mutual respect, Miss Teague,' Jo continued seriously. 'You know more about the village

149

and the children than I probably ever shall. I would like to learn from you.'

'You would?' The charitable corner of Miss Teague's heart was given an airing. Perhaps the advantaged Joanna Venner, rebel of her social class, actually did intend to inspire the children here.

She came forward, smiling pleasantly. 'Do take my hand. I shall be very pleased to be of service to you in any way I can, Miss Venner.'

Jo smiled into Miss Teague's dull eyes as they exchanged a polite salute, but she would never fully trust her.

The wind was growing ever wilder and sleet was once more consorting with the freezing rain. Wearing his heavy overcoat and trilby hat, Marcus was supervising the children leaving the school gates. A huge umbrella pulled down close over his head, he was absorbed in another planned escape from his mother – one he would never make.

'The children have all left, Mr Lidgey. So has Miss Teague. I am the last.' He did not respond. Jo put her own umbrella down and slipped her head in under his. 'Everyone has gone home, Mr Lidgey,' she repeated.

'What?' He saw her then, popping up at him out of nowhere. Shining with kindness, honesty, vitality. She was fresh and lovely. Pity he could not tell her so.

'Thank you, Miss Venner. I was deep in thought. It's turning into another stormy night. Can I offer you a lift home? I have a meeting with the headmaster of Pendeen Primary School in half an hour. I·shall be driving past Nance Farm.' It was an excellent opportunity to form a closer link with her.

A ride in a comfortable motorcar to Nance would be welcome in the gusty, wet weather but it would set the tongue-waggers into overtime. Jo did not care. It would appear churlish to decline Mr Lidgey's offer. He was always considerate towards her, always spoke with patience and sometimes humour. He reminded her a little of Alistair. Caring, attentive but often remote. Unlike her brother, Mr Lidgey often seemed tense. He would rub his brow and compress his eyes. A sufferer from violent headaches?

On the drive out of the village, Jo could almost sense the curtains twitching. Marcus, craving a cigarette but too polite to ask her if she would mind him smoking in the close confines of the car, guessed why she was craning her neck in all directions. 'We'll both be clocked out and I'll be clocked in when I return,' he said.

'Does it bother you? All the nosiness?'

'Quite often. I'm a very private person.'

Relaxing against the thick leather upholstery, Jo told him about her chat with Kenneth Willis, while following the measured movements of his hands on the steering wheel. Fine hands with long fingers, which gentled evocative music on the harpsichord, cello and violin. She had heard him play all three instruments during the play or dinner breaks. Passable on the violin herself, she had accompanied him once while he had performed on the harpsichord. His playing somehow always echoed a beautiful sadness. Eleanor had not been in the sitting room with them that one time and he had seemed a different man, calm, inspired, almost spiritual.

Celia must have spoken to him in connection with her donation to the school. She had probably liked him. Jo liked him.

'You drive so fluently. My brother drives like a lunatic.'

'Does it scare you?' He glanced at her.

'No.'

'I can't imagine it would.'

'Why?'

'If I may say so, I think you have a sense of bravado.'

From the security of the motorcar, she studied the weather-ravaged moor, the watchful tors, the hardy stone walls. 'Irene Trevail told you the truth. I used to run about this area with her sons like a wild moorland pony.'

'Are you close to her sons?' It bothered him, that she might be on friendly terms with other men. She had spent a lot of time with Luke Vigus. They seemed on rather friendly terms. Thank God the handsome dealer had taken himself off.

'Not really. I've had a violent quarrel with Lew Trevail

151

over his abandonment of Marylyn Vigus. He's hardly spoken to me since. I suppose it is none of my business.'

'No one can be sure he fathered the child.'

'She looks very much like Lew.'

'Then it must also be the case that she is very much like his brother. I've observed that they favour one another in features.'

'Russell? I didn't think about that possibility. Oh, dear. See what happens when one accepts gossip as the truth or makes an obvious judgement. Mind you, it is more likely that Marylyn is Lew's baby. Russell has been hankering after Sally Allett for some time.'

'His calls at the schoolhouse were becoming a blessed nuisance. Things are better now Sally is walking out with him.'

'I didn't know that.' She had been too preoccupied with Luke, the Vigus children and her pupils to take much interest in other events. She studied her companion. He seemed relaxed. She might not get a better opportunity. 'Marcus, I'd like to talk to you about our girl pupils. What more we could do for them.'

'I don't understand. I've thought through their lessons very carefully to equip them with all that's necessary for their future.'

'Well, yes, I agree, and please don't be offended, but have you considered that they should also be given encouragement of a different sort? More than what is expected of them?'

'Such as?' He frowned. He wasn't offended, but was sure he was about to hear some unrealistic ideas from the young woman who had enjoyed privileges and backing that the girls of Parmarth would never have any hope of receiving.

'We need to turn their expectations into something more than domesticity, marriage and motherhood. Worthy as all three occupations and institutions are, it's not for every girl. Given the right motivation, intelligent girls like Ann Markham could go out and make their mark in the world.'

Marcus smiled softly at her. Joanna was fired up with enthusiasm for her ideals. It was noble of her to be concerned

152

for girls who were usually thought of as the servant class, but she couldn't see that in a place like Parmarth her ideals were virtually pointless. 'I admire your intentions, Joanna, but putting them into action would be imprudent, and indeed seen as improper, in an area where even the boys face the prospect of poor employment, if they can obtain employment at all.'

'Don't be indulgent towards me, Marcus. If you don't agree with me then say so.'

The short distance to Nance was covered. 'What I shall say is that you would be doing the girls a great disservice in building up hopes in them that can only be crushed, making them more discontent with their lives. But I shall think again on the matter of the girls' education, see if there is something that might lift their lives above the mundane. We must discuss this again, pool our ideas. Does this suit you?'

'It does. Thank you, Marcus.' Jo was satisfied, grateful to him. The majority of teachers, male and female, would have accused her of being absurd and extreme. 'And thank you for the ride home.'

'Not at all. It was pleasant talking to you. If the weather turns really inclement I'll come and fetch you in the mornings, if you like. I used to do the same for Miss Choak, who lived on the outskirts of the village. No one should make a misconception out of that.'

'It would be very kind of you.'

After they had wished each other a good afternoon, Marcus drove on to Pendeen, praying there would be gales for the rest of the winter.

Next morning, the wind had died to a sulky whisper and a watery sun shone in the sky. It gave no cause for Marcus to drive to Nance Farm, to enjoy more moments alone with Jo, but Joel Willis's presence first thing at the school made him request her company at his desk.

'Miss Venner, do take a seat.' He pulled up a chair for her. 'This is Mr Willis, Kenneth's father.' Joel Willis refused to sit down, so Jo and Marcus remained standing.

'I'm pleased to meet you, Mr Willis,' Jo said evenly.

153

From his stance, she knew she was about to meet the kind of reproach and obstinacy that was the province of the insufferably proud. He was a big man, square jaw tracing a high line, shabby but clean. He pointed a work-grimed finger at Jo.

'You had a go at my boy yesterday.'

'I've already explained to you Miss Venner's reason for her talk with Kenneth yesterday,' Marcus said before Jo could answer. 'I support her entirely. I'm sure you agree that his constant exhaustion had to be brought to the light.'

'I can assure you I only wished to help Kenneth, Mr Willis,' Jo said.

'You're bound to say that, both of you.' Joel Willis's brooding eyes flitted from teacher to headmaster. 'Getting good marks on books is all you care about.'

'It is part of our job,' Jo explained. 'Kenneth is an intelligent boy. I've looked back over his past work and he's achieved some very good results. It would be a shame to allow his education to slip, don't you think?'

Joel Willis spoke to Marcus. 'You know as well as I do, 'master, that all the book learning in the world will do he no good in the end. I teach him lots of things when he's with me. I go through his numbers, tell him history, get him to read notices and old newspapers. He keeps up with the world, even though he ain't got much hope to live well in it. The best way for him to learn about life is the hard way.'

'That's all very well, Mr Willis,' Marcus said, 'but it is the law that children should attend school regularly. If you do not send Kenneth more often, the authorities will be in touch with you. They check the registers. No exceptions are made. And, of course' – he deepened his tone – 'there is Kenneth's health to consider.'

'I know that!' Joel Willis roared. 'What do you think I am? Cruel? I'll see he gets more rest. He'll come to school most days. Is that good enough for the pair of 'ee?'

'It's a start,' Marcus said dryly.

'It'll have to do.' Before pounding to the door, Joel Willis rounded on Jo, saying, 'You made my boy look at me like

I'm a devil to him. I'll never forgive you for that,' and stormed out.

Jo met Marcus's eyes. 'I sometimes wonder why we bother,' he sighed. 'Did he distress you?'

'Not in the least.' She smiled triumphantly. 'I knew he would be too proud to risk people saying he was neglecting Kenneth's health. Kenneth was getting desperate for enough rest and sleep. He will get it from now on, and inevitably his schoolwork will improve.'

'How astute you are,' Marcus said. 'You sound as if you almost enjoyed sounding him off.'

'I'm used to battling to get my own way. Sometimes, though, it's easier if you slip in by the back door.'

All Marcus could do was gaze at her in admiration, then he was disquieted. She was clearly too clever to fall for his mother's scheme. She would quickly detect if his interest in her was genuine and honourable. Actually, it was. He liked her. A lot. More than any woman he had known before.

Seventeen

'**P**eople are talking about Jo,' Lew remarked to Mercy. They were bringing up the rear of a procession of cows, on the way to the farmyard for milking. Darius Pendower was at the front of the herd, setting an unhurried pace. The two collies were darting up and down in attendance.

'What're they talking about her for?' Mercy strode along, stout stick in hand in readiness to prompt stragglers back into line.

'You know. They're saying she's interfering in people's lives.'

'How do they make that out, for goodness' sake?'

'Well, she made Joel Willis feel like a rotten father, and since Luke Vigus went on the road she's been giving Beth Wherry orders on what to do for the children. She's been in that stinking cottage every minute she's not in the school.' With narrowed eyes, Lew puffed on a cigarette. 'She won't last long in Parmarth the way she's going on. People won't put up with it.'

'Those being spiteful should put their hands in front of their mouths,' Mercy said crossly. 'All this being said, when she's only showing concern and kindness. And you, boy, are only telling part of the story because the maid's got you feeling guilty, and rightly so. It's your child she's trying to make things better for. 'Tis time you gave Jo the respect she deserves.'

'Huh! How many times have I got to tell you that the Vigus brat don't belong to me? I can have virtually any woman I like. Honestly, Mercy, Jessie Vigus? I just couldn't. Give me some credit.' Lew glanced behind them. There was very little traffic on the road, but it paid to check regularly nothing was rushing up on them.

Mercy peered down loftily on her nephew. 'Why should I believe you? You don't own up to none of the children you've fathered. You're too 'fraid you'll be call to recompense.'

Lew's face grew flushed and he did not reply. 'Mother sticks up for Jo but others think she's asking for trouble. She's even bought things for the Viguses. Betterfit she helped more deserving cases. There's plenty of honest, hard-working people in the village going through hard times.'

'Like Joel Willis? Who'll see it as charity and throw it back in her face. If you ask me, whatever Jo does she can't win. People were suspicious of Celia Sayce's generosity, and now they've found out she was involved with a married man, they want the school to get rid of everything bought with her money. Load of damn hypocrites.'

Lew kept a mulish silence as the herd turned into the farmyard and headed for their stalls in the shippen. Darius Pendower's working day was over and he left for home. Mercy put on her white coat. Lew fetched the milking pails and slammed one down in front of her.

Mercy grinned, exposing her big teeth. 'Gets to people, that maid does, but I reckon Parmarth won't get the better of her.'

Marcus hurried through the partition dividing the upper and middle classes, anxious to catch Jo before she left the school. She was repacking items laid out on her desk into a straw bag. Foodstuffs, disinfectant, dishcloths, all bought earlier in Pascoe's store. It appeared she was about to call at the Vigus household again.

He was desperate for her to ease off her association with the misfit family. His mother had slated him today over her absence at her side. Eleanor demanded he put a stop to this charity work and concentrate on beguiling her into his bed. He had tried to explain that he must progress slowly, but his mother stubbornly refused to agree that Joanna Venner would not be easily harnessed. From his considerable experience with women, Marcus sensed with despair that love and a husband were not on Jo's agenda. She had been at the school just a few weeks and had found her crusade, bettering the lot of a classful of mainly disadvantaged children.

'Mrs Lidgey was hoping to have your company for a little while this afternoon, Joanna,' he said mildly.

Jo's mind was on the rusks in her bag. Would Marylyn be able to eat one crushed in a little warm milk? From the advice she had sought from Verena Jelbert, Marylyn should be introduced to solid food. Would the buttons she had bought fit Molly's cardigan? 'Oh, I'm sorry, Marcus. What did you say?'

'I hope my mother is not going to be deprived of your company,' he entreated pleasantly.

'I went to the schoolhouse during the morning break,' Jo pointed out, picking up her handbag. She was eager to leave. Jo had arranged with Beth that she would make the children's teatime sandwiches.

'Yes, but that was only for a few minutes. My mother has long lonely hours to endure. She likes you, Joanna. If I may say so, she needs you.' He was concerned about the talk that was circulating. Those expressing admiration and wonder at her benevolence could all too easily change their views to agree with the malicious gossipmongers.

It frustrated him being unable to press again the protests that were indeed his duty as headmaster. For the sake of his mother's wicked scheme he could not risk antagonising her; he had to appear to be totally supportive. At this moment, she looked so appealing, smelled so attractively. She was like a delicate flower of rare configuration. He imagined crushing such a flower in his hand and waiting to see if the petals would unfold and regain their once perfect formation. Would some petals be lost? The stem snap in two? How much damage could the bloom of this young woman withstand?

'I'm sure Mrs Lidgey will understand that the greater part of my spare time is needed elsewhere for the moment,' Jo said, missing the hardness playing round his eyes and mouth.

It would have reminded her of the look a child bore when ripping wings off a butterfly.

The irony of her statement made Marcus gape at her.

Jo felt uncomfortable. He was right not to applaud her efforts with her two pupils. She was giving Rex and Molly too much of her time. But she was devoted to Marylyn, and being close to the children helped her feel close to Luke. She was missing him more than she had imagined.

Her sudden discomfiture made Marcus regret his sadistic thoughts. Putting his long sinuous fingers inside his waistcoat pocket, he produced his wallet and pulled out two folded one-pound notes. Reaching for her hand, he placed the notes on her palm, folding his hand around hers, very gently. 'I hope this will be of some help towards what you're trying to achieve for Rex and Molly.'

'Thank you, Marcus,' she said. His flesh was hot, strangely alive, as if pulsating with an unquiet energy.

'I hope all your good intentions will soon be accomplished.'

He let go of her hand and walked away. Then a distorted vision of his mother's face appeared in front of him, as real as the blackboard, as the wooden screen in the room. He saw Eleanor's carping mouth, heard her vicious demands. 'What have you achieved today? Did you mention the recital? Are you getting somewhere with her at last?'

He turned back, speaking in a voice that gathered strain. 'Joanna, you may be aware that a strings recital is to be performed at Penzance on Saturday afternoon, in the town hall. I know you appreciate good music. I'm thinking of attending. Would you care to accompany me?'

Jo would enjoy a social occasion, but she could not accept an invitation from Marcus Lidgey unless it concerned the school. She considered his motives. Any excursion would probably be diverting for him from the boring life he must lead. Did he simply want her company? She could not forget that he had a mistress. Her position, she hoped, disqualified her as a replacement for or an addition to the services he received from Sally Allett. Could he possibly be interested in her romantically? Marcus had supported her in her first

159

days here with understanding and kindness, had intimated he valued the presence of an equal in Parmarth, but from such a short acquaintance she could not determine what might be on his mind.

'Thank you for the invitation, Marcus,' she replied firmly, 'but I've already made plans for the weekend.'

Marcus watched her changing expression, shutting him off, her thoughts already moving elsewhere. He was filled with the crushing angst he had suffered so often as a boy, when his mother's secret violations had resulted in him feeling trapped, humiliated, contaminated, and at times suicidal.

A dangerous rage threatened to overwhelm him. He would not allow this sanctimonious little do-gooder, who had deliberately brought about her own inferior position in the world, who had money coming to her to sweeten her life, to make a fool of him. He would make it plain that he had no ulterior motive for inviting her to the wretched concert, and damn his mother's evil designs!

'As you please. Don't forget the school choir is singing an anthem in church on Sunday. Be sure you don't infect the school with head lice from your trips across the road.' His words were clipped, the last discordant.

Turning sharply, he returned to his own side of the screen, leaving Jo utterly bewildered.

Standing inside the headmaster's outdoor convenience, Marcus slammed his fists against the damp chilled brick wall, muttering under his breath, 'You fool! You stupid, ignorant fool. It was too soon to make a move on her. She's a colleague, a subordinate, for goodness' sake. She had no choice but to refuse.'

Of his mother: 'You bitch! You cunning, conniving bitch. It was your fussing and moaning which made me go ahead too fast, do the very thing which instinct told me would take time and careful planning.'

At himself: 'You've got to get away again before the bitch wrecks your life. In London, you were in control. The nightmares had stopped. She couldn't touch you, not in any way. You learned to respect yourself a little. You were your own man. But the minute she got you back she turned you into a frightened child again. Damn her! Look at yourself. See what she's doing to you? A frail old woman. Making you manipulate a woman into bed who'd despise you if she knew the truth. Joanna Venner would hate you for being so weak, so gullible, so pathetic. She doesn't give a damn about what her mother thinks of her. She broke free. You've got to break free. Stir yourself, man. Grow up again. Break free.'

Then he was weeping in despair. 'Oh, God, help me, help me.'

Brought back to Penzance by his mother's distressful letters over her bankruptcy, at one glance from her vengeful, pitiless eyes as she had slammed the door behind him, he knew he was her captive again. The very first time she had come to him had been at night. She had resumed her depraved habits. Now he had no self-respect, no hope. All he owned was the night.

Eighteen

After church on Sunday morning, Jo found someone waiting for her outside the churchyard.

'Alistair, you're a surprise.'

'Hello, little thing.' Her brother kissed her affectionately.

Jo kissed him back, delighted he was here. In plus fours, white scarf, pipe peeping out of the breast pocket of his mackintosh, and driving hat and gauntlets, it seemed to Jo that Alistair was slipping comfortably into the role of an old-fashioned country squire.

'I've brought a letter for you. Hop in the car. I'll drive you to the farm.'

'What makes you think I haven't got a luncheon engagement?' Jo said airily.

Alistair grinned. 'Word is your vicar's not at all sociable. It's unlikely there's anyone else in this place you'd dine with.' His eyebrows rose as he glanced behind her. 'Mind you, he's a cut above the others here. Any chance . . . ?'

Jo turned round. Alistair was peering at a man emerging through the lychgate. His dark overcoat, equal in quality to Alistair's more flamboyant apparel, his bearing slightly disdainful, made Marcus Lidgey a courtly figure.

Some of the females among the congregation were treating themselves to an appreciative perusal of him, in between speculating who the stranger was talking to the new teacher. He was on kissing terms with her!

When Marcus saw the stranger, with a hand resting familiarly on Joanna's arm, his face darkened. Damn it! Did the woman have a suitor? This wealthy toff, with the arrogant air of a young man finding life treating him exceptionally well. In comparison, Marcus, who had quickly regretted his exhibition of pique towards Joanna, and to make amends had expressed sympathetic concern for the Vigus children before the service, felt he stood little chance with her.

Striding towards them, he lifted his hat to her, prepared to determine the measure of his rival.

Jo was pleased to introduce the refined headmaster to her supercilious brother. Marcus was relieved at Alistair's identity.

Alistair raised his brows again, at the youth and stylishness of the headmaster. 'I'm pleased my sister isn't working among a lot of old fogies, Mr Lidgey. Lidgey, Marcus . . . let me see, the name is familiar to me somehow.'

'Lidgey is a fairly widespread Cornish name, Mr Venner,' Marcus said, dropping his eyes. 'You have arrived to dine with Miss Venner?'

Jo shot Alistair a hopeful look.

'Sorry, no can do. You're not married, Mr Lidgey?'

Jo wanted to elbow Alistair in the ribs. He had always been bluntly nosey. Pity it did not occur to him to be courteous to Parmarth's headmaster for her sake.

'No, I am not.'

Jo examined Marcus's face. Had Alistair offended him? He smiled very warmly at her. It was a nice smile, lifting away the tiredness around his dark eyes, making him more like the younger, hopeful version of him in the portrait in his sitting room.

'Did you go to the recital, Mr Lidgey?' she asked conversationally.

'Yes, I did. There was a rather fine interpretation of Bruch's Violin Concerto number one. I think you would have enjoyed it, Miss Venner. I hope the next time there is a musical treat, you will be able to find the time to accompany me.'

Jo regretted her curiosity. She could almost hear Alistair's mind ticking over, wondering if there was anything going on between her and Marcus Lidgey. If there was, he probably would not approve. A headmaster would not merit a high enough position in his, or their mother's, mind to commend him as a marriage partner for her. If she ever conformed to their idea of a suitable marriage, they would explain away her career as a spot of eccentricity. She could imagine their outrage if they knew she had a lover who was an itinerant half-gipsy.

'I'm sure you want to get on,' Marcus said graciously. 'A very good afternoon to you both.' He smiled at Jo again then walked away down the hill.

Alistair asked for details of his new acquaintance as he drove inconsiderately fast out of the village. 'He's got a good make of motorcar. How can a poor headmaster afford it, I wonder.'

'He's known better times. He's very accomplished. He was in London before. He came back to Cornwall for his invalid mother's sake. And before you start making silly assumptions, there is absolutely nothing between us.'

'I certainly hope not, Jo,' Alistair cried, bringing the car to a sudden halt, the engine spluttering out like a dying bronchitic. Jo was nearly thrown across the lacquered dashboard. 'I've just remembered where I've heard of him.'

'What are you talking about?' Jo shook her hand irritably, hurt in her reflex action to save herself. 'You very nearly caused me serious injury, you stupid fool.'

'Never mind that, little thing.' He rubbed her back to help her reclaim her breath. 'I was up in London when the scandal broke. Lidgey was thrown out of a top music college over an affair with another tutor's wife. There was quite a to-do. The husband shot himself. All very nasty. Stuff I heard in the club I couldn't possibly repeat to you. Dear God, Jo, you must take very great care you don't get involved with him. The man's a degenerate.'

'Really, Alistair, you must be exaggerating.' Jo felt a disquieting mixture of shock from the Bentley's violent stop and Alistair's revelation about her superior. Could it be true? She had no notion why, but some of the signals she had witnessed passing between Marcus Lidgey and Sally had made her feel uneasy. There had been moments, instances she had chosen to forget, when she had sensed that there was something *not quite right* in the Lidgey household.

'I'm not mistaken,' Alistair stressed. 'Marcus Lidgey. It's him. The right age. The right description. It was in the newspapers. It was said he had scuttled off out of the capital. What a fortunate thing I turned up today. He's a very presentable man, knows how to lay on the charm to the ladies by the way he kept smiling at you. You don't care for him, do you, Jo? Please say you don't?'

She had never seen her brother more intense. A frosting of ice fell away from her heart, her very being warmed through, to finally be sure her brother cared deeply for her. 'I can set your mind at rest, Alistair. It's going to be rather difficult teaching under Mr Lidgey's headship now. I often take tea with his mother.'

Alistair restarted the engine. 'He hasn't behaved improperly towards you, has he?'

'No. He's always seemed rather unassuming. Inclined to the occasional bout of capriciousness. Please don't tell Mother or anyone else about this. She would laugh at me if the headmaster of the school I teach in was dismissed within weeks of me starting here, and I don't think Mr Lidgey deserves to have the scandal follow him to Parmarth. He loves his mother so very tenderly.'

They were driving again. 'Well, I suppose, as they say, better the devil you know. You can look after yourself, and although I want nothing to do with Mercy Merrick, she's man enough, so to speak, to look after you. Promise me though, you'll be wary of Lidgey from now on?'

'Of course. Thanks, Alistair.' Jo pressed her face against his arm. 'I'm glad you understand my feelings.'

Silent for a while, Alistair asked quietly, 'Doesn't it feel odd living under the roof of Mother's old lover?'

'No. As we're speaking plainly, if she hadn't dallied with Bob Merrick, I would never have met Celia.'

'Oh, her.'

'Don't be like that. She was like a mother to me.'

Alistair's hand left the steering wheel to hold Jo's for a

moment. 'I do try to understand, Jo. Mother hasn't played fair with you. I hope Phoebe will be maternal towards our children.'

'Oh, Alistair, you'll make me feel emotional. Why couldn't we talk like this before? You're a good old stick, really.'

Alistair stopped the car beside the farm, grimacing at the base odours filling the air. 'Mother's been looking at property, Jo. Says she needs a retreat and Phoebe and I should have more time to ourselves.'

'Oh, really.' Jo considered this a move on Katherine's part to enable her to carry on her affairs all the more freely.

'Does Mother know you were coming here today?'

'Um, yes.'

'And did she send a message to me?'

'Not exactly.' Alistair cleared his throat and fiddled with his pipe.

'Well, never mind.' Jo rallied brightly. 'It's been a really lovely surprise, you turning up, Alistair. Will you come inside?'

'Afraid not.' They embraced. While Alistair reversed into the farm's entrance to turn the car, Jo waited to wave him goodbye.

He stopped a moment and beckoned to her. 'Oh, I nearly forgot to give you your letter. It was forwarded from your old address.'

'Are you comfortable, Mrs Lidgey?' Sally was settling her mistress for her afternoon rest.

'If it's the best you can do, I'll just have to put up with it.' Eleanor's head pressed down heavily on the pillows. 'Is Mr Lidgey in his study?'

'Yes, working on a science project.'

'He works so hard at the school and then worries over me. He could do with a rest too. Send him to me before you leave.'

Sally positioned a small hand bell, once part of a set that had belonged to the school, near Eleanor's hand. 'Beth will be here if you need to ring for anything.'

Sally went downstairs to the kitchen. Beth Wherry had almost finished the dishes. 'When you've scrubbed the sink and draining board and done the preparations for tea, you can put your feet up, Beth. Then you've only got to listen out for Mrs Lidgey's bell.'

'Yes, Sally.' Beth carefully put a plate in the rack above her head. 'See you take a good rest yourself.'

'You be careful you don't wear yourself out taking on all that extra work for the Viguses. Luke's practically getting a full-time housekeeper out of you.'

'I don't mind. I hated seeing the children suffer.'

'The trouble with you is, you're too kind.' Sally envied Beth's uncomplicated nature. The girl did not appear to mind drudgery. She was wiping the next dinner plate too slowly for Sally's impatient nature, the circular movements done almost reverently. The high-quality china plate must seem precious to Beth; she was gazing at the delicate red and blue roses and gold leaf pattern round the edge with pleasure. When she finished here later this evening, she would return to the warmth and affection of her family, then attend chapel.

Sally stirred up the energy to walk to her widowed mother's cottage, several dwellings away on the other side of the road. After giving her mother a third of her wages – Marcus paid her well – she was glad to let her mother wait on her.

'Joanna Venner's causing quite a stir,' Mrs Allett remarked, as Sally settled at the hearth. Sally had inherited her fair appearance and feminine body and the inclination to be brisk and pithy. 'You should have heard the minister going on about her this morning over what she's done for the Viguses. I reckon he wants us chapel folk not to let someone who's church do all the charity round here. But then she always was determined. She must have shook up Luke. He's worked in that cottage like a miner. She wants to watch out for his roving eye though. Handsome man like he could have quite an effect on her, even though she's bettermost of people like us.'

'I hardly think she's Luke's type,' Sally said disdainfully. She could not see Jo Venner paying clandestine visits to Luke's wagon as she had once done. Luke had been a very

167

satisfying, sensitive lover. Pity he had refused to let her join him on his travels. 'Jessie only gets out of bed occasionally now, doesn't do a thing for the children, but I expect they're glad of that. I watched her from the schoolhouse sitting-room window the other day. She was lurching off down the road, half-dressed, drunk as a lord as usual. Don't know where she was going. Don't expect she knew herself, come to that.'

'She'll come to grief one day and it'll be her own fault. Well, between Joanna Venner and the Wherrys, the kiddies should fare better. How's Mrs Lidgey today?'

'Same as usual. Bitchy one minute, quite pleasant the next. Her back's getting worse.'

Mrs Allett fetched two cups and saucers from the crockery cupboard, pausing at the sink to gaze out of the window. 'Russell's heading this way.'

'Oh, no,' Sally moaned wearily.

'You could do a lot worse, Sally.' Mrs Allett expressed an opinion Sally had heard before. 'He's thirty-two, looking to settle down. I know he can be hard and touchy, but he's not like Lew, still sowing his wild oats. He's got a job at the moment and is the sort who'll always seek work. He's persistent, it shows he really cares about you. It's time you thought about getting married. I'd like to have grandchildren before I'm too old to enjoy them. You could have your old bedroom. You wouldn't have to squeeze in with Irene.'

'I was hoping to do better than him,' Sally snapped testily.

'Who? There's no one else in these parts for you.'

'Afternoon, Sally,' Russell said cheerfully, after Mrs Allett asked him to step inside. Sally felt like laughing. He looked gormless, unsure of himself now they were courting. However, he was manly and distinguished in a second-hand, navy-blue blazer and grey flannel trousers, his dark brown hair brilliantined. 'Coming for a walk, Sally?'

'I'll put my coat on.' She sprang to her feet, eyeing her mother pertly.

'Lift me up and sit close to me, Marcus.'

'No.' Marcus had his hands inside his jacket pockets.

His mother detested slovenly habits. He was daring to be rebellious.

'Little bastard.'

'Not little any more, Mama.'

'What's got into you these past few days? Answering me back. Are you acquiring some backbone at last? I shall whip you.'

'You are not strong enough, Mama,' he said coldly.

Eleanor narrowed her eyes, snake-like. 'Whist! Your bravado never lasts long. Tell me again what you said to Joanna after the church service.'

Marcus became tense. Meeting Alistair Venner had changed things. 'I omitted to tell you that I met her brother. He was waiting for her. They are very close, as members of a family should be. It got me thinking again. What happened to my sister, Mama?'

'You never had one, Marcus.'

'So you say, but I remember her. I looked up her details, a long time ago. I've even been to her grave. Gabriella Lidgey. Died aged ten months. Why do you behave as if she never existed?'

'I loathed her. I was glad she died. Come to me, son. My darling boy. Love your mama.'

There was little change in his closed expression but Marcus's heart clenched painfully. He hid his disgust and the hatred that grew inside him with every passing hour. 'Why didn't it occur to me before? You had no use for her. Poor little Gabriella, but perhaps she was the fortunate one.'

'I forbid you to talk about her ever again.' Eleanor struggled to raise herself. 'Come to me. Now!'

'Never again, Mama. You can go to hell.'

It was the letter Jo had been hoping to receive. 'It's from a solicitor at Penzance, Mercy.' Jo passed the typed sheet of white paper to her friend.

Mercy declined to take it. 'What's it say?'

'It's asking me to get in touch with him. It says I'll hear

something to my benefit under Celia's will.' Jo leapt up from the kitchen table, bringing Kip and Hunter, dozing at Mercy's feet beside the fire, to rise and pace about expectantly. The cats, slumbering in the chimney, peeped out of offended eyes.

Mercy placed her big stockinged feet to rest up on the side of the range. ''Tis Sunday afternoon, maid. Sit down and relax.'

'I can't. I think I'll go over to Cardhu and take a look around again. I'll reply to the solicitor when I return.'

Mercy never idled her time speculating on something that would become evident all in good time. She stretched her long limbs. 'It's no good, I can't rest now. Think I'll go over to Stan and Ellie Blewett's for a yarn.'

After putting on her outdoor things, Jo found Mercy and the collies gone. What could Celia have left her, as the letter implied? She hoped it was the house. Please let it be the house. It was hers in her heart. As Luke was. Realising she had deep feelings for Luke brought Jo absolutely still. He was due back in three days. Now it seemed like three long years she still had to wait. She understood Celia's loneliness.

She was irked to see Russell striding into the yard. He looked furious.

'You lying little bitch! I've just found out from Sally that you never spoke to her about me. Why didn't you ask her to meet me at the mine ruins that time?'

'I've got better things to do than run your love life,' she answered darkly. 'Why should I do anything for you? Clear off, I'm busy.'

She turned her back on him, but he grabbed the collar of the Burberry coat and yanked her off her feet. Jo choked as it tightened round her neck. She kicked and struggled, but Russell dragged her through the yard, her boots scraping the cobbles. He stopped, turned her round to face him, and despite her wild attempt to fight him off, shook her until her woollen hat fell free and she turned a violent red.

'Get your hands off me!' she yelled.

Clutching the front of the coat, he hauled her off her feet

170

and spat in her face. 'Think you're really someone, don't you? Because that stuck-up schoolmaster and his mother's taken to you. Because some people think you're a bleddy heroine because you've stopped the sodding Vigus bastards starving to death. Well, you can't behave round here like you've been brought up in Court; there's pigs down the other ruddy end! Your plan to keep me and Sally apart didn't work. She's just agreed to marry me.'

Her air supply was being cut off by his vicious hold and Jo felt light-headed. Her sight dimmed. Suddenly he tossed her away, stood over her and laughed for several moments. As she gasped in air and her senses cleared Jo realised he had thrown her on the dung heap. With a hand to her burning throat she fought to sit up. 'Sally must be mad. I'll tell her exactly what you're like.'

'You cause trouble for me and you'll bitterly regret it.' He thrust out his foot and pushed her down to lie flat on the stinking dung. 'You're not quite the lady now, Jo Venner. You were a scraggy little kid and wallowing in cow shit is where you belong!'

'Hey! Get away from her.'

Jo heard the sound of boots running over the cobbles. It was Marcus Lidgey, sliding over the mud in his haste to reach them.

'Sod off,' Russell snarled at him, 'or I'll toss you in the cow shit too!'

'Get away from her, Trevail,' Marcus growled, hands extended, ready to grasp Russell by the throat.

'I'll not fight you wearing my best clothes, Lidgey. Just you keep away from Sally Allett. She's mine.' Russell stalked off, away over the fields.

Jo crawled down on to the cobbles and wiped some of the filth off herself.

Marcus reached for her hands. 'Are you hurt?'

'My throat feels like it's on fire,' she rasped. He pulled her gently to her feet. A rush of blood thundered in her ears. She moaned and closed her eyes. Marcus helped her inside.

Jo pulled off her coat and sat down at the kitchen hearth,

the comforting warmth of Mercy's home wrapping itself around her.

Marcus was pouring hot water from the kettle into a bowl he had found in under the draining board. He approached her with the bowl and a towel. 'It was a brutal attack, Joanna. May I ask what it was about?'

'Spite left over from our childhood, nothing to worry about,' Jo croaked. 'Marcus, there will be some tea left in the pot. Would you fetch me a cup, please?'

'Of course.'

Jo was trembling. He held the cup to her lips. She placed her hands over his. The tea was bitter but soothed her throat. Marcus wet the towel. He passed it to Jo and she rubbed at the muck on her face and hair. He brought the bowl up close so she could wash her hands.

'Thank you. I must get out of these filthy clothes. I'm afraid your clothes are soiled too.'

'No matter. Joanna, you have an angry mark on your neck. Will you unfasten your blouse buttons and let me see if it's serious?'

Jo lifted her fingers to her throat and undid the top three buttons of her linen blouse. When she pulled the sides apart, Marcus knelt in front of her to examine the wound. 'There's a deep welt. Trevail very nearly drew blood. It must be very tender. I suggest you bathe it.'

'Yes, of course. Thank you for your help.' She refastened the buttons. 'Why are you here, Marcus?'

He sat down on the bench. 'I'll come straight to the point. Your brother recognised my name, didn't he?'

Jo nodded. Alistair had said this man was a degenerate. Yet he had touched her, studied her exposed skin with modesty, and a natural gentleness. She felt no threat from him, but neither did she welcome this interview.

Marcus coloured. 'Forgive me, this is embarrassing for you. You will understand that I have to know if you intend to report what you have learned to the local authorities. They are not aware of the circumstances that forced me to resign from the music college.'

172

'Actually, I can't see that it's anything to do with me.'

He did not bother to hide his relief. 'Thank God. A fresh scandal would ruin me. I'm not proud of what I did. I confessed my dishonour to my mother immediately. She has forgiven me. You will appreciate that I am eager to make her last years as contented as possible.' His guts lurched at the lies.

Jo now had the reason for him teaching in a position inferior to his accomplishments and experience. The chances of his disgrace coming to light were fewer in such an isolated area. She could think of no comment she should make.

'I hope this will not affect our professional relationship,' Marcus said. He was squirming on the bench like a schoolboy caught in the act of something odiously disgusting. 'What I am going to say next is difficult for me but I'd like to be completely honest with you. My mother is harbouring notions that you and I will form a romantic alliance. I admire you, Joanna, but I swear that I will never compromise you. In fact, I'm hoping we can be friends. Otherwise, it will be impossible for us to work side by side. I'm hoping that with everything out in the open, you will not ever misunderstand my intentions or misconstrue anything I say to you. I'd like to tell you what happened in London.'

Jo sighed. When she had sought the teaching post here she had envisaged difficulties, but nothing of this sort. Apart from being faintly disgusted by him, it was hard to know what she thought of this man, while he was looking at her so pathetically, pleading for her understanding. Not long ago he had been her rescuer; Russell might well have given her a brutal kicking. If she wanted to make successful advances with her pupils, she could not treat the headmaster as a social leper. Was it possible for them to be friends? Lew was a friend. Perhaps she could think of him rather as she did the kinder Trevail brother; another man of libidinous appetites.

'You don't have to tell me anything, Marcus.' She really did not want to hear about it.

'But all kinds of things may go through your mind. There will be times when you may not be able to look me in the eye, and I won't know what to say to you. Please.'

Jo was reminded that it was a sexual indiscretion by her own mother which had led to her achieving her aims, and she was living under the late Bob Merrick's roof. Marcus Lidgey had positive aspects to his character. He cosseted his ailing mother, was an excellent teacher, could resume an outstanding career. He deserved a hearing.

'Well, I think we could both do with a tot of Mercy's medicinal brandy, if you can find it in the cupboard. I'm still feeling shaky.'

Marcus went to the oak cupboard, his thoughts racing. He was in the presence of an uncomplicated, circumspect woman, of a sort he had never met before. He was suddenly burning with desire for her.

'Don't,' he mouthed anxiously to his treacherous body.

Keeping his back towards her, he quickly located a nearly full bottle of brandy but pretended to search among crockery, ornaments, old letters and other miscellanea to find a pair of tumblers until he was under control.

The strong smell of alcohol spread through the kitchen, clearing Jo's head. She sipped the potent red liquid from the glass he handed her.

Marcus held his glass in his palms. Meeting Jo's steady gaze, he cleared his throat. 'I cared very much for the married lady. We met at the college, following a student concert. She was fair and lovely. Her husband was a lot older than her, a cantankerous stuffed shirt. He was unkind to her, left her on her own for hours. We found we had a lot in common, were easy to talk to and laugh with. She and her husband had a violent row. I came across her weeping in St James's Park. I won't deny I sought an affair with her. I was intoxicated by her.'

'You fell in love.'

'Love? What is that?' He stared into the fire, sizzling and crackling behind the grid of the range. Jo had the impression he was somewhere else, somewhere he could not quite reach. He returned to her. 'Where was I? The husband, he found out.

174

Couldn't take the shame. He shot himself. I resigned before I was dismissed from the college.' He switched off again.

'And the lady?'

'Oh, yes. She wanted to make a fresh start on her own. I respected her wishes. Shortly afterwards I returned to Cornwall, then my mother had her fall. We are not financially independent. I needed to earn a living. I obtained the headmastership of Parmarth. We've lived here rather quietly for the last year.'

'A year that has been stultifying for you?'

'Yes, I won't deny it. One day I'm hoping to get a better position. I would like to join an orchestra as second violinist or cellist. I'm hoping people will have forgotten about me by then.'

'And what about Parmarth?'

'I shall give my best efforts to the school while I'm its headmaster. Do you intend to stay here for good?'

'No. Actually I have plans to found a school for girls, but not for some years when I shall have the means. Until then, I'm still keen to do something for the children of the village, particularly Ann Markham who is above average intelligence. I can remember the Solace Mine being worked. For a short time I knew Parmarth when it was busy, alive. It's sad and humbling to witness what's happened to its inhabitants.'

Jo pulled at the clothes chafing her skin. The stench from them was steamy and offensive in the cosy kitchen. 'Marcus, I really must ask you to excuse me. I need to bathe and change.'

'Yes, of course. Thank you for listening, for not being judgemental. Good afternoon, Joanna.'

It was after Jo had put Mercy's enormous hip bath to use, was wrapped in her dressing gown and dabbing a soothing ointment of soapwort on her throat, that she realised this new informality with Marcus Lidgey would inevitably bring about more unrealistic expectations in his mother. Might even lead to unwelcome complications.

Dismissing the thought, she replied to Celia's solicitor. Then she lingered over her drawing of Luke.

175

Nineteen

'Tell me what my daughter's up to these days, Mardie.'

Through cracked eyelids, Mardie Dawes glanced up as she gathered her tarot cards together. For her fortnightly appointments at Tresawna House, she wore a clean blouse and splashed her hands and raddled face with water and scented soap, making her more tolerable to be close to. 'Strange, you suddenly asking about she. Did something in the reading put Joanna into your mind?'

'No, and I'm still waiting for this wonderfully rich man to come into my life who you keep promising me,' Katherine replied coldly. She stretched out her silk-encased legs, where she reclined on the couch in her bedroom. 'With Alistair well matched, I was simply wondering if my recalcitrant daughter has made any progression on that front. You should know all about her.'

'I keep my eyes 'n' ears open.'

'I don't suppose she would be the slightest bit interested if a young blood danced attention on her anyway,' Katherine muttered crossly, regretting bringing up what was to her a boring subject. 'All she cares about is her pathetic career.'

Sitting at a small round table in a darkened part of the bedroom, illuminated enigmatically by candlelight, Mardie was pleased to be in the position to spring a surprise. She interlocked her bony fingers over the pack of cards. 'Actually, the girl's got herself a man.'

'What?' Katherine spilled the glass of white wine in her hand as she jerked herself up to a sitting position. 'Who is he? Why didn't you tell me this when you first arrived, damn you?'

'He's nobody you'd approve of, Katherine. His name's Luke Vigus. A most handsome fellow. He's a travelling man, lives most of the time on his wagon and is light-fingered. His drunken mother and her three other young snotty-nosed brats live in a hovel in the village.'

'If you're telling me the truth, what on earth does Joanna see in him, for goodness' sake? Has she gone mad? The wretched little bitch. I'll have to send Alistair to her to put some sense into her stubborn brain.'

'Won't do you no good, Katherine. Like I said, Luke's all man; you'd like him for that. He's got an amiable nature underneath his wild ways. He's a wandering soul, mind, can't see him staying interested in Joanna for long.'

'I don't care if this reprobate ends up breaking her heart!' Katherine snapped angrily. 'But it could ruin her chances of making a good marriage.'

'When are you going to learn that you have no influence over the maid? Interfere, and you'll only drive her deeper into his arms.'

'Blow it. Why couldn't there be someone at least remotely suitable in that God-forsaken village for her? There would only be the vicar, but he's an old man, isn't he?'

Mardie eyed Katherine shrewdly, knowing she did not really care about her daughter's prospects of making a good marriage. She simply hated Joanna being independent, making a success of her life. 'There is someone. The school-master. He's the same class as you, expert at playing and teaching music. A fine-looking man he is too, not yet forty. He'd definitely suit your tastes in bed, my dear.'

'How do you know this?'

'You know I make it my business to learn everything about everybody in Parmarth. I asked about him in Penzance, where his mother comes from. There's a nice juicy scandal in his past.'

'You evil witch.' Katherine picked up her beaded purse, took five pounds out of it then passed it to the fortune-teller, who rapidly slipped it down inside her bodice. 'I suppose you're blackmailing him too.' Until William Venner's death,

Mardie had obtained hush money from Katherine over her affair with Bob Merrick, then continued to demand half the funds to keep quiet about the two abortions she had performed on her.

'Not him. I wouldn't get away with it. I wouldn't even dare spread rumours about he.'

'Why not?'

Mardie tapped her head. 'Touch of madness, dangerous.'

Luke raked out the ashes of the fire, put more coal and furze on the glowing embers then employed the bellows until he had created a good blaze. When he stepped back, he nearly fell over Molly, who had crept up behind him to crouch in her usual spot. She howled in pain, clutching her scuffed hand to her scrawny chest.

'Bloody hell, Molly. Can't you watch where you're going? I'm sorry. Are you hurt?'

Keeping her head bowed, Molly nodded miserably, making the yellow ribbon Jo had bought for her fall out of her thin mousey hair. Clutching a scrap of cloth for comfort, which had become a habit of hers, and sniffing back tears, she flopped down on the cushion next to the hearth.

'Let me see,' Luke said.

Rather than holding out her hurting hand, Molly curled herself into a tight ball.

'Please yourself.' He turned to Rex, who was copying out a simple nursery rhyme, which Jo had set exclusively for him, in large shaky handwriting. 'Go and get the baby from Mrs Wherry.'

'You get her,' Rex muttered, without looking up from his labour, his brow furrowed in concentration.

'Do as you're bloody told, or I'll clout you round the ear.'

'I'm doing this.'

'Rex!' Luke marched to the mirror on the wall and combed his hair.

Moments later, his younger brother was still sitting at the table. 'Rex, go and get Marylyn. I'm warning you. Off your ass, now!'

'You shouldn't swear. Miss Venner says you show yourself up for an ignorant fool when you swear. And this is more important than getting ready to go down the pub, spending all your money.'

'You little runt! I'll tan the skin off your backside.' Red-faced, because Rex had shamed him, but disinclined to pass over the issue of his cheek, Luke leapt across the room, grabbed Rex by the back of his shirt collar and dangled him up high in the air. 'Do as you're told, or you'll be sorry.'

Struggling, his sallow, elfin face indignant, Rex shouted, 'Why don't you go and fetch Marylyn for a change? You don't do nothing when you're here but give orders.'

'Shut up, Rex.' Luke shook him. 'You'll wake up the old woman and she'll be down here making you wish you'd never been born.' He put the boy down and cuffed him across the top of his head. 'I spend money on you, your sisters and this miserable place, never forget that. I could walk out the door this very minute and never come back, then where would you be? Bundled off to an orphanage, and they're terrible places. You won't get nothing to eat. You'd—'

Molly began to sob. 'Oh hell,' Luke hissed. 'Now she's off. Molly, I didn't mean it. I'll always make sure you've got a proper home. Whenever I'm on the road I'm always thinking about you. I promise I'll always come back. Look, I won't go down the pub tonight. I'll stay in. Where did I hurt you just now? Show me?' He was actually going to Nance for a secret rendezvous with Jo; he'd have to wait for Molly to fall asleep.

Staying huddled, Molly's tears persisted.

'She's been crying all day,' Rex said.

'Why?'

'She don't want to go to school no more. She gets teased.'

'Well, she must learn to hit back. Crying like a baby won't help. You're there, Rex, stick up for her. Belt the culprits.'

'I do when I hear them.' Rex balled his fists. 'But I can't be round her all the time.'

'I'll ask Miss Venner to do something about it.' Luke approached Molly. 'Did you hear that, Molly? I'll ask her

179

to stop the bullies, and if they don't, then I'll smack 'em into order myself. Right?'

Molly looked up at him from huge baleful eyes. 'Here, take this.' He removed the rabbit's foot from around his neck. 'It's lucky. Nothing can hurt you when you're wearing this.' Molly continued to stare at him. He dropped the pendant over her head. 'You'll be all right. Better now?'

Finally she nodded, giving one last noisy sniff. Luke smiled at her. 'Good girl. Glad we've got that straightened out.'

When he stood up, he was annoyed to see Rex had gone back to his writing. 'All right, I'll get the baby this time.'

'We're heading for disaster!' Keane Trevail thumped the kitchen table. 'I'm telling you, Abner, there won't be a tin mine left in Cornwall the rate it's going. They've been picking the eyes out of the mines for years.'

'You don't think the Geevor'll hold on?' Abner Jelbert gulped down a second mug of bitter brew from Irene's teapot. 'It's got good management.'

'Maybe it has, but what can they do against a world slump? It's on its way, I can feel it in me water.'

'That's what Mardie said too when she read your palm last month.' Irene glanced up from her knitting.

Keane made an impatient rumbling sound in his throat and ignored her. 'The moment the Geevor can't meet its working expenses they'll be finished. They did a lot of development two years ago, but will it pay off?' He was mainly an optimistic man but he was getting troubled again at the depressing outlook of the industry which now employed only one of his sons – a crime in his opinion. Today he had heard that another young family was about to move out of the village, dwindling the number of children attending the school by three. There had been a time, less than fifteen years ago, when there had been over seventy children running through the school gates. If things went on like this the services of one of the teachers might be dispensed with. It would be a shame if Jo Venner lost her job, and she doing so well for the children.

180

The pride deeply embedded in the miners of the St Just area was not to be found in Abner. When the Solace Mine had been 'knocked' he had found no success in getting another job as a boilerman and had contented himself by scratching about for odd jobs or drawing the dole. However, he put on a sorrowful face at the injustices of life. 'Good job my father isn't alive to see this day. Would've broke his heart. Nearly all his grandsons going off to work in a different trade, Arnold no prospects of getting nothing decent at all. It's a comfort to me now that he died how he'd lived, down the mine, where a Cornishman belongs.'

'Many a good man saw the end of his life or hopes and dreams underground, but it was better'n this. Whatever work men find, it doesn't pay as well as down the mines,' Keane rejoined with a strong sense of grievance. He pushed his mug towards the end of the table for a second refill and sent Abner's empty vessel after it.

Irene hated this constant stirring of her ageing bones. 'You'll be up and down the garden all afternoon, Keane.'

'That's my problem,' her husband said grumpily.

While Irene topped up the heavy cloam teapot with hot water, he recounted the sad tales that came to his lips with ever-increasing regularity. 'My grandfather was killed when the boiler house blew up in 1904, along with Caleb Wearne and three other men drying out their clothes. John Allett suffocated in bad air; never saw his maid born. Young Harry Pascoe was crushed in a rock fall first day down. His uncle and brother was with him and my younger brother, Tom. Billy Bawden fell away, dizzy, from the ladders down Pike's Shaft, and so did Mark Penrose and Charlie Burthy.' Keane noisily swallowed a mouthful of tea.

'Not forgetting Stan Blewett whose eyes were blown out in a gunpowder blast.'

'Now he could smell out tin like a dog. I belonged to visit he. Haven't been out much this winter with my creaky bones.' Keane's craggy face brightened. His old friend, who lived topside of the church, was someone else he could indulge his reminiscences with, and Ellie Blewett employed a better

181

hand at making yeast buns than Irene. 'Think I'll go up to his place after dinner.'

He rolled a cigarette, and Abner, chuckling, screwed up his ill-favoured face. 'Arnold don't half give that Jo Venner the runaround at school. Gillian too. She's got 'em readin' better, mind, but we've had two notes sent home complaining about their behaviour. She's got some hopes if she's expecting Arnold to settle down. I could whip the skin off his backside but he'd still have the last word, cheeky little bugger.'

'She shouldn't spend so much time hanging round the Viguses,' Irene said. 'Even goes into Mrs Wherry's to see the baby most days. And she's getting too close to Luke, if you ask me.'

'People got a lot to say but many think she's the best thing to ever come to Parmarth,' Abner said thoughtfully. 'She's an uppity madam but she could fall under Luke's spell.'

'So you think so too. Well, Mercy's sure there's something going on between them. She come across them together in the barn the other night; unusual place to confide in a teacher. And Jo's got drawings of Luke in her room. Lew saw them when he went upstairs to use the toilet. He's thinking of having a word with Luke. Why don't you go with him, Keane?' Irene challenged her husband. 'Put Luke straight about her.'

''Tisn't nothing to do with we,' Keane objected, wiping his runny nose on his jumper sleeve. 'Why don't Mercy put her straight?'

'She's tried to. Jo won't listen.'

Spying a rush of counter-arguments to his protests, he sighed and patted his congested chest. 'Don't go on, Irene, I know you like the maid. I'll see what I can do.'

Twenty

In contemplative silence, her heart aching with grief, love and gratitude, Jo drew near the front door of Cardhu. She had the keys clasped in her hand of the property she now owned.

That morning, Luke had taken her to the solicitor at Penzance. The solicitor explained Celia had left Jo her entire estate, which included fifteen thousand pounds and many valuable pieces of jewellery, which had been placed for safe-keeping in a bank.

Alone for this pilgrimage, a lump of emotion grew in her throat as she entered the house. The curtains were drawn, the atmosphere still and dark, and she half-expected Celia to meet her, smiling affectionately, arms extended to embrace her.

Putting her coat next to Celia's in the hallway, Jo moved slowly through the downstairs rooms, disturbing the dust that had gathered in the few weeks the house had been unoccupied. Her shoes tapped on the tiled floor of the kitchen. She opened the biscuit barrel in the kitchen and was delighted to discover it contained ginger fairings, the regional delicacy Celia had introduced her to. At home, as a child, Jo had been denied the treat of nibbling biscuits. In the sitting room she touched an unfinished work of tapestry, the last book Celia had been reading and the Broadwood piano where they had played duets together. On the wall was the portrait Celia had painted of Jo in the garden last summer, the painting Luke had seen.

Upstairs, in the main bedroom, she gazed down sadly at the bed where her friend and mentor had died alone, from natural causes the post-mortem had revealed.

Before leaving Cornwall for teacher-training college at Bristol, Jo had read to Celia when she had been ill in bed, those occasions becoming more frequent as the years had worn on. Celia had become prone to chest infections. Jo was racked with guilt at all the time Celia had spent alone – it was over sixteen years since Sheridan Ustick had died – but Celia had urged her to make a good start in her career. Celia's unselfishness must have left her unbearably lonely, just how Jo was feeling now.

Jo was facing the full-length wardrobe mirror. The bedroom door was ajar, and in the mirror's reflection she saw it softly open wider. Then the room was filled, like an anointing, with gardenia perfume. Jo turned, stretching out her arms, her heart suddenly overwhelmed with joy. 'Oh, Celia, you've come to say hello. I should have known you'd be here.'

The perfume remained strong for several moments. Jo sat down on the side of the bed, feeling warm and wanted and loved. Close by was the first photograph she had seen of Sheridan Ustick: a middle-aged man with a sanguine expression, neat moustache, and a smile Jo had felt she could trust.

Heavy footsteps were coming up the stairs. Jo was not afraid. Whoever the trespasser was, Celia would protect her. She walked to the landing and as she looked down the stairs her heart leapt with joy. 'Luke! I was hoping you'd come.'

'I didn't know whether I ought to intrude.' He gave her his striking smile. 'I was worried about you, sweetheart. You were so quiet on the way back from Penzance, but you look happy now.'

'Celia was here. I smelled her perfume, felt the essence of her.'

Ascending to the top step, he leaned forward and kissed Jo's lips then glanced about warily. 'She might not like me being here. She'd hardly think me good enough for you.'

'I've thought about what Celia would say about us. As long as she knew I was happy it would be all that mattered. Come and look round.' Jo took his hand and led him into the bedroom she had just left.

Luke studied the distinctly feminine room: flowing, snowy white drapes, shiny brass bedstead. 'You should live in this sort of place.'

'I shall keep it as a haven to return to after I've founded a school at Penzance. I hope you'll see Cardhu as a haven too, Luke.' They had discussed their future relationship, acknowledging they were two very independent people, content to remain lovers. They had both sworn fidelity.

'The moors are my haven, Jo.' He paused. 'And wherever you are.'

'Really?' Jo hugged him, completely happy. She had a career which fulfilled her, faithful friends, a home now with roots and blissful memories, and with Celia's money added to her trust fund, a small fortune. She could put her plans for the school into action any time she liked. Most importantly, she had something very special with the man at her side.

There was a sudden intense sadness and an uncertainty in Luke's stunning blue eyes. 'Are you sure about being involved with me, Jo? You have all this, I've just got a covered wagon to live in, or a stinking hovel. You're honest. I've thieved all my life and no one trusts me. You're a schoolteacher and I can't even read properly. And people are getting suspicious about us. They'll be warning you off me; there'll be trouble at the school.'

'I don't care about the differences in our backgrounds, Luke, and as for anything else, when I'm with you it simply doesn't matter.' She pulled his head down and kissed him fiercely.

Enfolding her in his arms in the way of a man desiring a woman, Luke returned her passion. It was a chilly pre-spring day, but they were quickly warmed through.

Jo said, 'Do you want to see where I used to sleep? There's four bedrooms but Celia only furnished two of them.'

'Lead the way,' he said, smiling.

In the room next to Celia's, while she pulled back the curtains to let in the light, he sat down on the small double bed. 'Soft and comfortable. I can imagine you sleeping here, your sweet little face peeping out the covers. I've never slept in a proper bed but I don't feel I've missed out. Gran gave me everything that was really important. She would've liked you.'

'Tell me about her, Luke. How did she die?'

'It was 'flu.' His expression was a series of sadness, regret and poignant amusement. 'I burgled a house in Germoe the night she was took bad. The coppers couldn't prove it, but they battered on the door and watched my every move while I kept vigil over her. I think she would've been tickled at how I made sure I'd never be arrested. Just before the lid of the coffin was nailed down I kissed her one last time and slipped the cache of jewellery inside her nightdress. Gran rests decked out like a lady.'

Jo smiled at his tale but grew serious. 'Did she ever worry that you'd be sent to prison?'

'Yeh.' And he was serious. 'I don't do break-ins any more.'

'I feel I knew your grandmother. She passed on all her good ways to you.'

'I'll never meet your mother but I can see Celia Sayce in you. She was a real lady. I first met her when I was travelling back this way. She was out walking and stopped me and asked if I could get hold of tapestry silks for her. I told her to make out a list and I'd go over to St Ives that afternoon. She invited me inside the house, didn't keep me on the doorstep. She led the way to the sitting room even though I insisted the kitchen would do. While I was waiting for the list she gave me a delicious drop of rum. Didn't have a snobbish bone in her body. I enjoyed talking to her.'

'Did you think she was lonely?' Tears pricked Jo's eyes.

Luke went to her. 'I thought she had a loneliness about her but she wouldn't want you to feel guilty about it. This house is her gift to you. Enjoy it. Her love for you was the most important thing and love goes on for ever.'

'Thanks, Luke.' Her voice came husky with emotion. 'You've said just the right things.'

Putting his palm on the small of her back he pulled her in closer to him. While gazing into her eyes, he brought her hands up to his lips and delicately kissed each finger and the soft flesh between them.

Jo stroked his face with all tenderness, then their lips met and they were feasting on each other, clinging, embracing, searching. He led the way to the bed and started to undress her.

Jo froze. She needed his touch, his loving, but their previous encounters had not allowed them the freedom of being naked. Rushing out of the hidden darkness of her mind was the old insecurity about her body, cruelly undermining her confidence. Surely Luke would find her body flat and unfeminine. He was well built, perfectly formed, totally masculine, while she was formed as a female on the brink of womanhood.

The buttons of her blouse were undone and he was pulling it off her shoulders. Jo was filled with bolts of panic. Luke would see the shape under her chemise amounted to no more than two insignificant points.

She pulled her blouse out of his hands.

'Jo?' He looked tender, concerned. 'Are you going shy on me?'

'Yes,' she said shakily, moving out of his reach. 'I want you, Luke, but the thing is, you may not find me very interesting with no clothes on. I've not got much of . . . of what a woman should have.'

'What?' He gave a puzzled laugh. 'I don't understand.'

Trying desperately not to weep in shame, she explained, 'I haven't any curves, Luke. I'm not much like a woman.'

A smile full of caring and loving lit up his rugged face, and Jo felt she could drown in him. 'Of course you're a woman. I've felt your body in my arms. You're beautiful and feminine and everything I desire. Please don't torture yourself over something that isn't true.'

'But all my life my mother's told me no man would ever find me attractive,' Jo cried.

'Who do you believe? Me or your mother?'

It was his look of such passionate concern that swept away all her years of secret misery. 'You, darling.'

A deep intimate silence descended on them. He smiled deeply and it was devastating, vanquishing her fears and inhibitions for ever. Her desire now was an unstoppable force. Perfectly comfortable while he slowly undressed her, she undid his shirt buttons and pulled it off him. She rubbed her palms over the smooth bronzed skin of his body, feeling the powerful conformation of the muscles of his arms and shoulders. He was flawless, wholesome, extraordinarily beautiful. He was central to her every sense. She let the scent of him wash over her. As he moved, the crisp black hairs on his forearms grazed her skin, making her shiver deliciously. Kissing his body was different to kissing his lips, it was so much more personal. She was finding out all there was to know about him. Each of his touches was like an act of worship, his fingertips so sure and clever. Moment by moment he was inflaming her, creating sensations unspeakably fine in every tiny part of her.

Luke's deep blue eyes took in a long lingering look all over her. In comparison to his, her skin was soft and creamy pale. 'You are beautiful,' Luke whispered through their heat, their passion, his hands expressing his love for her. 'Shaped in absolute perfection.'

Jo experienced another rush of desire, an unprecedented hunger. Surrendering to the emotion, she took his dominance, his physical strength. As he lay over her, they became lost in a stream of loving, of honouring, of total sacrifice that seemed to have no end.

Long after their sequence of blissful climaxes was over their touching and giving continued. 'You OK, my love?' Luke whispered.

She traced a finger down his gorgeous face. 'It was perfect, Luke. You're perfect.' She now totally understood Celia's choice to stay in her loneliness, wanting no one else after her lover's death. But that was because Celia had been so deeply in love with Sheridan Ustick no one else could have taken his place in her life.

Jo snapped her eyes shut, afraid to let Luke look into her eyes and read her thoughts. She recognised the truth behind her hunger for him was born out of more than a mutual enjoyment for love-making. She had never meant it to happen, and it scared her – she was in love with him. An aching sense of isolation overwhelmed her. She had prided herself on being in control of every aspect of her life but instead she had been naive, blind, foolish. To fall in love with such a restless spirit was going to cost her very dear. Luke had been honourable in pointing out the negative side of their involvement but to him this was just an affair. She should tell him to go, that it was over between them, and she would continue to do her best for Rex and Molly at the school. But she loved him and she couldn't bring herself to desert tiny, needy Marylyn. Until she was forced to she could not make these sacrifices.

Twenty-One

L uke hitched Lucky to his wagon at the back of the forge for the last time. When he came back to Parmarth from now on, he would stop at Cardhu.

He became aware two men were watching him.

'How're things with you then, Luke?' Keane Trevail asked with a false smile. His hands were stuck carelessly in his coat pockets but his watery eyes were sharp. His flat cap was pushed back from his brow.

His face expressionless, Luke closed the canvas at the back of the wagon then moved forward and readjusted the straps of Lucky's harness. 'Fine, thanks, Keane. Couldn't be better. How are you? And you, Lew?'

'Aw, got nothing to grumble about,' Keane said, attempting to swagger as in his younger days.

Lew gave a curt nod. 'Off on your travels again, I see. Where you doing business these days?'

'Oh, all over. Anywhere between St Ives and Penzance. Around Mount's Bay. Further afield.' Luke smiled coldly. He knew why the Trevails were here. They had bragged in the pub they were going to warn him off Jo. 'And Nance. I do a lot of business over at Nance.'

Lew's haughty sneer turned ugly. Springing towards Luke, finger pointing, he threatened, 'That's what we're here for, Vigus. To tell you to keep away from Jo Venner and don't have her in your house no more.'

Luke casually folded his arms, but his fists were balled. 'So you've finally worked up the courage to have your say, have you? It's none of your business. Now bugger off the pair of you, before you say something that'll make me really angry.'

'She's too good for the likes of you. People are talking about her. You'll ruin her reputation. We're not going until you swear to leave her alone,' Keane thundered, the effort making him cough hoarsely, 'or you'll be bleddy sorry.'

'No,' Luke stated harshly. 'If you set yourselves on me, it's you who'll be sorry. And what are you going to do anyway? An old invalid and his yellow-bellied son, who spends all his energy shagging anything in a skirt, including my whore of a mother. Have you forgotten, Lew, that you and Russell tried to turn me out of Parmarth when I first came here? Just because you didn't like the cut of me? I beat the guts out of the both of you then. Now, if you two don't want to make bigger fools of yourselves, get off home. And one more thing, leave Jo out of this.'

Luke's demeanour was so threatening, Lew threw an uncertain look at his father. He was not afraid of a fight, but Luke had a brutal way of grinding his fists into an opponent's body, and he could be handy with the hunter's knife he kept concealed about him. He could see it had been a stupid idea to confront Luke. Luke and Jo were both too headstrong to be chivvied away from anything they were set on. But Lew felt protective towards Jo. Everyone he had spoken to had agreed something should be done to distance her from this ne'er-do-well. Lew consoled himself that at least he and his father had made an attempt to shield Jo from any trouble.

Keane scowled at his elder son, feeling let down. If Lew had had half the grit of Jo Venner, he would have laid Vigus out in the dust.

To save face, he spat heavily on the cobbles. 'We've said our piece. If you've got one decent bone in your body you'll keep away from the maid. You're no bleddy good and never will be, and you've got no right to risk ruining her life. Reckon you'll be on your way for ever soon, and good riddance to you.' He jerked his head at Lew, and they slunk away.

Luke leapt up on the wagon, furious, indignant, hurt. He had no intention of ruining Jo's career, her life. It would be wise on Jo's part, however, to drop him. Perhaps, when he was back here, he'd find out she'd come to that decision. He hoped not. He'd never felt so close to a woman before. He'd

191

never needed one before to approve of him, admire him. Be in love with him. This last time they'd been together, something had happened to draw them closer, bound in some special way. Sort of bottomless, spiritual.

Closing his eyes he prayed in the way Gran had taught him. Please, God, make something happen to make it work.

One afternoon, after the children had been dismissed, Jo and Miss Teague sat opposite Marcus at his desk for the teachers' weekly meeting. Jo had a pen poised over a notebook and was making regular jottings as they discussed the merits and misdemeanours of various pupils.

Jo reported in disgust, 'Arnold Jelbert pushed muddy stones down the back of Molly's dress during playtime this afternoon. He never stops tormenting the poor girl.'

'I shall take it into account tomorrow when I speak to Arnold on another matter. Please remember, Miss Venner, that he is not responsible for all the mischief in the school,' Marcus said firmly. He had intimated before that he thought Joanna was getting somewhat overconcerned at Arnold's continual high jinks.

'It is bullying, Mr Lidgey,' she emphasised, 'and should not be tolerated.'

'I am not powerless to deal with it,' Marcus said rather curtly. Powerless only to break the cruel hold his mother had over him. He and Jo had been coolly polite in their communication over school affairs since his refusal to allow her to host parents' meetings at Nance. 'The school is the only place for such a consideration, and anyway, it would be a waste of time. The bi-annual meetings I trouble to take are very poorly attended.'

'We'll move on to the end-of-term Easter service,' Marcus said, glancing at his wristwatch.

'We always put a lot of effort into the school play, sports day and the celebrations for Empire Day,' Miss Teague told Jo. 'And we have a special Easter service, with a display of maypole dancing beforehand.'

'Do the parents attend, Mr Lidgey?' Jo enquired.

'They are invited but few bother to turn up.' He raised his dark eyes in a dismissive gesture she found greatly irritating. Not all the parents shared Jessie Vigus's attitude to parenthood, she would like to point out. Yesterday, Mr Moore had turned up at the school asking about a music scholarship for Adam; the fact that Adam did not possess the talent if a scholarship could be procured for him was not the point. She watched as Marcus tapped his fountain pen on the desk, was sure she heard him sigh.

Did he feel the children of Parmarth were not worth him keeping up his best efforts? To help her class with the art of conversation she had introduced a five-minute slot, twice a week, called 'Discussion time'. Miss Teague had raised her eyebrows at this. On the first occasion, Jo had brought up the subject of farming, inviting the children to contribute. Most of them had looked blank at what was required of them, so used were they to being told what they should think. Then Ann Markham had talked about how hard her father worked on Boswella Farm. Once the others realised they could say what they liked, and on subjects they could bring up themselves, Jo had encouraged them to let their imaginations fly. She had even got some of the shyer children talking to the class.

Marcus gave nothing away as he made his own notes. 'Miss Venner, you will supervise the building of an Easter garden. All classes can make paintings on seasonal subjects. The school orchestra will be employed and the vicar will end the occasion with prayers.' He gathered up his papers, putting them into his briefcase.

Jo understood his eagerness to go home. At dinner time, Eleanor had suffered greatly with pain in her back and her breathing had seemed troubled.

Molly was slow at putting on her coat and woollen bonnet, and Arnold Jelbert, Adam Moore and two other boys waylaid her at the school gates.

'Last out again,' Arnold jeered. It had been raining all day and he kicked icy water from a puddle at her legs. Molly wailed and the boys giggled. 'No one wants to walk home with you, Molly Vigus. You stink. You've got fleas.'

'Leave me alone,' Molly cried, 'Rex will be waiting for me.'

'No, he won't,' Arnold hissed. 'We told him you've gone on to Mrs Wherry's. He's doing the errands Luke left him. You're all alone with us, pissy-pants.'

Molly backed away. 'M-miss Venner and Mr Lidgey are inside. I'll scream and you'll be caned again.'

'Get her before she gives us away,' Arnold ordered his gang.

A grubby hand was clapped over her mouth, her arms were pinned behind her back and the four boys dragged her down to the bottom of the boys' playground. Molly was too scared to struggle. She went limp, eyes bulging with terror. She was brought to the slatted door of the coal house, a low building with a sloping roof, attached to the boys' block of toilets.

'We're going to throw you in there, Miss Pissy-pants,' Arnold sneered, 'where no one can smell you, you filthy pig.'

Gibberish emitted from Molly's throat. Urine trickled down her legs.

'You beastly bitch!' Arnold howled, yanking open the coal-house door. 'You deserve to be eaten up by the coal-house bogeyman. He won't leave a scrap of flesh on your bones. You'll be nothing but a skeleton, Molly Vigus, rattling round in the darkness for ever and ever.'

The boys threw Molly inside. 'L-let me g-go,' she pleaded, her arms outstretched as she tried desperately to get past them.

'Get in there!' Arnold roared, ripping the rabbit's-foot pendant from her neck and pushing her down on the coal heap.

The other three boys began to chorus, 'Pissy-pants! Pissy-pants!'

Molly was petrified, then Arnold ran at her and she found her legs and started scrabbling up the hill of coal. Slipping and sliding, her legs and hands were becoming scratched in her madness, and blackened blood trickled from the wounds.

194

Arnold slammed the door on her.

Jo was walking out of the teachers' entrance with Miss Teague, putting up her umbrella, when they heard the anguished screaming. It sounded like a child in abject fear. The two teachers traded worried glances, then thrusting her things into Miss Teague's hands, Jo ran in the direction of the screams.

She saw Arnold Jelbert and his gang banging and kicking on the coal-house door, shouting obscenities to someone they had imprisoned inside. Then she recognised Molly's terrified voice.

'Get away from there at once, you little savages!' Jo shrieked in shock and anger.

The boys scattered. She wrenched open the door and saw Molly crouched pathetically on the coal heap. Even in the dark confines and the girl's dirty state, Jo could see blood on Molly's hands and knees. She must have been trying frantically to escape the suffocating blackness.

Arnold and the three boys were about to slink off. Her feelings almost out of control, Jo grabbed Arnold's shoulder and shook him. 'How dare you hurt her like this, you little beast! I'll see you're punished more severely than you've ever been before.'

For one terrible moment she had the urge to slap the boy's smirking face. He was staring insolently at her, then her expression must have changed because he paled and began to tremble. She snatched Molly's pendant out of his hand. 'You're the most despicable child I have ever come across and you are a thief.'

'Let him go, Miss Venner,' Adam whimpered at her. 'We didn't mean her no harm.'

Before Jo could answer, her fingers were prised off Arnold's shoulder. Marcus pulled her away from the culprit. 'I'll deal with this, Miss Venner,' he said, stilling her protests with a look that had warning in it. 'You boys go home at once and tell your parents what you have done. I want you all in school early tomorrow morning. Miss Teague, escort them off the school grounds, please.'

Jo had not wasted any time. She was scrambling over the coal towards Molly. The little girl was sobbing pitiably. 'It's all right, Molly, dear. I'm coming for you. I'll take you home.'

Lifting Molly into her arms, she made the precarious journey back down the coal heap. Pieces of coal fell into her boots, ripped her stockings and savaged her feet.

Her eyes still ablaze with fury, she faced Marcus in the rain with Molly clasped against her.

'Give her to me,' he said.

She ignored his outstretched arms. She knew he was displeased with her reaction to Arnold's bullying. 'There's no point in us both getting dirty,' she said, scowling.

'Do as I say,' he ordered. 'She may need a doctor and there's a telephone in the schoolhouse.'

'She's my responsibility.' Molly was clinging to her and it would only add to her fears if she relinquished her. Jo desperately needed to take off her boots and tip out the coal hurting her feet. The rain was sending black rivulets of coal dust down over Molly's stricken face and Jo's hands and raincoat.

'Joanna, be sensible. You may be closely connected to the family but on these premises Molly is my responsibility. The Vigus house, I'm told, hasn't even got a proper kitchen sink in it and both you and Molly need attention.'

Miss Teague returned. 'Go to the schoolhouse, inform Sally Allett what's happened and instruct her to prepare the necessary ministrations for Molly and Miss Venner, please, Miss Teague,' Marcus said.

Miss Teague trotted off dutifully again.

'You can't carry Molly with your feet in agony,' Marcus said. His eyes had not left Jo's face, but he was aware of her resting first on one foot then the other.

Jo could not argue. In addition to nearly weeping over poor Molly's plight, she was fighting back tears of pain as the coal rubbed her raw flesh. With the greatest reluctance she made to hand Molly over to him.

When Marcus tried to receive her, Molly shrieked and put a stranglehold on Jo.

'It isn't going to work,' Jo cried, trying to loosen Molly's grip so she could breathe properly.

'Calm yourself, Joanna. Lean on me for support and I'll see to your boots.'

Lowering himself, he put an arm round Jo's waist. She rested against his shoulder, and he lifted each of her feet in turn, unlaced and took off her boots and tipped the coal out of them. The cold, wet, coal-dusty ground was less painful to her flesh as he put her feet down.

'There's too much grit inside your boots to enable you to walk in them,' he said, straightening up and keeping his arm round her. 'I'll carry you both.'

'But—'

He ignored her protest. Jo hoped no one saw them as he lifted her and Molly up into his arms, strode through the playground and took them round to the back of the schoolhouse.

Sally had the back-kitchen door open and ushered them into the kitchen. Beth was hovering, ready to be given orders. Marcus placed his light, double burden down carefully on to a chair which had been placed beside the table. Bowls of steaming water, towels and rags were waiting.

'Miss Teague,' Marcus said, 'would you mind making two more little journeys, please? To fetch the pair of shoes Miss Venner keeps in the school, then to go to Molly's home and fetch clean clothes for her.'

'Of course, Mr Lidgey,' and she hurried away again.

'I'll leave you in Sally's capable hands, Miss Venner,' he said, and Jo looked up from lifting dirty hair away from Molly's face to see his caring expression. It was how he looked at Eleanor, or was it? 'Before you leave I would like to see you in my study.' He asked Sally about Mrs Lidgey and was informed she was sleeping in her room, then he left the kitchen.

'Poor little mite,' Sally said as she knelt and undid the buttons of Molly's cardigan. 'Arnold Jelbert wants a good

197

belting.' Now the headmaster had gone, Molly became more pliable and allowed Sally to ease her off Jo's lap.

It was a great relief to have the clinging child's weight removed from her. Jo looked with dismay at her raincoat. 'It's ruined,' she sobbed angrily, wresting herself out of the garment.

'Here, Beth,' Sally said, 'you finish with Molly. She knows you better than me. Then give her an iced bun from the larder. Miss Venner needs my help.'

Molly stopped crying and went meekly to the quiet girl she trusted. Her eyes looked enormous and pathetic in her blackened face. Jo's heart lurched at the sight.

'Why are children so cruel?' she sighed as Sally helped her to remove her stockings. Jo flinched as the wounds on her feet stung in a bowl of warm water.

'We're all born with spite and malice inside us,' Sally said. Standing behind Jo, she pulled off her hat and tidied her hair.

'Her clothes won't be no good any more,' Beth said, holding the girl's ripped, coal-marked and urine-stained bundle at arm's length. 'What shall I do with them?'

'Burn them,' Jo instructed. 'Thankfully they aren't her best clothes and she's got other things to wear.'

When Molly was washed and wrapped in towels, her cuts and grazes bathed and dabbed with iodine, and Jo's feet were attended to, Miss Teague, flushed and excited, came back with the results of her errands. 'I had to fetch Rex from Mrs Wherry's to get the clothes. I couldn't make their mother understand why I was there. He was about to come looking for Molly. I've brought you my summer coat to borrow for your journey home, Miss Venner.'

'Thank you, Miss Teague. I'll return your coat tomorrow.' Jo was grateful the incident was coming to an end.

'Mrs Wherry will be here shortly to take Molly to her house.' As there was nothing else Miss Teague could do, she went straight to the sweet shop, to inform Paula Hadley about something odd Jessie Vigus had said to her.

Mrs Wherry came in through the back door a few minutes

later. 'I heard Arnold howling as I passed the Jelberts,' she said. 'Sounds like Abner's giving the little brute just what he deserves.' She waited for Beth to complete getting Molly dressed. 'Are you all right, Miss Venner?'

'I am now, thank you, Mrs Wherry. Sally's just making me a cup of tea and then I have to see Mr Lidgey. I'll come to your house in a while, if I may.'

'You're very welcome. You look quite worn out by what's happened. Make sure you get some rest.' Mrs Wherry left with Molly, who, still trembling from her ordeal, was nibbling on her iced consolation.

Beth, who had made no comment throughout the entire proceedings, soothing Molly and working in her calm methodical way, cleared away the bowls of dirty water then resumed her chores in the back kitchen.

Sally sat down at the table and poured tea for Jo and herself.

'I think Mr Lidgey will take me to task.' Jo sighed wearily. 'He was angry at the way I lost my temper with Arnold.'

Sally put her head to the side, holding her cup midway to her lips. 'And I bet he won't do anything of the sort,' she said bitterly. 'He'll be all sweetness and light to you.'

'Why do you say that?' Jo frowned at the maid's tartness.

'For someone as intelligent as you are, you can't see what's standing out a mile, can you? He wants you.'

'You are mistaken, Sally,' Jo replied crossly. This sort of jealous spite was the last thing she needed. Right now she was feeling responsible for Molly's plight, having promised Luke she would ensure the children would come to no harm at school.

'You'll see. He'll be making a move on you soon.'

'You have an overactive imagination. He wouldn't do anything of the kind.'

'Oh, wouldn't he?' Sally scoffed. 'He has a great appetite for that side of life. He made advances to me the first night I slept in this house.' She went bright red and glanced down in her cup. 'He succeeded and I've been keeping him happy until recently, when I realised there was no

199

future in it. He's after you, believe me. It's what his mother wants too.'

'Mrs Lidgey is an old lady, and old ladies who have nothing to occupy themselves tend to shore up romantic notions.'

'If you don't take me seriously then you're already a lost cause. I know him, he'll take a risk of this kind but he'll be very careful not to do anything you could complain about. His sort are good at covering things up. You can please yourself, but for your own good, keep your distance from him. You've too much to lose. He's certainly not worth it.'

'Thank you for being honest with me, Sally. For telling me how you see things, but you have no need to be concerned about me.' She eased on her shoes and picked up her handbag, umbrella and Miss Teague's coat. 'I'll go to the study now.'

Walking gingerly, she paused at the door. 'Sally, you gave me a warning, perhaps you'll allow me to give you one. Be careful of Russell Trevail. He can be cruel, he hurt me not so very long ago.'

'I can handle him. Sometimes a woman has to settle for what she can get, but not you. You could do really well for yourself.' Sally's aggressiveness eased a little. 'While we're on the subject of men, remember that Luke Vigus isn't the right man for you either. And before you protest there's nothing going on between you, it's all round the village that there is. I don't understand why you're wasting your time with him.'

Faced with the fact that the truth was known Jo made no denial. 'Luke is a good man, Sally.'

Jo had no idea how much her expression, as she mentioned Luke's name, gave her feelings away. Sally shook her head. 'Well, fancy that. You're in love with Luke. His nibs doesn't stand a chance with you after all.'

'I won't deny I'm in love with Luke. The gossips might as well get their facts right about our relationship, but I'll confide this in you, Sally: there could never be anything of that nature between Mr Lidgey and me.'

A minute later Jo knocked on the study door and went inside.

Marcus rose from his desk, where he had been filling in the school log. 'Are you feeling better, Joanna?'

'I'm perfectly all right, thank you, Marcus. About Arnold—'

'I'll call on his parents this evening,' he said. 'You must try not to let your emotions run away with you. You have a tendency to do that.'

Jo offered no response. Her emotions were not his affair.

'Sit by the fire.' Marcus smiled warmly. 'You're shaking. You're welcome to stay and have supper with us.' He was journeying back to the feel of her in his arms. Twice now he had held her against his body. The first time had led to arousal but this time he had kept control. Even so, he could not aspire to marry her. She was too good for him. His mother would have to think of another evil plan to reverse her fortunes. Even if he could persuade Joanna to become his partner, he distrusted himself not to abuse her in the years ahead. He knew Luke Vigus meant something to her; even that scoundrel was more worthy of her than he was.

Now came another injustice, another aching void to add to his perpetual distress. Suddenly he knew he was in love with her and must keep his feelings a secret. Being alone with Joanna was a sweet torment, but he must settle for being only her friend.

'Thank you, but I really just want to go home to Nance.'

'Mama will be disappointed.'

'I shall see Eleanor tomorrow. I've promised to help her sift through her wardrobe and bring out her cooler clothes ready for the better weather.'

'That is very good of you.'

He was making polite conversation, even seemed a little uncomfortable with her. However he had behaved with Sally and his previous paramours, Jo was confident she would never find him a threat.

'When are you to move into Miss Sayce's house?'

'Quite soon. It may seem strange but I'm not in a great hurry to leave Nance. I've really enjoyed living there.'

'Not at all. Miss Merrick has been a loyal friend to you.

201

I've never had a friend, except for you.' He looked down at the floor.

'One day I'm sure things will get better for you, Marcus. If I can do anything to help . . .'

'Just play along with my mother's belief that we're closer than we really are. I swear I shall never ask anything more of you, Joanna.'

While a frowning Rex and a mournful Molly, who gave an occasional sob, tucked into the tea Mrs Wherry served them, Jo cradled Marylyn in her arms.

'Molly's got deep scratches on her hands and knees and she's still in shock.' Mrs Wherry stroked the little girl's shoulder. 'She won't be able to go to school tomorrow. She can come in here with me and Marylyn.'

'Thank you, Mrs Wherry,' Jo said, crooning to the baby, who was daily growing healthier under the other woman's care. Molly would never catch up on her lessons, but right now she needed mothering rather than schooling.

''Tis time the 'master did something about that Jelbert boy.' Mrs Wherry bustled to the table with more food; the children were getting good value for Luke's three shillings a week. 'Before Arnold does something really dreadful to her. Dear little maid's got enough to put up with, having no father and a useless mother. I'm glad Luke's pulling himself together at last and taking proper place as head of the household, but he isn't always here. I s'pose Arnold took advantage of him being away. Luke would've boxed his ears. When's he coming back?'

'I don't know,' Jo said, kissing the tiny face that so closely resembled Lew's. Marylyn gurgled contentedly.

'Thought he'd have told you that,' Mrs Wherry said, standing back from the table to get a better view of Jo's face.

Jo ignored the remark. She was not about to suffer another warning over Luke.

'He'll be back when he's sold all that scrap metal he bought,' Rex piped up, helping himself to more bread to wipe round his soup bowl. He eyed Jo in an acerbic manner. 'I'm in charge when he's gone.'

'Of course you are, Rex,' Jo said, hoping the confidence she showed in the boy would lead to her gaining his trust. Rex had still not forgiven her over his caning. Understandable with the injustices he had borne in his seven years.

'Can I get you something to eat, Miss Venner?' Mrs Wherry asked kindly. 'I can reheat the soup.'

'No, thank you. I must be going soon.' Jo cuddled Marylyn in tighter, reluctant to let her go, wishing she had more time to spend with her. She left with only a simple goodbye to Rex and Molly. Rex would have baulked at a fuss and Molly looked to Mrs Wherry for the reassurance she needed outside the school premises.

Jo decided to call on Jessie Vigus, to discover what effect her drinking was having on her. She opened the door to the cottage.

Jessie was downstairs, slumped on the couch in her tatty blue dressing gown, a half-filled gin bottle clutched in one greasy paw, but looking reasonably sober. The appalling smells of stale alcohol and her unwashed body stretched across the room, which despite Beth's efforts was none too clean and tidy.

'Hello, Jessie. How are you?'

It took a few moments for the alcoholic to register Jo's presence. 'Why ask?' Her voice was sarcastic and sharp, not its usual drunken slur. 'Who do you think you are, coming here with your hoity-toity voice and ways. You don't give a damn about me, do you, you uppity bitch?'

Jo looked at her dispassionately. 'No, not really.'

'Where're my children?'

'Luke's away working. The little ones are safe with Mrs Wherry.'

'Safe? Safe from what?'

'I'd better go.'

'Safe from me, that's what you meant,' Jessie screeched, levering herself up from the couch. Jo was unprepared for her fleetness as she charged at her. Jessie grabbed her by the head with her free hand, dislodging her hat and yanking on her hair. 'You interfering bitch! You've stolen my kids. You've made Luke hate me.'

Jo gagged on the woman's sour breath and pushed her away. Unsteady, Jessie hit the floor in a heap. Gin slopped out of the bottle and she wailed as she righted it. She took a long swig of the pale greenish liquid, then swore profanely at Jo. 'You'll come to grief one day. You'll get what you deserve.'

'I did not take your children away from you,' Jo hissed. 'If you were a proper mother instead of a drunken slut they'd be with you now.'

'Think you're spotless, don't you?' Jessie's voice rose insanely where she lay sprawled on her back. 'Well, let me tell you this, Miss Lady Muck, you're no better'n me. You dangle your bait in front of men, you're a whore just like the rest of us. I know what you do with my son.'

Snatching up her hat, Jo ran out of the cottage with the woman's demented screams chasing after her. 'You're a whore, Joanna Venner!'

'Good heavens! What's happened?' Davey Penoble came out of the forge. Alarmed at Jo's flushed face and tangled hair, he noted the unfamiliar coat she was wearing.

'Do you know what that wretched woman in there has just called me?' she fumed. 'A whore! I don't mind her calling me an interfering bitch, but not a whore. How do I deserve that label?'

'Simple enough,' Davey said soothingly. 'She struck out at what she knew would rile you most. You're honest and decent, the exact opposite of her. Don't let it upset you.'

'Well, it has, especially coming so quickly after Arnold Jelbert terrorising poor little Molly again. Have you heard about it?'

'Of course, it's all round the village.' There was also talk of how one day soon Jo would come to regret her association with every member of the Vigus family.

Davey's company as he walked beside her up the hill was

204

comforting. It made Jo realise just how much she was missing Luke, who occupied nearly all her thoughts. Where was he? What was he doing? She could hardly wait to be close to him again.

Twenty-Two

'When are you and that Venner girl going to announce your engagement?' Eleanor snarled from her bed. She was wrapped up tightly in the sheets.

'All in good time, Mama.' Marcus looked down on her coldly from the foot of the bed.

'I understand, my darling boy.' She smiled whimsically. 'Joanna will take a while to harness. I'm very tired. Kiss me goodnight and let me get my rest.'

Marcus abhorred the very thought of touching her marble-cold skin, but she was offering him an early escape tonight. A swift peck on her cheek and he could get away, perhaps enjoy a quiet drink in the pub.

The instant he bent his head to kiss her, Eleanor whipped out the silver-backed hairbrush she had hidden under the bedcovers and brought it down viciously on the side of his head. With her other hand she grasped his groin, squeezing and twisting his most tender flesh.

He yelled in pain and humiliation, struggling to wrest the hairbrush out of her hand while fighting off her vice-like grip on his body.

'You vile bitch!' he wailed.

At last, the almost superhuman strength Eleanor had called upon deserted her. She dropped the hairbrush, but not before she had beaten him on the chest with it and rammed the handle into his stomach.

Marcus leapt back in panic, unable to catch his breath. His mother was the epitome of all things corrupt and evil. Now was the time to rid himself of this lump of debased filth.

Rearing towards the bed, he yanked the top pillow out from

under her, making her head jerk to the side. He thought he had broken her neck, achieved his aim, but she rolled her head and sour-sweet breath puttered out between her lips. He threw the pillow over her face.

A pain shot through his guts as if they had been penetrated by a red-hot arrow. She had hurt him more than he'd thought. Groaning in agony, he doubled over, slipping to the floor. His eyes closed and his senses left him.

When he came to, his mother had managed to replace the pillow under her head. She looked serene, her gleaming hair formed around her head like a halo, as if to mock him. 'You haven't got the courage, you bastard. Make sure you have good news for me soon. Now get out and lick your wounds elsewhere. You make me sick.'

Stumbling to his room he lay in torment on the bed. Hours passed. Sally retired without calling goodnight to him. She had as little as possible to do with him these days. Marcus was utterly panic-stricken. When she married Russell Trevail and left the schoolhouse, how would he cope with his mother? He could not bear to do the intimate services required by an invalid. His mother would enjoy making him perform every unpleasant task, and she would turn them into something else, something sordid and unthinkable. Yet how could she? She was old, in constant pain and becoming frail. She should not be able to make him do anything unless he wanted to. But she had power over him. A little while ago, he could have suffocated her. Not meekly left her room. His mother would never die. She would never leave him in peace. He sank into despair. Contemplated killing himself.

Finally he rose, stripped and washed his abused body, almost scrubbing off his flesh in a crazed attempt to purge the corruption his mother had left on him and in every fibre of his being. Then dressing in clean clothes, he crept outside to his car and drove about all night.

'Jo! You'll be late if you don't get a move on,' Mercy yelled up the stairs.

After a restless night, Jo awoke slowly, at first thinking

Mercy's voice was part of her nightmare, in which Jessie Vigus murdered her children, including Luke, in a drunken rage. Then Eleanor Lidgey was rearing over her on two good legs, forcing her to put on a black wedding dress and walk up St Lubias's aisle to marry Marcus. When she reached Marcus's side he had contorted like a changeling, and she had been faced with a small frightened boy as her bridegroom. His pitiful weeping had left her feeling darkly troubled.

Reading the time on her little clock, she threw back the covers and scrambled out of bed. Splashing water over her face, she dressed hurriedly.

Mercy popped her head round the door. 'Be careful, my handsome, when you walk to school today. Lew's just come in and said he's found a dead sheep. Been savaged. Looks like a rogue dog done it. If it's hungry, it's possible it might attack someone.'

'I'm sorry, Mercy. It's one more worry for you hard-working farmers,' Jo sympathised. She pulled a chunky cardigan out of a drawer; it was a lovely spring day and it would do in place of Miss Teague's coat. She realised then she had left her ruined raincoat in the schoolhouse. 'I hope this will be a better day than yesterday,' she muttered grumpily. 'Has the postman called?'

'Yes, nothing for you though. Surely you're not expecting Luke to write to you?' Mercy replied brusquely.

Jo ignored her.

'I've got your breakfast ready. If you hurry you'll just be on time.'

'Thanks, Mercy, you're a gem.'

Mercy heard something and left the room. She called out from the landing window. 'You might not have to rush after all. Your headmaster's just pulled up in his car.'

'Oh? I hope nothing's wrong. Eleanor hasn't been well lately. She spends most of the time in bed now. Mercy, will you show him inside, please?'

Mercy did as she was asked, then went outside to supervise Kizzy Kemp in the dairy.

Jo joined Marcus in the kitchen. He was standing, head

slightly bowed amid the hotchpotch of furniture. 'Good morning, Marcus. Is Eleanor ill?'

'Good morning, Joanna. I hope you don't mind me calling on you. Mama had a bad night. I've had no sleep. I had to get out and clear my head. I've been driving around and stopped here on the way back.'

'Are you well?' She went closer to him. He was ashen and she spied a livid red mark beside his ear. 'You're hurt. How did it happen?'

'Arnold Jelbert has started bullying me.' He smiled. It was a wan and sickly smile, and Jo wasn't fooled by the joke.

'Marcus, tell me what happened.'

He could not meet her eyes. 'Sometimes Mama can't help herself and she lashes out.' He pressed both hands to his face, clearly embarrassed. 'I'm sorry, I shouldn't bother you with my troubles. I should have driven past the farm.'

'No, I'm glad you're here. We're friends and I'd like to help. Mercy's just made me some breakfast. Why don't you join me?'

He hesitated and she held out her hand to him. He gripped it quickly, as if she had thrown him a lifeline, and he allowed her to lead him to a chair.

Kip and Hunter pattered into the room and while they sniffed and examined the newcomer, Marcus responded to them wholeheartedly.

'The dogs like you.' Jo poured tea for them both and offered him the plateful of thick wedges of toast and marmalade Mercy had left for her.

'Thank you. As a child, I always wanted a dog. Mama would never let me have one.'

'You could have one sometime in the future,' Jo said. 'It will give you something to look forward to.'

'Yes, I could,' he said. 'Thank you, Joanna. You give me hope.' He consumed his part of the breakfast in reflective silence, and Jo sensed it best to leave him to unwind with his thoughts. She slipped out of the room to collect her hat.

When she returned, ready for the drive to school, Hunter

suddenly jumped up and put his heavy front paws on Marcus's chest. It snapped him out of his morbid cogitation over last night's humiliation and he was able to laugh. 'Perhaps I will get a dog one day. A faithful companion like Hunter or Kip is just what I need.'

As they drove to the village the sun was caressingly hot. Birds were singing, the verges were awash with celandines and wild garlic, and gorse was splashing its vivid gold on bank, field and roughland. Tangy moorland scents were scattered on the crisp breeze. The wildlife settled the spirits of the man and woman in the motorcar.

'There's something I have to tell you,' Marcus said. 'The authorities have contacted me about the Vigus children's attendance at school and I have replied that all is satisfactory in that respect. It's entirely your doing, Joanna. I do admire you.'

'Thank you. I want to do my best for all the children. Ann Markham is particularly bright. I'd like to talk to her parents about a scholarship to grammar school.'

'I wouldn't advise it. It would be unrealistic. You'd only build up the girl's hopes for nothing and put an unfair burden on her family. Her parents could not afford the extra finance for her uniform, books and things. I've talked to two fathers about sending their sons to study mining at Camborne. It would give them a good future, even though it would almost certainly mean them moving overseas to achieve success. Both men said it was out of the question.'

'Perhaps something could be set up to help children like Ann and the two boys. Miss Sayce left me some money. Would you support me if I set up a trust fund?'

'If you're sure it's what you want to do, I shall be totally behind you.' It suited him to think of her money being used to benefit the children of Parmarth rather than to finance his mother's wantonly sought exit from the moors.

'I want so much for him to get married,' Eleanor said, propped up against her pillows.

210

After taking tea with Eleanor, Jo was emptying her wardrobe, laying the winter garments in a trunk, which Sally and Beth had dragged in from the boxroom.

'I'm sure Marcus will find the right woman one day,' Jo replied, putting a fur coat into the trunk.

'He already has. You, Joanna. You're perfect for each other. When are you going to realise it?'

'Marcus and I haven't known each other long, Eleanor,' Jo hedged. The pretence with Marcus that they were on closer terms was becoming increasingly awkward. Was it right to lie to an old woman to make her final years more comfortable? To feed her false hopes? And it was only a matter of time before Eleanor got to hear of her relationship with Luke. Recalling how miserable Marcus was this morning, and believing Eleanor might have struck him partly out of frustration that there was not yet an announcement, she decided to tell her the truth.

She approached the bed. 'Eleanor, Marcus and I are close friends, but I don't think there will ever be anything more between us. You see, I've formed an attachment with another man and I love him very much.'

'You mean the rumours about you and that gipsy are true? You have no intention of marrying my son?' Eleanor's eyes enlarged to twice their normal size and glittered strangely.

Jo backed away. Eleanor was frightening. 'No. I'm sorry if that was the impression I've been giving.'

'You little bitch! You've been enjoying the hospitality of my house and all the time you've been playing me for a fool. Isn't my son good enough for you? You won't find another of his calibre prepared to marry a plain little shrew like you, with a common whore for a mother and a trollop as a best friend!'

Shocked at Eleanor's malice, Jo somehow managed to keep her composure. 'Well, you've certainly revealed your true colours, Eleanor Lidgey. I've always thought there was something wrong here, now I know what it is. It's you. You're selfish, mean and spiteful.'

Jo expressed her next thought angrily. 'Was it you who spread the gossip about Celia Sayce?'

'Yes and I'm proud of it. Communities should know what sort of people they have living among them. Now get out of my house, Joanna Venner, before I throw something at you.'

Twenty-Three

'Look in particular for anything you're unfamiliar with, children, and we'll try to identify it together later,' Jo instructed her class.

She had taken the children a little way on to the moor for a nature study. Some of the children had sketchbooks and pencils for drawing the rocks, flora and wildlife, others were making notes. A few had old toffee tins to carry back specimens or jars to collect frog spawn. She had shown them where she remembered looking among the stones of the Cornish hedges for signs of stoats and weasels. They'd all had fun sending sticks and leaves down the stream which trickled slowly down the valley.

'Can some of us climb to the top of Fox Tor, Miss Venner?' Arnold asked politely, a tactic he had acquired, for Jo could be very strict with him. 'I can draw a good picture of the whole village up there.'

'We're studying nature, Arnold,' Jo reminded him firmly.

'There's some funny-looking moss up there. I can draw that. And I bet there'd be grubs under the stones. We can bring some back to examine.' He turned on an innocent expression.

Jo knew he and the more energetic children were excited to be out of the classroom and needed to spend their energy. It would be wise to allow Arnold, and those he stirred into mischief, to wander the short distance rather than risk them picking on Molly. Always nervous, Molly was keeping very close to Jo, and had already received jibes for putting nothing more exciting than grass in her toffee tin. She was more interested in the picture of the two fluffy white kittens on the lid.

'Very well, Arnold, but I shall expect good results from you and those who accompany you. You must keep in sight at all times. When I wave my handkerchief, you must come back at once.'

Nine boisterous children, including Rex, began the scramble for the small tor up ahead. The remainder of the class scoured the immediate vicinity, where the stream formed a pool, offering a habitat to a large quantity of unhatched tadpoles.

Sitting on a granite boulder where she could observe all her class's activities, Jo sketched a pile of flat discus-like heavy stones, which nature had arranged one on top of another and which were encrusted by an interesting skeletal bright red lichen.

Molly perched on a smaller boulder nearby and drifted off into a daydream.

Jo pointed to a patch of sphagnum moss. 'Why not put some of that in your tin, Molly?'

The little girl looked at her vacantly for a moment then obeyed, soon drifting off into her own little world again. Jo let her be. She drew Molly sitting on the boulder, with the stream in the background. Molly looked tranquil in a yellow dress and white cardigan, a large gold-coloured ribbon fluttering in the breeze on top her head.

It was calm and peaceful, the sky was pale blue with soft white clouds gently skimming the heavens. The breeze was warm and ambrosial. For many of the children this was being taught at its best. They would gain nothing from the nature study itself, indeed they already knew all the names of the specimens they were drawing and collecting, but the occasion would stay in their memories as pleasant and worthwhile for all time. A short escape from the harsh realities of life.

Ann Markham whispered in Jo's ear, 'Miss Venner, look over there.'

'I see it. Thank you, Ann.'

A hundred yards away, Mavis Best had discovered a hare hiding in a boat-shaped depression of its own making. Mavis was standing absolutely still and the hare was lying motionless, its long black-tipped ears held back, its huge

214

yellow eyes wide open. Turning swiftly to a new page of her sketchbook, Jo dashed off a drawing of the girl and the hare. Suddenly the hare sprang up and made its escape, its long brown body quickly disappearing behind a blaze of gorse.

'Did you see it?' Mavis delightedly called to her teacher and friends.

'We did,' Jo replied, holding up her sketchbook for Mavis to see. 'And I've got a good drawing of you both.'

A strange panting sound suddenly came from behind Jo. Molly turned round first and then screamed, leaping towards Jo and grabbing her skirt. A quiver of fear leapt up Jo's spine.

A large black shaggy-coated dog with a white front and white-tipped tail was creeping up on them on its haunches, in the way of a collie stalking livestock. The dog was slavering, its long tongue hanging out over sharp yellow teeth. There was dried blood on its jaws and the whiteness of its heaving chest. The creature was hungry and dangerous.

'Quickly, children, get behind me and we'll try to back away from it,' Jo said urgently, pushing Molly behind her. Molly was sobbing in terror.

At the sound of Jo's voice, the dog mounted menacingly on all fours, snarling and growling low in its throat. Jo wondered frantically if any of the children had something to eat on them which she could throw to the dog. She took one step backwards and the dog, gnashing its awesome teeth, leapt forward several inches. Any moment now and it would launch itself on her or one of the children.

'Run, children! Run away quickly!' she shouted, thrusting Molly's hands from her skirt. Rushing forward, screaming at the top of her voice, she waved her sketchbook in the air then threw it at the dog. Chaos broke out. The children, except for Molly, who curled up on the ground in a frightened ball, and Norman Pascoe, who would not get far with his stick, ran away screaming and shrieking for help.

The dog barked and snarled. Shouting and screaming at it, Jo picked up anything to hand and hurled it at her attacker, praying it would send the creature scurrying away. Stones and twigs landed hopelessly in front of the dog. One stone hit its chest and it yelped in pain. Then, in fury, it propelled itself in the air straight at Jo.

Jo ran, in a direction away from the children. Using all her experience of the moor, she leapt from boulder to grassy tussock, careful not to imprison her feet in a rabbit hole or trip over a root, but she knew she could not outpace the dog. She heard its heavy breathing and its pounding paws gaining on her. Closer and closer. The dog's teeth clamped over the hem of her skirt and she was nearly shaken off balance.

Screaming in panic, she tore on in desperate flight and the hem tore free.

Vaguely she was aware of more children's screams, then a barrage of stones just missing her. Arnold, Rex and the others had scrambled down from the tor and were throwing missiles at the dog.

'Get out the way, miss!' Arnold shouted shrilly.

Jo veered to the side and, still running, glanced round to see what was happening, fearful for the children. She stopped. Panting, she watched in horror, then relief, as Arnold, Rex and their companions, whooping and catcalling, bombarded the rogue dog with rocks and stones. Finally, growling and yelping, it slunk away, seeking refuge on the open moor.

'Miss Venner!' Rex ran to her. 'Are you hurt?'

Jo's arms were reaching out to him and the other children. Her eyes filled with tears. 'Is everyone all right? Was anyone hurt?'

Nine small pairs of hands were comforting her. 'We're fine, thanks to you,' Rex said. 'You saved the others. You were some brave.'

'It's you children who were brave,' Jo breathed emotionally. 'We'd better get back to the others and then hurry to the school. We must reach safety in case the dog returns.'

'If it does it'll get more stones chucked at it,' Arnold threatened dramatically. 'Three cheers for Miss Venner.'

Jo was powerless to stop the children's noisy exhilaration. It would take hours for them to calm down. There would be many excited and outlandish accounts of the dog's attack in the homes of Parmarth this evening.

Jo gathered all her class together, and holding Molly's hand and her ruined sketchbook she led them back to the school, all nervously straining their eyes for signs of the wild dog. Long before they reached the protection of the school walls, a party of adults, Marcus at the head, came to meet them. Abner Jelbert had a shotgun hanging over his arm. The children whose parents were present ran to meet them.

Marcus rushed to Jo. 'We heard the commotion all over the valley. What happened?'

Before Jo could relate the tale, Arnold piped up, 'That dog what's been killing the sheep attacked us. Miss Venner saved us by making it run after her. It nearly tore her skirt off.'

'Good heavens!' Marcus gasped, louder than all the other exclamations that ensued. Jo's face was red and perspiring. Taking her sketchbook from her, he gave her his arm and escorted her to the school.

After a debriefing, which the worried parents piled into the school to listen to, Marcus dismissed all classes for the day. The children were divided into groups, with an adult to oversee them safely home. Joel Willis was not expected back from the Carn Valley Stamp until late so Miss Teague took Kenneth to her cottage.

Jo kept Rex and Molly with her. Rex stood guard over her and Molly clung to her hand. 'I can hardly believe it's happened,' Jo said, when Marcus returned from the school gates. 'One moment we were all enjoying the afternoon and the next we were in deadly danger. I must tell Mercy about the attack as soon as possible.'

'I've seen to that. Russell Trevail was on his way to the schoolhouse to see Sally. I've asked him to send Beth here to take Rex and Molly along to her mother's house. Trevail has gone on to Nance Farm. He said his aunt would organise a hunt for the dog. Every available man and gun will be abroad until the creature is caught.'

Beth arrived. 'Thank you, Beth,' Marcus said. 'I'm sure your mother won't mind receiving the children early today.'

'Of course she won't,' Beth said. 'Sally's making tea. I'm sure Miss Venner could do with a hot sweet cup for the shock.'

'Thank you, but I don't want to leave Rex and Molly,' Jo said, shivering violently.

'You're in no state to care for the children,' Marcus said, pulling Molly away from her. 'They'll be fine with Mrs Wherry. You can see them later.'

Jo was feeling faint and reluctantly admitted the sense of his words. After persuading Molly to go with Rex and Beth, promising she would join them shortly, she walked with Marcus to his sitting room.

Sitting on the sofa, she sipped the tea Sally had left for them, the cup rattling on the saucer as her hand trembled. 'I've never been so scared in all my life. If it wasn't for Rex and Arnold and the others I could have been torn to pieces and then the creature might have gone after one of them.'

'But it didn't and apart from being badly shaken you're safe.' Marcus was standing close at her side. 'Would you like a little brandy?'

Not wanting any more tea, she passed him the crockery. 'No, thank you. I'll be fine when I've stopped shaking.'

'I'll drive you home when you're ready.'

'Thank you, Marcus.' Leaning towards him she rested her face against his arm.

She did not hear him catch his breath, nor was she aware of him fighting his confusion. Should he shift away from her or was he able to innocently give her the comfort she was seeking? A vision of his mother jeering at his dilemma filled his mind. Before meeting Joanna he had never been plagued with the torment that he might hurt a woman. But he had deliberately hurt Sally. He was in love with Joanna. Would it make a difference?

He sat beside her and tentatively put his arms around her, but stayed a little remote, concentrating on his breathing to still his thumping heart. She stayed against him for two, long, bitter-sweet minutes, in which neither spoke or moved,

218

in which he triumphed, which in turn gave him hope that a small part of him somewhere was wholesome.

Sitting back against the sofa, Jo said, 'Your mother may not be pleased that I'm here, even in the circumstances. Has she been giving you a difficult time?'

'Telling her the truth was the best thing you could have done,' he said softly. Eleanor had hardly spoken to him since Jo's revelation. 'Mama will come round when she's over the disappointment of there being no chance of a romantic union between us.' It hurt him to actually put it into words.

'I suppose she's clingy because you're her only child.' To avoid upsetting Marcus, Jo had not revealed the extent of Eleanor's spite to her. 'Miss Teague keeps asking me why I don't take tea here any more.'

'I'd noticed that.' Marcus smiled. 'I've explained it's because of my mother's failing health.' If only it would fail more quickly. Sometimes Marcus suspected Eleanor was only pretending to be in such pain in order to spring some despicable surprise on him.

'I think I'd like to see Rex and Molly now, and then go home to Nance if it's convenient.'

'Of course, but you may find yourself alone. I shall be happy to stay with you.'

'Thank you, you're so kind.' Jo shivered again and looked wistful. 'I wish Luke was here.'

'I'll see you to Mrs Wherry's, then get the car ready,' Marcus said in an efficient tone. Every time she mentioned Luke Vigus, his views on the roughcast dealer plagued the tip of his tongue, but Joanna would fight off his condemnation of the man in her life every bit as fiercely as she'd fought off the wild dog.

Twenty-Four

V ery awkwardly, grimacing in pain, Eleanor sat up in bed and rang her bell insistently.

Sally walked into her bedroom, a minute later. 'Yes, Mrs Lidgey?'

'I want to get out of bed and get dressed, Sally. I'll wear my green crêpe dress.'

'Has the pain eased at last?' Sally asked, pausing at the wardrobe door.

'It's bearable.'

'It's a pity the doctor couldn't do more for you. It's not right you should have to go on suffering like this.'

'We're all a martyr to something,' Eleanor snapped. If she and Marcus weren't so damned strapped for cash she could consult a top specialist. The country doctor who came over from Pendeen was dithering, apologetic and almost useless. Her body had long mastered the analgesic he prescribed. She had considered obtaining a herbal remedy from Mardie Dawes but did not trust the woman to give her something non-addictive.

'Is there any news of Luke Vigus?' she enquired. She did so every day.

'Not yet. I saw Jo Venner coming out the side door of the pub last night. I think she was waiting for a phone call from him. She was looking disappointed. He'll stay away for as long as he can. The green crêpe dress, you said?'

'Yes, it will do, dear. And my jet brooch. What do you think of this romance between those two, Sally?'

'Best of luck to her. She'll need it with him. Luke's a heartbreaker. Mind you, I should think she'll soon get over it. If she can fight off a wild dog she should be able to cope with anything.'

'You admire the girl? I thought you considered her a snob and was glad I no longer entertain her.'

'To be honest I don't like her much but, yes, I do admire her. She's done something with her life.'

'She was fortunate to have been born into a well-to-do family. You have always had to work hard, Sally.'

For less restriction, Eleanor wore few undergarments. Sally passed her a pair of French knickers, in feminine ivory silk and lace, then fastened her stockings with garters decorated with hand-made rosettes. Eleanor gingerly smoothed a full silk slip over her damaged hip, willing the pain shooting up through her spine to ease. Sally fastened the row of glass buttons at the back of the dress, then opening Eleanor's jewellery box, took out the oval-shaped jet brooch, surrounded by tiny diamonds. Eleanor pinned it to the left side of the white tie on her dress.

Sally's eyes lingered on the brooch.

Eleanor touched it. 'You like this, don't you? It's your favourite among my jewellery.'

'It's beautiful,' Sally said wistfully. Russell had given her an engagement ring but it was only a second-hand one he had bought off a tinker, and not very big or pretty.

'It's worth a lot of money. It's a pity I have no one to leave it to.' As Sally rose, after putting Eleanor's shoes on her, Eleanor reached for her hand. 'You deserve a reward for all the hard work you've done for me. I know I can be a trying old woman at times.'

Sally could not disguise her hopes. 'You mean . . . ?'

'I never forget people who are loyal to me. I'm going to confide in you, Sally, the reason why I don't like having the Venner woman in my house. My son was hoping to marry her. She flirted shamelessly with him, building up his hopes, then cast him aside like a scrap of rubbish for this fling with that no-account bastard gipsy. Marcus has taken it very hard. I'm becoming increasingly worried about him. He's taken to spending less time with me and I can't read his moods as I

221

used to. He either plays his music for hours or wanders off on the moor alone, and I'm terrified until he comes back while that savage creature is still at large. Could I ask you to keep an eye on him and report back to me what he does, where he goes? And watch that little flibbertigibbet too? I don't want her upsetting him again.'

Sally's eyes were glued to the brooch. The money from the sale of the exquisite piece of jewellery would set her and Russell up for life. It would be easy money, there was very little she could report. Marcus behaved impeccably towards Jo. There was no evidence of Jo ever playing games with Marcus's heart. As with any woman foolishly in love with an unsuitable man she was quietly waiting for Luke to come back. Sally would have to be careful not to cause trouble for Jo. No one approved of her romance with Luke, but she was quite the heroine in the village since saving the children from the savage dog.

'I'll do anything I can to ease your burden, Mrs Lidgey.'

'Thank you, dear. I knew I could rely on you. When I've done my hair, you can call for Marcus to carry me downstairs.'

'He didn't come home for dinner. The school's busy today, getting ready for the end-of-term service. Beth and I can manage between us.'

Eleanor's face darkened at being snubbed once more by Marcus. Nevertheless, she smiled at Sally. 'You can help me into my wheelchair then fetch my hat and coat.'

'You're going outside?' Sally was surprised. Although Mrs Lidgey frequently asked questions about the villagers, she'd never once expressed the desire to mix with them. She was more of a snob than Jo Venner.

'I think I'll attend the Easter prayers at the school.'

Eleanor arrived at the school, with Sally pushing her wheelchair, as the maypole dancing finished. She ignored the children and the few parents who were present. After speaking briefly to the vicar, her eyes lingered beadily on Marcus before flicking insidiously to Jo.

222

'The Easter garden is magnificent, Miss Venner. You are very clever. I was wondering, has Luke Vigus returned from his travels yet?'

From the smirk on Sally's face, Jo guessed Eleanor was getting her to pass on details of her private life. 'The children worked hard on the garden, Mrs Lidgey. I'm so pleased you like it,' she said graciously.

'Take Mrs Lidgey into the school,' Marcus barked crossly at Sally. 'You must not allow her to catch a chill.' He stalked on ahead of them.

'Well, that was rude,' Sally exclaimed indignantly.

Underneath the blanket over her lap, Eleanor was shredding her hands.

'Try not to lose your patience with her,' Jo whispered to Marcus as he looked over the music for the hymns.

She had the notion Eleanor was expert at making Marcus feel guilty for his moments of nettle, and he would then put himself into the awful position of working extra hard to make it up to her. Such a waste of his time. It was a pity he didn't see fit to trundle her off to a nursing home. Some mothers were not deserving of unbroken care and devotion.

Marcus made no reply – what could he say? Eleanor would make him suffer for it later. She made him suffer all the time.

Eleanor's words over Luke taunted Jo. He had failed to telephone her as arranged last night. Where was he? Was he safe and well? She ached for his return.

When the gathering was assembled in the upper class-room, the short Easter service began. Marcus, Adam Moore, Jane Lawry and Susan Wherry played string instruments in accompaniment to Miss Teague on the harmonium. The occasion was finished off with prayers performed solemnly by the Reverend Mountebank, who wished the children a happy holiday and exhorted them to attend the Easter services in the church, ignoring the fact there were Methodists present.

Jo closed her hymn book and swung her eyes to Molly to see if she appeared comfortable.

223

'Checking on your ready-made family again?' Biddy Lean suddenly positioned herself in front of Jo.

'I think you've said enough, Mrs Lean,' Jo returned smartly. Biddy's loud voice had ensured others were staring and listening to them.

'People think you're a saint, but they'd change their minds if they knew you and your man were encouraging his mother to drink herself into an early grave.'

'I suggest you go home, Mrs Lean,' Marcus interrupted harshly. 'I think the village has heard enough of your spiteful remarks.'

'You're a troublemaker, Biddy Lean,' Verena Jelbert said. 'And a liar.'

'A liar, am I?' Biddy snapped, her eyes seering into Jo's angry face. 'Luke Vigus pays Mardie Dawes to leave drink for Jessie every day. Your perfect Miss Venner knows all about it. Ask her. She can't deny it. Jessie even boasts about it.'

In the corner of her eye Jo saw Miss Teague gasp triumphantly then lean over the wheelchair to titter to Eleanor.

'I won't deny it,' Jo said firmly. 'It wasn't an easy option for Luke but it was the only one he could think of to stop Jessie selling everything he provides for the children.'

Verena Jelbert looked shocked at the revelation but again she came to Jo's defence. 'And you've all seen for yourself that it's working. I don't think this is a subject that should be discussed in front of the children.'

'Nor do I,' Marcus's voice boomed, halting the rush of opinions. The vicar was sidling away, but his pale face was a contortion of outrage. Marcus would have to call a meeting with Mr Mountebank as soon as possible, and Joanna had some smart talking to do if she was to keep her position at the school. 'It's past school hours and there's clearing up to be done. I suggest everyone disperses for their homes.'

'Wheel me towards Marcus,' Eleanor ordered Sally.

'You must dismiss that young woman at once,' she hissed at him. 'Or the vicar and villagers will lose their trust in you, then what will happen to us?'

'I will do what I think is necessary, Mama,' he said

tightly. 'Now you must excuse me. I shall be busy for some time.'

The clearing-up was done without a word passing between the three teachers and Frank Burthy. Miss Teague was too nervous to look Jo in the eye, but she left the premises with her chin pointing upwards.

Jo finally approached Marcus when he was standing alone at his desk. 'Please accept how sorry I am that Biddy Lean made her announcement in the school, in the presence of invited company.'

'I hardly know what to say to you, Joanna.'

'What are you thinking?'

'Now that you've asked I shall tell you. I'm astonished that you are in agreement with Luke Vigus over his unorthodox plan to provide his siblings with a better standing of living.'

'Luke got the idea from something I said.' Jo was ashamed it was she herself who had caused these hostile feelings against Luke.

'It's hardly a recipe to lead Jessie Vigus into the realms of good motherhood,' Marcus said sternly. 'You will have lost a lot of support today and it will not be easily overcome if you continue your alliance with Luke Vigus. You do see that one's private life matters very much in such a small close-knit community?'

'I understand all the implications.' Jo swallowed the bile in her throat. 'Do you think I shall face being hounded out of the village?' It would be a source of celebration for her mother, and his, and Jessie Vigus. All three women loathed her.

'To be honest I don't know.' A wave of panic washed over him, making him clench his fists to stop himself rocking on his feet. He could hardly bear the thought of not seeing Joanna nearly every day. She was the only person who brought sanity into his wretched existence. 'I shall fight in your corner, of course, and after the tumult has died down, I'm sure many of the parents will remember that not so very long ago you put yourself at great risk to save their children's lives. The Methodists will prove to be the greatest opposition and the vicar is going to be very difficult. He's always concerned about his standing.'

'You make it sound like it's your fight too.'

Their eyes locked. 'Oh, Joanna, if you only knew how much it is. I don't want to lose the only friend I've got.'

'Thank you, Marcus. Whatever happens, let me assure you that you'll never lose my friendship.'

He was silent for a moment, then, 'And Luke Vigus?'

Jo met his eyes levelly. 'I don't wish to discuss my involvement with Luke, only to say that I will never give him up.'

He nodded briefly, accepting the statements. 'I hope I will see something of you during the holiday. Perhaps we could go riding together.'

'I'd enjoy that.'

His face lit up. 'I shall look forward to it.'

They left the school together.

'Hello there!'

All her worries vanished for the moment. Overjoyed to see it was Luke hailing her, she hastened out of the gates to him.

Marcus watched them with envy and a terrible sinking feeling in his heart. How could Joanna throw herself away on such a worthless individual?

Jo was eager to be alone with Luke but first she must say good afternoon to Marcus.

Luke eyed the approaching schoolmaster but did not speak to him.

'Are you back for long, Vigus?' Marcus asked abruptly.

'I shall be around for a while,' Luke replied, looking at Jo and not the headmaster.

'Good heavens!' Marcus exclaimed, staring wide-eyed across the road. 'Isn't that your mother, Vigus?'

'Bloody hell,' Luke hissed. 'She's wandering off again.'

Jessie was lurching down the road, her dressing gown open, exposing all her raddled hide. Luke darted across the road and tried to get a grip on her. Jessie spat and swore, lashing out and butting him in the chin with her forehead. She raked her broken fingernails down his face.

As if a silent signal proclaiming a drama had been given

226

people were suddenly about. Abner Jelbert started catcalling. 'How can you bear to touch the filthy bitch, Luke.'

'Get in here and shut your ruddy mouth!' Verena was heard shouting to her husband. She was watching the scuffle from a window.

Abner ignored her. 'We all know your lady-love's in league with you over your mother's booze. You'd better keep your head down, boy.'

Jo pleaded with Marcus. 'We must help Luke get her inside.'

'Of course.' Marcus's long legs ensured he beat her to the struggling couple. Because he had no other option, he caught Jessie in a stranglehold from behind and lifted her off her feet. 'Come now, Mrs Vigus. Calm down. You're making a spectacle of yourself.'

'Bastard!' Jessie howled, gouging at his hands. 'You're all bastards.'

Luke grasped her wrists and tried to hold her arms still, but she kicked him viciously in the shin and he fell back, crumpling against the wall.

Jo opened the door to the tiny cottage. 'Marcus, drag her inside.'

He obeyed, and as Jessie's feet combed the dust, Jo tightly grabbed her ankles. Despite her thrashing about, they managed to get her to the couch and threw her down on to it. It winded her, and Jo hastily pulled the dressing gown decently together.

Luke half-fell through the door and slammed it shut, drowning out the gales of laughter outside.

'Are you all right, Luke?' Jo went to him.

He nodded breathlessly, rubbing his painful shin. Blood was trickling down his face and neck. 'God damn her! I'll take her upstairs. I can't bear the sight of her.'

Jessie had fallen into a kind of daze. Lifting her over his shoulder, Luke mounted the rope ladder.

'Something must be done to stop her leaving the house in that condition,' Marcus said, examining the stinging, bloodied digs in his hands.

'I can't see what, except for tying her up,' Jo replied grimly. 'She was probably making her way to Mardie Dawes for more gin or some herbs to drug herself with. Luke says she's often in pain from the long-term abuse of her body.'

Marcus glanced round the room. It smelled every bit a fetid shanty. 'Marcus, it was good of you to help, but Luke is terribly embarrassed. Would you mind if I asked you to leave before he comes down?'

'You shouldn't stay in a place like this, Joanna. It must be crawling with vermin.' He wound his handkerchief around his hand that had been scratched the most. 'You're going to very much regret your association with this family.' He went back to the school, his soul heavy with a crushing sadness over all he could not have now and in the future.

'Thanks for getting rid of him, Jo,' Luke murmured when he came down. They immediately embraced. 'I feel humiliated that he should see my mother like that.'

'He is sympathetic about it, Luke.'

'Perhaps. He was certainly disgusted. I can't blame him for looking down on me too with the way I've let her behave, the way I've let the kids be treated. Oh, God, Jo, when will it end?'

'It will end one day, Luke, and in the meantime I'm here for you.'

Bracketing her face in his hands he kissed her very tenderly. Jo tasted his lips, felt the wonderful familiar impression of his body against her. The kiss deepened and deepened, love, passion and need their only communication.

When their lips finally separated she kissed him again. 'I'm just reminding myself you're really here.' She smiled up at him. 'Luke, is your leg hurting?'

'Not so much now,' he murmured huskily. 'All the time I was away I kept asking myself how could I leave you. But, Jo, the instant I stepped inside this house I felt I just had to get out again. I'm going to have to find a permanent solution for the kids to be looked after. I can't bear this situation any longer.'

A loud thump came from overhead and Jessie, who had fallen off her mattress, screamed obscenities.

Letting Jo go, Luke limped to the rope ladder and gripped it savagely with both hands. 'You rotten stinking bitch. I swear if the drink doesn't take you soon I'll kill you myself.'

Twenty-Five

Mercy put the last of Jo's luggage down in Cardhu's hallway, then raised her eyes to the ceiling. Jo and Luke were in the kitchen and they were kissing again, laughing like a pair of adolescents. Their steady stream of embraces was growing almost indecent. There was no use in asking them to stop, they both wore the same hopelessly devoted, doe-eyed expression as her brother had had when looking forward to a meeting with Katherine Venner.

'Oh, Jo,' Mercy whispered sorrowfully. 'I wish you could see he'll bring you nothing but trouble.' The way Jo was behaving at this moment meant an unplanned pregnancy was probably not out of the question.

Jo had only managed to keep her job through Marcus Lidgey's wholehearted support for her teaching accomplishments, and by her agreeing to the vicar's restrictions that she must not set foot inside a pupil's house unless in the company of Miss Teague or Mr Lidgey. In view of her selfless action on the day of the savage dog's attack, most parents were prepared to give her a second chance. But they would not tolerate another scandalous incident. Beth was only allowed to continue work at the Vigus cottage on the condition Luke bought no more drink for Jessie.

'Jo, is that kettle boiling yet? I'm getting parched,' Mercy bawled along the passage.

The couple finally parted and she made for the kitchen and the mug of tea promised half an hour ago.

While Jo made the brew, Luke leaned against the draining board. After transporting half a dozen sacks of coal to Cardhu and tipping them into the coal house, he had carried scuttles

230

of coal inside and lit fires in all the rooms to air the house. His hands, face and shirt were blackened. He gulped down the tea, unconcerned at Mercy's disapproving glare, making a point of not dipping into the tin of homemade cake the farmer had brought with her.

Jo arranged a bunch of daffodils and catkins in a crystal vase. 'We'll soon have plenty of hot water, thanks to you, Luke.'

'Good.' He sniffed under his armpit, eyeing Mercy in equal disdain, only his expression held amusement. 'I need to clean up. Think I'll take a bath before I go, never used a proper one before.'

Mercy exhaled a long breathy sigh. 'I'm sure Jo's grateful for your help but there's no need for you to hang about.'

Luke finished his tea. 'You might as well go, Mercy. I intend to stick around long enough to spend time with Jo alone.'

'S'pose you'll be off on your travels again soon. Don't know why you bother to come back. Them poor kids hardly ever see you when you're here,' Mercy fulminated.

'I'll be here all through the Easter holiday. My affairs don't concern you. Haven't you got a wild dog to catch? Heard it had one of Dick Markham's prime ewes last night.'

'Where did you hear that, as if I didn't know? Down the pub, probably on your umpteenth beer.'

'Please don't fall out, you two,' Jo implored them. 'My moving in here is a cause for celebration.'

'I'll have to be going anyway,' Mercy said, heading for the back door. 'You're a fool to trust him, Jo. I've said it before and you choose to take no notice, but the only promise you'll get out of him is a short-lived one. Don't make yourself a stranger at Nance.'

When Mercy had gone, Jo returned to Luke. 'Don't let Mercy upset you. She's only being a friend.'

'Do you share her views? And the others? That I'm no good? That I'll soon desert you?'

'No, darling, of course not.'

He gazed at her a long time, his face working, as if he was

231

having difficulty forming the next words, but for Jo they were the words she had been longing to hear. 'I couldn't bear it if you thought badly of me, Jo, because I love you.'

'I love you too, Luke. I love you now and I always will, nothing that happens will ever change that.'

Their embrace was long and tender, putting the seal on their declaration. Then he laid his mouth over hers in a long sensuous kiss. He felt her tremble, recognised her inward sigh. 'I'll clean up, then you can join me upstairs.'

They had made love several times in the past few days, here in the house, in Luke's wagon, on the moor, each occasion as special as the first time. Jo was in a state of ecstasy now she knew he wanted more from her than the joining of their flesh. While he bathed, she locked the doors in case word of her move had got about and she received curious visitors.

On the landing, wearing only a towel, Luke linked arms with her. He stopped at the door of the main bedroom.

'This is Celia's room,' she said.

'It's your room now. I'm sure she'd approve of you taking the man you love in there.'

'Yes, you're right, darling.'

Inside the bedroom, Jo touched the satin bedcover. Like Celia, she would know the ecstasy of having her lover lie here with her, and the loneliness when he was far away.

They fell naked and laughing on to the bed, kissing softly at first, then letting passion build and burn, enfold and inspire them, transport them where it may.

Luke became contemplative. Jo was so fragile, it was as if he could run his fingers right through her, break her, then remould her to his own design. But there was no need for that, she was wonderfully unique. She was strong, an ocean of love, a storm of hope, come into his life to fulfil him.

The only contact she could feel was his warm sweet breath fanning her face. 'Luke?'

He smiled in the way he kept exclusively for her.

She took his lips hungrily, seeking to place the heat of her love inside him and take away all the hurt and pain he had known. Like the distant wind soughing through the

232

empty spaces on the moor, she sighed, 'Luke, I love you. Please . . .'

Taking ultimate possession of her, he received his reward, her moan of rapture. As always he kept one hand moving over her body to heighten her awareness and pleasure. She arched herself towards him, giving herself to him more and more, carried away on a sea and sky of perfect motion.

Luke understood her voyage completely, why she wept as he took her into timelessness and total inner liberation. In this woman beneath him, her mobility in perfect rhythm with his, he felt them join totally as one.

Later, as he tenderly dried her tears with the pads of his thumbs and kissed her one last time, she curled into him, drawn to the hope of a wonderful future, his love for ever.

'You all right, my love?' He asked her this every time they made love.

'Mmmm.' Dreamily she moved closer against him. 'I don't think many people are blessed with the way we make each other feel, Luke.'

They stayed quiet. They slept. They awoke and made love again and this time he showed her how to take the dominant position. Then once more he sought her reassurance. She kissed his hand. Words were not needed.

Back down in the kitchen they made a meal of the food Jo had brought with her from Nance and they took it, with the beer Luke fetched from the wagon, into the sitting room. Both ravenously hungry, they cuddled up on the sofa and quickly consumed the bread and ham and preserved-apple pie.

'We'll have a wonderful night too, my love,' Luke said.

Jo looked him in the eye. 'Don't you intend going home today?'

'No, why should I?'

'Luke, what about the children? I've been feeling selfish keeping you away from them for so long.'

'They're fine. Mrs Wherry will take Marylyn home at six. Rex can watch her and get Molly off to bed.'

'But they're only children.' Jo frowned. 'Rex is too young for that sort of responsibility. They need you.'

233

'Don't be bossy, Jo,' he crooned, blowing on her neck. 'I'll see them tomorrow. They manage when Beth's not there.'

'But that's the point, darling. They shouldn't have to manage—'

'Don't spoil the day.' He pulled away from her. 'I'm trying as hard as I know how to make things better for them.'

'For them or for you, Luke?'

He leaned forward on the sofa, his arms resting on his knees. 'Why are you nagging me? No one really cares about the little sods.'

'Luke! That's not true. Listen to me, I'm sorry, I didn't mean to make you feel guilty.' Putting her hands on his tense shoulders she spoke close to his ear. 'I've got an idea. Bring the children here for the rest of the holiday. We can be one big family together. The change will do them good, specially Molly.'

'This place is too fancy for them.' He shook his head, as if trying to dislodge a torment, refusing to look at her. 'You can't give them a taste of this then shove them back in that bloody pigsty. Besides, you're not thinking straight. You're their teacher, the vicar wouldn't like it. For crying out loud, Jo, why can't you leave this go? Why must you pick away at me? The kids are all right. I pay Beth and the Wherry woman well for feeding them. I'll do more, I swear. I'll think of something. Just leave it. Understand?'

'Do you love the children, Luke?' Jo's voice was calm but her heart was uneasy while waiting for his answer. She had not realised quite how much a burden his brother and sisters were to him. She had rubbed at the sorest spot of his selfishness. 'You cuffed Arnold Jelbert for bullying Molly that time and issued all manner of threats to him, but you didn't comfort Molly.'

He raised his dark head, gazing at her out of great solemn eyes. 'I care about them, that's all. That's the truth, whether you like it or not. I've only ever loved two people, Gran and now you. Isn't that good enough for you?' Before she could reply, he groaned, as if cut to the bowels. 'I don't know what else I can do, Jo. I'm asking around to find the kids a new home. Where they'll be well cared for. Where I can visit them. I don't ever intend to desert them. What I can't do is be a father to them. I don't ever want to be a father!'

'It's understandable that you feel this way,' Jo cried, irked at his self-pity. 'But it doesn't excuse you leaving the children alone while you're in Parmarth.'

Tears formed in Luke's eyes. 'So you do think of me in the same way as the others. I should've known I'd never measure up to your standards. It was just a silly dream, that we had some sort of future together. I'm sorry you ever got involved with my family.' He was on his feet, ready to leave.

Jo sat stunned, unable to believe that so soon after proclaiming their love they were quarrelling heatedly. Then she was beside him, gripping his arm. 'I won't let you go like this. I love you, Luke, whatever your failings. But you are a good man, I believe that with all my heart.'

He stared down on her. Small, barefoot, only half of her clothes on, tears on her face, she looked rather like a child. A vulnerable needy child, same as the ones he wanted to offload on to others. He loved her so much then he thought his heart would shatter. 'Let me go, Jo. I'm no good for you. I'll only hurt you.'

'No! If you walk out on me I'll follow you wherever you go. I'll find you, no matter how long it takes. We've been joined as one and there's no going back for me. I want you, whatever you're like. I can't live without you, Luke! I won't!'

Luke suddenly crushed her in his arms. 'I could never give you up. You're right. I ought to go home to the kids. Just let me stay with you a little while longer.'

235

Twenty-Six

Luke carried Marylyn to the Wherrys' house. He was not holding his baby sister close, unaware of her panic that she was about to fall. Fretting wildly, her arms flailing, she hit him on the chin. It hurt a lot.

In his ignorance, Luke considered she had done it in spite. 'Stop it. For goodness' sake, I'm doing my best for you.'

Mrs Wherry took Marylyn from him and the baby settled at once in her arms. 'That's better, my handsome. I'll take care of you now.'

'She's always crying,' Luke grumbled.

'She's teething, Luke.' Mrs Wherry, thickly bodied and conservatively dressed, tut-tutted at him. 'You should be more patient with her.'

Luke put his hand in his trouser pocket. 'Here's your pay.'

'Thank you.' Mrs Wherry expected him to leave immediately, as he always did when he brought Marylyn to her, and she was surprised he was still cluttering up her kitchen a few moments later. 'Did you want me to feed Rex and Molly? I thought you were staying home this morning.'

Embarrassed at the woman's tart tones, he cleared his throat. 'You're good to the kids. I'm very grateful to you. I guess you're getting fond of them.'

Mrs Wherry eyed him. 'I suggest you bring what's on your mind out in the open.'

'I was wondering if there's any possibility you could take the kids on for good. I mean, come to live with you. You've got a big enough house. They like you and Beth. Molly feels safe here. I'd pay you well. I can even give

236

you a lump sum upfront if you'd need to get anything in for them.'

Mrs Wherry put Marylyn down on the mat to play with the few makeshift toys she kept for her, then folded her arms. 'And then I suppose I'd never see you again.'

'No, I promise it won't be like that. I'll be back this way regularly.'

'To see Miss Venner, I suppose. That maid hasn't kept the sense in her head the good Lord gave her. I doubt if she'd see you for long either. I'm sorry, Luke, you've asked me a favour so I'll say my piece. Even if I wanted to agree with your request, I couldn't take the children away from their mother, as bad as she is. They're your responsibility, not mine and Beth's. We'll go on with our present arrangement for the children's sakes. You should really be thinking of settling down.'

'But I've got to go away to work,' Luke bellowed, frustrated, humiliated. He couldn't take much more. 'There's no damned work round here, you know that! I don't want the kids left alone with my old woman any longer. It's not my fault she's a rotten mother. I'm trying to do the right thing. Can't you give me some credit?'

'Calm down, Luke.' Mrs Wherry raised her voice. 'I won't have you shouting in my house. I understand your problems, up to a point, but I can't help you.'

Luke felt the whole world was against him. 'I'll come back for the baby this evening.'

He strode outside, feeling the need to thump his fists into something hard to assuage his anger. How dare the bloody woman make that crack about Jo? He'd never desert her. One day he'd make these nosey, self-righteous villagers admit they were wrong about him where she was concerned.

His hands trembled as he lit a cigarette. He rubbed his fingers over his face. The stress of trying to care for his brother and sisters was getting to him. He had been in a nervous state since his quarrel with Jo yesterday. He hated her seeing his worst traits so clearly.

237

Twenty-Seven

M arcus carried his mother's breakfast tray downstairs to the kitchen. The plate was cleared. Most days his mother kept to her bed, but her appetite had picked up and he despaired that she would ever weaken and die. On a positive note, he was sharp enough not to step close to her and she had been unsuccessful in laying her hands on him throughout the holiday. The days were passing relatively peacefully. He tended the garden and rambled on the moors. Played for hours on his harpsichord and violin.

The only blight was Luke Vigus being home, but last night, at the Engine House, Marcus had overheard the other man talking of spending the following afternoon with a fellow dealer at Pendeen. At last, he had the opportunity to take the promised horse ride with Joanna.

In the pub, Marcus had taken his glass of brandy to a secluded table to study the man who had no notion he had an inactive rival for Joanna.

Luke was playing cards, a cigarette dangling from his lips. He was clean and acceptably dressed, but his language was coarse and ill-used. His fiercest critics did not frequent the pub, and he was thoroughly at home in the company of his male neighbours, swapping jokes and ribald stories. To Marcus's mind, hardly an intelligent word passed his lips. His beer glass was refilled at a rapid rate. He did not seem the type to settle down to wife and hearth, to give a woman the respect and cherishing she deserved. Marcus had finished his drink in perplexity. He could not see what appeal the other man had for Joanna. But who knew what went on in private? The villagers would suffer enough shock to last them a lifetime if they discovered how his mother had abused him nearly all his life.

Beth Wherry was alone in the kitchen. 'Mrs Lidgey was tempted again then, sir?' she remarked modestly.

Engrossed in his thoughts, Marcus almost missed her childlike voice. Although very quiet, Beth had an abundance of good sense. He had come to realise it was her ability to switch herself off from her surroundings which made people accuse her of being simple-minded. She was a very good cook and now shared the job with Sally. Honest and ordinary, her faith unshakable, she never complained and always saw the better side of people. While Marcus did not appreciate her slipping into his mother's room and praying over her while she slept, he valued the peaceful atmosphere she brought to the house.

'Yes, Beth, she likes your light pastry particularly.'

'I'll get a fresh chicken from Nance tomorrow. Make some hearty broth for her.' She looked for his approval, treating him as if he was her headmaster and she his pupil.

'Good.' Marcus stared at her. Her voice was immature, so soft, a murmur, barely above a whisper, and it gave him an idea. Hope at last? It required serious thought. He would have to tread carefully to win Beth's support while at the same time keeping her trust.

'How are you coping with your other job as nursemaid to the Vigus children, Beth?' Marcus said, his eyes directly on his young skivvy. The whole village was agog with the news, of how last Sunday Luke Vigus had attended chapel, wearing a suit, while his brother and sisters had been baptised. Of course, Luke Vigus's only intention had been to keep Beth and her mother's services.

'I enjoy it, sir,' Beth said. Mr Lidgey had taken to pausing in her company for little chats. She sensed he was lonely and she was happy to ease that for him, but she always felt strangely disturbed by him and was glad when he moved on. Beth was too naive to recognise the stirrings of infatuation. 'Do you want me to make you some coffee?'

'Yes, please. Is Vigus about to leave Parmarth again?'

'I don't know, sir.'

'You are charitable to sleep in that place. I understand his mother still manages to be continually inebriated. I wish you well of it, Beth. I've seen the unpleasant conditions in the cottage.'

'Mrs Vigus is no trouble when she's in that state,' Beth said, as she made the coffee. It was true, Jessie had neither the strength nor the coordination to be a worry. Beth suspected Luke was somehow keeping his mother in drink. 'It gives me the opportunity to pray for her soul.'

Shortly after lunch, which he ate alone in his study, Marcus was on his way to Nance Farm on foot to collect a horse for himself and lead another to Cardhu for Joanna. On reaching the patch of willows Mardie Dawes frequented to peddle her wares, he looked about warily for her. His heart missed a beat when he spied two pairs of eyes blinking at him through the foliage.

'Rex. Molly. Good morning to you.' He presumed correctly that they were hiding from him.

Molly remained camouflaged. Rex emerged sheepishly, then stood up on the bank, face dirty, short trousers muddy and ripped, staring insolently. 'Morning, sir.'

'Are you enjoying the holiday?' Marcus asked him conversationally.

'Yes, sir.'

'You will be careful on the moors? The ruins of the Solace Mine are obvious, but there are many shafts which are concealed and dangerous.'

'I know where they are,' Rex boasted.

'I'm pleased to hear it. How is your mother?'

'She's gone off again. Luke was cooking our dinner before he went to Pendeen on business, but he's out looking for her.'

'I hope he finds her safe and well. Well, I must be on my way. I'm going riding.' He left the little brother and sister astonished that he had stopped and chatted in such a friendly fashion.

As Marcus continued towards Nance his mind was full of

Luke's character. He was surprised to learn he had actually been cooking the children a meal but there was very little else to recommend him. How was it possible, Marcus asked himself, that he did not allow himself the same consideration as Vigus did? To love Joanna, to form a relationship with her, perhaps even be her lover. Was he not being too hard on himself? He was sexually amoral but was he allowing this harsh fact to overshadow what was good and honourable in himself? He had been celibate for some weeks now, the longest period in his adult life, and he was not finding it as difficult as the loneliness of being without the companionship of a woman.

I'm the one rejecting the idea of having Joanna for myself, he told the remoteness of the moor. If Luke Vigus can have her, for all his faults and worthlessness, why not me?

Russell rolled off Sally for the second time in half an hour, bruising the new curling green fronds of the ferns.

Sally straightened her clothes then laid her head on his stomach, which was agitating in the aftermath of their fierce exercise. She stared up moodily at the inner walls of the mine ruins. Russell was clumsy and too lazy to learn what pleased her.

'When are we getting married?' Russell asked suddenly.

Sally made an impatient noise. 'I've told you before. As soon as Mrs Lidgey's given me what she's promised.'

'You can't believe the likes of her. She won't give you an expensive piece of jewellery just for carrying tales. You can still work for the old woman after we're married, just in case she keeps her word.' Russell was impatient to make Sally his wife, afraid she would forsake him and go off with someone else, or make her way to Penzance to work in a pub, as she had threatened during a teasy moment.

'Stop grumbling, Russell,' she exclaimed, 'or I'll go home.'

There came a peculiar cackling sound above them. The couple looked up. Silhouetted against the engine-house wall was a figure, breathing heavily, hideous. Sally screamed in terror.

Russell pushed her aside and leapt to his feet. 'Bloody hell, what do you think you're doing, spying on us, you old hag? Get away! Luke's looking for you.'

'Having a bit of fun?' Jessie Vigus tittered, swaying on her bare feet. 'Can I join you?' She was in her soiled blue dressing gown.

Sally scampered away on all fours, huddling against the engine-house wall. 'Get her away from us, Russell.'

'You heard me,' Russell shouted at the intruder. 'Get back home, you beastly witch.'

Jessie ripped open the tie of the dressing gown and pulled the garment apart. She was naked underneath. 'C-come on, Russell,' she hiccupped. 'Enjoy yourself with me. It'll only cost you two shilling.' She stretched out her withered arms to him. 'I know you like a good romp.'

'Shut your mouth!' he shrieked, pushing the loathsome woman away from him. 'You know what I'll do to you if you make trouble for me.'

Awash with gin, weak from virtual starvation, Jessie fell like a stone. She groaned, struggled to get up.

'Stay where you are!' Russell drew back his foot and kicked her viciously in the head.

Sally crept up to him and grabbed his arm. 'You've hurt her.'

'Shut up.' In dread, he bent down to the mother of his child and gingerly touched the side of her neck. Thank God, she was breathing. 'She's out of it. Sleeping off another drunken binge. We'll leave her here. She can't come to no harm in the fresh air.'

Sally was still shaking minutes later as they tramped back to the village. 'She was like something out of a nightmare.' She clung to Russell's arm. 'I don't want to go there again. I'd be too afraid she'd turn up. You don't think she was watching as we . . . ?'

'No, she would've jumped out on us before.' Russell's thoughts were coldly alert. 'Don't tell anyone we've seen her. She could accuse me of assault.' It would be thought she had fallen down in a drunken stupor.

*   *   *

Jessie regained consciousness twenty minutes later. She took her painful headache for granted, the same result after every drinking bout. The wind was picking up and howling through the mine ruins. Afraid the mine knockers – malicious sprites – would come for her and cast her down into the blackness, she levered herself up on her elbows and gradually, swaying, lurching, got to her feet. Dizziness overwhelmed her and she lost her bearings. She stumbled about, the bright sunlight and the pain in her head forcing her to keep her eyes closed.

Minutes later, she screamed and screamed as she plunged down the one hundred and thirty-five fathoms of Pike's Shaft.

Twenty-Eight

Rex passed Jo a note just before she took afternoon registration. 'It's from Luke,' he whispered, eyeing the class warily.

'Is it about why Molly's not attending today?' Jo opened the note. There was nothing written about Molly. It was a plea from Luke for her to see him as soon as possible. 'Thank you, Rex. Would you like to wait here a minute then take the register to Mr Lidgey?'

Rex smiled broadly. She had offered him the most prestigious errand. Although Molly was still having difficulties at school, and was often poorly and absent, because Rex never backed down when Arnold and his gang teased him, he was gaining their respect. He could cope with very easy sums, and while unable to master 'big words' in reading, his writing had improved.

'Thank you, Rex.' Marcus ran his eyes over the boy while taking the register from him. He had become one of the cleanest and tidiest children in the school, thanks to Beth and her mother, and the gentle concern of the young woman in the next classroom.

After the children had gone home, Jo quickly packed away the last of the things from the girls' needlework class. Miss Teague admired the little pinafores they were making. 'Whose is the one with the pretty cross stitch on the bib?'

'It's Gillian Jelbert's. Believe it or not, she's quite artistic. I'm sure she'll win the needlework prize at the end of the year for her fine sewing. She would make an excellent tailor with proper training. I'll suggest it to her parents. Well, I must get on.'

Jo was eager to see Luke. The words of his note had haunted her all afternoon. 'Dear Jo, Please come over strait after school. Need you. Luke.' Could it have something to do with Jessie's disappearance? With no clue to her whereabouts as darkness fell on the day she had wandered off, Luke had called on Davey Penoble and half a dozen other men and formed a search party. They had drawn no luck nor on the subsequent day, when the constable had been informed, and after a week it was assumed Jessie had roamed too far this time and was lost for good.

'I must be going too,' Miss Teague said, smiling faintly. 'I've a letter to post. Still no news of Mrs Vigus, I suppose?'

'No, I'm afraid not.' Jo hid her impatience. No one in the village cared about Jessie Vigus. Miss Teague was only after gossip. Jo was concerned that evil whispers were changing lips. Lew had refused to join in the search for Jessie. 'Luke's probably done her to death. There's plenty of mineshafts he could've chucked her down and there's the cliffs to push a lying old bitch like she over. If so, she deserved it and he deserves the right justice for it.' Jo had warned him to keep his dangerous, unfair opinions to himself, but there were moments when she recalled Luke's threat to kill Jessie.

Marcus appeared brandishing some mail in his hand. 'Miss Teague, did I hear you say you are going to post a letter? Would you kindly take these too?'

'Certainly, Mr Lidgey. Good day to you both.'

At the last echo of Miss Teague's footsteps, Marcus smiled at Jo. 'Could I detain you for a few moments, Joanna? Now that the final legal requirements for your trust fund are set up, I think now would be a good time for you to approach the Markhams and bring up the subject of an assisted scholarship for Ann.'

Jo was filled with anticipation at the good her gift might bring. 'I wish to remain anonymous, Marcus. It's likely to cause complications if people know I am behind it. They could spurn it as charity, and I'm not a favoured person in the village at the moment. It would be better if you saw the Markhams.'

'I think that would be wise, but don't worry, the locals will come round to admiring you again, as you so richly deserve. I wish there was at least one boy worthy of a scholarship this year, but Norman Pascoe's written work is beginning to look promising.' He wanted to keep her talking, he enjoyed her company so very much, but she was ready to leave. It would be a long session marking exercise books for him, then afterwards anything else he could think of to delay going home.

To hurry things along while waiting for Jo, Luke gave Rex and Molly their tea, sent Molly to bed and Rex outside to play, then he fetched Marylyn from Mrs Wherry. He made his own front door as Jo hurried across the road towards him.

'Is something the matter?' She took Marylyn from him and entered the tiny cottage.

'The Welfare people were here this morning.' He sighed long and hard as Jo showered Marylyn with affection. 'Someone's told them my mother's gone missing and how she was living before she disappeared. How I was giving her booze every day.'

Jo's heart sank. 'I see. And?'

He shook his head angrily. 'I told them it was a lie about the drink but I don't think they were convinced. They aren't happy about the situation, even though they could see the place is no longer in squalor, that Mrs Wherry's practically fostering the kids and Beth's sleeping overnight while I'm away. I said Beth gets the kids to Sunday School. It wasn't good enough. They said I've got to make proper permanent arrangements for the them.

'But I have to go on the road, Jo,' he cried despairingly. 'I can't sell enough goods round here to come home every night.' He probably could, but the thought was abhorrent to him. 'I can't let the kids go into an orphanage. It'd be the end of Molly and I might never see 'em all again. What can I do?'

246

Jo felt as if she was losing all her energy. 'Let's sit down and talk about it, Luke. I'm sure we can come up with something.'

They sat on the couch, Marylyn on Jo's lap. Before he said another word he gave Jo an earnest kiss.

'One thing's for sure,' Jo said vehemently, making Marylyn chuckle by tickling her dribbly chin. 'I'll never let Marylyn be brought up in an orphanage, and I couldn't bear that for Rex and Molly.'

Luke lit a cigarette. He tugged on a tress of hair falling in front of Jo's ear. 'I could tell that interfering bunch of bas— official nosey parkers, that you 'n' me are getting married. They'd leave us alone if they believe a respectable schoolteacher is to become the kids' new mother.'

Jo's jaw dropped. 'Luke, I—'

'I know you don't want to give up your job.' He smiled disarmingly. 'We could just say we're getting married soon to get the Welfare off my back. Things should settle down then and we'll carry on as now. You don't object to that, do you, sweetheart? It's not really a lie. We haven't talked about it but I s'pose we'll get married one day, won't we?'

'I want nothing more than for us to get married in the future, darling. But the present situation for the children shouldn't be allowed to carry on. Luke, now your mother seems to have gone for good, have you considered getting in touch with your cousin at Germoe?'

'Maud is very duty-conscious but why should she help me? She's miles away and probably has a family of her own.'

Jo asked him carefully. 'Do you ever wonder who your father is?'

'I'd break his bloody neck if I knew,' he said heatedly. 'My mother was only a fourteen-year-old maid when he went with her. It ended with me being born and her downfall. I hope he's dead.' He secretly hoped his mother was dead and her body would never be found so he would not have to fork out for a funeral. It would be too awful, damned unfair, if she returned and caused more complications. 'Anyway, you're forgetting, the kids all have different fathers and Lew Trevail doesn't recognise Marylyn. It's my problem, Jo. With your consent I'm sure it'll be sorted.'

'I understand how you feel. Luke, I have had another idea. You've been looking for someone to take on the children, but why not buy a house and employ a nanny to care for them? I don't mean the sort of nanny that I was used to, but a kind and caring woman, perhaps a couple, who would rear them properly as if in a family. Please don't be offended at what I'm going to say next. You haven't got the sort of funds to buy a house. I have. I'd like to buy a house for the children.'

Luke was quiet for a while, smoking heavily, his features rigid. 'No. I won't have that. They're not your flesh and blood.'

'It's what I want to do, for them and for your peace of mind, darling. I didn't have to get involved with you. It was my choice and I'll never regret it. Let me do this for all of you.'

'No,' he repeated firmly, crushing the cigarette butt between his fingers. 'It's a good idea and I love you for thinking of it but I won't have you taking over my responsibilities. I could rent something bigger and better than this place. I'll advertise in the newspapers for someone like you spoke of, someone looking for work and a place to live.' He got up from the couch. 'The Welfare should be satisfied with that once I've got the kids out of this godforsaken dump. They left their address. I'll write to 'em later. You'll have to help me with the right words.'

Jo reached for his hand and kissed it tenderly. He seemed depressed. She knew her suggestion had eaten away at his pride. 'I've got some stationery in my handbag.'

Rex came in from his play as she was giving Marylyn her evening bottle. 'Where's Luke?' he asked cautiously.

'He's seeing to Lucky. He'll be back shortly,' she replied.

He was looking at the stationery she had put on the table. 'You got a spare envelope?'

'Yes, of course.' She took another envelope out of her handbag. The boy hid it behind his back. 'Are you going to write to someone?'

'Father Christmas,' Rex said, looking down awkwardly. 'He always forgets to come here. I thought I'd send him a letter early this year.' Jo stroked his arm sentimentally, and acutely embarrassed, he added, 'You won't tell Luke, will you? He'll laugh at me.'

'I promise I won't say a word. Here you are.' She gave him a spare stamp. 'Do you know the address?'

'Yes. The North Pole. I'll write it upstairs.' He paused at the rope ladder. 'Thanks, Miss Venner.'

'I'm happy to help in any way I can, Rex. You only have to ask.'

'You're better than my mother,' he said ardently. 'I hope she never comes back!'

As he climbed up to the loft, Jo thought it unlikely Jessie would be found alive and she felt a moment of pity for the contemptible woman.

Twenty-Nine

Fern Field was more overgrown than Katherine Venner remembered, but she had not forgotten a single moment of her assignations here with Bob Merrick. It was difficult at first to distinguish the path to their old meeting place. She forced her way through a mass of flowering brambles and clumps of dark green ferns to reach the centre of an accommodating assemblage of giant boulders, the silent stones which had hidden her and Bob as they had laughed and loved together.

With her clothes snagged and exposed skin scratched, she sat down on the dry firm ground, resting her face on her drawn-up knees. She was wearing jodhpurs, a light jacket and headscarf; years before it had been a long-skirted riding habit and formal hat.

She had come back here but Bob was dead. Shot and killed while going over the top of one of those barbaric trenches in the Third Battle of Ypres. He would still be alive if he had listened to her pleas not to enlist, but Bob had wanted 'to do his bit', even though he was in a reserved occupation; no shame attached to farming throughout the war. She regretted not coming back before. No one would know the grief she had borne. The granite enclosure was a secret memorial to Bob. If only she could sculpt his name on a boulder, with the words from one of the love poems he had penned for her, poems she still kept.

Katherine pulled at moss and foliage, sifted through small stones, pushed her fingers into the recesses between the boulders, searching for anything that might have been left by Bob, his tobacco pouch, a handkerchief, a small tool from the farm, but there was nothing.

Her heart heavy with disappointment, she leaned back against the hard granite, where once she had pressed into his warm body. She could almost see him, bounding down towards her from the top of a boulder, smiling in the adoring manner he had kept just for her. Magnificently built, a lion of a man, a touch of barbarian in him, his earth-brown hair thick and unruly. He had been a powerful lover, yet tender and discerning. And she had loved him intensely. Katherine wept for her lost love and the hollow years she had lived without him.

Since Bob's death she had not kept a lover for long and now she desired a change from the aspiring young artist currently sharing her bed. Mardie Dawes' account of Marcus Lidgey appealed to her. It would amuse Katherine to seek the attentions of her daughter's superior. She stayed for an hour in homage to Bob, then squeezed back through the broken ferns and brambles for the ride to Parmarth.

She had tethered her pony near a patch of rosebay willow-herb, several yards from the field gate. It was concealed from sight by a low hill and she was alarmed to hear it whinnying violently. Katherine was almost too nervous to make the climb and approach her mount. Then she sucked in her breath and her heart raced with terror. 'Oh, my God. Swallow!'

The pony, helpless in its tethered state, was being attacked by a dog, a large black and white rough-coated creature. The cries of the pony and the savage growls of the dog chilled Katherine like nothing had ever done in the past, even news of Bob's death. The dog's jaws and front quarters were crimson with blood. Blood oozed on the pony's flank, splashing down its front legs, then the dog leapt upwards and Katherine knew it would rip out Swallow's throat. There was nothing she could do. Hands to her mouth in horror, she was powerless to stop the vicious beast from killing her pony.

A shot rang out, the sound reveberating round the moorland, from hill to tor, and Katherine screamed. The dog yelped and was hurled away from the pony by the blast from a shotgun.

Frozen on the spot, Katherine stared at the smashed and blood-soaked body until someone touched her arm and she lurched forward in fear.

'It's dead,' Mercy said bluntly. Leaving Katherine to follow in stunned silence, Kip and Hunter on her heels, she bounded down the hill to the witless pony, which was jerking its head wildly as it sought to break free from its reins.

'Th-thank God you came along, Mercy.' Katherine shuddered, holding herself while she took in the enormity of Swallow's gaping wounds.

'Lucky for you I tracked down the animal who just killed two of my sheep, or you'd be dead 'n' all by now.'

'How is Swallow? Will she have to be shot?'

Mercy caught hold of the reins, but the pony could not be calmed. Its injuries were grotesque, bones were exposed. 'I'm afraid we can't help her. Stand back, I'll do it now.'

Katherine pushed the shotgun up in the air, making Mercy step back awkwardly. 'Are you sure? She's a thoroughbred.'

'Are you bleddy mazed, woman?' Mercy fumed. 'You nearly got yourself shot. Course I'm sure, I wouldn't shoot a good animal for no reason. She's suffering. If you don't want to watch get out to the road.'

Crying in shock, Katherine stumbled to the gate, yanked it open, ran several yards along the road and fell backwards against the hedge. She clapped her hands over her ears but was too late. A second shot rang out like a dreadful off-key bell. She was sobbing uncontrollably when Mercy joined her.

'You'd better come to the farm. I'll get my nephew to bury the dog but he'll have to get help to cart the pony to the knackers.'

Katherine pulled a handkerchief out of her jacket pocket and dabbed at her streaming eyes. 'I-I'll pay for the time and inconvenience.'

'You will not. Bob would've expected me to look after you.'

'I don't want to go to the farm. I want to see Joanna.'

Mercy stared at her. 'Did I hear right? She'll be in school. Home time's not for a hour and half yet.'

'I'd rather go there, nonetheless.'

'Well, if that's what you want. What's your game? I'll walk to the village with you, make sure you get there all right with the state you're in.'

'Thank you, Mercy. I really did love Bob, you know.'

'Yes, more to his pity,' Mercy replied harshly.

Marcus slipped home during the afternoon play break to collect a project on Ancient Rome he had forgotten. Beth was in his study, dusting and sweeping.

'I'm sorry to disturb you, Beth. I shall only be in your way for a minute.' He smiled warmly. He had been studying her carefully for some time, nurturing her with gratitude for all she did at the schoolhouse, giving her the occasional unremarkable gift when Sally was out of the house. Beth never refused someone a favour. Could he persuade her to do what he had in mind?

Beth waited unobtrusively for him to leave, redusting a stack of music sheets on a shelf.

'I saw Luke Vigus leave with a full wagon this morning. Are you sleeping over with the children tonight?'

'Yes, sir, he'll be away three days this time. He's working the Penzance area,' Beth replied shyly.

Marcus paused with the project in his hands. 'How do you find this child-minding?'

'Sometimes I have a bit of trouble getting Rex off to bed.' The girl smiled to herself. 'But Molly's good as gold. Little Marylyn's so sweet and rarely wakes up through the night. It's not a very nice place though. I find it difficult climbing the rope ladder with the baby.'

'Be careful you don't tire yourself, Beth. You do so much for everyone.'

Jo was supervising play in the girls' playground, holding one end of a long skipping rope. From the corner of her eye she spied Molly hanging back. 'Come along, Molly. Get into line behind Ann.'

Molly shook her head and began to cough, a hacking

congested sound. Jo made a mental note to take her to the doctor herself if Molly was no better in a couple of days.

Two figures were coming through the gates, one leaning against the other. Gasping in surprise, Jo stilled her hand and the rope fell on top Jane Lawry's head. 'Aw, miss.'

'I'm sorry, Jane. Ann, take the rope from me, please.' She rushed to meet Mercy and her mother, alarmed at Katherine's ashen face.

'Oh, Joanna.' Breaking free from Mercy's supporting arm, Katherine ran and threw herself at Jo, holding on to her body, resting her coiffed head on her shoulder.

Jo was overwhelmed by the fact her mother was actually seeking comfort from her, then she was fearful. 'What's happened? Is it Alistair?'

Katherine began to weep, so Mercy answered. ''Tisn't your brother. Can't say in front of the kiddies. Do you think Mr Lidgey will mind if we take her to the schoolhouse?'

Marcus had witnessed the scene for himself and overheard Mercy's question. 'Of course I don't mind. Take Mrs Venner into the sitting room. I'll ask Miss Teague to take over your duties for the rest of the afternoon, Miss Venner. You children, don't stand and stare, go about your play.'

Jo and Mercy escorted Katherine to the schoolhouse and Marcus joined them a few minutes later, carrying a tray with a glass of brandy on it. 'I thought you might be in need of this, Mrs Venner.'

'Thank you, Mr Lidgey,' Katherine said in a weak voice, holding out her shaking red-varnished fingertips for the brandy. 'I'm sorry to put everyone out. You see, I've had a terrible shock. You tell him, Joanna, dear.'

Jo told him the tale Mercy had just related to her. She was eyeing her mother suspiciously. Katherine had been fond of her pony but she was playing the distraught female rather too convincingly. For Marcus's benefit? Her loving-mother routine was not fooling Jo.

'But that's terrible,' Marcus sympathised. 'Thank goodness the beast has been killed at last. Is there anything I can do?'

'No,' Mercy said. 'I must be going. Will you still be coming over to Nance for tea, Jo?'

Jo lifted her brows to enquire from her mother what were her intentions. 'Oh, do you mind changing your plans, Joanna? I've ridden over from St Ives to tell you that I've moved into a cottage there. It's in a lovely quiet spot where I can enjoy the tranquillity. Could you ring for a taxicab and accompany me home?'

'I'll come with you, Mother,' Jo said blandly. Could her mother be feeling lonely now she was living on her own? Did she need her daughter after all these years? Jo thought not. It was more Katherine's style to dash her off a note with her new address, or even more likely to let her learn the news from Alistair. The most likely explanation was that this visit to her old lover's stamping ground had gone horrifically wrong. Perhaps she had heard about her romance with Luke from Mardie Dawes' runaway tongue and had come to challenge her over it. Jo would brace herself for that possibility when they were alone. 'I'll come over to Nance for supper, Mercy, and stay the night, if it's OK with you.'

'See you later then, Jo,' Mercy said, leaving without bidding anyone much of a goodbye.

'Perhaps you'd allow me to drive you home, after I've dismissed the school for the day,' Marcus offered.

'You are very kind, Mr Lidgey, isn't he, Joanna?'

When Marcus drew his motorcar up outside the high gates of the four-bedroomed thatched cottage Katherine was renting at St Ives, she insisted he come inside with Jo and look over her home. Katherine had been disinclined towards conversation as she sat beside Jo on the back seat of the Ford coupé, but she chattered enthusiastically as she led the tour of the rooms. Set in a dell which afforded a sweeping view of Porthminster beach, the cottage was charming. It was fully furnished in sturdy dark golden oak, willow-patterned crockery was set on the dresser and light floral curtains and white lace hung at the windows. Baskets of logs and pine cones stood on the slate hearth.

Katherine explained, 'I've employed a daily help to do the

domestic work. Don't you think Meadowsweet is a wonderful name for the place, Joanna?' She omitted that Alistair was paying the rent and all other expenses.

'Very nice, Mother.'

'I wanted a complete change, to strike out while I'm still young and active.' Katherine took off her jacket and thrust out her chest, then smiled with all her feminine charm at Marcus, who was listening politely to the two women. 'Would you mind excusing us for just a moment, Mr Lidgey? I need Joanna to help me change out of these clothes.'

Upstairs in Katherine's bedroom Jo pulled a crêpe de Chine dress out of the wardrobe and helped her mother into it. Every now and then Katherine gave a shiver of shock but Jo did not feel entirely sympathetic for her over her ordeal. She was waiting for her mother's helpless expression to change to one of furious indignation. 'What are you up to, Mother?'

'I don't follow you.' Katherine slipped her feet into a pair of very high-heeled shoes and set about reapplying her make-up.

'You have nothing to say to me?'

'What about? You know my opinion on your teaching, your continuing disobedience towards me.' Katherine teased her hair into shining controlled waves and dabbed a musky perfume on her wrists. She wanted Marcus Lidgey to notice her when she went downstairs. 'Oh, I've caught up with you now, Joanna. You're assuming I came to Parmarth to take you to task over your affair with that gipsy fellow. Yes, I know all about your man.'

Jo studied her mother suspiciously. 'You're not going to astound me, are you, by saying you don't mind?'

'Joanna, you've forgotten I know what it's like to fall for a handsome working-class man, though yours sounds more lowly than Bob Merrick was. Bob meant more to me than anyone else in the world. Enjoy your affair, Joanna. Don't forget you can carry on with it after you marry. If you get yourself into a delicate condition consult Mardie Dawes. She's sorted out a couple of unwanted little problems for me over the years.'

256

'Is that the reason why you allow her to come to Tresawna?'

'Mardie requires hush money, so try not to avail yourself of her services or you'll end up funding her gambling stakes.'

'I shall never need to have anything to do with her.' Jo's intention was not to conceal that Luke was her lover, she could not countenance ridding herself of his child.

Katherine pursed her painted lips. 'We'd better go downstairs, it would be impolite keeping Mr Lidgey waiting any longer.'

Marcus had been gazing distractedly out of the front window, anxious to leave and enjoy the drive back alone with Jo.

Katherine sat down on a tapestry-covered wing-back chair, crossing her legs extravagantly.

Jo stayed on her feet; she did not intend to stay here long. 'Won't you be lonely here, Mother?' She was curious. Katherine had always demanded lots of company in the past.

'I shan't stay here all the time. Actually, I've got a little cat to keep me company. He's called Tuppence because he's so tiny. Be a dear, Joanna, and see if he's hiding in the garden. I'd love for you to see him before you leave.'

Jo followed the request. Meadowsweet must have been empty for years. The back garden was choked and overgrown. An archway sagged under the weight of masses of rambling roses. There was a rockery which had almost disappeared under heather, daphne, saxifrage and horned violets. Rows of raspberry, gooseberry and blackcurrant bushes were tangled and the rhubarb plants had giant leaves. This place would have spurred Jo's imagination if she had been brought here as a child.

It was a pity Molly had never seen such a delight. She made up her mind to take Molly and Rex on a picnic to Porthmeor Cove on Saturday or take the bus to St Ives where the forlorn little girl could enjoy the sandy beaches.

Rising to her feet, watching from the mullioned window, Katherine waited until Jo was searching for the kitten at the

257

bottom of the garden. 'Can I get you a sherry or something, Mr Lidgey?'

'No, thank you.'

'You've been so kind, Mr Lidgey.' Katherine gazed into his eyes. Such perfect velvety blackness, and so beautifully tragic in their appeal. 'Joanna is so happy at the school and now I can see why.'

'Joanna has brought innovations to the school. Her class is devoted to her,' Marcus said, eyeing Katherine to see if the facade she was giving as a loving mother would slip. He had heard about the bad feelings between Joanna and her mother and sensed this woman was as devious and manipulative as Eleanor. Why had she come to Parmarth? To persuade Joanna to give up her career? Perhaps she had heard about Joanna's attachment to Luke Vigus, but there was no sign she had taken Joanna to task when alone with her upstairs. 'You must be very proud of her, Mrs Venner.'

'I am indeed. She was such a bright child. Would you like to see some photographs of her? I've got some recent ones of her taken at my son's wedding.'

'I'd be delighted to.'

'Oh, dear, I haven't unpacked them yet. You are most welcome to call again to see them. I'd be interested to hear everything about Joanna's time at the school. I'd ask her, but she would find it embarrassing. We must exchange telephone numbers in case I want to pass on a message to her. I shall expect a call from you in the very near future.'

Marcus was filled with unease and was relieved when Jo came inside with a tiny, white, half-grown cat in her arms. 'He was shy at first but I managed to coax him out from the roots of a lilac tree. Shall I take him to the kitchen and feed him for you, Mother?'

'No, thank you, darling. I feel quite well now and can manage. You had better run along. Mrs Lidgey will be expecting Mr Lidgey.' Now she had accomplished the first part of her plan, to meet Marcus Lidgey – and he was going to be a satisfying challenge, more reserved than she had imagined – she did not want Jo under her roof a moment

258

longer. Jo's youth and shining prettiness irritated her, as did her poise and confidence.

Silly little bitch, Katherine thought, glaring at Jo as she waved farewell at the front door. You think you've got the world at your feet. No woman did. Not even one with a career and money and ownership of a house.

'You're not at all like your mother in looks,' Marcus said as he made the car crawl along the quiet road. He was recalling Katherine's hard, over-made-up face and fat breasts straining at her dress.

'What did you think of her?'

'She seems charming, I suppose.' He thought her insincere, a social climber and a bore. 'Tell me about your childhood, if it's not an imposition.'

'I had mixed blessings really, a perfect childhood in comparison with some of my pupils' lives.' She launched into an account of her mother's uncaring attitude, her association with Celia. Marcus listened attentively, gaining insights into what made up Joanna's character, why she was so strong-willed. Because Katherine Venner obviously despised Joanna, he despised the whorish woman.

Beth arrived at the Vigus cottage at seven thirty. It took a lot of gentle persuasion to get Rex to wash before he climbed the rope ladder at nine o'clock for bed. While he was undressing, she tucked Molly into the bed they shared, top to tail, where she had lain, feeling poorly, all evening. Beth sat on the camp bed which Luke had provided for her. He had propped his mother's mattress on its side against the wall, giving more room in the cramped space. She told the children the tale of Holiburn the giant, read the account of the Good Samaritan from the Bible, finally saying a prayer over them. Then she climbed down the rope ladder to Marylyn.

The baby, now a bonny eight months old with soft reddish-brown hair, was wakeful. Beth played with her for an hour, then sang softly while giving her last bottle. When Marylyn was settled in her cradle upstairs, Beth made herself a mug of hot chocolate and finally put her weary feet up on the couch.

She went to bed at ten thirty, much later than when at home for her parents retired early. After kneeling beside the camp bed to say her prayers, she climbed in under the rough covers. People told her she must be mad sleeping in this pokey little cottage – a hovel or a pigsty, they called it – but Luke paid her two shillings each night she slept here and he had promised he would soon find somewhere better for the children to live.

In the middle of the night Beth was running to the school-house in her nightdress, crying in panic.

Thirty

The front door of Nance Farm was suddenly being battered on. The dogs created a noisy din in the kitchen.

Jo followed Mercy downstairs, both in nightclothes. Before she opened the door, Mercy passed the lamp to Jo and picked up the heavy shapeless lump of iron used as a doorstop.

It proved to be Marcus causing the commotion. Mercy invited him inside, but reckoning it was Jo he had come to see, she left it to her to ask why he was calling so urgently at this ungodly hour.

In the dull orangey light, he faced the two women in the hallway. 'I remembered you were staying the night here, Joanna.'

Jo stared into his grave face. 'What is it? Is Eleanor ill?'

'I haven't come about my mother,' he said in the soft, precise manner of someone making sure their every word was clearly understood. He was having difficulty meeting her eyes.

'Is it Luke?' Jo started forward. 'Have you heard something about him? Has he been hurt?' Mercy took the lamp back, instinctively putting an arm round her.

'It's not about Luke.' Marcus shook his head sadly. 'Can we go into the kitchen and talk?'

'No!' Jo cried nervously. 'Tell me now. What's happened?'

He swallowed hard and reached for Jo's hand. 'A short time ago Beth Wherry came running to the schoolhouse for help. Joanna, my dear, I'm very sorry to have to tell you this but little Molly is dead. It appears she died in her sleep.'

Gripping his hand in shock, Jo felt as if she had been hit

by a tremendous breaker of freezing cold water. Her mouth went dry and she had difficulty speaking. 'W-what? No! It can't be true.'

'Come on, my handsome, into the kitchen,' Mercy said. 'It'll be warm in there.'

'N-no. I must get dressed. I have to go to Rex and Marylyn.' Scalding tears of grief fell down Jo's face. How could fate have been so cruel to Molly? She'd had a terrible start in life, suffered constant ill health, fear and humiliation. And now this. Her young life suddenly snatched away.

Still clutching Marcus's hand, she appealed to him. 'Thank you for coming, Marcus. Did you come in your motorcar? Will you drive me to the village?'

'I asked Davey Penoble to drop me off here.' He gave her a smile full of understanding and sympathy. 'He's gone on to the Penzance area to locate Luke. I'll wait for you to get ready and walk with you to the village.'

As the three set off for the village, dawn was beginning to streak the sky, a cold banner of red in the glowing yellowy-whiteness. Jo held Mercy's big rough hand, and when Marcus offered her his arm she gladly took it.

Her mind strayed again to Molly's misery. Her fearful, distrusting, scabby little face when she had first seen her. Her constant discomposure at school, where she had been so unmercifully bullied. Blood and coal dust all over her when she had been thrown into the coal house. Pleasures had been few in her short life. The hair ribbon Jo had given her, a bag of sweets, an iced bun, a second-hand dress. Despite Jessie's neglect and cruelty towards her, she had asked Jo only two days ago when her mother was coming home. Thank God she had known the kindly attentions of Beth and Mrs Wherry.

Suddenly, Jo sobbed, 'Did she suffer?'

'No,' Marcus replied, his voice choked with emotion. 'I've seen her myself. She looks very peaceful. I waited for the doctor to confirm she had slipped away then I left Beth and her father with her. Rex and the baby have been taken to Mrs Wherry.'

When they got to the Vigus cottage, Marcus stayed down-stairs. Mercy climbed the rope ladder after Jo. Beth and John Wherry were sitting either side of Molly's body. Beth was looking fairly composed now the terrible shock of her tragic discovery had abated a little. John Wherry, who had lit candles all round the room, had an open Bible on his lap.

Jo hugged Beth. 'Are you all right?' she whispered through her tears.

'Yes.' Beth nodded, her childlike voice trembling. 'Something woke me up. I felt I had to check on the children and . . . it was Molly. I knew at once she'd been taken, God bless her. She's with Him now.'

Jo fell on her knees and gazed down at Molly's sweet pale face. She looked as if she was sleeping. Jo stroked her hair and kissed her cold cheek. 'Oh, Molly, my poor dear Molly.' Then she turned to Mercy and cried her heart out in her arms.

Luke turned up shortly before midday. Jo was sitting on the settee in the Wherrys' parlour, holding Marylyn very close on her lap. Rex was clinging to her, as he had done the moment she had arrived here early in the morning. Mrs Wherry discreetly crept away to her kitchen.

Sobbing wretchedly, Rex left Jo's side and ran to his elder brother, who looked ashen and gaunt, his pale blue eyes almost colourless. Luke hugged him briefly then went to Jo. They embraced but he pulled quickly away. He paced up and down the short room, his boots slapping down on the worn linoleum. He ran his hands through his hair. Extracted a cigarette out of the packet he pulled from the breast pocket of his shirt with trembling fingers. Jo made to check him, changed her mind and choked on the unspoken words. The air undulated with tension.

Luke glanced at her, his eyes filled with tears. He swallowed heavily to forbid them, shook his head, looked out of the window, ran his palm over his face. Finally, he turned back to Jo.

'Where is she? I went home and she's not there.' His voice was husky with emotion. And anger.

263

'She's been taken away, darling.' Jo stood up. She wanted to hold him, shower him with comfort. 'The coroner ordered it. They have to find out exactly how she died.'

'What! She doesn't deserve that. To be treated like a slab of meat in an abattoir.' He swore and Jo had the notion he wanted to beat his fists into something, anything to ease his pain and fury. 'Davey Penoble said she died in her sleep, peaceful and no pain and all that rubbish! He made it sound like she'd received a blessing, not died in a stinking hovel.'

'Luke, stop it,' Jo implored him. Mrs Wherry peeped into the room, worried over Luke's anguish. Jo passed Marylyn to her. 'Think of Rex. He mustn't hear things like that.'

'Why not?' Luke bawled savagely, glaring at Rex who was backing towards the door. Jo went to the boy, put her hands on his shoulders and he halted, watching Luke from frightened eyes. 'It's the one lesson in life he should learn, that life's a bloody torment and then you die and turn to dust.'

'Take no notice of him,' Jo whispered in Rex's ear as Luke continued to rant macabrely. 'Luke's grief-stricken. Molly's in heaven now, safe and well with the Lord Jesus. She'll always be happy, no one can ever hurt her again.' Jo prayed she had soothed away some of the boy's horror. 'Go to Mrs Wherry, she'll take care of you. I want to speak to Luke.'

Before he left the parlour, the look Rex gave his brother was consumed with hurt and accusation.

Jo closed the door and faced Luke. His handsome features were taut and uncompromising, the skin stretched white over his high cheekbones. It was as if he had closed a door inside himself, shut part of himself off from her. Life had returned to his eyes, but they held nothing appropriate to the tragedy. He had already lost the consoling numbness associated with the death of a loved one, and he was looking at her in the same way Rex had just looked at him. She was desperate to go to him, and she needed his arms about her too, but she felt that if she touched him, something inside him would snap, something bad would be brought to the surface. She loved this man so much it was an agony to have to stand back as if she was nothing more to him at that moment than Molly's teacher.

'I'm very sorry, Luke. I'm convinced there was nothing anyone could have done for Molly. It was better that Beth was with her than your mother. Davey was right. She did look peaceful, there was even a little smile on her face.' The tears pressing at the backs of Jo's eyes began to fall; she could not stop them even if she wanted to. 'She looked lovely, like an angel.'

'She died alone,' Luke breathed bitterly.

'No, she didn't. Beth prayed for her just before she went to sleep. God was with Molly. If you can't turn to me, Luke, at least comfort yourself with that.'

At last he came to her, putting his hands on her arms. There was so much he wanted to say but he would choke on the words. A thousand times he had wished to rid himself of his sisters and brother. He knew if he had fixed it for them to be fostered he would have seen less and less of them.

When Davey Penoble had found him in the Admiral Benbow in Penzance, his first thought at the news was that at last he was free from one of his responsibilities. He'd hated himself for it immediately, but the thought had been there, thrust to the surface, and he had seen into his own soul as clearly as if looking into a mirror. It was seamed with utter selfishness. He had always prided himself on his masculinity, but he wasn't a man. A real man shouldered his burdens, no matter how unpleasant and hard they might be, and it wasn't as if Rex and Molly and Marylyn weren't ever going to grow up and make their own way in the world. Only Molly was not going to grow up at all now. He should have been at home with her. It was his fault she'd died, he must have wished it on her. And now he had scared Rex with his morbid ravings and lost his brother's respect.

He squeezed Jo's arms. He did not hurt her, but he had the physical strength to. Yet she was stronger than he ever would be. He had always known it. He wasn't good enough for her. Maybe she knew it too, but she loved him nonetheless. And he loved her. He could not give her up any more than he could help himself for not caring enough for his siblings.

Jo could not bear his silence and moved in to his body.

The familiarity of him was balm to her aching heart. She prayed his fit of frenzy had assuaged his despair, that he would apologise to Rex, hold the boy, reassure him.

Luke was feeling iron-cold but it helped to hold the woman he loved and needed, to bring her against him, feel the delicate body that so willingly yielded to him. 'I'm sorry, Jo.'

'It's been a terrible shock,' she said, trying to look up into his face.

Luke could not let her see his weakness. He kept her head clamped to his chest. 'I suppose I'd better make some arrangements.' Yes, do the necessary things, go through the motions, for the sake of the others. He kissed Jo's lips briefly, then left for the hovel Molly had died in.

Marcus was on his way home during the school dinner break, and saw Luke coming out of the tiny cottage across the street. Luke ignored him, making for Lucky tethered to the chapel railings. Marcus walked rapidly to catch up with him.

'I would like to offer my deepest condolences over Molly's death, Mr Vigus.'

'Thank you for your help.' Luke kept his eyes on the ground.

'Have you received any information?' Marcus persisted. He was not in a position to be with Joanna, but he had to know exactly what was happening.

'I phoned the doctor and he told me they've taken Molly to Penzance hospital. I'm going there to see her and arrange to have her brought home.' Luke was uncomfortable in the other man's presence. Marcus Lidgey had not shirked his duty, he was caring admirably for his ailing mother.

'I'd like to offer you unlimited use of my motorcar and telephone. Can you drive?'

'Yes, but I'd rather use my horse and the pub telephone.'

'Miss Teague and I have divided Miss Venner's class between us. I've told her she must take off as much time as you have need of her.'

Luke nodded curtly and stalked off.

Marcus ate his lunch alone at the dining table. When Sally

266

came to collect the dishes, she said frostily, 'Mrs Lidgey's asking to see you.'

'Tell her I'll be along directly.'

'You're going this time then?' Sally rattled the plates on to the tray. 'I was beginning to think you didn't care about her no more.'

You behave as if I don't exist, she mused bitterly, but you talk to Beth all the time these days. Good thing for her she doesn't sleep in this house or she'd have you knocking on her bedroom door, as plain and as religious as she is. Anyone would think it was her sister who'd died this morning, the fuss you made of her. It's time Mrs Lidgey knew about this.

'Of course I care about her.' Marcus lit a cigarette. He would make a point of taking his time to go to Eleanor.

'You've got a strange way of showing it. She's always asking for you and you can't be bothered with her.'

Marcus found Sally's remarks and ill humour objectionable, but he did not remonstrate with her. His mind was too occupied working out his plan. 'The doctor said she must have as much rest as possible. You know what she's like when I'm with her. She tries to do too much and when I chide her she loses her temper with me. Getting into a passion isn't good for her. But you're right, perhaps I've overdone staying away from her.'

Anxious to get a higher professional opinion on the condition of his mother's health, Marcus had paid an orthopaedic specialist to come to the house for a consultation. A week ago, Dr Mark Richardson, sleek in a grey, pin-striped suit and waistcoat and ink-blue bowtie, pedantic and methodical, had made a detailed examination of Eleanor, to which she had eagerly submitted. His opinion was that she needed regular manipulation of the spine by an expert hand, complemented by a particular brand of medicines which he alone could prescribe (at an exorbitant price, Marcus was certain).

For Marcus's ears alone, he had pontificated, 'Your mother's age has taken a toll on her condition. If I had been consulted at the time of her accident and my treatment had been followed she would be much more mobile and in far less pain. You will see she gets the therapy I've recommended?'

'Of course. But her general condition is quite well?'

'You have nothing to fear there, Mr Lidgey. Your mother's heart is very strong. She has years left in her.'

The prognosis had left Marcus with no alternative. Eleanor must be helped on her way out of this world.

Precisely ten minutes passed before he went into the sitting room, where Eleanor was lying on the sofa, propped up by a mass of pillows. Her dress, hair and make-up were immaculate as usual, but pain worried the corners of her eyes, paled her temples.

She examined him steadily. 'I knew you would not stay away from me for ever, my son. When is the treatment Dr Richardson prescribed for me going to start?'

He stood well back from her. 'He left the arrangements to me. I don't intend to do any such thing.'

'Bastard!'

With Joanna in his thoughts, he found the strength and calm he needed. 'For what you've done to me you deserve to suffer all the pain in the world. It should have been you who died today, not an innocent little girl.'

'You may wish that with all your heart but I have great strengths within me. Come close, Marcus.'

Putting his hand under his chin in a thoughtful expression, he frowned slightly. 'Do you think children go straight to heaven, Mama? Or do you think wronged ones, like my little sister, Gabriella, stay earthbound, desperately hoping to gain the love of those who hated them?'

'No one really has a soul, Marcus.' Eleanor smiled maliciously. 'The only life we get is what we have while we're breathing. Gabriella isn't breathing. She was eaten up by the worms long, long ago.'

'Her body perished, but sometimes I have this fancy that I hear her voice, like a quiet murmur, calling to me. She knows I would have loved her dearly. One day I'm going to kill you, Mama.'

'You haven't got the courage.' Eleanor laughed scornfully.

268

'You and your pathetic schemes. I've seen the way you look at me, plotting inside your silly head.'

'Oh, I'll do it, and without laying a finger on you. I'll tell you something else. I mean to have Joanna as my wife, and honourably. I'll not fail. Now I really must go back to the school. Enjoy a restful afternoon, Mama.'

It was late evening when Luke got back from Penzance. He went straight to the Wherrys' house, knowing Jo would stay there with Rex and Marylyn. The Wherrys gathered in the parlour to hear what he had to say.

Luke was badly shaken. 'I waited for the results of the tests. Molly died of something called an aneurysm. A blood vessel swelled inside her and ruptured, hitting her heart. They said she was probably born with the weakness. It could've happened any moment. They said she didn't suffer. It wouldn't have woken her.' His eyes shone with tears but he refused to give way to them. 'I've arranged for Molly to be brought home tomorrow and to be buried next Monday.'

'At least you know what happened, Luke,' Jo said quietly. 'I hope you will take comfort from it. Talk to Rex now. He needs you.'

'Poor little Molly.' Mrs Wherry dried her eyes with her hanky. 'You can leave Marylyn and Rex with us for the next few days, Luke.'

'Thanks,' Luke replied briskly, almost as if he had no feelings on the matter. 'Do you want to stay here, Rex?'

'Yes,' Rex answered sullenly, leaning into Beth, avoiding Luke's eyes.

'I'll fetch some things for you. Come to the house tomorrow afternoon if you want to see your sister in repose.' He looked at Beth. 'I'm sorry you found Molly dead. I should've been there with her.'

To Jo, 'I've hitched up my wagon. I'll take you back to Cardhu.'

Luke left his wagon in a sheltered hollow near Cardhu and stalled Lucky in the old stable behind the isolated grey house. Jo made coffee and she and Luke sat in the kitchen to drink it. Neither of them was hungry, but she nibbled on a ginger fairing. It brought her comfort, remembering how Celia had often given her the biscuits as a token of care.

Luke had fallen into silence again, but Jo's thoughts centred on the little dead girl. Poor dear Molly, even if she had been blessed with a loving mother and enjoyed better health, she probably would have died in this way.

Luke said suddenly, 'I can't let Rex and Marylyn go back to that cottage, Jo.'

'Of course not. I understand, darling.'

Luke fell into desperate thoughts. There was only one way now to give Rex and Marylyn a stable future. He and Jo must marry as soon as possible. But it would mean Jo forsaking her career. She was prepared to do this in the future, when the school she was planning was well under way, and keep to the administration side of things. He wanted to marry Jo, with all his heart he wanted her, but he did not have the right to spoil her life. A knot was forming around his heart and pulling tighter and tighter.

Jo was reading his mind. And she feared, as Luke did, Jessie returning and plunging Rex and Marylyn back into their old way of life. Jo would fight to prevent Jessie doing this, but the children had already suffered too many traumas. They deserved a stable life, a full-time mother.

'We'll have to get married, Luke.'

He reached across the table for her hand. 'You must think this through carefully, Jo. You'll have to make a big sacrifice. You'll be tied down with two kids while I'm away on the road. I don't want you to be unhappy, to come to despise me.'

'It won't be such a big sacrifice to marry the man I love, darling. I can't pretend it will be easy giving up my career, but I'll gladly do it for you and Rex and Marylyn. I love them too. We could always meet you on your travels and sometimes even go with you.'

'I'm sorry, Jo.' Luke shook his head, downcast, regretful. 'I'm too selfish to refuse your offer.'

'We'll make it a simple affair. The children can move in here as soon as I've worked out my notice. Rex will get used to it. Marylyn won't know any different. We'll have a wonderful future, Luke. I promise.'

He gazed a while into her eyes. 'Can I stay tonight?'

She kissed the hand holding hers. 'You didn't need to ask that, darling.'

They lay in each other's arms unable to sleep, and in the long dark soul of the night, Jo heard a catch in Luke's throat.

'What is it, Luke?' she whispered.

His voice emerged beset with tears. 'God help me, but I've been thinking it's the best thing to happen to Molly. She couldn't cope at school or with the world. She had no future to look forward to.'

'We have to believe that God knows what's best for all of us.'

'Yes,' he sighed deeply, then groaned in anguish. 'Oh, God forgive me. Molly's dead and while she was alive I rarely held her or kissed her. I didn't even speak to her much, except to order her about. She must have wished every day of her life she'd never been born.'

He wept finally and Jo cradled him to her. 'You mustn't feel guilty, Luke. You did your best.'

'But I didn't, Jo,' he cried against her soft flesh. 'I resented the kids for tying me down. If it weren't for them I would've gone off and lived my own life.'

'But you didn't leave. Although you weren't there all the time, Molly knew she always had you to turn to. If there had been no one in Parmarth for you to come back to, you would never have met me.'

'I can't bear that thought,' he said, flinching. It was some moments before he composed himself. 'I swear I'll never let you, Rex or Marylyn down. You have my word, Jo.'

Thirty-One

U nder a scorching sun, wearing a black dress and small sunhat, Jo arranged gardenias on Celia's grave, now graced by the granite headstone Jo had provided. She stayed in ponderous stillness for some moments, then on slow, heavy legs walked round to the little mound created in the churchyard only yesterday.

Molly's grave was covered with wreaths and posies. More flowers, cultivated and wild, were lined neatly nearby on the grass verge. Shocked by the suddenness at which death had snatched away an innocent child from among them, nearly all of Parmarth had turned out for the funeral. Marcus had closed the school for the day and many of the pupils had been there. A mass of black-clad figures blighting a magnificent afternoon in June.

The largest wreath was from Luke, Rex and Marylyn. The villagers had decried Jo's name being written on it too; as if it really mattered, Molly was dead, and although the villagers had no knowledge of it yet, Jo was to marry Luke with haste and become foster-mother to Rex and Marylyn. Molly did not need more flowers today, but before going to the schoolhouse to hand in her resignation, Jo had needed to pick gardenias and white dwarf roses from her garden and to make this dual journey.

Luke had said early this morning he'd find the money to pay for a headstone and have 'A Little Moorland Rose' sculpted on it. Then he had left, saying he had business he must see to.

Jo understood. He needed to be alone, just as she needed to look down on Molly's little grave to believe her tragic young pupil was really dead. Perhaps Molly was with Celia now and Celia was looking after her. A childless woman and a motherless child. It was a consoling thought.

Her mind echoing with repressed silence, Jo knelt and carefully moved aside the wreaths on the centre of the grave, then pushed the clay vase she had brought with her into the dark, dry earth. She made a second trip to fetch water at the back of the church, from the iron pump beside the sexton's shed. The water sparkled silver and brilliant as it poured into the rusty watering can, making a pounding noise, like thunder over the moors on a sweltering summer day. Everything Jo saw and heard these last few days seemed brighter, more resounding, more obvious, as if life itself was trying to break into her numbness and disbelief and assert it was still there.

Tears came in a rush again and Jo wept in the shady privacy. She put her hand in under the mouth of the pump and let the water wet her skin. It was icy cold, pumped up from a natural stream several feet underground. The water was down, down in the deep dark silence. Like Molly. Death was cruel, as life sometimes was. Certainly life had been cruel to Molly.

And people were cruel. Very cruel.

Yesterday, after the vicar had intoned the final prayer, Luke and Rex, who was standing stonily beside him, took their last look down on the little white coffin. People had seemed reluctant to slip away and leave them to quietly bear their loss, as if wanting to come to an understanding of the tragedy for themselves.

Keane Trevail had said loudly, after glancing up at the clear blue sky, 'She deserved this good weather. Goodness knows the poor little maid never had much sunshine in her life.' His eyes pounced on Luke, declaring who he thought was responsible for his sister's misery. Assenting murmurs and stares had come in a relentless volley.

Breaking down in grief, Rex ran off, disappearing among the graves. 'Can't you damned people wait till you get outside the churchyard,' Luke seethed.

Standing close to Luke, Jo slipped her hand inside his. 'Don't, Luke. Let's just leave.'

'If you have any decency at all, Joanna Venner' – Biddy Lean pushed to the front of the crowd – 'you'd let go of his hand and give him his marching orders. We don't want his sort in Parmarth, and if you keep on with his company you won't be fit to teach our children.'

Murmurs of agreement echoed round the churchyard again. Jo was furious, but before she could say anything in her or Luke's defence, somehow a whisper of a voice broke through the tension. 'It's you people attacking Luke and Miss Venner at this saddest of moments who have no sense of decency. They both did all they could for poor little Molly.' It was Beth who had spoken. With her family, her mother holding Marylyn, she slipped quietly away to host the wake at their house – if there was now to be a wake.

Marcus, who had enjoyed his rival's shortcomings being aired in public, coughed authoritatively, as if sharing his housemaid's views, then he immediately left to go off by himself. An exodus of red faces shied away after him. But Jo knew the villagers were only sorry to have been shamed in the churchyard. The insults would be offered again. It was ironic; she was giving up her teaching career anyway.

After an apologetic clearing of his throat, the Reverend Silas Mountebank also beat a hasty retreat, and Jo and Luke were alone. Alone with their painful emotions. The funeral had changed from an occasion of mourning into a disaster.

'That's right, clear off and leave us alone, all of you!' Luke swiped angry tears from his cheeks. 'I'm going to throw their rotten flowers away. I won't have them put on Molly's grave.'

Jo used force to stop him lunging at the floral tributes. 'They're for Molly, darling. Don't let them upset you.'

Still looking as if he wanted to trample the multitude of flowers, Luke stalked away through the graves as Rex had done, to scale the churchyard wall.

'Luke, wait for me.' Jo was unable keep up with his long, furious strides and she fell behind, watching his rigid back, her heart wrung in pieces over his suffering. She had been forced to hold her own feelings in check since Molly's death for he had given way to so many different moods. For three days he had sat in his old home over her open coffin, refusing to go outside until it was time to follow her to the churchyard. He had thrown away the rabbit's foot he'd given her – it had not brought her any luck – and put a tiny silver cross around her neck, and a white rosebud in her hand. Jo had sat in the cottage with him, watching him smoke and drink beer, unsuccessfully coaxing him to eat, and only to avoid more gossip had she made her way home to Cardhu each night.

Luke charged on, tramping across the moor, not stopping until he'd reached the same spot at the stream where Jo and her class had encountered the rogue dog. Jo came hurrying up to him, her face flushed. He saw how upset she was and knew he should take her in his arms, but right now he couldn't bear to be touched. The funeral had become a fiasco, a bloody joke! The woman he loved had been ostracised in front of the whole village just because she was his. Was he a piece of dirt? That was how those self-righteous bastards had spoken about him.

'We have to go to the Wherrys' house, Luke,' Jo pleaded breathlessly.

All Luke could do was vent his frustration and fury. 'No one will go there. No one will see all the food I've provided, enough to have kept Molly well fed for a month. There's plenty of food and heaps of flowers for her grave. Molly had to wait to die before she had anything in plenty!'

'Stop it, Luke. For pity's sake, you'll make yourself ill.'

'Later today I'll take the kids' things out of that blasted dump and I'll never set foot inside it again,' he snarled, referring to the little cottage. 'I'd like to burn the wretched place to the ground!' and he let out the foulest oath. 'I'll bring Molly's stuff to Cardhu. Will you keep it for Marylyn? She can have it when she's older.'

'Of course.' Hot and perspiring, Jo took off her hat and unbuttoned her coat, worn just six months ago at Celia's funeral. 'Don't you think you ought to find Rex?'

Luke peered at the heather-laden hills, the hazy sky, the hard outline of the tors, anywhere but at Jo. At times like

275

this he could not bear the good sense he saw in her face. With a mighty sigh, he forced himself to speak calmly. 'He'll eventually make his way to the Wherrys'. I'll take his things there, and apologise to the Wherrys about the wake.'

'The Wherrys will understand. What will you say to him?'

'I know what you're getting at, Jo. I need to talk to Rex, put things straight. I'll do it, I promise.'

Then he'd gone to her, gathered her into his arms, so much in need of her comfort. And Jo had responded by trying to blanket him with her love.

Later in the day Luke had spoken to Rex in the Wherrys' house, but what had passed between the two brothers he would not say. After a restless night, he had hitched up his wagon and was gone.

With a start, Jo realised the icy water was spilling over the rim of the watering can and her arm and shoes were getting soaked. She stopped pumping.

Something prodded her shoulder. She turned round and with the greatest dismay saw it was Mardie Dawes. She smelled like rotting fish and was wearing a grubby, low-neck blouse. Her exposed neck and sunken chest were riddled with thick purple-blue veins. Her bare toes were malformed, peeking out like lumps of raw meat from the scuffed leather of her sandals.

'I'll carry that for 'ee,' Mardie squawked, her bony hand reaching out to lift the watering can off the pump.

'I don't need any help,' Jo said tartly. Wrenching the watering can down, splashing the overflowing water, she rudely pushed past Mardie.

Thick-skinned at her hostile reception, but her eyes marked with menace, the fortune-teller rambled along at her side. 'The Vigus maid had a good send-off. Beautiful flowers. I would've come back to the wake, but thought I wouldn't be welcome.'

'You were right, Mardie. And I don't ever want to see you on my doorstep. Would you mind going away. I want to be alone.' They were nearing Molly's grave and Jo stopped, having no intention of sparring with this wretched nuisance beside the sacred little place.

'You are alone.' Mardie edged closer to her. 'All alone. Luke Vigus quickly took himself off. Everybody said he would. You expecting him back?'

'Of course. It's none of your business.'

'I don't agree with the others. I reckon he cares for you and will come back. You love him very much, don't you? You are, after all, giving him what your mother gave Bob Merrick. But I wonder just how much you think Luke is worth.'

'What are you talking about?' Jo snapped. She would not tolerate one more insult to Luke's character. He may not have been a model father figure to his siblings but he had never made them work so hard they couldn't stay awake at school. He wasn't cruel to animals. He wasn't openly conducting an affair with a married woman. And he'd never cruelly ostracise someone in public.

Mardie tapped her skirt pocket and there was a jingle of loose change. 'You've got money, missy. Are you willing to part with some of it to keep your precious Luke out of trouble, from dangling on the hangman's rope?'

'What?' Jo wanted to scream but she kept her voice to a furious whisper.

'Luke killed his mother. I saw him do it, up at the mine ruins. He threw her down Pike's Shaft.'

'How dare you say such a thing! Get away from me.'

Mardie grasped Jo's wrist, making her drop the watering can, the water splashing over both their feet. 'Jessie don't rest, she walks the moor. She wants justice. Keep a watch for her in that lonely house of yours.' Mardie looked her most cunning and heartless. 'Somehow she might get word of her fate to the police. They wouldn't be a bit surprised to learn Luke's done away with her. He threatened to do it often enough and there's plenty of people who heard him.'

Thrusting Mardie's hand off her, Jo turned scarlet with rage. 'Luke didn't mean it. He wouldn't hurt anyone.'

'Are you sure about that, missy? How well do you think you know him? He was out on the moors alone, supposedly looking for her the day she disappeared. There's enough circumstantial evidence to make sure he's convicted and hanged.'

'The law may not see it that way.'

'The question is, are you willing to take the risk?'

Jo could not answer. She wanted to throw her hands round the old woman's neck and cut off her breath for telling these wicked lies. Lies? She had heard Luke herself threatening to kill Jessie. Had he become desperate enough to carry it through? Throwing Jessie down the mineshaft carried little risk, if one wasn't seen. But people often threatened to kill when they were angry. They never had the slightest intention of actually doing it. She, herself, was so livid that right now she felt like lashing out at Mardie over her cruelty at waiting until now, when she was at her most vulnerable immediately after Molly's funeral, to try to blackmail her. Had Luke allowed his hatred of Jessie to grow out of control? No, it was unthinkable.

It troubled her there was so much animosity against Luke at the moment that a police investigation could be very damaging for him. In a voice pained and hoarse, 'How much?'

'This is a serious matter.' Mardie's soulless eyes glittered malevolently. 'Not in the same league as adultery. Celia Sayce paid me well not to tell the village of her sordid affair so she could live here peacefully. I would've asked hush money off you to keep her reputation intact if that damned Lidgey woman hadn't realised who she was and blabbed about it. Keeping my mouth shut this time will mean saving Luke's life. The price of that comes high. A lump sum of two hundred pounds and then twenty a month. He's worth it, isn't he?'

'You rotten, evil bitch!'

'I'll call at Cardhu tomorrow evening.' Mardie cackled. 'Give you time to go to the bank.'

'Don't you dare set foot on my property,' Jo snarled. 'I'll meet you at the willows, at six o'clock. Now get away from me.'

'If you don't show up I'll be making a phone call to the coppers the same evening, and the only place you'll see your lover after that is in court,' Mardie warned coldly. She picked up the watering can and thrust it into Jo's hand. 'Enjoy the sunny afternoon, Miss Venner.'

Jo had no idea how long she stood there, rigid in shock and disbelief. When someone softly called her name she cried out in alarm.

'Joanna, it's me,' Marcus said, suddenly there beside her. While Jo was a small figure in black, he looked cool and commanding in light slacks and a cricket jumper, the sleeves pushed up past his elbows. 'I've just passed that fortune-telling misfit. Has she upset you?'

On his way home after a routine meeting on school affairs with the vicar, he had cut through the churchyard, and behind the cover of a yew tree had overheard every word of the conversation between Joanna and Mardie Dawes. He would say nothing about it, but he was not going to allow Joanna to be blackmailed.

'She was taunting me about Molly's death.' Tears sprang to Jo's eyes. This latest blow, and having to keep it a secret, was more than she could bear. 'People have been so unkind.'

'You've lost your water,' he said softly, relieving her of the watering can and offering her a consoling arm. 'There's a seat near Molly's resting place. I'll take you there then get more water. You're shaking, you need peace and quiet.'

'Thank you, Marcus.' Numb and confused, she leaned against his arm. 'I . . . I was coming to see you after I've finished here.'

'Is there something I can do for you?' He held her trembling hand. 'You only have to ask, nothing is too much trouble for a very good friend.'

Jo sat on the bench, frozen as she recalled every mean word Mardie had said, terrified over the blight the blackmail would bring to the future.

When Marcus came back with the water, she gazed down at the dwarf roses she had left beside Molly's grave. 'Would

279

you mind, Marcus? I've put a vase there. I don't think I can manage at the moment.'

'Of course. I'd be happy to.' He knelt and filled the vase with water, arranging the white roses inside it with meticulous care. 'They're very pretty. Molly would have liked them.'

'I wanted to bring something personal for her.' Jo shuddered, as if the weather had turned cold and unfriendly, but the sun was a golden globe in the bluest of skies.

'It's been a trying time for you. My mother is in bed. Will you come to the schoolhouse and have some tea?'

'No, thank you. I'd rather stay here. I need the fresh air. Will you stay with me? I don't want to be alone right now.'

'I'll stay as long as you need me.' He sat close beside her. 'How can I be of service to you?'

'What?' Jo said vaguely.

'You were coming to see me,' he reminded her gently.

'Oh, yes.' She took a small white envelope out of the pocket of her dress and handed it to him.

Marcus looked at his name and address on the envelope, written in her flowing hand. 'Is it an invitation?'

'No. I'm sorry because this is going to cause you great inconvenience. It's my resignation. I want to leave the school in three weeks; it will nearly be the end of the term. Luke and I are getting married. We're going to provide a stable home for Rex and Marylyn.'

It was like a blow to Marcus's heart but he worked hard not to show it. 'If I may say so without seeming heartless, is making a home for the children a good enough reason to get married?'

He flinched at her reply. 'It isn't just that, Marcus. Luke and I are deeply in love. We have been for some time. I know people don't approve of our relationship but I don't care.'

'It is a shame to have to give up your career. You are an exceptional teacher and will be an enormous loss to the school.'

'Some people won't think so,' she said bitterly.

'I don't think it is you they have anything against, Joanna. Their views are . . .' even though he wanted to shout from the church turrets that she must be out of her mind to marry a man who was a self-seeking failure, he would not say a word to hurt her. It would not further his hopes to win her for himself.

'Their views are understandable? Well, whatever they think I don't agree with them. No one knows Luke like I do. They haven't seen his gentle side. They don't care that he's been hurt and humiliated. I want to go home now. Will you walk with me until I'm out of the village? I don't feel strong enough to face any more animosity alone.'

'I've got lots of time to spare. I'd be delighted to see you safely home.'

Marcus would have liked to linger at Cardhu but Jo said she needed to rest.

A few minutes later, standing on the bridge, he pulled out the envelope containing her resignation, crumpled it in his hand, and tossed it into the stream.

Jo went upstairs to her bedroom; it would be hers and Luke's permanently soon. Tomorrow she would have to hand over the first instalment of the blackmail money to keep Luke out of prison, to keep him free and alive. He was worth it, he was worth anything. Whatever Luke might have done it would make no difference to her. Her love for him was unconditional. And she knew in her heart he was not a murderer. He was not a violent man. He was kind and tender, and at times childlike, with good reason to hate his mother.

Feeling utterly alone, she picked up a shirt Luke had left behind, then curling up on the bed she hugged it to her body and cried for hours.

Thirty-Two

Returning home, Marcus went straight to his study. Lighting a cigarette to calm his nerves, he looked up the telephone number Katherine Venner had given him. She was his best hope in stopping Joanna's wedding. He had the notion Joanna would marry in secret to prevent family intervention.

'Mr Lidgey, Marcus,' Katherine gushed familiarily over the telephone. 'At last, I was beginning to think you were ignoring me.'

'Not at all, Mrs Venner. I do apologise. I've been pre-occupied with my mother's needs and a tragedy in the village.'

'How is Joanna?'

He restrained his anger at her false motherly interest. 'Quite well, I think. She's grieving terribly over the little girl. I suppose you are busy preparing for the wedding. It will be a rush for you.'

'What wedding?' Katherine enquired brusquely. 'Are you telling me Joanna is getting married?'

'You mean you know nothing about it?' Marcus returned as if surprised. 'Joanna's wedding to the local itinerant dealer, Luke Vigus. You do know she has an attachment to this individual?'

'Yes, I've been informed about it.' Katherine could not hide her rage. 'Can you tell me why she has suddenly made up her mind to actually marry this rag-and-bone man?'

'I feel uncomfortable at imparting this news to you, Katherine. It is really none of my business. It's a consequence of Vigus's younger sister's death. Joanna is giving up her career to become mother to Vigus's remaining younger brother and baby sister. It's very noble of her. She will be a tremendous loss to the school.'

'She's what! Children!' Katherine exploded. 'I'm so sorry, Marcus. I didn't mean to shout at you. You will understand, of course, that all this is a terrible shock to me. I must inform my son at once. Alistair will put a stop to this nonsense. Oh, damn, he's in Scotland at the moment, not expected back for a few days. I'll telephone him anyway, he can write to her. I'll go to Cardhu tomorrow, although it won't do the slightest bit of good. Joanna won't listen to me, I'm afraid. Thank you for ringing me, Marcus. If I get the opportunity perhaps I could call on you? I'd be most interested to meet your mother,' Katherine ended on a hopeful note.

'My mother is indisposed at the moment. I wish you well in talking some sense into Joanna. Vigus is totally unworthy of her. Goodbye, Katherine.' Marcus put the receiver down. He couldn't stop trembling. Stubbing out the cigarette, he put his hands to his temples, feeling the beginnings of another violent headache.

The old miner's cottage was the epitome of gloom, waste and desolation. Neither stones nor ashes had been laid to form a proper path to the front door of weather-bleached wood. If there had been a flower or vegetable garden created by the former inhabitant it was now under a tangle of weeds, ferns, nettles and brambles. Marcus's eyes flicked to the two small, glassless windows. Dark curtains flapped in the wind.

Mardie Dawes was at home, either inside the cottage or in a nearby dome-shaped granite construction. He had heard her singing an indecent ditty to the tune of 'Onward Christian Soldiers'. The shrill singing started up again. She was in the outbuilding, which was about ten feet high and incorporated a misshapen chimney and a narrow slit for entry and exit. He assumed it was where she made her illegal gin.

'Mardie Dawes,' he called out.

There was the sound of something clattering to the ground, then swearing and muttering. Marcus waited.

Mardie crept out on to the moorland dirt, grimacing, showing her yellow teeth. She stayed close to the strange building, eyes glowing with suspicion. 'What can I do for you, Marcus Lidgey?'

'You don't seem pleased to see a customer, Miss Dawes.'

'You want to buy something?' Mardie asked nervously.

Marcus glanced coldly round the vicinity. 'I should imagine it is the only reason for someone venturing here.'

'Love potion, is it?' Mardie was a little less fearful of him, but she marvelled that no one else had ever grasped the madness in this man's face. 'I saw the way you looked at the Venner maid in the churchyard this afternoon.'

Marcus came closer. He wasn't sure which smelled worse, the woman or her illegal brew. 'I'd like a bottle of your best gin, Miss Dawes,' he said as pleasantly as if he was in the best society.

'I didn't take you for a tippler of that kind.' Mardie laughed tensely.

'Actually, it's for someone else.'

'Oh, I see. Give me a minute. I'll fetch one out to you.' Ducking her head under the low portal she disappeared inside the still-house.

Marcus followed her. The construction was dark and shadowy, the walls mouldy and running with condensation. He did not notice the overpowering stink of fermenting alcohol.

Snatching up a bottle of gin from a bench, Mardie squealed to see him so close to her. Backing away from him, she held out the bottle at arm's length. 'Take it. You can have it for nothing, being a new customer.'

The bottle in his hand, Marcus yanked out the cork which he threw to the ground. His eyes, like sharded ice, bore into the old woman. 'Were you telling Miss Venner the truth about Luke Vigus killing his mother?'

Mardie stepped back until her spine was pressing against a bench, on which a row of bottles and flagons of gin vied for space with herbal potions and lucky charms. Her eyes were steadily growing in size. 'I . . . I don't know what you're talking about.'

'Then let me refresh your memory.' His voice was low and deadly. 'This afternoon, you subjected Miss Venner to the horrors of blackmail in the churchyard. Was it true what you said?'

'No! No, it wasn't.'

'Then who did kill Jessie Vigus?'

Mardie stared at him, searching his mind.

'Well? Speak, I'm beginning to lose my patience!' he snapped.

'No one killed her, she fell in.' Mardie was blubbing rapidly. 'I'm sorry, honest I am. I'll tell Miss Venner it was all a mistake. I'll tell her I'm sorry.'

'It's too late for that, Mardie Dawes.' Marcus reached inside his coat pocket.

'Keep away from me!' Mardie yelled like a demented savage, her arms shooting out and sending her wares crashing to the floor. She could back away no further and fell to the ground in terror. 'Don't hurt me. I know you're in love with Joanna Venner. Let her go on believing Luke might've done it. That way she'll turn to you. I promise I won't bother her no more.'

Marcus glared down at the woman huddled beside the bench, clawing at the dirt. 'With you gone there will be no witness either way and she'll always doubt Vigus's innocence. You hurt Joanna. You caused distress to the woman I love.'

Holding the bottle upright he shook gin over Mardie.

'Stop! I said I'm sorry. Oh, God help me.' Mardie screamed in desperation as gin flowed over her face, splashed on her clothes, arms and legs.

When the bottle was empty Marcus stood back. 'You shouldn't have made her suffer. I can't bear anyone hurting her.'

Mardie screamed madly as he produced his cigarette lighter.

'I'll be doing the world a favour getting rid of you. You deserve to be dead like Jessie Vigus. You're both scum. Neither of you are fit to live near honest, decent people,

285

people who care about children and don't do terrible things to them. No one's going to mourn your death.'

Bending down, he lit the hem of Mardie's skirt.

She shrieked and tried to beat out the flames that shot up the alcohol-soaked material. Reaching past the flames Marcus lit her hair. Soon she was a screaming, writhing mass of burning.

Tearing his eyes from her crazed dance of death, he bolted out through the narrow slit and raced off over the moor. He did not stop until he'd scaled Carn Galver, where he looked down with cold satisfaction as the dome-shaped building, a ball of fire, collapsed in a glowing heap.

Thirty-Three

L uke was leaning on the quiet bar of the Admiral Benbow at Penzance, in the company of a few dockers and seamen.

He was on his third pint, silent and morose, when the landlord laid a newspaper down in front of him. 'Have you seen today's news? There's been another tragedy in Parmarth.'

His confidence struck low, Luke was in no mood for more bad tidings but his eyes caught the headline the landlord was pointing to. 'WOMAN DIES IN FIRE ON MOORS'. He read on, then muttered scathingly, 'Mardie Dawes. Good riddance to her. Hardly in the same league as my sister's death.'

'You knew this Dawes woman well, did you?' the landlord asked.

'She was a damned nuisance. Reckoned she could tell fortunes but was a fake. Think yourself lucky, Mike, she never frequented your pub. Had a bad gambling habit. She'd have sold her soul to put up her stake money.'

'Says there' – the landlord tapped the newspaper – 'she must have had an accident with the home-made liquor she was making. Went up like a light. The likes of her don't do my trade no good. Oh, well, that makes three sudden passings-on now. I take it your mother's not showed up?'

'No, and I'm not going to waste my time wondering what happened to her.' Luke downed the last drop of the pint and lit a cigarette. He shook his head when Mike made signs enquiring if he wanted a refill. 'Make it a large whisky this time. I need something to feel warm inside.'

'Feeling poorly, are you?'

Luke stared into space. 'No. I've got a lot on my mind.'
'Like what?'

Luke lifted the glass of whisky and swished the amber-gold liquid about inside it. 'Like I'm getting married in a couple of weeks' time.'

'What?' Mike's jaw fell open.

'Eh?' gasped a drinking acquaintance nearby who had been listening in on the conversation. 'You? Getting married? I don't believe it.'

'Sometimes nor do I.' Luke shook his head.

'If you feel like that then don't go through with it,' the drinker said sympathetically.

Luke knew him as an amiable young man who sometimes found employment on the docks, weighed down with the burden of a wife and six children. Luke sold him cheap knick-knacks at Christmas for his family. He often bought him a drink but so far today had not extended the hospitality.

''Tisn't like that, mate,' Luke said hastily. Visions of Jo flooded his mind. Jo laughing, crying, angry, wistful, intense, tireless, caring, loving. He loved every part of her. He missed her so much at that moment, wanted desperately to be with her. He had left her without a proper goodbye, and with all the wedding arrangements to make. 'I love her very much. All I want is her. When we get married I'll be rearing my brother and baby sister too. Never bargained on that.'

'And it's a bit frightening for you? I can understand that.' The young father nodded. 'Don't worry. You'll soon take to it. Me and the missus have never had anything much but we always get by. 'Tis hard bringing up a big family but we don't regret a single one of ours. They've brought their love with them and that's all that matters.'

'I hope you're right,' Luke said quietly. 'What're you having to drink?'

The young father asked for a pint of bitter. After the landlord had pulled it, and accepted a drink for himself, he folded the newspaper and threw it aside to wrap rubbish in later, its contents old news, already forgotten. Thoughtfully, he wiped down the counter. 'Things have a way of working out for the best, Luke.'

'Yeh, guess so, Mike.' Luke's familiar friendly smile finally returned. He thought fondly, Jo will always be mine and I will never, ever, leave her.

Thirty-Four

In the larger of the two unfurnished bedrooms at Cardhu, among Celia's trunks, dance dresses and tennis rackets, things Celia had not used for the last three decades of her life, Jo was making decisions. This room was to become Rex's. She would ask Luke to carry the stored items up to the attic. Rex would have a new bed and new clothes. Nothing flashy, just the same as the other boys in the village but better quality than what he'd been used to all his life. He would have lots of toys and board games, and she would encourage him to play boisterously and have fun, just as Celia had done with her.

Jo hoped Rex would be easily persuaded to leave Mrs Wherry's house, where he and Marylyn had lived since Molly's death. He had made no reply when she told him she and Luke were to marry, that he was to live at the big house, with her as his mother. Nor did he ask why she was breaking this news to him instead of Luke or why his brother had gone away. The boy did not seem to care. Jo would make him care. And she would teach him how to live without Molly and to accept her love.

She moved on to the other spare bedroom. Square and compact, it would be Marylyn's nursery until she was old enough to take over Jo's old room. A cot would fit nicely facing the window. Jo would fetch her dolls and Noah's ark and rocking horse from Tresawna House. The furniture would be white, and Jo would paint fairy motifs on it and bright murals on the walls. Luke would baulk at the money she intended to spend on the children, but she was determined to have her way. Once they were married, Rex and Molly would be *her* children.

She had already spent money on the projects. It was market day at Penzance and she had travelled there early that morning on Mercy's farm wagon to buy paint and yards of curtain material. Making a note of the measurements for the curtains, she was ready to go to Mrs Allett's to ask her to make them up.

Every few minutes her thoughts turned to Luke, hoping he would return soon, unaware of how close she had been to him a few hours ago. At times, the disappointment of giving up her career threatened to crush her, but she was looking forward to making her vows to Luke and taking over the care of the two children she had come to love.

'I miss you so much,' she whispered, remembering Luke's smile, his touch, how complete she felt when he was near. Her teaching was a small sacrifice for what she would receive in return. She had made several more drawings of Luke and kept them in a folder. She turned over the pages. For some of the pictures he'd posed for her, in others she'd captured him unawares, in many different moods. Her favourites of him were drawn out on the moors, where he was at his best, relaxed, content.

She realised someone was knocking loudly on the front door.

'So you are in,' Katherine said crossly when Jo opened the door. 'Why didn't you answer at once?'

'I didn't hear you. I'm busy, Mother, about to go out,' Jo replied impatiently.

'Wherever you are going it will have to wait. I have to speak to you. Well, show me into your sitting room.'

When Katherine had been admitted into the hall, she swept off her gauzy summer hat and dropped it on the hall table.

Sighing heavily – her mother was obviously set on a confrontation – Jo led the way into the sitting room. Katherine twirled round, eyeing everything.

She sat down snootily on the sofa and crossed her ankles. 'You have a good cleaning woman at least,' she remarked, looking down her nose.

'I do my own cleaning,' Jo said tartly. 'Do you want some tea?'

'Of course, as long as it's not some cheap, tasteless, local preference you have in. I've had to call for a taxicab to bring me here and it was an uncomfortable journey. When I telephoned Tresawna House for the motorcar, I was informed that Phoebe had the use of it. Off to Truro to do some shopping apparently.'

'The motorcar belongs to Alistair. You can't swan about in it as you please now. How is he?'

'If you ever bothered to call at Tresawna you'd know. He's in Scotland, which is why this duty call has fallen on me.'

'I didn't think for a moment you came to see me out of fondness. So, why are you here? If it's to cause trouble you can take yourself off again.'

Rising demurely, Katherine patrolled the room, flicking and prodding at things that had belonged to Celia. She weighed a Dresden figurine in her hand. 'I've come to stop you ruining your life and I think, for once, your late friend would have agreed with me. Is this ornament made of paste?'

Jo rescued the figurine, a favourite of Celia's. 'So someone's run to you with the news of my forthcoming marriage. It'll do you no good to argue with me. You can shout and scream, but I won't change my mind.'

The next moment Jo felt the full force of Katherine's hand across her face. 'You dare speak to me like that! I won't have it, and I'll never allow you to marry a common thief and drag the Venner name through the mud. Mardie Dawes told me how this Luke Vigus makes his living.'

'I don't care what she said to you,' Jo shouted, hand to her stinging face. 'I'm marrying Luke and you can go to hell! And Mardie won't be able to cause any more trouble. She's dead. Burnt to death in a fire at her home yesterday.'

Katherine gazed at Jo. 'Well, it's good to know that one of my problems is finally over,' she said without compassion.

'Get out of my house.' Jo pointed at the door.

'You'll receive a visit from Alistair in a few days. You

had better not dare to defy him as you have me. Goodbye, Joanna. It's unlikely I shall darken your doorstep again.'

'You had better not,' Jo yelled after her, 'and heaven help the busybody who told you about the wedding when I get my hands on her.'

Katherine collected her hat, and having had the foresight to wear walking shoes, set off for the village.

Jo unconsciously turned the figurine over and over in her hands. With Mardie Dawes dead, Biddy Lean was the most likely culprit to have caused this trouble for her, but Biddy had probably not heard the news of the wedding yet. Only a few people knew. The vicar, the Wherrys and Mercy. It wouldn't have been the vicar. Could it have been one of the others, thinking they were acting in Jo's best interests? All of them had tried vigorously to get her to change her mind. Perhaps Lew had found out from Mercy and told Keane. Perhaps one of the Trevails had informed Katherine. Despondently, Jo acknowledged she did not trust even her friends in Parmarth.

'There's a fine-looking lady at the front gate, sir. I think 'tis Miss Venner's mother,' Beth said, from the window of Marcus's bedroom. She was putting away his laundered shirts in the chest of drawers. He had followed her into the room on the pretence of collecting some sheets of music.

'I really don't want to see her,' Marcus said, peeping out from behind the net curtain. 'Tell her I've gone out and you don't know when I'm expected back.'

'But it's lying, sir.'

'I know, Beth, but I've got a dreadful headache and I can't face her tittle-tattle. Tell her you'll leave a message for me. Run along and pop outside before she disturbs Mrs Lidgey's afternoon rest.'

'Yes, sir.'

Marcus watched darkly as Beth reached Katherine Venner halfway along the concrete path. Sally had gone to fetch the grocery order at Pascoe's store and he had taken the opportunity to speak to Beth alone. It seemed every time he spoke to the girl these days, Sally was eavesdropping on him. Now another chance had vanished thanks to the damned Venner woman.

He heard her arguing with Beth but was unable to make out the words. The breath jammed in his lungs when she entered the house, practically pushing her way past a stunned-looking Beth. He dared not move in case the floorboards creaked and gave him away. Minutes later, he heard the front gate bang and saw Katherine Venner marching up the village hill.

He dashed down to the kitchen, knowing Beth would head straight there. 'What did she say? Why did she come inside?'

Beth, face flushed in guilt, was clearing away the flat irons she had just used. 'She was angry with me. I hate lying. I hope she didn't realise I was. She wanted to phone for a taxicab. I said she could wait here till it came. I thought it was only right because she said Miss Venner was out as well, but she left in a huff. I think she's going to wait outside the village. She should have made sure people were at home before she sent away the taxicab she came in.' Beth blushed furiously and looked even more unhappy. 'I'm sorry, sir. I shouldn't have spoken about the lady like that.'

'No, no, Beth, it was a fair thing to say. I'm sorry I've made you feel uncomfortable but it was only a little fib really. Now, I—'

Sally could be heard hefting the box of groceries on to the back-kitchen table. Marcus sighed in frustration. 'Well, I'd better let you get on, Beth.'

Alone in his study, he paced up and down. He hoped the Venner woman was lying about Joanna being out, that she'd had the chance to demand she reconsider marrying Luke Vigus. But in reality, he knew Joanna's determined nature made it unlikely any appeal her mother made would change her mind.

It would have been wise to see Katherine Venner and establish if anything had in fact passed between her and Joanna, but he had been afraid. He loathed being chased after by a woman, especially one so blatant. Katherine

Venner made him think of sex. He had been thinking about it a lot lately. Desiring it. Fighting the desire. It was a fight he must win.

For the next few days he had to behave with utter decorum, with a cool, calculating mind. Everything vital to him was at stake.

Thirty-Five

The telephone rang and rang in the schoolhouse.

'Get that, Beth, for goodness' sake. Don't let it keep ringing,' Sally shouted from the upstairs landing. She returned to Mrs Lidgey's bedroom, where she had been massaging the old lady's back, an extra duty she had been given every day.

Denied the expert manipulation Dr Richardson had prescribed, Eleanor was hoping the simple massage Sally was able to apply would ease her pain, give her more mobility. She was lying face down on a bath towel on the bed, her head turned to the side.

Her anger at Marcus's continuing rebellion was making her fly into rages, and yesterday, when Sally had unwittingly caused a dart of agony to shoot up her spine, she had lashed out and struck her in the stomach.

Sally had yelled out and retaliated in a fit of furious temper. 'If that's the way I'm going to be treated in this blasted house I'll walk out this very minute. I'm sick and tired of being used and abused by the people living here.'

'Calm down.' Eleanor had quickly apologised. 'I didn't mean to hurt you. You're talking about yourself and Marcus, aren't you? I'm sure you must know that I realised you'd had an affair with him and that he cast you aside when he'd had enough of you. Men are like that and I'm afraid my son is no different. You're right, we have been treating you unfairly. It's time you had a little reward. Fetch my jewellery box.' She had given Sally a pair of pearl-drop earrings.

The earrings were more beautiful and expensive than anything Sally could hope to own, except for the promised brooch, but she was not grateful or pacified. The brooch held less appeal now and she was seriously considering giving up her job when she married Russell at the end of August. Unable to fathom the discordant relationship between Marcus and his mother, she'd had enough of this household.

'Is that girl capable of taking a message, Sally?' Eleanor asked.

'Just about,' Sally answered gruffly, 'but I couldn't go down with oil on my hands.'

'Of course not. Is Marcus still hanging around her?'

'Yes.' Sally poured more lavender oil on her hands and began rubbing Eleanor's shoulder. 'Every opportunity he gets. I saw him give her a bunch of roses from the garden yesterday to take home. "For your mother," he said. It didn't fool me. He's after her. It's shameful.' Sally's belief was he would make do with Beth if he couldn't have Jo Venner.

'Oh, no, you're wrong there.' Eleanor swivelled her head round as far as she could. 'Beth's a child. He only likes women, and he couldn't bring himself to go near a virgin. He's got this thing about not touching the untainted.'

Sally got on with her task but concentrated on her thoughts. Marcus had taken an instant liking to Jo Venner and he was showing even more interest since – it was obvious to Sally that Jo was sleeping with Luke Vigus – Jo had lost her virginity. Sally's expression showed distaste. It wasn't natural. What was the reason then, for Marcus spending so much time with Beth? Maybe she really should get out of this house.

Beth was nervous of the telephone, but she memorised the message from the caller and passed it on to Marcus the moment he came home at the end of the school day. 'Mrs Venner rang again, sir. She said, will you please return her call when you come in. She sounded like it was urgent.'

'Thank you, Beth. I'll do it later,' he lied. He smiled down at his housemaid. 'How are you? I hope you did not find Mardie Dawes' funeral too taxing this morning.'

'Oh, no, sir. It was very quiet.' Beth lingered to chat with him, but as always kept busy with a little housework, this time polishing the hall mirror, where she could see his friendly reflection.

'How many mourners were there?'

'Just myself and my mother and a couple of strangers. It was all over very quickly.'

'Good. You are very caring, Beth. Always willing to do what you can to ease another's misery. I'd like to talk to you about something of that nature, if I may.' Marcus saw movement on top of the stairs. Sally was glaring down on them. He whispered to Beth, 'Later, when there's a quiet moment.'

'Of course, sir.'

'Bring some coffee to my study in a little while, please.'

Beth was making the coffee when Sally flounced into the kitchen. 'Who was that on the phone just now?'

'Mrs Venner. Miss Venner's mother. Shall I make enough coffee for Mrs Lidgey too?'

'Never mind that. You took your time telling Mr Lidgey about the phone call, didn't you?'

'Did I?' Beth put the coffee pot down in surprise.

'Oh, don't go all gormless on me now. You know what I'm talking about. You're always hanging about him. Spending ages when you take things into his study. Whispering together in corners. Your mother wouldn't like it.'

'Sally, I—'

Beth was clearly upset by Sally's harsh words but it only annoyed Sally more. The girl had always worn her soft fair hair in two childish plaits but had changed it to a more becoming, single plait. She'd bought a new dress of a more mature style than what she usually wore. She did not look so daft now. It could even be admitted she was rather pretty. Lew Trevail had started casting his eye in her direction, to which she was oblivious. It was different when she was near Marcus. She glowed. She had a tremendous crush on him.

Sally should warn her that her feelings could grow out of control and she might end up looking a fool, or worse. She should be kind to the sweet, inoffensive girl, but she couldn't stop her jealousy breaking out. 'You'd better start pulling your weight round here, my girl, or I'll tell Mrs Lidgey you're hankering after her son and then you'll be out of a job. Then what will your father say? And the rest of the village? You work your fingers to the bone elsewhere but I'm left to do all the dirty work here. You haven't got to empty Mrs Lidgey's pee and the rest of it. You haven't got to hump her about every day, like I have, making my back ache.'

Her neat chin wobbling as she tried not to cry, Beth gazed down on the spotlessly clean kitchen floor – the floor she got down on her hands and knees each day to scrub and polish. 'I'm very sorry, Sally.'

'I'll take his coffee in to him this time. You keep your mind on your work from now on and I'll say no more about it. Thank God it's my evening off. I can't wait to get out of this damned place.'

Beth stayed petrified in misery until she heard Sally coming back, then she snatched up a dishcloth and wiped over the oven.

'Don't forget, Beth, Mr Lidgey is old enough to be your father.' Sally slammed the back door on her way out.

'Yes, Sally.' Giving Sally enough time to walk round the side of the house and through the front gate, Beth ran to the outside toilet. Falling back against the door she sobbed into her hands.

Not for one moment had she really considered Mr Lidgey in any other light than as her employer. He was a man she respected. Yes, she had noticed he was good-looking in a dark brooding way, but she had never thought to have him for herself. Had she somehow behaved wrongly towards him? If so, he was kind enough not to have mentioned it. He treated her rather like a child. Whatever she was doing, however, she was being unfair to Sally. That wasn't right. But she couldn't ignore Mr Lidgey when he was speaking to her. It would be bad manners. She cried over her dilemma.

Five minutes passed before she dried her eyes on her apron and opened the closet door to return to her duties.

'Oh!' Her hands flew guiltily together in front of her body.

Marcus observed her protective movements. 'So this is where you are. I've been looking for you. Why have you been crying?'

'I, um . . .' She could only lie her way out of the situation, but one would not form on her lips.

'Are you feeling unwell?'

'Not really. I . . .'

'Come inside, Beth. You look tired. I fear that lately we have been overworking you.'

Nervously fiddling with her hair, she walked meekly in front of him to the kitchen. Marcus knew she would find it unsettling to be invited into the sitting room so he pulled out a chair at the table. 'Sit down, Beth. I'll get you a drink of water.'

The glass of water was put into her hands and Beth thanked him quietly. She took a sip but only because it was expected of her.

'What's upset you, Beth? You can trust me. I won't tell anyone.' He lowered himself until their eyes were on the same level, speaking as if addressing his youngest, shyest pupil.

'I'm afraid I can't say, sir.' It was too personal and she did not want Sally getting into trouble. Sally had only flown at her because she was overworked and tired.

'It is something you can talk to your mother about?'

Her mother was understanding. Astute and wise, the minister called her, always to be relied on to give advice with love and compassion. She wasn't the kind of person to jump to ill-judged conclusions, she wouldn't misinterpret Mr Lidgey's kindness. She would tell Beth if she was doing anything wrong. 'I'll talk to her when I get home.'

'Good girl.' Marcus glanced at both doors, looked out of the window, making sure no one was about. Then he pulled up a chair and sat close to the girl. 'I like talking to you, Beth. I'll tell you why.'

A little concerned at the sudden change in his manner, Beth eyed him nervously, steeling herself for what might come next.

'The fact is you remind me of the little sister I had.

Gabriella died when she was very young, suddenly in her sleep. She was the sweetest child, bright and full of life.'

Beth smiled sadly, feeling honoured by his words.

'Do you remember what I was saying to you earlier? About how kind and helpful you are? Beth, would you do something to help Mrs Lidgey? She's suffering terribly and I have an idea to ease her pain, not her physical pain, but her emotional agony of losing Gabriella. I fear she will not be able to endure much more and you are my only hope.'

'I pray all the time for Mrs Lidgey, sir. I don't think there is much more I can do.' Beth frowned.

'Oh, but there is. What I'm about to tell you is in the strictest confidence. No one else knows about Gabriella, it would cause untold distress to my mother if people started to gossip about her. You see, my mother blames herself for Gabriella's death. She's never really come to terms with it. No matter how I try to reassure her, she believes her fall down the stairs was a punishment for Gabriella's sudden end and she'll be punished again after she dies. I'm worried her obsession is getting out of control. You may have noticed that she's been upsetting Sally with her violent moods and she often takes me to task.'

'But it's the vicar who'd be best at comforting her,' Beth said. 'He should make sure she understands that if she accepts the Lord then all her sins will be forgiven and she'll spend eternity in heaven.'

'I'm afraid Mrs Lidgey doesn't trust the Reverend Mountebank.' Marcus peered all round again, praying that they would not be interrupted by the dreaded sound of his mother's bell summoning him to her bedside. She had taken a sudden exception to Beth, insisting he go to her when Sally was out of the house.

'Let me tell you a little tale. A few years ago I knew a kind old gentleman who was dying. His family sent for his son in India. It became obvious that sadly the old gentleman would die before his son arrived. As he lay on his deathbed he kept crying out for his son. Eventually a young man in the room could stand it no longer and he knelt beside the old

gentleman's bed and said, "Father, it's me. I've come home."'
Marcus was satisfied Beth was gazing at him from wide
emotional eyes. 'And do you know, all the old gentleman's
moaning and wrestling ceased and he died shortly afterwards
with a smile on his face.'

'That's a wonderful story, sir.' Beth gave a breathy sigh, so
enraptured by the story she had forgotten there was a reason
for it being told.

She had taken the bait. All he had to do now was to get
her to agree to his plan. A plan that would, with luck and
perseverance, send his mother off her head and he could have
her committed to an asylum, or better still it might lead to her
death from a seizure. At the least, it would give her a fright.
She so richly deserved to be made miserable.

'I'm going to ask you, Beth, to do a similar thing for
my mother. Although, thank God, she is not near the end
of her life, she needs comfort and of a sort only you
can give.'

'I don't understand.'

'Beth, my dear, if you were here at night you would hear
my mother calling out for Gabriella. You have a soft quiet
voice. I want you to speak to my mother, concealed of course,
as if you were Gabriella. If she believes Gabriella has come
back and forgiven her then she'll rest easy and will sleep
better. I'm sure of it. I'll tell you exactly what to say and
coach you on how to say it.'

Totally astonished at his request, Beth could only stare at
him.

'Will you help, Beth?' he prompted with a coercive smile.

'I . . . I don't know.' Beth swallowed nervously. 'It sounds
a bit wrong to me.'

'I know it's a deception but it will be done with the very
best of intentions. Please don't say no, Beth. It would mean
so much to me to see my mother at peace.'

'I meant it'll be like calling up a spirit.'

'No, it won't.' Marcus put authority into his voice and
reached forward and took her hand. 'You can't really let Mrs
Lidgey go on suffering, can you? Can you, Beth?'

302

Beth was more confused over this than by her troubles with Sally. 'I'd like to help, sir, bu—'

'Good girl, I knew I could rely on you. Come back this evening at seven o'clock. It will give us plenty of time before Sally arrives to take up her duties.'

He squeezed her hand and Beth experienced a series of tiny hot tingles shooting up her arm.

When he had gone, she found her coordination had almost left her and the last of her work was performed clumsily. She knocked the cup on Mr Lidgey's coffee tray and it fell to the floor and broke into several pieces. She would get a severe scolding from Sally over the accident but somehow she didn't care – Mr Lidgey would not mind at all.

Thirty-Six

At six thirty, Marcus went to Eleanor's room. She took off her spectacles and put down the book she was reading. 'Good heavens, what have I done to deserve this honour?' she said acidly. 'What have you got there?'

Marcus tossed a bottle of pills on the bed. 'The painkillers Dr Richardson prescribed. He'll think it odd if I don't get the new pills he wanted you to have. Why don't you take the lot?'

Returning her spectacles to her nose, Eleanor read the label. 'Pass me some water.'

'You've got a glassful beside you.'

'I want some fresh water. Is it too much to ask?'

'Yes. I'm busy. Don't ring for me,' he said at the door. 'I'm doing something really important.'

'Marcus, you worm, I want something to eat. Fetch me something at once.'

'You'll just have to stay hungry. Sally can see to you when she comes back.' He left the bedroom door ajar.

His face a cold expressionless mask, he walked slowly down the stairs to wait for the pills to take their course. Eleanor always ill-advisedly took a double dose of whatever she was prescribed and these particular pills, when taken without due care, apparently produced a hallucinatory effect. Very useful when Beth began to pretend she was Gabriella.

Seven o'clock chimed on the clock in the hall. Two more minutes passed. Beth was late. Unusual for her. He paced the passageway. Peered out of the window beside the front door. Please, please, any minute now she would come into view. Fumbling in his pockets he produced his cigarette and lighter.

304

While his head was bent over to light the cigarette, the sound of someone in the kitchen made him jerk and he hastily dropped his lighter.

Wiping away the sweat which had broken out on his forehead, he ran to the kitchen.

'Beth, at last— What are you doing here?' His disappointment made his insides feel as though they were contorting into knots.

'I've sent her home.' Sally tilted her head to the side. 'I was unnecessarily sharp with her this afternoon and I couldn't get it out of my mind. Beth's such a sweet soul, an innocent. She doesn't deserve to be made unhappy, so I encouraged Russell to go the pub tonight and I made my way to her house to say I was sorry.

'I met her on her way here. She couldn't look me in the eye and lie about where she was going. I asked her if her mother knew where she was off to and, of course, she said no. I told her if that was the case then it wasn't right and she should go home at once. She didn't argue for long, she's too pure-hearted for that.'

Trembling visibly, Marcus was tongue-tied.

Sally began to advance on him. 'So, Marcus, why did you want Beth to come here in secret? Your mother and I were talking about the pair of you this afternoon. She doesn't reckon you're after the girl's body. I was glad to hear it. What other way were you planning to corrupt the poor girl?'

Sally was moving closer and closer to him. Marcus remained at a loss for words. His plan was in ribbons and he couldn't think lucidly. Except for how foolish he was. Foolish to think anything he had schemed would succeed. How could he have thought for a second he could rid himself of his mother? And why did he destroy Joanna's letter of resignation? And telephone her mother in the hope she could remove Luke Vigus from the scene? All he had accomplished was to pressure an innocent young girl into doing something she would have no part in if she knew the truth. He had wanted to make Beth an accessory to murder. Unforgivable. He deserved to have Sally here now mocking him.

He couldn't breathe and ripped the tie from his neck, tore at his collar buttons. Panic was reaching down to his bowels. He was afraid he'd go mad, never get a grip on himself again.

Sally was a breath away from him. 'You miss me, don't you? I've heard you tossing and turning at night. Not in your nightmares but because you need a woman. You need me, don't you, Marcus?'

'Get away from me,' he hissed wretchedly.

'No. Why should I? You used me when it suited you and now it's my turn. I've been missing the times we had together. Russell doesn't do the extra things you showed me. If you don't fill me with pleasure tonight, I'll go straight to Beth's father and tell him I stopped you seducing her. You'd be finished here then, Marcus. Finished everywhere.'

Blood filled his face. He couldn't breathe, he was going to die. 'Don't . . . please . . .'

'You hurt me once, but you're just a little boy inside, aren't you? I see it all now. A mother's boy, trying to break free from that horrid old woman upstairs, but you can't, can you?' Sally slid her palms up over his chest, ran a fingertip along the contour of his chin. 'I know what you like, Marcus. I know how you like to be touched, where you like to be kissed. We're going upstairs now and you are never going to forget the next hour or so.'

He lay awake for hours after Sally left his room. Violated, in anguish. His head ached so acutely he felt like banging it again and again into the wall until he reached blessed oblivion. Another woman had degraded him and he had timidly allowed it to happen. He had called Luke Vigus worthless, but that was the label he deserved himself. He was pathetic. Hopeless. His life was completely hopeless.

Finally he got off the bed and put on his nightshirt. He had drawn two prescriptions of his mother's new pills. Creeping to the bathroom, he filled his tooth glass with water and carried it to the bed. There was only one way out for him now.

He tipped all the pills into his hand.

306

Thirty-Seven

M arcus must have dozed off while lingering over his last thoughts, his final prayer, for he was awakened by shuffling and sighing. Someone was moving towards the bed. Sally was coming back. Before it was too late, he lifted his hand to bolt down the pills.

A sharp knock on his hand sent the pills scattering in all directions.

'Not yet, my son. I haven't finished with you yet.'

He was so frightened at seeing his mother wielding one of her walking sticks at him he spilled the water over the bed. 'Mama!'

'I heard you with Sally. She's a woman who knows her own mind. You're the sweepings of a man, Marcus.'

'H-how did you get in here?'

She hobbled the last few inches to the bed and flopped down on it. 'It was agony but I decided to come to you as you refuse to come to me. Take off that wet nightshirt.' She was reaching for him.

A vision of the aversion of Joanna's face if she saw him like this, loathing him for his weakness, his terrible shame, was more than he could bear.

Screaming in despair, he lashed out at his mother.

She crashed to the floor. Lay in a heap on the rug, her negligee spreading out from her legs like the petals of a fading flower.

Huddled against the headboard, Marcus stared down at her in the lantern light, terrified she would get up and come after him again.

Sally pounded into the room on bare feet. 'God in heaven

what's happened?' Falling to her knees she picked up her mistress's hand. It was warm and limp. 'Mrs Lidgey? Mrs Lidgey?'

Filled with fear, Marcus edged nearer to the scene on his bedroom floor.

Sally glanced anxiously at him. 'She's not moving. What happened here? What's she doing out of bed? I didn't hear her ring. Marcus? For goodness' sake, say something!'

Realising he was in shock, Sally sighed and gently shook Eleanor. 'Mrs Lidgey. Wake up.' There was no response.

Apprehensively, she felt about the woman's head and discovered a large lump, wet with blood, where she had struck the heavy carved leg of the bed in the fall. Sally put her head gingerly on Eleanor's chest. 'I can hear a faint heartbeat.'

'No!' Marcus howled in despair.

'I'm sorry, Marcus. She's badly hurt. Go downstairs and ring for the doctor.'

Sally saw the pills scattered on the mat beside Eleanor's flung-out arm. Lifting up the bedspread and looking underneath the bed she picked out more pills in the dim light. 'What's been going on?'

She noticed Marcus's wet nightshirt and the wet bedcovers. 'You were going to kill yourself. That's it, isn't it? She's your mother and somehow she must have known and came in to stop you, but fell over. Oh, Marcus, why? Because of me? Because of my threats? I was angry with you. I would never have said anything to Beth's parents. Come on, pull yourself together,' she pleaded, 'and ring for the doctor.'

'I can't.' He wept feebly. 'I'm scared.'

'All right, I'll do it. Get some blankets and cover your mother. Keep her warm.'

Eleanor raised her head and Marcus held his breath in terror. 'M-Marcus . . .' A long rattling moan escaped Eleanor's lips and her head fell back with a thud.

Marcus gave a strangled cry, hardly daring to hope it was the last sound his mother would ever make.

Sally froze for a moment then pressed two fingers to

Eleanor's neck, searching for a pulse. 'I . . . I can't feel anything.'

After a while, Marcus croaked, 'Mama?'

Eleanor was motionless.

He stepped away from the bed and stood behind Sally. 'Listen to her heart again.'

Sally did so and shook her head when she looked up at him. 'Nothing. I'm sorry. She's dead.'

'Are you sure? Are you absolutely sure?'

There was no life in the hand Sally was holding. She lowered it to the floor. 'Yes, I'm sure.'

Marcus hurled himself out of the room and leaning on the banister of the landing let out a peculiar howl. Freedom at last and more by way of an accident than by murderous design.

Sally mistook his whoop of triumph and the tears he wept for intolerable grief. 'I'm so sorry, Marcus. I know things weren't easy between you both lately but I know you adored each other. I'll phone for the doctor. Before he gets here I'll change your bed linen. You get dressed. No one will ever have to know that you were thinking of taking your own life.' She hesitated. 'You won't do anything silly while I'm downstairs, will you?'

He shook his head, drying his eyes. 'I . . . I'll be fine. Don't worry.'

When Sally was downstairs he returned to his room, skirted the inert figure on the floor and picked up the lantern. He was afraid, but he had to make sure his mother was really dead and not playing a cruel trick on him.

In the glow of the light he saw her eyes wide and staring, slightly rolled upwards. Her face was waxy and a little contorted. He prodded her. Lifted up her hand and let it fall. It hit the floor with a hard knock. She was dead. Thank God, she was dead!

Before Sally got back, he picked up Eleanor's body and carried it to her room. Laid her on the bed, closed her eyes and folded her hands on her chest. He fetched a bedspread from the linen cupboard and covered her neatly up to the waist. He would get Sally to comb her hair, make her look her best. He knew he should not have moved Eleanor – but a grieving son could not be expected to behave sensibly in the face of tragedy. It would be easy to play the part expected of him until after the evil old woman's funeral.

By lashing out in fear he had accidentally killed his mother. It didn't matter how. She was dead and at long last he was free. He recalled from the back of his mind that he had killed Mardie Dawes and gained the truth about Jessie Vigus's disappearance and had done nothing to remove suspicion from her son. It did not horrify him. He felt no shame. He had done a good thing. They were bad women and deserved violent deaths. The world was better off without them, and Joanna would be better off without Luke Vigus; pray something would happen to separate her from that no-good wretch.

Thirty-Eight

The school was closed until after Eleanor's funeral. This new tragedy, added to the death of Molly and Mardie Dawes and the mysterious disappearance of Jessie Vigus, caused a sullen gloom and sense of unease to permeate the village.

Jo now found herself, since her first banns had been read in church, the subject of sympathy from some who greeted her when she went to the schoolhouse each day to offer Marcus comfort and friendship. She was also called a brave soul or a fool for 'taking on the Vigus young 'uns'.

After leaving the schoolhouse on the third day following Eleanor's death, instead of going home Jo went to Heather Cottage. Mercy was there, drinking her sister's bitter-strong tea. Irene fetched another cup.

'You're very welcome, my luvver. 'Tis good to see you, though you're looking peaky. Sure you're eating enough? Have a slice of hevva cake. You need building up. Keane's out, so we women can enjoy a natter.'

'Had any word from Luke yet?' Mercy asked bluntly.

'Yes,' Jo said, swallowing a mouthful of Irene's delicious homemade cake. 'I'm expecting Luke back today. When I leave here I'm hoping to persuade Rex to come to Cardhu with me to welcome him.'

'Hardly likely from what I hear,' Mercy muttered.

'He'll come round,' Jo said, only half-confidently. 'Irene, I'm here to invite you and Mr Trevail to my wedding. There will be a small reception at Cardhu afterwards. You've always been kind to me and I'm hoping you'll set aside your feelings about Luke and wish us well. I believe in Luke totally, and

311

when the village sees how committed he is to our marriage and future that we'll be able to live at Cardhu contentedly. If not, it will be Rex and Marylyn who will suffer.' She added tartly, 'People have had a lot to say about Molly's misery.'

Irene coloured. 'We'd be delighted to come. Like I said to Keane the other day, you're giving up everything and taking on a lot, but you can't help who you fall in love with. Good luck to you is what I say, Jo.'

'Taking on a lot of trouble, more like,' Mercy mumbled disagreeably.

'Please, Mercy, let's not quarrel.' Jo appealed quietly but there was fire and conviction in her eyes. 'You've been a very good friend to me but I love Luke and if I'm forced to, I'll choose him above our friendship. Will you come to the wedding?'

'I'll be at the church,' Mercy said. 'I always stand by my friends. And I'll be around to help pick up the pieces when he breaks your heart.'

There was a tense silence, then Irene said, 'How's the 'master today, Jo? Life will be different for him from now on. Sally's moved out, well, she had to, of course, or people would gossip. Dear little Beth's taking Mrs Lidgey's death hard.'

'He's bearing up very well, Irene. Sally was terribly shocked at what happened. Beth's deeply concerned that Mrs Lidgey died unhappy.' Jo did not welcome the atmosphere at the schoolhouse that was stealing over her again.

Over the last three days, Marcus had revealed little emotion but some terrible dark secrets. He was pale, his eyes heavily shadowed, but he appeared quiet and contemplative. He had told her he had sent off his resignation. 'I posted it at the same time as yours. I held on to yours for a while, hoping you'd change your mind.'

'Where will you go?' Jo had asked.

'Far away from here. I shall never teach again.'

'You'll miss Eleanor.'

'Well, that's the standard thing to say at a time like this, but I won't miss her at all. She was selfish and cruel and she ruined my life. I'm ashamed to admit it but I was afraid of her.' He looked intently at Jo. 'She was even glad that my infant sister, Gabriella, died. She hated Gabriella.'

Thinking he was under more strain than he was showing, Jo said carefully, 'Marcus, are you aware of what you've just said?'

'Yes,' he replied, strangely calm after making such a shocking statement. 'She told me from her own lips. Do you want to see her in her coffin? It's in the dining room.'

'No, I'd rather not.' Eleanor Lidgey a heartless mother? Was this why Marcus had always seemed hunted, dispirited? If he wasn't confused and rambling, thank goodness Eleanor was no longer in a position to hurt him. At times Jo had been worried he was heading for a complete breakdown.

'The undertaker did excellent work on her. She looks highly beautiful. I like to look down at her corpse and know only the shell is left of the evil woman who terrorised me, who turned me into someone unfit to be near other people.'

'Don't, Marcus.' Jo was appalled at his jubilant tone, then his bizarre expression. 'You'll make yourself ill if you go on this way, and what you're saying about yourself is not true.'

'If you knew the whole truth you wouldn't say that, Joanna.' Pain burned behind his tragic dark eyes.

'I don't believe there is anything bad about you, Marcus. I respect and value you. You must take a long rest and look only towards the future.'

'I'll try. It helps, having others to think about. Beth will be out of a job when I leave. I owe her and Sally a great deal.' He had chosen to forget Sally's callousness with him; she was keeping his suicide attempt a secret. 'I'll divide my mother's jewellery between them. That's fair. I'll sell everything else, except for my violin. Start again. The world's a huge place . . .'

On each visit he'd drifted off into an introspective silence and Jo had quietly left.

Jo bribed Rex to accompany her to Cardhu with the promise of sweets and a comic. He chose nut-and-raisin fudge and *The*

Union Jack, fronted by a story of Sexton Blake. In the rare position of having the upper hand over someone, he also wheedled a bar of Fry's chocolate out of her.

'Those old biddies in the shop were talking about us,' he grumbled angrily, dragging his heels behind her up the village hill. In the last few days he seemed to have grown older in his ways and increasingly bitter.

'I'm afraid they talk about everyone, Rex.' Jo slowed to his pace and tried an encouraging smile. 'They're bored and small-minded. We should simply ignore them. How do you feel about living at Cardhu? You'll have a large room all to yourself, and books and toys and you can have a bicycle, and a pony too if you like. I'm going to ask Beth to work there. You like her, don't you? She's a good cook, you and Marylyn will never go hungry again. And I'll always be there to teach you new games and take you to the beach and on outings. We'll have a wonderful time. We could go away on holidays. Go to London and see where the King lives. Would you like that?'

Rex stayed stonily quiet and Jo was concerned she had overdone her eagerness to make him look forward to his new home. 'Have you nothing to say, Rex?'

He thrust a cube of fudge into his mouth, chewing with exaggerated slurping noises and swallowed it loudly before answering, 'You've said nothing about Luke.'

'Oh, you noticed. I omitted him deliberately because you become difficult when his name's brought up. It's time you forgave him, Rex.'

'He don't really want me and Marylyn.'

'He does,' Jo stressed. 'How can I convince you?'

Rex shrugged his shoulders.

'Please give our new life together a chance, Rex. We'll all have to adjust to a lot of changes.'

'Mrs Wherry said you're doing a grand thing giving up being a teacher for us. Miss Venner, will you teach me my lessons from now on? I hate the bloody school.'

Jo ignored his bad language, he had sounded so fierce and rather desperate. 'You can call me Jo now. I'm afraid you'll have to got to school, Rex. It's the law. But I can coach you at home and then you won't have any difficulty keeping up with the others. You might even be top at some subjects. We'll work hard together in Molly's memory, shall we?'

'I s'pose so.' Then, not unlike his headmaster, Rex slipped into a world of pensive thoughts. Some he shut out of his mind, others he brooded on.

An unoccupied Bentley was parked near the turning from the main road for Bridge Lane. Assuming the driver was hiking the moors, Luke took little notice of the motorcar and continued on to Cardhu.

Home. As the wagon lurched over the uneven ground, he tried to warm to the reality of the house becoming his home. A fine building of stone, bricks and mortar was not an acquisition he had ever desired, but at least Cardhu was set in isolation on the moor, away from prying eyes and smart mouths. Gardening, house-painting, general repairs might not be so daunting, so restricting, once he got started.

The enthusiasm he was trying to work up stayed steadfastly elusive, but Jo would always be here, that was what mattered.

He was not pleased to see a young man looking out of the sitting-room window. No doubt the owner of the flashy car. The first glance Luke got of the stranger, when he stepped outside into the brilliant sunlight, left him in no doubt he was Jo's brother. He shared many of her features.

Luke expected trouble from Alistair Venner and had no intention of listening to any warnings. Bringing the wagon close to the garden wall, he leapt off and began unhitching Lucky, coldly eyeing the man now sauntering slowly towards him, puffing on a long-stemmed pipe, hands casually in the pockets of his ridiculous plus fours.

The two men were in complete contrast. Luke, broadly built, rough clothes, dusty from travelling, dusky gypsy looks, unyielding deportment. Alistair, pale, softly honed, immaculately turned out, arrogantly relaxed.

'We obviously can dispense with introductions, Vigus,'

Alistair said, standing relaxed as he watched Luke's impatient movement while he groomed his horse with a handful of straw. 'Have you any idea where Jo is? I was hoping to find her at home. The doors are unlocked.'

'Wherever she is she won't be long coming back. She's expecting me,' Luke replied tersely. He patted Lucky's rump and the horse, tossing its long neck, walked off to graze.

'There's no point in beating about the bush, is there?' Alistair took the pipe out of his mouth. 'If you really love Jo you'll do the decent thing and bugger off before you wreck her life.'

Luke would have preferred to meet the other man with a stream of heartfelt abuse, but he wasn't about to fall into the trap of being accused of proving the point that he wasn't good enough for Jo. 'It's none of your business.'

'I won't stand by and allow Jo to throw away her teaching career. She worked damned hard to achieve it.'

'Jo knows what she's doing. If you really love her you'll agree to give her away at our wedding. She's sure to ask you, now you've actually bothered to visit her home. And before you move on to the next thing you're bound to say, I can't be bought off. I love Jo, she loves me. We're getting married and you'll just have to get used to the idea.'

'Luke! Alistair!' Jo's slight figure came rushing up the last few yards of the lane.

Luke broke into a dash for her. They met and he swept her up off the ground and kissed her lips.

Hugging tightly, laughing, kissing, it was some time before they separated. Time enough for Alistair to see he had a futile task ahead in convincing his sister to cancel the wedding, but he had to try. He had always known that if Jo fell in love it would be with a man the antithesis of what he or his mother was hoping for her.

Arm in arm with Luke, Jo beckoned Rex to them and the group walked to where Alistair was waiting. She held out her cheek to him. 'I take it Mother sent you, Alistair.'

He kissed her. Tried to pull her away from Luke, but he wasn't prepared to let her go. 'You don't look particularly well for a future bride, little thing. You're even thinner than before.'

'There's been a lot of tragedy recently, Alistair. The whole village is suffering under the strain. I am very much part of the community.' A pang of sorrow hit her heart for her last statement was untrue, but hopefully once she was married and things had settled . . .

'This must be the younger brother.' Alistair turned his eyes on Rex and received a similar hostile reaction to Luke's. 'Please accept my condolences on your sister's death, young man. You too, Vigus.'

'Checked up on us, have you?' Luke challenged him. 'Think you know how we tick?'

'I know enough to have formed a clear opinion of you,' Alistair replied astringently.

'Rex, this is my brother, Alistair,' Jo said quickly, sensitive to what had passed between the two men before her arrival. If only she could persuade Alistair to give her marriage his blessing. It would help soothe the difficult period ahead while the necessary adaptations were made.

She smiled enthusiastically. 'There's one more little person you need to meet, Alistair. Marylyn. She's being looked after in the village at the moment. She's eight months old and absolutely adorable. I'm looking forward to being her mother. Shall we all go inside?'

'I'd like a few minutes with you alone, Jo,' Alistair said immovably. 'I'm sure you won't object, Vigus. I am the head of my family.'

'Come with me, Rex. Take a look in my wagon. I've brought back some things for you and Marylyn,' Luke said tightly, unwillingly relinquishing Jo.

Alone on the hard stony ground with his sister, Alistair opened his mouth to speak.

'Don't say a word,' Jo cautioned severely. 'I've heard all the doom-laden warnings. Nothing will make me change my mind. I'd marry Luke no matter what. I couldn't live without him.'

'The fellow's handsome, I grant you that. He's got the sort

317

of virility women go for, but surely not you, Jo? I'd have given you more sense. Why can't you see this marriage can only end in disaster? Apart from his dubious background you must have very little in common. You'll end up like Celia Sayce. Lonely and unloved, except you will have two children to bring up and perhaps more if you have your own.'

She could still feel the imprint of Luke's body against her, feel his arms enfolding her in his love. 'Luke will never leave me. Alistair, as surely as I know the sun will rise every morning, I know Luke loves me. He's not perfect. He has faults and weaknesses but I love him nonetheless and always will. We will be happy. Please be happy for me. And Celia was never unloved. Sheridan Ustick loved her until the day he died. I loved her.'

'For goodness' sake, Jo, you've only been in Parmarth for six months! How could you possibly give up your teaching for a common family, a scoundrel? I can't make sense of it. You know it's utterly absurd or you would have told me about it immediately. Were you going to wait until after the wedding to tell me?'

'No, of course not. You know I'm not a coward. Mother turned up here unexpectedly first. If you'd only try to get to know Luke, you'd see the good in him. He's bound to take exception with you coming here like this. He should be getting encouragement and friendship.'

'You know that's impossible. How could you suggest it?'

'Because if you make me choose between you and Luke, I'll choose him.'

Sighing resignedly, Alistair said, 'Well, it looks as if I'll just have to leave you to it. At least you'll have a decent house to live in. I stole a look around inside. You will have domestic help?'

'Yes, of course. Alistair—'

'You realise I can't bring myself to give you away?'

Jo swallowed her terrible disappointment. 'It matters very much but I accept it.'

'You're so strong, Jo.' Alistair squeezed her shoulder. 'I

only hope you never have to call on all your resources. Keep in touch, eh?'

Pecking her cheek, he walked away and Jo knew he was cutting himself off from her for good. She had expected it, but it did not help her bear the pain of his rejection.

'He's gone?' Luke said softly, a minute later.

'He won't come here again,' Jo said, choked with emotion, turning to him for comfort.

'I'm sorry. I didn't think about the probability of you marrying me costing you your family.'

'Well, I only ever really had Alistair. Hopefully we'll exchange the occasional letter. At least I'll never have to see my horrid mother again.' She smiled up at him through her tears. 'Anyway, welcome home, darling. I've missed you so very much.'

They kissed tenderly, then their deeper feelings led to a passionate embrace.

Jo pulled away from Luke. 'It's important we include Rex in all our decisions or he'll find it hard to settle into Cardhu. To think of me as his foster-mother, or sister-in-law or whatever. I'm going to cook the three of us a special meal, then we can all sit down and discuss the wedding. Are you going to ask Rex to be your best man?'

'There's no one else. I'll freshen up then show him the stable and the pocket of land I've earmarked as a paddock. I might keep horses to sell. Marylyn's well, is she?'

'She's fine, sitting up properly now and making lots of interesting noises. While you're having a bath, I'll show Rex his room. It'll help him feel at home.'

Luke glanced behind him. Rex was sitting on top of the garden wall reading his comic, his urchin face sticky from the sweets he was devouring. Beside him was the red and blue kite Luke had bought for him. 'I wanted to do this at a more romantic moment. I've got something for you, my love.'

He produced a ring box and Jo took a deep breath. He opened the claret-coloured velvet lid and an exquisite emerald-and-diamond ring sparkled in the sunlight. 'Oh, Luke!'

Taking her left hand, he took the ring out of its velvet bed

319

and slipped it on to her finger. 'There, it fits perfectly. Do you like it?'

'I love it,' Jo exclaimed and the rigours of the past few weeks fell off her face and she was wholly radiant. 'And I love you, Luke. Thank you. My ring is beautiful.'

They kissed passionately, forgetting the time, forgetting they had company.

Watching them morosely on the wall, Rex screwed up the comic and threw the kite to the ground.

'Where were you earlier today, sweetheart?' Luke asked after they had eaten and Rex had gone outside to examine Jo's old toys in the outhouse.

'I called on Irene Trevail, to ask her to come to the wedding. Mercy was there too. We shall have some guests. Before that I called at the schoolhouse to see how Mr Lidgey was.'

'What do you mean? Ill, is he?'

'Didn't Rex mention that Mrs Lidgey died three nights ago? She took a bad fall, hit her head and died shortly afterwards.'

'Another death? Mardie Dawes must have put a hex on this place. People are dropping off one after the other.'

'Well, if she did, she became one of her own victims.'

'In a while, I'll take Rex back to Mrs Wherry and pay her for the kids' keep.' He gave Jo a heart-stopping smile and placed a circle of tiny kisses behind her ear. 'Then you and I can be alone.'

After a long, breathless kiss, Jo said happily, 'I'll call Rex inside so we can discuss the wedding arrangements and decide when he and Marylyn will come here to live.'

Rex lost interest in the toys and was staring gloomily at the kite, making up his mind whether to play with it or break it up. Luke couldn't buy his cooperation.

He swore under his breath at the sight of a smartly dressed man and woman walking towards the house. More of Miss Venner's rotten stuck-up relatives come to look down on him. He made to take to his heels, off and away over the moors.

'Hey there, wait a minute! Are you Rex Vigus?' the woman called out.

Thirty-Nine

R ex led the strangers into the sitting room. The man took off his bowler hat. 'These people have come to see us, Luke.' Rex's voice was filled with fear and suspicion as he edged away from the couple.

Luke took in the couple's formal clothes, their air of something between gentility and rigidity. In their mid-forties, the woman was tall, stout, stiffly hatted and carried a large handbag, the man was short and thin with a trim moustache.

Luke got up from the sofa and adopted an aggressive stance. 'Are you from the Welfare?'

'Don't you recognise me, Luke?' the woman replied in a broad regional accent. ''Tis cousin Maud.'

Luke looked closely at the woman. 'Maud. What are you doing here? Did you hear about the wedding?'

'We haven't heard nothing about a wedding, have we, Godfrey?' She glanced at the man, who was grinning self-consciously. 'I got a letter, from the boy here.' After pointing at Rex, she produced a sheet of paper from her formidable handbag.

Jo frowned, recognising her own stationery. She stood beside Luke.

Maud handed Luke the letter. 'Read it. It says, "Dear Maud, Mother's gone. Need help. From Rex Vigus." And in brackets, "Luke's brother". So I've come looking for you to see what this meant.'

When Luke had read the letter, Jo took it from him to do the same.

'What's this all about?' Luke turned on Rex, who had gone red in the face and looked guilty and defensive.

'I remembered Mother talking about a cousin called Maud,' Rex said in a small voice.

'So what of it?'

'She sent us a Christmas card once. It's the only one we ever got. And Mother got angry about it, saying Maud was, well . . .' His blush deepened.

'Go on, Rex,' Maud said briskly. 'I'm pleased to make your acquaintance, by the way. I didn't know you existed until I got your letter. I can imagine what your mother said about me, we never got on. I'm interested in what she could have said to make you write to me.'

'She said you were a church woman. Some church people are good. When Mother went off I was afraid we little ones would be taken away and stuck in a home. I thought you might help, I . . .' He petered out, snivelling huge tears, afraid he had caused terrible trouble and would be punished.

'Well, if me and Godfrey – this is my husband, Godfrey Redstone, by the way,' she announced for Jo's benefit, 'can help, we will. That's why we're here. I'm sorry your letter took so long to reach me, Rex. You'd addressed it to, Cousin Maud, Germoe, and you see, we'd moved four years ago to Helston. It took the Post Office a bit of investigating to catch up with me. We drove to the village first. An ugly little man, who said his name was Jelbert, directed us here.'

'I'm so glad you've come,' Jo said, smiling at Luke's relatives, 'but everything's going to be fine from now on. I'm Joanna Venner, Luke's fiancée, and we're getting married in a few days. You're just in time to be invited to the wedding.'

'You've got a lot of news to catch up on, Maud,' Luke said. 'You'd better sit down.'

'I'm glad to hear you're settling down at last, Luke,' Maud said when the gathering had taken seats. Unsure of his position, Rex took refuge close to Jo. 'I'd never have thought it of you the last time I saw you. Must be nearly ten years ago.'

Jo could see Maud was the sort of staunch woman, apt to hand out well-meaning advice, that Luke would have avoided.

322

'And you living in such a splendid house too, Luke,' Maud went on, gazing appreciatively round the room.

'The house belongs to Jo.' Briefly, Luke filled his cousin in on the events since Jo's arrival at Parmarth.

'Lucky for you Miss Venner came here then. I'm not surprised Jessie would come to grief one day,' Maud said. 'I'm so sorry to hear I had another little cousin and I'm too late to meet her. We'll visit Molly's grave before we go. And call at this Mrs Wherry's house to see the baby.'

'Molly's headstone's just been put up,' Luke said.

'Well, Luke,' Godfrey Redstone said, 'you've got a pretty, very suitable bride. It seems all is working out. I'm happy to see Maud had no need to be alarmed.'

'When I got Rex's letter,' Maud broke in, 'I took it for granted you could look after yourself, Luke. We were thinking, if it was necessary, of offering the children a home. We can't have any of our own, you see. A great disappointment to us. We have a grocer's shop in Helston and live in a big house there. There's plenty of room. But we can see their future is settled now.'

Luke was looking at Godfrey and Maud intently. The couple exchanged downcast looks; another disappointment. 'It's good of you to get in touch, to make this offer. The kids belong here now.'

'I don't want to live here,' Rex wailed suddenly. 'I'd still have to go to that rotten school every day where me 'n' Molly was teased, and see the beastly place she died in. I want to get away from here, for good!' Deserting Jo, he stood contentiously beside Maud's chair.

'Don't be silly, Rex. You've heard what I've just said. You're going to live here with me and Jo.'

'I don't want to live with her,' Rex fiercely pleaded with his cousin. 'She's not our sort and her family don't want nothing to do with us. She's nice but she'll want me to be different to the other boys. I won't fit in nowhere. I haven't even got Molly now.'

'I'm sorry, Rex,' Maud said, glancing uncomfortably at Jo. 'You've asked for my help and I have a duty towards you and Marylyn but I can't interfere. Luke is your next of kin.'

Huge tears splashed down over his cheeks. 'But Luke doesn't really want me. He likes his freedom too much. Nor does she, not really. She wants to stay a teacher. She'll end up hating me for making her give it up. They never planned to get married till Molly died. I want to get away from here. That's why I wrote to you. I hate the village and I hate this place!'

Her face weighty and troubled, Maud brought the boy's head on to her shoulder and comforted him with soft pats. 'Seems to me he may have made some good points, Luke, Miss Venner. I think we should chew this over.'

Forty

Jo couldn't recall how long she had been standing on the cliff edge near the Solace Mine. She let the thundering sea hundreds of feet below continue to drown out her thoughts, her humiliation, her feelings of rejection. She loved Rex, but he did not love her in return. In fact he had very little respect for her. He had expressed the wish never to see her again, because she was part of Parmarth, part of his life in which he had lost Molly, the only person he had ever loved or needed. Jo felt guilty at how little thought had been given to the tragic boy's loss at Molly's death. How ironic, that it was she herself who had taught him the words of the letter that would take him and Marylyn out of her life for ever.

Lifting her hand to brush away her bitter tears, for a moment Jo wanted only to be part of the surging force of miles and miles of ocean.

Someone nudged her arm.

'Joanna, what are you doing here?'

She did not reply but slipped her hand inside Marcus's, and there they stayed in silence. In empathy. Staring out across the ocean. Then, glancing at his remote, pain-filled, gaunt face, Jo knew he had told the truth about his mother.

'This is one of my favourite spots,' he murmured. 'I come here to watch the sky and the sea. The clouds drifting across the heavens. I look down at the rocks and the waves, and I long to be a cloud. But I'm always a helpless piece of rock, overpowered by the mightier waves.

'So many times I've tried to pluck up the courage to jump off the cliff and end my life on those rocks, let the tide wash me away for ever. Now I don't have to do it. She fell. She released me. One day I shall totally experience the reality of it. Sometimes, like today, I just feel numb, unreal. As if I'm not actually here.'

'Nothing Eleanor did to you was worth killing yourself over, Marcus.'

'She stole my innocence. She made me weak. Made me hate her and hate myself. I don't know if I shall ever come to terms with it.' He looked at Jo strangely, as if pursuing something profound. 'Or do you think we are what we are because it's how we would have turned out anyway? Despite our upbringing?'

'We must be partly how people mould us and partly our own ongoing personality, I suppose. It's how I see myself. How I see Luke. You can fall in love with what you want to see in a person, or you can look deeper and love him anyway. For all he is and always will be. My mother rejected me but I had Celia. Jessie rejected Luke but he had his grandmother.' Now she hoped Rex's new life with Maud and Godfrey Redstone would bring enough good things to prevent him from being a lifelong victim, and Marylyn the security she deserved.

'I've had no one like that, Jo.' Marcus wept softly and Jo knew he was on the edge of despair.

'I know, Marcus. I'm so sorry. But you'll always have me as a friend. And there's Beth. I've noticed that she's good for you. Try to look forward, not back. Eleanor's dead and so is the hold she had on you. When times are bad cling to that.'

Jo shivered. The sun was beginning its nightward journey. The wind was buffeting them. Somehow they had crept closer to the cliff edge. 'It's time we were going home, Marcus, to face what the rest of our life might bring.'

They did not part hands, but walked silently until separating at the paths which would take one to the village, the other to Cardhu.

Forty-One

G rim-eyed, Luke faced his cousin on her doorstep in the wide, quiet Helston street. 'I've brought these toys over from Cardhu. Jo wanted the kids to have them.'

'At least come inside for a minute, Luke,' Maud Redstone coaxed him, where she stood on the passage runner in a starched white apron, holding Marylyn. 'You haven't said goodbye properly to the children yet. Rex is playing in the back garden.'

'No, it's better I just go, Maud. I'll come back and see them after a few weeks.'

'Don't be hurt, Luke. Rex is only a child.'

'He's had a terrible start. He didn't deserve to go on suffering, Maud. I should've packed up the kids and moved them away the moment I stepped inside Jessie's door. I let them carry on living in squalor and Molly her last days in misery. Now we're split apart. It's guilt I'm feeling and rightly so.'

'The good Lord will forgive you, Luke. You must forgive yourself.' Maud always spoke plainly. 'So what are you going to do now? Let it ruin the rest of your life? Or the young woman's who's seeing fit to marry you?'

Reaching out Luke touched Marylyn's hand. 'No, Maud, but you taking the kids has changed things. Jo and I have a lot of talking to do. And in time, I'm hoping Rex will come round and we can be close. That suit you?'

He left quickly, but instead of making his way back to Cardhu, he headed off for Penzance. Before he and Jo had that long talk they both needed time alone.

Forty-Two

Katherine smiled maliciously as she put the telephone down. She had been speaking to Alistair. He had made enquiries about his sister's wedding and discovered it had not taken place today. Luke Vigus had fobbed his brother and sister off on a relative and hadn't been seen in Parmarth since. Joanna's house and money and future fortune were, evidently, not such a draw. She was all alone.

It was tempting to travel to Cardhu and torment her, but Katherine's recollection of her own humiliation by the headmaster after her last excursion there made her fume and decide against it. She had not been deceived by the maid's story that he was not at home. On the other hand, now his clinging mother had been laid to rest and the school holidays had started, he might be more receptive to her approaches. Baiting Joanna was hardly worth the bother, but Marcus Lidgey made a most alluring quarry. He was attractive, pensive, and according to the late Mardie Dawes, his sensitive hands were as adept in intimate matters as they were accomplished on musical instruments.

Katherine's young artist lover had learned nothing from her. She needed a master in the art of loving. It could prove a triumph to make one more advance on the elusive Marcus Lidgey, especially if Joanna was feeling vulnerable and turning to him for comfort.

She returned to the telephone, but this time she would make him come to her.

'I'm going out, Beth.' Marcus anxiously jangled his car keys in his hand. 'You take some time off, there's nothing urgent to do here. I'll finish my packing when I return.'

'If anyone asks, can I say where you're going, sir?'

'Just for a drive.' He smiled to hide his worries. 'It's too lovely a day to stay stuck indoors.'

'Good for you.' She smiled from the kitchen table, where she was preparing a vegetable salad for his lunch. 'You shouldn't hide away. If you wait two minutes I'll make some sandwiches for you to take with you.'

He sat down for a moment and watched her patient movements. 'I can't face people. The last days of term were hell to get through.'

'You will say goodbye to the villagers before you leave?'

'I know my manners, Beth.' He grinned wryly. 'You're turning into a little nag since Sally's left my employ.'

'I'm sorry, sir. I let Mrs Lidgey down and I don't want to do the same to you.'

Tucking the sandwich tin under his arm, he took her by the shoulders. 'Mark my words, Beth. I don't mind what you say to me, and I've told you many times that my mother died at peace with herself. She came to my room the night she died to tell me she felt Gabriella had forgiven her. It was your prayers that worked. Now, have I convinced you, my dear?'

'Yes.' She smiled shyly up into his eyes. 'I wish you weren't leaving.'

'I have to. There's too many sad memories for me here. My dear Beth.' He bent forward and placed a peck on both her cheeks. 'There are only two people I shall really miss when I leave here. You're one of them.'

'I came straightaway, Mrs Venner,' Marcus said the instant he was inside Meadowsweet. He had walked the last mile to avoid his motorcar being seen outside the cottage and giving rise to gossip. He mopped up the sweat on his brow and neck. 'Your call about Joanna left me very concerned.'

Stroking Tuppence the kitten, which she was holding against her breast, Katherine peered at the flesh revealed by his open-necked shirt. 'I'm sorry if I alarmed you, Marcus. My son was informed that you are leaving Parmarth very soon and I'm anxious to discuss Joanna with you. She stayed on at the school and worked out the end of term, I understand. Do you happen to know her plans? I'd hate to see her burying herself away in the remote countryside like that Sayce woman did.'

'Joanna has not talked about her personal life to me,' he replied aloofly.

He would not tell this salacious woman anything about his close relationship with her daughter. Every word Joanna spoke to him, every smile she gave him, every moment she was near him was too precious to be defiled. He had called at Cardhu to offer her companionship over her cancelled wedding. All she would say about the cancellation was that it had been a mutual agreement between her and Vigus and they planned to discuss their future together soon. She was putting on a brave face but he could see her unhappiness. Sense her utter loneliness. He felt she trusted him. They were becoming closer.

Marcus was beginning to feel he had a future. He was leaving Parmarth and only Joanna knew his destination. He was to rent a house at St Ives. And from there he would wait and watch for what Joanna would do, and when she had decided, he would set himself up as a private music tutor, close by her. They might even have a future together. Fate seemed to be arranging things his way. He would not let anything spoil his chances. Not her damned mother, who revolted him with her designs on him.

Designs on him! Panic ripped through his mind. She had procured his presence here. Had he walked into a trap, like the ones his mother had so cleverly and cruelly laid for him?

His senses highly alert, he took a good look at Katherine Venner. Her frock was cut very low at the front, her cleavage thrusting out and upwards. She was heavily made-up, overscented. Her strappy, high-heeled sandals revealed bare painted toenails. And from the beguiling widening of her eyes, she not only wanted him, she was on to his suspicions.

'I . . . I think I ought to go.'

'But why? You've only just arrived, Marcus.' Smiling alluringly, Katherine put the kitten down and gave up all pretence of being concerned about her daughter. 'Let me get you some iced lemon tea. You look hot and bothered, as if you need to unwind.'

'No, thank you. I'll see myself out.' Marcus stepped back, his hand reaching for the door handle, but Katherine's actions were quicker. Her hands were on him.

'Come now.' Her voice throbbed with desire. 'Surely you don't really want to go. I did not think I'd have to chase you quite so literally.'

'Don't.' Marcus pushed her hands off him.

Laughing in sultry amusement, Katherine twisted a strand of her dyed red hair. 'I don't think you're normally so restrained. A man like you, who I'm reliably informed is a connoisseur of delicious acts in the bedroom, must be ill or under extreme stress to decline the invitation from a lady of similar needs and expertise.'

'Actually, I'm in love,' Marcus threw at her.

'What? You hardly ever leave Parmarth. Who could you have possibly fallen in love with?' She studied his serious face, then she gave way to hysterical laughter. 'Oh, don't tell me you've fallen for Joanna? Surely not? It's unthinkable. She's plain and dreary. Only her money could make a man . . . Ah, so that's it, is it? Your mother's left you penniless. Well, I suppose you're a cut above that gipsy fellow.'

Then, stung by his latest rebuff, she lowered her voice to a sarcastic hiss. 'But not much. If she does take you on, you'll be able to show her a thing or two the gipsy wouldn't know about. How do you think Joanna will like being—'

'Shut your filthy mouth!' Marcus bellowed, turning purple with rage. He couldn't stand the very thought of himself contaminating Joanna. 'You bitch! You disgusting whore! Don't you dare speak about Joanna like that.'

His body shook. His breathing came in laboured groans. His eyes seemed to swirl in their deep sockets, as cold as ice, as if devoid of balance and soundness.

331

Katherine remembered the other statement Mardie Dawes had made about him. 'Touch of madness. Dangerous.' Had the dead blackmailer been correct?

Her heart fluttered in panic. Ominous fear pricked its way into her guts. 'Like you said, Marcus, I think you had better go.'

He stood with his feet planted apart, gradually unlocking the white fists he had made. 'But I thought you wanted me to stay, Katherine. I was only using foul language to get us in the right mood. Let's go upstairs. I'll give you the best time you've ever had.'

She was torn, whether to insist he go or to take advantage of his change of mood. He didn't look angry now. In fact, his eyes were sad and haunting. Katherine liked to control men and this man appeared to have something of a lost boy about him. Mardie Dawes hadn't mentioned this aspect of his character. She had probably been mistaken or lying about him being mad.

'Follow me,' she commanded.

As each high-heeled foot left a stair, his took its place behind her. Katherine felt his hot breath on her back and shivered deliciously. Once at the top, he gripped her wrist and spun her round to him.

'Want to play rough here, do you?' She was bringing her arms up to clamp round his neck with the intention of roughly kissing his mouth, but he caught her other wrist in his hand.

'You shouldn't behave like a slut. You're a mother. You're Joanna's mother! And you treat her like she's filth. If you were good and kind and decent you would see her as she really is. Gentle and lovely and feminine. You've made her suffer in the past and want to do so again, but I won't let you. Never again!'

Katherine was engulfed by stark naked terror. This time his eyes blazed so brightly they looked as if they'd been blasted into his skull.

A scream built up inside Katherine's throat but had no time to reach her lips. He thrust her violently down the stairs.

Bump, bump, bump, she went down over each step. Ending up at the bottom in a sprawled heap, face down on the sheepskin rug.

Marcus went to the bathroom and carefully washed his hands, to get the taint of this woman off him. Walking down the stairs, he stepped over the still body and outside into the clear hot air.

He set off along the road, head up, taking long strides. He saw the birds in the air, cattle and sheep in the fields. After a while it seemed he was the only human in the world. He felt peaceful.

Then this was gradually overtaken by an alien energy, which did not fill him with hardiness but was draining him. There was no breeze to cool his burning skin and suddenly he was sweating feverishly and panting like an old dog. The verges were awash with the pungent smell of cow parsley, campion and wild herbs. It made him cough and fight to breathe.

When he reached his motorcar he fell into the driver's seat. Saw the sandwich tin on the next seat. Why had he come here? Presumably for a picnic. He couldn't remember leaving the schoolhouse. He put his hands on the steering wheel. Why were they shaking? Where the hell was he? His head ached, waves of agony searing into his skull. Resting his head in his hands he closed his eyes.

He must have fallen asleep. When he next looked through the windscreen dusk was stealing over the landscape. Moments later, he was terrified. He had forgotten who he was.

Forty-Three

'Joanna! Joanna! Wake up, please.'

The desperate cries and sounds of something hitting her bedroom window woke Jo in the middle of the night. Unnerved, she crept out of bed and peeped out of the window.

There was a tall shadowy figure standing on the front lawn, silhouetted by the moonlight, about to throw another missile at the window.

'Luke, is that you?' she called out warily. But she knew the figure wasn't Luke and she felt vulnerable for the first time since living in isolation.

'Joanna, come outside.' The figure dropped to his knees. 'I need you.'

'Marcus! Wait there, I'll come down to you.' He was evidently in the throes of another anxiety attack. Beth had arrived in the late evening, worried by his long absence. What had he been doing all this time? Lighting the lantern, slipping into her dressing gown and slippers, Jo rushed downstairs and unlocked the front door.

She hurried to Marcus. He was slumped forward on the lawn, face in his hands. 'What is it, Marcus? Where have you been? Are you ill?'

'Yes – I mean I don't know,' he whimpered, looking up slowly, beseeching with outstretched arms for her to come to him.

Putting the lantern down on the grass, Jo knelt in front of him, bringing his head to rest against her shoulder. He clung to her. 'I went out. I can't remember why or what happened. Or how long I'd been away. I came across the motorcar. And

334

then I couldn't remember who I was. I was scared out of my mind. Somehow I drove back here, stopped at the foot of the lane. I had to come to you, Joanna. Please help me. I fear I'm falling into a deep bottomless pit.'

'You're safe now, Marcus. I'll take care of you, I promise. You're cold, shivering. Come inside. I'll get you some brandy.'

'No, please, I'd rather stay here. Don't let me go, Joanna. Don't let me fall.'

'I promise I won't let anything happen to you, Marcus. You can trust me. We'll stay here and talk if that's what you want.'

'I want . . .' His voice was like a small abandoned child's. 'I want you to love me.'

'I do love you, Marcus. I love you as a close friend. I won't let you down. Relax, breathe slowly. I'll stay with you.' She stroked his hair, rubbed his shoulders. His shirt was wet with perspiration and his skin underneath was chilled.

He was silent for a while, then his next words came wretchedly. 'Am I going mad?'

'No, of course not, but you're close to a breakdown. Marcus, tomorrow I want you to see the doctor. Will you do that?'

'He can't wash away my shame and degradation.'

'You've got nothing to be ashamed about. You were devoted to Eleanor. You did everything for her that a son could possibly do.'

'She did things to me that a mother should never have done.' He sobbed into the bodice of Jo's nightdress, gripping her so firmly she felt her breath would soon be cut off. 'She . . . she made me do things to her. She used me. Hurt me. Made me an animal. Turned me into filth. Do you understand what I'm saying? Do you realise now what I've become?'

In horror, she saw clearly the terrible hold Eleanor had had over her son. Every odd thing Jo had witnessed in their relationship fell into place. It was why Marcus was a shadow of the man he should be, but despite his terrible secret, he was good and thoughtful. She was overwhelmed with compassion for him.

Swallowing the painful lump rising in her throat, Jo gently used her fingers to wipe away his tears. 'Oh, Marcus, I'm so sorry. I had no idea you were going through something so horrendous.'

'I wanted to kill her, Joanna. I made plan after plan but I never had the courage to go through with them.' He wept in torment. 'She knew and she taunted me. The one time I came close to getting rid of her it all went wrong. I had nothing to live for. The night she died I was going to take my own life, but she stopped me. She was going to defile me again and I pushed her away and she fell to the floor and died.'

He gave a peculiar laugh and shook with a dreadful passion in Jo's arms. 'I wish I'd crushed her to death with my bare hands. She should have suffered more at the end.'

'Don't say any more, Marcus. Just keep telling yourself that it's over now. You're in a bad state because you've been keeping it all locked up inside you for too long. Don't punish yourself like this.'

He groaned suddenly, as if not hearing her words of hope and encouragement. 'Don't hate me, Joanna, now I've told you the truth. Don't despise me for my weakness. I couldn't bear that.'

'I don't think any less of you, Marcus. It wasn't your fault. Eleanor was an overpowering woman. Now you must take the long rest you deserve, look towards the future. I'll help you in any way I can.'

His body crumpled, his face sliding down on to Jo's breast, taking her dressing gown and nightdress off her shoulder and bringing his skin into contact with hers. 'I love you, Joanna,' he murmured. 'I wish you loved me as more than a friend. It's my biggest regret.'

Oh, no, Jo whispered to herself. If he meant, or believed he meant, his declarations of love, it would exacerbate the situation. Her posture was becoming increasingly uncomfortable and Marcus was getting heavier, dragging her down. Soon she would be in a lot of pain. And he was burying his lips into her breast. She feared he would desire comfort in a way she was unwilling to give.

'We can't stay out here all night, Marcus.'

He tugged her closer to him and she bit her lip to forestall a cry from the agony shooting up her spine. 'No.' His voice was muffled against her flesh. 'I won't be able to breathe if we go inside. We must stay here.'

Jo could no longer bear the pain she was in. She tried to ease him away from her. 'I have to get up, Marcus. My back's hurting.'

She could not shift him and he clung to her with more intensity. 'Marcus, please, you're beginning to hurt me.'

No response. She was forced to wrest his hands away from her and push on him with all her strength.

Marcus staggered and fell on the dew-laden ground. He howled like a wounded animal. The lantern tipped over, the flame puttered out.

'I'm sorry,' Jo said quickly. 'I just had to move.'

Stunned, sitting up, shaking his head to clear his bewilderment, he rubbed his raw elbow. 'You hurt me,' he wailed like a petulant child.

'I'm sorry,' Jo repeated, rising to her feet. 'Marcus, I can't deal with this out here. I'm getting cold. Please let me get dressed and I'll walk to the schoolhouse with you.'

He got to his feet, lurching as if drunk. Her body was outlined by the moonlight. Small, delicate, womanly. She was trembling, breathing heavily. Then she wasn't the woman he loved any more. She was looming in the darkness. Menacing. Procuring a situation to humiliate him. 'Don't tell me what to do!'

Jo leapt at his sudden fury. 'I didn't mean to sound bossy, Marcus. Please listen to me.'

'No! I won't. You women always want to do things to me. All of you. Even you. Just like she did this afternoon.'

'Who are you talking about, Marcus?' Jo tried to keep the alarm out of her voice. Instinct made her walk backwards. 'Where did you go today?'

'She lied to get me to go to her house. Told me she was

worried about you. But she only wanted to have me in bed. She wanted to hurt me. Make me feel ashamed. The evil bitch.'

'Who?' Jo shouted to break through his crazed ramblings. 'You're not making any sense.'

'Your mother!' He swore profanely. Then he was coming after Jo.

Somehow she made her feet move faster. He was growing increasingly deranged and she was very frightened. She had to get into the house and slam and bolt the door on him.

'Marcus, calm yourself. I'm your friend, remember. I want to help you, not abuse you. A minute ago you said you loved me. Did you mean it?'

He hesitated. 'I . . . I . . .'

She was on the path running alongside the flower borders. The front door was just feet away. She took another step backwards but her foot landed awkwardly and she was falling, hitting the ground.

Marcus was there, standing over her. Jo was sitting, leaning back on her hands, her chest heaving. She couldn't make out his features in the darkness but could see the outline of his head, turning from side to side as if perplexed. Then she knew what she must do. It was when he felt threatened he became demented.

It was not difficult to cry like a child, hurt and afraid. 'Help me, Marcus.'

He crouched beside her and she felt his harsh breath on her face. 'Joanna? What happened? Oh, God, I've hurt you, my only friend. I'm sorry. Forgive me. Oh, God. Oh, God . . .' Then he backed away from her, scrambled to his feet and hurtled off into the night.

Jo got up, ran inside and secured the house, listening anxiously in case he came back. She had been very scared but did not blame Marcus for his actions. His mental breakdown wasn't his fault. The blame lay wholly with his cruel, wicked mother. She felt such a strength of sorrow for him, and then for Luke and herself. The three of them had one thing in common; all their troubles originated from their mothers.

Time passed. Where was Marcus now? The moors and cliffs held many perils for an unbalanced man. He needed help. She got dressed. When fragments of dawn began to breach the darkness she hurried to the village.

Forty-Four

N ot a whisper of wind stirred the long grasses or sighed against the stones on top of Carn Galver. The minerals in the rocks, scoured and burnished by the sun, glinted like tiny stars. Insects, too flimsy to flit in the warm air high above the roughland, cradled in the yellow petals of tormentil or on grey-green foliage. Luke flamed the last of a cigarette, let the breath out slowly then rubbed the stub out between thumb and forefinger, putting it into his shirt pocket. He could never spoil the grace and beauty of the carn.

He was sitting on the sheltered spot where Jo had sketched him on that wintry day, where he had first kissed her, where they had first made love. In the fragrant openness, in the quiet, he let his mind drift over his beautiful memories of her. Those searching, caring, lovely green-flecked eyes. The delicacy of her soft skin. Her unique tender femininity. She was perfection. His soulmate.

Another lasting impression of her nudged aside these pleasant ramblings to haunt him. Her look of hurt and dreadful sadness at losing Marylyn and Rex, when he had so readily agreed to Maud's offer to adopt them. He'd argued it was for the best, Rex wanted to go anyway, and now Jo could continue to teach, not give up her cherished career. He'd tried to make it sound noble. They'd still get married, any time they liked, they just didn't have to rush through with it now.

Jo's face had also shown the humiliation of a jilted woman, despising his weakness, his selfishness. Could she ever trust him now? Forgive him? Was she bitter? No, not bitter. Jo was the one with loyalty and honour and strength. She cared about others, like poor deranged Marcus Lidgey, now incarcerated in an institution. He'd heard the schoolmaster had been found by Beth on the cliff edge near the mine ruins, his face glazed over, his mind completely shut off from reality. She had been able to take his hand and lead him back to the schoolhouse, apparently the only one he responded to now.

Slowly, as if surfacing from the depths of the ocean, Luke came back to the reason why he was here, to think over how he could ask Jo to forgive him. And then how to say goodbye to her, before allowing her to get on with her life. He'd go far away where he could never hurt her again.

A small shadow blocked out the sun. He glanced up and there was Jo. Hands in her cord trouser pockets, she was gazing down on him solemnly.

'Don't get up, Luke. I'll join you.' She sat down close to him, but at an angle where she could see his face.

Her hands rested either side of her on the ground. He took the one nearest him in a warm clasp. 'This is the best place for us to talk, Jo. Think you should go first.' He closed his eyes a moment, as if steeling himself.

Jo had been watching him for some time. For the past few days she'd gone over every aspect of their relationship. Her anger at his eagerness for the solution that Maud take the children had faded, and then the hurt, and gradually everything else that was sad or wrong had seemed unimportant, especially in the light of tragic Marcus's misery. She'd stood outside her house, remembering the time she'd first seen Luke, her immediate attraction to him; how light-humoured he had been then.

She'd climbed the carn today to relive the precious moments spent with him here, and when she'd seen him, so alone, thoughtful, downcast, vulnerable, she'd longed to run to him, comfort him, plead with him never to leave her again for she loved him so much. But she knew him through and through; she must not take the initiative again, the superior position, or their love, their future, would be lost. Luke must be allowed to regain his pride. He needed to feel strong, needed her to see him as strong if their relationship was to work.

341

She pressed back on the grip of his fingers. 'I know you can imagine how I've been feeling, Luke. All the lonely days and nights, the regrets and recriminations. But I promise you my grief is gone and only my love for you is left.'

He sighed from the bottom of his soul. 'I don't deserve your love, Jo. Never have, never will. I must leave and let you get on with your life, get on with your teaching, build your school. I'm sorry you ever got involved with me. You came to Parmarth to be with Celia but her death ruined that for you. You inherited her house, planned to live there as my wife, the kids' mother, and I ruined that for you. Didn't even give a chance to see if it would work out for us and Rex and Marylyn. I've come between you and Mercy Merrick and your brother. Because of me you can hardly show your face in the village or enjoy Cardhu, Celia's gift to you. People were right, I've ruined everything for you. Please believe me, I love you more than anything and always will. I never meant to hurt you but I should've walked away. We must say goodbye, Jo. You must start all over again without me. You do see that?'

'I love you for thinking this way, Luke, it shows how much you care, how unselfish you really are. Now tell me if you still want me. Don't say what you think to be the best for me, tell me the truth.'

'Yes, Jo, of course I still want you.' His eyes had never looked so deep, so despairing. 'Nothing will ever change that.'

'Well, I still want you. I love you and I need you. Things aren't as bad for me as you think. Mercy and the villagers got together and have asked me to stay, and the school board have asked me to reconsider my resignation for the sake of the children; the school doesn't want to lose two teachers in such tragic circumstances. I'm staying on, Luke. To try to right my mistakes and the damage and confusion recent events have left here. I'm not running away and I don't believe you should either. I've always believed you are a good man and I want you to prove it to yourself and the people of Parmarth. To Rex and Marylyn. Of course the best thing for them was to go to Maud; she's family, and they will have more in common with her than with either of us.

'If you leave me there will be a terrible void in my life that no one else can fill. I need you, Luke, I want to lean on you. You see, Marcus Lidgey told me that he was cruelly abused all his life by his mother and I believe that it was my own mother who somehow pushed him towards a total mental breakdown. I don't know exactly what happened and I doubt if the truth will ever be revealed.'

'That's terrible. I heard about your mother, how she's paralysed from the neck down after an accident in her house. How are you coping with that?'

'Not at all well. She's also lost the power of speech, Luke. She's back at Tresawna House, under nursing care twenty hours a day. I called there to see her. She went berserk, thrashing her head about and glaring at me as if she wished me dead. It was horrible. Alistair's advised me to stay away from her. I can't honestly say I'm sorry about that, but' – tears glittered on Jo's lashes – 'there was never any real reason for her to hate me, Luke. I've been hurt again by my mother's hateful behaviour and I need someone to help me come to terms with it.'

Luke's heart was filled with emotion. He was reaching for her. 'Don't cry, sweetheart. If you need me then of course I'll never leave you. But I'm weak and flawed. How can I be enough for you?'

'You just are, Luke, because you're you. The man I fell in love with despite everything. The only man I'll ever want.'

'Come to me then.' She moved into his arms and he held her tight. 'I'll never give you up, Jo. I'm not going to live out of a wagon for the rest of my life. I swear that somehow I'll make a proper life for us and when you're ready we'll make that final commitment.'

She hugged his strong body, burning an impression of him into her soul. 'I trust you to keep your promise, Luke.'

A new road lay ahead of them now, one where they knew they would meet more pitfalls, more obstacles to their union, but whether together or apart, they would always share the

343

same journey. For now, not talking, quite still, they let the quiet of the day join them in an unbreakable bond.